CW00953000

OTHER BOOKS BY THIS AUTHOR

Broken Faith
Walking the Labyrinth
Kicker's Journey

REVISED EDITION

COMING HOME

LOIS CLOAREC HART

AUTHOR'S NOTE

I chose to leave the anachronisms of 2001 in place in this revised issue of *Coming Home*. That means there are references to movies and books of 1999–2000 and a lack of common technology such as smartphones, Netflix, and Facebook. While these aspects do date *Coming Home*, they don't change the essence of the story or the timeless nature of love between three good-hearted and well-intentioned characters caught in an impossible situation. Because *Coming Home* and its companion novel, *Broken Faith*, comprise the beginning of a roman-fleuve, which finds later expression in *Walking the Labyrinth*, I kept the natural progression of events, even if they're suspended in the amber of an earlier era.

ACKNOWLEDGEMENTS

Coming Home was always a labour of love — love remembered and new love found. When I originally wrote the story, my late husband was in the last months of his long and relentless battle with multiple sclerosis. I met my wife-to-be when she was assigned to edit the first incarnation of this book. Day still reviews every word I write, and I am so thankful for her and all the treasured friends *Coming Home* brought into my life. Day and Kathleen GramsGibbs are my not-so-secret beta team. They catch my mistakes, correct my grammar, push me gently to better paths, and laugh in all the right spots. They are a joy to work with, and I am deeply grateful to both.

For this third revision of *Coming Home*, I again had the pleasure of working with Ylva's superb senior editor, Sandra Gerth. She'd already done the arduous slog of breaking my bad habits when we revised *Broken Faith* last year, which made this time around a breeze. Sandra, thank you for your patience, tact, and humour. Many authors don't enjoy the editing process, but under your auspices, I've found it to be a delight. I look forward to future collaborations.

DEDICATION

In loving memory of BJ,
who was Rob.
1943–2001

CHAPTER 1

J AN LOOPED HER ARMS UNDER Rob's, tucked her head next to his, and braced herself. "Are you ready, love?"

"I'm ready."

"Okay, here we go." Jan began the simple transfer from Rob's wheelchair to his recliner.

They were in mid-lift when Rob's involuntary leg spasm threw them off balance. Jan tried a mid-air reverse but was unable to get him back into his wheelchair, and they tumbled to the floor.

"Oooph." Jan stared up at the ceiling. *This day is not getting off to a good start.* At least she'd managed to keep Rob on top this time. "Are you all right?"

"I think so. I must say, you dance divinely, my dear."

"Gee, thanks." Jan eased out from under Rob and knelt beside him. She rolled him on his back, straightened his limbs, and checked for any obvious signs of distress, knowing that his multiple sclerosis-induced paralysis could mask an injury. "It looks like you survived our nosedive all right. Now we have to figure out how to get you up in your chair." She grabbed a cushion from the couch to slide under his head.

Rob looked up at her. "Do you think Andrew might be home?"

Jan shook her head. "No, he'll be at work by now."

"You could ask Victor."

She raised an eyebrow.

"You know he's always eager to help us."

"Rob, he's got to be eighty if he's a day."

"I know, but maybe between the two of you?"

Jan stroked his hair. "Not your best idea, love. Victor would try, but I'd be afraid to hurt him." She ran through her list of options. *I could call Kate or John, but I hate to ask them to leave work.* "I think we're going to have to contact the fire hall again."

"I know you don't like to do that." Rob leaned his head into her caress. "I'm perfectly comfortable here. We can wait until Andrew's home from work."

"No way am I letting you lie on the floor all day." She dropped a kiss on his forehead and stood to get the phone. About to place the call, she glanced out the window. Their letter carrier had just turned into the front gate. "I wonder. All I can do is ask, right? If she turns me down, I'll call the firefighters."

<hr />

Terry whistled as she walked up the Spencer walkway. She'd made good progress on her route that morning. *I should be done early today. Lots of time to write later.*

It was a sunny, mid-summer day with nothing to slow her down except the usual challenge from the McFarlane's noisy dog. He lunged at her from the end of his chain every time she entered his yard.

Striding on automatic pilot, she appreciated the absence of any obnoxious mutts in the Spencer yard. Their green-and-white bungalow was surrounded by spruce trees, lilac bushes, and well-tended flowerbeds. *It's peaceful. I like it.*

Terry occasionally saw Mrs. Spencer tending those beds. The woman always had a smile and a pleasant greeting for her.

When Mrs. Spencer opened the front door and stepped out, Terry held out several envelopes. "Good morning. Lovely day, isn't it?"

Mrs. Spencer accepted the mail. "Please, I hate to bother you, but would you mind helping me? My husband's fallen, and I can't get him back into his chair by myself. If you could lend me a hand, it would only take a moment."

"Umm, sure. No problem." Terry followed Mrs. Spencer and slung the mailbags off her shoulders in the foyer. She walked into a sparsely furnished, book-lined living room.

A tall, thin man with a shock of thick, brown hair hanging over his eyes lay on the floor. He smiled at her. "Are you my knight in shining armour?"

Terry grinned. "Well, I can't say I've ever been called that before, but let's see if we can't get you back in your chair. Mrs. Spencer, you'll have to talk me through this. I don't want to hurt your husband while I'm trying to help." She started toward him only to duck as two feathered missiles shot over her head. "Whoa, what was that?"

Mrs. Spencer shook her head. "Oh, dear. I'm so sorry. That's Jamie and Xan, our budgies. They're not used to strangers, so I guess you scared them."

"I scared *them*?" Terry spied two sets of inquisitive eyes peering at her from the top of the nearest bookcase. "They won't strafe me again, will they?"

"No, they should be fine now," Mrs. Spencer said. "I really appreciate you lending a hand."

"I'm glad to help. What would you like me to do?" Terry crouched beside Mr. Spencer's legs.

Mrs. Spencer took up a position near her husband's upper body. "When I say go, we're going to lift him into the recliner. If you grasp him under the thighs, make sure your knees are bent, and don't lift with your back. It should go smoothly. Wait until I get set here." She lifted his head and shoulders, rested them against her body, and got a firm grip on his forearms. "Ready?"

Terry nodded. "Ready when you are." *Jesus, I hope I don't hurt him.*

They lifted him off the floor and angled him toward the recliner. They got him partway into the chair before Mrs. Spencer took over.

Terry backed away to give her room to maneuver. She knocked over the footstool that had been in front of the rocking chair next to the recliner, which sent the book and newspapers piled there to the floor. "Damn. I'm sorry."

"No harm done." Mrs. Spencer adjusted her husband's body upright.

Terry picked up the newspapers and book and raised an eyebrow when she noticed the book's cover. "I'm afraid I lost your place."

Mrs. Spencer eased her husband's legs out and crossed them on a pillow. "That's okay. I can find it again easily."

Terry set everything back on the righted footstool. "I like Laurie King's *Martinelli* series, too, though I didn't think the second book was as good as the first."

"I've only just started this one," Mrs. Spencer said. "But I'm looking forward to checking out her other books as well. Anyway, thank you very much for giving us a hand. We really appreciate it."

Mr. Spencer nodded. "You can be my white knight any day."

"Not that I mind riding to the rescue," Terry said. "But try to stay off the floor for a while, okay?"

"Okay, but you know you get a whole different viewpoint from the floor. You should give it a try sometime."

Terry tilted her head. "To expand my horizons?"

"Exactly. People get in such ruts." His bright blue eyes twinkled.

Mrs. Spencer eyed her husband. "Rob, I'm sure she has to get back to work."

"I do, but it was a pleasure to meet you both." Terry walked back to the door, re-shouldered the mailbags, and turned to leave.

"Thanks again," Mrs. Spencer said.

Terry waved and started back down the path. She resumed her route on automatic pilot mode. *Kind of funny that a straight, suburban housewife would read lesbian mystery novels.* She shrugged and turned into the next walkway. *No biggie, I guess. Judging by their bookcases, she obviously loves to read, and King is certainly a good writer.* She smiled. *Who knows? Maybe someday my books will be on her reading list. It could happen.*

A week after his unfortunate tumble, Rob sat in the living room while Jan cut his hair. He squirmed as she ran the clippers up his neck.

"Am I tickling you?"

He shook his head. "I was just thinking about the first time you cut my hair — what was it, about eighteen years ago now... and all the grief it caused me at work."

"Oh, my God. That had to be the ugliest haircut in the history of man, whitewalls and all. I was so afraid that you were going to tell everyone at work that I was the one responsible for it."

"Well, considering that I'd have had to explain why I was fraternizing with a corporal outside of work hours, I thought discretion was called for. Besides, I knew it'd grow back in eventually, and you did improve with practice. It certainly saved me the aggravation of finding a wheelchair-accessible barber."

"True, but I don't know how you put up with all those months of wisecracks while I practiced." Jan put a final flourish on her work and whipped the towel off his neck. "There you go, love, you're all neat and tidy again. No more looking like Saddam emerging from his rat hole." She held up the hand mirror for Rob to check the results.

"Looks good. You should think of taking up a career as a barber."

Jan's smile faded. "I already have a career—looking after you."

Which isn't going to last forever, no matter how much you want to deny it. Rob's gaze softened. "And you're wonderful at it. I really don't pay you enough."

Jan dropped a kiss on his head. "As long as you keep up my book allowance, we'll call it square." She wheeled him back to his easy chair.

The transfer went smoothly, and Jan went to get him a coffee.

"Could you flip the news channel on for me, hon?" Rob asked when she returned.

"Sure. By the way, you did remember that it's my respite afternoon today, right? Donny will be here in a couple of hours." Jan tucked Rob's fingers around his covered cup, balanced it on his chest, circled it with a towel to hold it in place, and positioned the straw in his mouth. "I picked up a couple of DVDs for you guys. Lots of explosions and mindless sex to keep you riveted."

"Hey, I have a sensitive side, too, you know."

"Better not let your old wingmen hear that, or they'd never let you live it down." Jan winked and started back to the kitchen, walking through a patch of sunlight that illuminated her hair.

Well, I'll be darned. I see some silver threads in with the red.

I probably better keep that to myself. Rob shook his head. *Where have the years gone? You were so young when we met. And weren't the odds stacked against us? But you hung in there.* He chuckled.

Jan looked over her shoulder. "Did you say something?"

"No, I was just thinking back to when we met."

"Are you fixating on those old haircuts?"

Rob shook his head. "No. I was thinking about how unlikely it was that we'd end up here, together, all these years later. I was so bitter after Tess dumped me. I blamed every woman for the way she treated me. I don't know how you put up with me in the aftermath…or why."

Jan crossed the room to kneel at his side. "You had reason to be bitter. She let you down when you needed her most."

"That's what I used to think, too."

"You don't still?"

"No, not really. I mean she married me when I was a healthy, young fighter pilot. I certainly wasn't that by the time she left. How can I blame her for bailing?"

Jan ran her fingers through his hair. "Did you forget that part about for better or for worse? She certainly did."

"Most people would've under the circumstances."

Jan shook her head. "I don't agree."

"You've seen the stats, hon. So many marriages crumple under the strain of this disease."

"They're just numbers, Rob. They don't have anything to do with us."

"I know." He pressed his face against her hand. "I may never know why you said yes to that first date, let alone to my proposal, but I know without you I'd have ended up in an institution a long time ago. I just worry — "

"Stop right there." Jan shot him a stern look. "We've been

over this a million times. I'm perfectly happy with my life, and I'm not missing out on anything. Got it, Major?"

"Got it, Corporal." *Except a career and children and freedom.* Rob accepted the straw Jan put to his mouth and took a mouthful of coffee. "So what time is Donny going to be here?"

Jan rose to her feet. "By noon. I've got some errands to run and I'll have lunch out, but I've left soup and sandwiches for you guys."

"Sounds good." Rob sipped his coffee and watched the news as Jan returned to the kitchen. The more restricted his body became, the more interested he'd grown in world events. The latest developments in the Middle East and the escalating chances of war there were his current preoccupation.

The closest he'd come to actual combat was when Russian tanks had moved in to crush the Prague Spring in 1968. He had been a rookie pilot, newly posted in Europe at the time, and all NATO forces had gone on high alert in case those tanks moved beyond Czechoslovakia's borders. It had been a tense but exciting period.

Engrossed in the news, Rob's mind flitted between the current Mid-Eastern imbroglio and that of long ago when he had been one of an elite band flying countless reconnaissance missions close to the Iron Curtain. Closing his eyes, he lost himself in memories of flashing over fog-filled valleys in razor-winged jets, of lighting afterburners to rocket heavenwards through the clouds, and of facing down MiGs over invisible borders.

He started when Jan took the cup from his hands. "I'm done?"

Jan shook the cup. "Feels like it. Would you like another?"

"No, thanks, but I think my bag needs to be drained." Rob nodded at his leg.

"I'll go get the bottle." She crossed the room and turned down the hallway.

Rob cast a rueful glance after her. *From soaring above clouds to needing my urinal bag emptied. Yes, I've certainly done well by you, love.*

CHAPTER 2

TERRY STEPPED OFF THE BUS, started down the street to home, and wiped her brow. *Ugh, dog days of summer. I should just swipe one of Michael's Coronas and spend the rest of the afternoon in the hammock.*

When she reached her house, her kid brother was sitting on her front step.

"Hey, Jordy. I thought you had to work today."

Jordy grinned and scrambled to his feet. "Gary wanted to change shifts with me because he's got a date this weekend, so I'm off tonight. I decided to see what you guys were doing, and Michael said he was fixing a picnic to go down to River Park. He invited me along, so I've just been waiting for you."

Terry slung an arm around his shoulders. "Well, if Michael's done the picnic packing, then we don't want to miss out. I have to shower first, though. Is Claire coming, too?"

"Yeah, she's off work today." He bounced up the stairs at her side.

Entering the house, Terry hollered for her roommates.

Michael poked his head out from the kitchen. "Honestly, woman, are you trying to raise the dead?"

"Sorry, I was just wondering how much time I have before we leave for the park."

"I need about twenty more minutes, so yes, you have time for a shower." Michael returned to the kitchen, and Jordy followed him.

Terry climbed two flights of stairs to her garret at the top of the house to get ready.

Half an hour later, the four of them piled into Michael's Pathfinder and drove to the welcome coolness of River Park and a shaded table close to the water's edge. The Bow River was low and placid at this time of year, but the breeze was a welcome relief as Michael started unloading the big cooler.

Terry took a cold stuffed pita and eyed Michael's famous lemon sponge cake. *Glad I didn't pack the picnic. It would've been bologna sandwiches and Cokes for everyone.*

"I forgot to tell you that Marika phoned just before you got home today," Claire said. "I told her that, as far as I knew, you would be home later on."

Terry groaned. "Damn. I wish you'd told her I'd be out tonight."

Claire's eyebrows rose. "Excuse me? I did not know you were avoiding her."

Michael grinned. "Yeah, Ter, what's up with that?"

"You know darned well I've been ducking her for a couple of weeks now. Jesus, I went out with her for one measly month, and now she won't let go. I mean, we had fun and all, but I wasn't looking for a wife."

"It's that old second date, U-Haul syndrome," Michael said. "You all take things way too seriously."

"Oh? Like you weren't mooning over that Owen creep for months last semester?" Terry snagged a cherry tomato from the vegetable tray and threw it at him. "If he'd crooked his little finger at you, you'd have bought him a mansion with a mountain view and moved in with dogs, quilts, and copper pans."

Michael caught the tomato and popped it in his mouth. "Can't argue with that. And I do appreciate the tough love, though it was damned hard at the time."

"I know." *I'm so glad you finally bounced that gold-digging low-life.* "But lots more fish in the sea, right? Especially for someone like you."

"Enough about my woes." Michael flashed a smile. "Let's talk about your love life instead. What's so bad about Marika? She's gorgeous, and she's crazy about you. What's the problem?"

"The crazy part."

"Huh," Michael said. "I guess it would be. So how'd you two meet anyway?"

"It was all Lisa's fault." Terry sighed. "She set us up on a blind date. Said she thought Marika would be just my type, but all I wanted was some fun. I'm not into getting serious with anyone, and she was. Lisa told me that Marika was asking about me at Oly's after the game the other night. I just wish she'd start obsessing about someone else and leave me alone."

"I'm sorry I told her you'd be home tonight," Claire said. "I didn't realize she had become a problem. Perhaps you should go over to your parents' place for the evening in case she comes by."

Jordy's expression brightened. "Yeah, Terry. Why don't you? Alex and Diane are bringing the babies over tonight. You haven't seen them for a couple of weeks."

"Good point." *It means another night without getting any writing done, but I can make up for it this weekend.* "Okay, buddy. Why don't you and I head over there after we get back to the house?"

Jordy beamed, and the conversation moved into a discussion of the upcoming academic year. Terry listened idly, her gaze drifting over the park as Michael and Claire discussed shared courses and professors.

She scrutinized an auburn-haired woman who sat a short distance away in a lawn chair under a tree. "Hey, I know her."

"What did you say?" Jordy took another pita. "You know who?"

"Remember me telling you about the man I helped lift off the floor last week?" Terry pointed at Mrs. Spencer. "Well, that's his wife. I wonder what she's doing here all by herself." She swung her legs out from under the table and stood. "I'll be back in a few minutes. Don't eat all the cake on me." She started over toward Mrs. Spencer, not entirely sure what she was going to say or even why she was approaching her.

In the week since she had helped the couple out, Terry had thought about them often. She had been impressed with Mr. Spencer's upbeat optimism and good humour, even while he lay on the floor as helpless as a turtle on its back. Unusual people fascinated her, and he appeared to have the soul of a hero inside that devastated body.

Mrs. Spencer had also made an impression. The woman's obvious affection and solicitude for her husband and the lively intelligence that illuminated her face made for an attractive mix.

"Hi." Terry dropped to the grass in front of Mrs. Spencer. "I saw you from our picnic table and was just wondering how your husband was doing. No after-effects from his fall, were there?"

"Oh, hi." Mrs. Spencer closed her book. "Thank you for your concern, but no, he's fine. I really did appreciate your lending a hand, though. I was going to have to call the fire department if you hadn't come along."

"No problem at all. By the way, we haven't really been introduced, although I know you're Mrs. Spencer." She held out her hand. "Terry Sanderson."

"Jan Spencer." She shook Terry's hand. "And I apologize for not asking your name earlier."

"No worries. Is Mr. Spencer around somewhere?"

"No, Rob's at home with a caregiver. I take one afternoon off a week, and today was so nice that after my errands I decided to come down to the park and read for a few hours."

"It's nice that you can get away now and then. I'm sure you can use the break. No Laurie R. King today?" Terry looked at the hardcover that Jan was holding. "Oh, Carol O'Connell. Yeah, I know her books. She's a terrific writer, and I love her *Mallory* series. I don't think I've read *Judas Child* yet, though. Is it as good as her others?"

Jan nodded. "I was disappointed at first when I saw a new Carol O'Connell and it turned out not to be one of the *Mallory* books, but *Judas Child* is every bit as good as her other ones. I was looking forward to another visit with Mallory and Charles, though. They have such a fascinating relationship, don't you think? Of course, nothing about Mallory is conventional, which is why she's such an intriguing character. In a way, she's such an amoral genius that you wouldn't think you could relate to her, and for me, I always have to have at least one of the main characters that I can relate to or I don't enjoy the book. But her friendship with Charles really humanizes her."

Terry blinked at the torrent of words. *So much for her being shy.* "I know what you mean about relating to your characters. I've often wondered how authors handle writing despicable characters doing repulsive things. You'd think that if they couldn't relate to them, they'd have difficulty making them real to the reader, wouldn't you?"

Jan tilted her head. "You sound like you've thought about this a bit. Are you a fellow bookworm?"

Terry smiled. She kept her writing aspirations strictly to

herself, out of an almost superstitious fear that she would jinx her work. "I do enjoy reading a lot, though I don't think I'm quite in your sphere of 'worminess.' It's difficult sometimes to get any peace and quiet at my place to settle down and read without interruption for long periods."

"Do you live in a noisy apartment building?"

Terry shook her head. "No, but I might as well. I share a house by the university with a couple of third-year students. I took the top floor because I thought it would be the quietest, and it is for the most part. But Michael—he lives in the basement suite—he likes to entertain." She laughed. "Actually, I think he's majoring more in partying than business."

Jan smiled. "That could catch up to him."

"True. He comes from a pretty wealthy family back east, and I know his father has high expectations. Sometimes I think he came west for university just to get out from under his parents' eyes."

"Is your other roommate also a party animal?"

"No, Claire is pretty quiet compared to me and Michael. She takes her studies seriously. She's originally from Quebec, but she wanted to improve her English, so she decided to go to school here."

"You're not in school, are you?" Jan asked. "You don't look much older than a college student yourself. Or have you found a way to combine school and work?"

Terry leaned back on the thick grass. "Up until a few months ago, I was a student, but I graduated with my M.A. from the U of C this year."

"What's a university grad doing delivering mail? I'd have thought you'd want work in your field of study."

Terry sighed. "Now you sound like my parents. They couldn't believe I'd spent six years in university only to pound the pavement every day in the service of Canada Post. But

I'm really enjoying it. The job pays well, which is important because I have a ton of student loans to pay off. It keeps me in great shape, and I have loads of time just to think. Frankly, I'm all schooled out. I may not spend the next thirty years of my life doing this, but for now it suits my purposes." She didn't mention that she had plotted the first four chapters of her book while walking her route in Jan's neighbourhood. "Do you mostly read mysteries, or do you like other genres, too?"

Jan smiled. "I've enjoyed everything from Stephen King to P.G. Wodehouse and from newspapers to comic books. As long as it's well written, it's a safe bet that I'll like reading it."

"What about speculative fiction?" Terry had the glimmer of an idea.

"I don't read as much of that as I once did, but yes, I've always really enjoyed writers like Stephen R. Donaldson and Dave Duncan. Donaldson was the very first one I read, and his *Thomas Covenant* series hooked me right from the beginning. Duncan is a true pleasure as he's so much fun to read. I loved his *Seventh Sword* series. For pure fantasy, I'd have to say Charles de Lint is my all-time favourite. I used to live in Ottawa, and I'd look for the places he wrote about in *Moonheart* and *Jack the Giant Killer*. I thought it was so fascinating to read fantastical stories set in my own town."

"I know what you mean," Terry said. "For awhile I wouldn't read anything but writers like Terry Brooks and David Eddings." *And then I found Naiad's lesbian romances and all bets were off.*

"So did you finish work early today?" Jan asked.

"No, I always start early on hot summer days so that I'm usually done not long after noon." Terry pointed back at the picnic table where Michael, Claire, and Jordy sat. "Would you like to join us? We have lots of food, and Michael is a terrific cook. You're welcome to share if you'd like to."

Jan's gaze dropped, and she ran a hand through her hair. "Thank you for the invitation, but I have to be getting back now. It's almost time for the caregiver to leave, and I hate to be late." She removed her reading glasses, closed her book, and put it in her bag. "It was nice talking to you, Terry. I'll see you around." She folded her lawn chair and walked toward the parking lot.

Terry watched her go, then returned to the picnic table.

The others looked up at her arrival.

"Sooooo?" Michael waggled an eyebrow at her. "Who was that, and since when did you get it on with older women?"

Claire smiled. "Oui, now I know why you are avoiding Marika."

Terry rolled her eyes. "No, you have it all wrong. I just wanted to check that her husband was okay after his fall."

Michael and Claire nodded and returned to their conversation.

Jordy studied Terry.

"What?" She scowled at him. "Do I have something on my face?" *God, I hate it when he does that. It's like he can see right through me.*

"No. Nothing on your face. Nothing at all."

CHAPTER 3

E MILY SMILED AS HER TWO youngest progeny bailed out of Terry's beloved ancient Toyota. *When that car finally gives up the ghost, she'll hold services for the dearly departed.* Hands immersed in a sink full of bubbles, she watched them amble through the backyard to the house. She finished stacking the dishes in the rack and picked up a towel to dry them just as they burst into the kitchen.

"Hi, Mom." Terry kissed Emily's cheek. "Still doing dishes the old-fashioned way, I see."

"I'm perfectly capable of washing and drying a few dinner dishes, daughter-dear." *They'll never understand that this is meditative for me. It's my window of peace in the day.* "Alex, Diane, and the twins will be over in about half an hour. Can you stay long enough to see them?"

"I'm all yours for the evening. Actually, Jordy told me they'd be here. I haven't seen the babies for weeks now. I'll bet they've doubled in size."

"Well, not quite doubled, but close enough," Emily said. "They've already outgrown all the clothes I took them a month ago. You've got some time until they're here. Why don't you go out and say hello to your father? He's in the garage working on the lawn mower again."

"I don't know why he doesn't just break down and buy a new one."

Emily smiled. "Oh, like you'll break down and buy a new car?"

"That's different. The Tin Can is a classic."

Jordy snorted. "More like a relic."

"Hey! If you ever expect to borrow it again, you'll show a little respect." Terry punched his shoulder. "I'm going to go harass Dad for a bit. Give me a call when they get here, okay?"

Emily nodded, and Terry headed back outside to the garage. She turned to Jordy, who was sitting at the table, munching on fresh chocolate chip cookies. "Don't eat all of them. I made them especially for company tonight."

"Since when was Alex company?"

"He's not, but you know Diane is still shy around this crew, so I like to make an effort when she comes by." Emily often wondered if her daughter-in-law would ever feel comfortable with the rambunctious family she had married into. Still, she and Alex seemed very happy together, and the twins were, without question, perfect grandchildren.

"Hey, Mom? I think Terry's having a problem with one of her exes. Do you remember the tall blonde she went out with a month or so ago?"

"Which tall blonde? You'll have to be a little more specific than that."

"You know who I mean," Jordy said. "Terry brought her here for Sunday dinner one time. Her name was Marika."

Emily frowned. "I thought they broke up a few weeks ago. I distinctly remember feeling relieved when Terry told me that one was history."

"Well, she is as far as Terry's concerned, but Marika won't leave her alone. She keeps calling her all the time, and she's keeping tabs on her through Terry's friends."

"I doubt there's too much to worry about. Your sister

manages to juggle her social life pretty well, but keep your ears open. If it sounds like things are getting out of hand, tell me about it. Just don't let Terry know you're looking out for her. You know she's convinced that it's her job to watch out for you."

They exchanged smiles.

The doorbell sounded.

"Oh, they're early." Emily dried her hands. "Run and tell your father and Terry that Alex and his family are here."

Jordy ran off to the garage, while Emily opened the front door to her oldest son with his arms full of baby and a diaper bag. Two steps behind, Diane followed with another baby in her arms. Emily reached out to take her granddaughter from Alex and ushered them into the living room.

Alex and Diane settled on the couch with audible sighs of relief.

Gordon, Terry, and Jordy came in from outside.

Terry took the other twin from Diane and looked at the baby in her mother's arms. "Have I got Kerry or Kelly?"

"You've got Kelly," Diane said. "It's actually pretty easy to tell them apart when they're together. Kelly's far more demanding than Kerry is. I think she must take after your side of the family."

Emily chuckled. *Good point. Lord knows we aren't the quietest clan around.* She surveyed the room. Alex and Diane relaxed on the couch. Gordon sat in his armchair, sipping his ever-present cup of coffee, and Terry and Jordy played with Kelly on the floor. *And I wouldn't change a thing.*

Terry looked up at Alex. "How's work going, bro?"

Alex draped an arm around Diane. "Actually, it's been murder this last month or so. Remember I was telling you about doing a job for that rich old lady in Mount Royal?"

"I remember. What happened?"

"This woman cannot make up her mind." Alex shook his head. "She had us import Italian marble tiles for her, but then, when we've got them two-thirds installed, she decided it wasn't the right colour. Doesn't go with the rest of the décor, she says. Fine, she's paying for it, so we rip the bloody things out and reorder in the colour she wants. They come, we start laying them, and damned if she doesn't change her mind back to the original colour. I sent Noel to run interference because if I'd had to deal with her again, I think I'd have killed her."

"Don't worry about it," Gordon said. "When Jordy graduates next year and joins the company, we'll put him in charge of public relations. He's much more of a people person than you, Matt, or Duncan."

Emily stiffened and looked at Jordy. He and Terry exchanged a glance. Gordon assumed that Jordy would join his three older brothers in the family business when he finished high school, but that wasn't Jordy's dream. Only she and Terry knew that he wanted to go to medical school and eventually become a pediatrician.

I'm going to have a fight on my hands when I confront Gordon, but come hell or high water, Jordy is going to get his chance. Emily sighed. *It's going to break Gordon's heart, though. He's dreamed about all four of his boys being in the business with him since Jordy was born.*

Gordon had been very disappointed when Terry appeared to waste her education by taking a job as a carrier. Emily didn't quite understand it either, but she assumed that Terry just needed a break after six intensive years of university and would eventually go on to make use of her degrees.

Emily had hoped to leave the confrontation a little longer, but it wasn't fair to either Gordon or Jordy to allow the situation to go on as it was. Jordy was already filling out his application. *I need to speak to Gord soon.*

"Uh, I think a change may be in order here." Terry held Kelly at arm's length and deposited her in Diane's lap.

Diane took the baby, grabbed the diaper bag, and headed for the washroom.

Gordon smirked. "What's the matter? Can't handle one little dirty diaper on your own?"

Terry sat on the arm of Gord's chair. "Careful, old man, I don't see you offering to do diaper duty either. I'll have you know it's in the Aunt's Handbook that we're only required to change diapers when parents of said child are not in the immediate vicinity."

"Well, I'll have you know that the Grandfather's Handbook outranks the Aunt's Handbook," Gordon said. "And since I did many years of diaper duty on you brats, you need to have a little respect. Besides, I can remember changing you and Matt in thirty seconds flat with my eyes closed in the middle of the night."

Terry groaned. "So you say, but I haven't seen you change Kerry or Kelly once. It's always up to Mom or Diane."

Gordon turned to Emily. "Honey, tell this daughter of yours how proficient I was when the kids were little."

Emily tilted her head. "I do have to admit you were a mean diaper changer, although there was that time with Alex when you couldn't find the pins and you duct-taped his diapers on him."

Alex shot a scowl at Gordon. "Dad!"

Gordon grinned. "Well, it worked, didn't it?"

Emily rolled her eyes. "Yes, until it was time to change him again and I had to cut his diapers off."

"I'll bet you never did that to Duncan or Matt," Alex said, amidst the family's gales of laughter.

"Nope," Gordon said. "I refined my technique with Duncan, and by the time Matt and Terry came along, they had a wonderful invention called disposables."

Turning to Emily, Terry asked, "Speaking of Duncan and Matt, are they coming for dinner on Sunday?"

"Duncan and Karen are coming, but I haven't heard from Matt yet."

"Not likely to either." Terry grimaced. "Matt will make up his mind five minutes before dinner, drop in without a word, and just assume you'll have a place for him."

"I always have a place for all you kids, you know that." Emily hated the friction between Terry and Matt. *They're so blessed competitive.* Matt was the most troubled of her children, but while the boys all made allowances for him, Terry never cut him an inch of slack. When she came out to her family at sixteen, Matt was the only one who tried to use her revelation as a weapon against her. It had infuriated Terry, and the bitter edge between them hadn't eased with time.

Emily had accepted that the best she could hope for from these two was an armed truce, but she was adamant that the family home be a neutral zone. Since she had lost her temper at the pair a year ago in a spectacular display of maternal rage, both Terry and Matt had done their best to be civil in front of her, but she was under no illusions that the war had ended.

Terry yawned and ruffled her father's thinning grey hair. "I'd better be getting home. I'll see you on Sunday, okay? What time should I be here?"

Emily stood, shifted her granddaughter to one hip, and walked Terry to the door. "Drop over whenever you like, and bring the others if you want to. We'll probably eat about six."

"Okay. I'll check with Michael and Claire. I'm sure they'd love to come."

Emily hugged her goodbye, then turned back into the house to rejoin the rest of her family.

CHAPTER 4

D ESPITE HER FATIGUE, TERRY'S PACE didn't slacken as she worked her way through her route. *I shouldn't have stayed at Mom and Dad's so late last night.* Though only mid-morning, it was already a very warm day, and the weather forecast promised another long, hot August week.

Her next bundle of mail was for the Spencers. She turned into the bungalow's walkway, pleased that the couple was in the front yard.

Rob sat in his wheelchair in the shade by the front door, watching Jan work in the flower gardens. "Hey, it's my white knight."

Terry grinned. "If I'm the white knight, does that make you the damsel in distress?"

"If you put on the armour, I'll put on the dress."

Jan stepped out of the flowerbed, dusted her hands off on her shorts, and reached for the envelopes that Terry extended to her. "Don't mind that husband of mine. He's feeling his oats this morning."

"No problem. It's too nice a day not to feel great. So is he the foreman of this endeavour?"

Jan laughed and shook her head. "What Rob knows about flowers could be contained in a thimble. I'm afraid he's strictly a spectator when it comes to horticulture."

"Aw, c'mon." Rob's eyes twinkled. "I'm not that bad. If nothing else, I can order a mean bunch of flowers."

"Yes, you can, love. You are one of the world's finest flower givers." Jan looked at Terry. "He once got a little carried away, and I came home from work to find six dozen long-stemmed roses waiting for me. You could smell the scent a mile away, and we ended up handing out roses to just about everyone who came by the apartment, even the solicitors."

"So he's really a romantic at heart, is he?"

"Well, I wouldn't ask him to write a poem, but he does all right for himself."

"Hey, I can write poetry," Rob said. "Don't you remember those squadron songs I made up?"

"Rob, honey. That wasn't poetry. Those were the grossest limericks set to music I've ever heard. Face it, you weren't exactly Robert Frost."

Terry had to get back on her route, but this was her chance to present the idea she'd been considering since the day she'd met Jan in the park. "On a whole other topic, you know how you mentioned the other day that Charles de Lint was one of your favourites?"

Jan nodded.

"Well, he's doing a reading of his latest book at Chapters on Thursday night, and I wondered if maybe you guys wanted to go and then maybe grab some coffee afterwards."

Jan shook her head. "Thank you for the invitation, but Rob doesn't care for fantasy, and I can't leave him alone."

Rob gazed at Jan. "Hon, why don't you call Donny and see if he can make it in the evening instead of the afternoon? Then you could go to the reading with Terry."

"Are you sure? You wouldn't mind?"

"No, I don't mind at all. It'll be good for you to get out.

Give Donny a call. Tell him I'll spot him five points. He lost three out of five games last week, and I bet you anything he'll be keen for a rematch."

Darn. He'd have been a hoot to have along. Oh well. At least Jan can come. "Why don't I give you my number, and you can let me know if things work out all right? If they do, how about I pick you up around seven on Thursday?" Terry pulled a pencil out of her pocket.

Jan handed her one of the envelopes.

Terry jotted down her contact information. "I'll be looking forward to hearing from you, and I hope you're able to go. I think it'll be an interesting evening." She touched Rob's arm. "Thanks for being flexible."

Rob shook his head. "No, thank you. Jan needs to get out and see people more often. She shouldn't be stuck at home with me all the time, but I haven't been able to convince her of that."

"I'm not 'stuck' with you." Jan laid a hand on his shoulder. "I'm where I want to be, and you know that."

Sounds like a longstanding disagreement if I've ever heard one. "I'd better get back to work. You have a good day." Terry started back down the path.

"See you on Thursday."

Terry answered Jan's call with a wave and turned up the street with a lighter step. *I'm looking forward to this.*

———◆———

Thursday night, Terry stood in front of her closet and glared at her wardrobe. She had already chosen and then discarded three pairs of pants. *Oh, for heaven's sake, just pick something.* She closed her eyes and grabbed.

Terry opened her eyes. "Okay. That'll do." She donned a pair of faded but clean khakis. Then she chose a dark blue, short-sleeved cotton shirt and held it up while she looked in the mirror.

"I'm sure your date will be impressed." Michael stood in her doorway, smirking.

Terry scowled at him in the mirror. "It's not a date. I'm just meeting a friend for coffee at the bookstore."

"Uh-huh." Michael sauntered over and perched on the side of the bed. "I've seen you take less time dressing for a wedding. So who are you meeting?"

"You remember the woman from the park last week?" Terry finished buttoning her shirt. "I ran into them on my route a couple of days ago, and I asked her and her husband if they'd like to go to the de Lint reading. He wasn't interested, but she was, so I'm picking her up at seven."

Michael arched an eyebrow. "Since when do you go out with married women?"

"I told you. It's not a date." Terry turned to face him. "Have you ever met someone—or in this case two someones—and just, I don't know, connected? Like you know you're destined to be friends? I want to know them better...both of them. They're quite the pair. They seem like a perfect team, and they're so comfortable together. In a way, they remind me of my folks."

"So Jan's a mother figure?" Michael asked. "Cuz you've already got a pretty cool mom."

"No, of course not." Terry ran a brush through her hair. "You know, just because I'm meeting a woman for an evening out doesn't mean there's anything romantic about it. Can't you be around good-looking men without lusting after them?"

"Nope."

Terry laughed. "Silly me, I forgot who I was talking to."

She glanced at her watch. "Yikes, I've got to get going, or I'll be late. I'll see you later."

She pulled up in front of the Spencer house a few minutes after seven and walked up to the door.

It swung open, and a burly man smiled at her. "C'mon in. Jan will be ready in a minute. We kind of got behind the clock, so she's running a little late. I'm Donny, by the way, and I take it you're Terry?"

"I am. Hi, Donny." Terry followed him into the living room. "I hear you're planning on beating the pants off Rob tonight."

"I heard that," Rob said. "Just for your lack of faith, I'm going to sic the birds on you."

Terry ducked and looked around for the feathered duo. They sat calmly on the top of their cage, eating a piece of oversized lettuce that poked through the bars. "Looks like they don't listen to you very well." She settled onto the couch to wait for Jan.

"No one does. Who'd ever believe I was once a senior officer with airmen grovelling at my feet and hanging on my every command?" Rob grinned at the snort from the hallway.

"No one who ever knew you while you served, that's for sure." Jan entered the living room, tucking her green, silky T-shirt into tan slacks. "There was a reason you were called Major Marshmallow." She glanced at Terry. "I'm sorry to hold you up, but I'm ready to go now."

Terry stood. "That's okay. We've got lots of time."

Jan walked over to Rob and kissed him goodbye. "Have fun. I won't be too late."

Donny arranged the dominoes. "Take your time. I need to teach your husband a little humility."

"Fat chance," Rob said. "Prepare to lose your shirt and probably the rest of your apparel, too."

"I didn't know you two were playing strip dominoes." Jan winked as she turned to leave. "Do try not to shock the neighbours, okay?"

Terry held the door for Jan. The men were already arguing over who got to go first. "Are they always this combative?"

They walked down the path. "Always, but it's good for Rob. He was intensely competitive as a pilot and a sportsman, and now he needs other outlets. I'm not much help. I don't have a competitive bone in my body, so Donny is the perfect caregiver for him. I like him to have male companionship, too, since he's mostly stuck with me."

Terry opened Jan's door, then walked around to her side. "I doubt he'd ever call it being stuck with you. He seems to be pretty happy you're around."

Jan slid into the front seat. "I know that he is, of course, but it's hard for one person to be everything to another person, don't you think?"

Terry pulled away from the curb. "I suppose. I think of everyone in my life, and they all fill different roles for me, so it's hard to imagine having only one person in your life." She flashed Jan a smile. "But if it has to be only one person, I'll bet Rob's darned glad that it's you."

"Thank you. That's very sweet."

Fifteen minutes later, Terry pulled up in front of the huge bookstore. The parking lot was crowded. Chapters, with its co-located Starbucks, was a popular gathering spot even without a reading scheduled. Terry found a spot and parked.

A refreshing blast of cool air hit them when they entered the store.

"I may just sleep here tonight." Terry tugged on her collar.

"I take it you don't have air conditioning where you live?" Jan asked.

"Not in the whole house. I do have a temperamental window unit that works sporadically. That can be a problem when you're living in an attic in August." Terry led the way to two seats in the rear. "I'll get us a couple of ice cappuccinos, unless there's something else you'd prefer?"

"That's fine. Let me give you some money for it." Jan started to open her purse.

"No, don't worry about it. You can get the next round." Terry stood in line to get the cappuccinos and watched Jan eye the shelves of books around her. *I'll bet she's spent quite a few dollars in here.* Once she'd been served, she returned to their seats and handed Jan her cappuccino.

"Thanks. You know, I think something may be going on. I've been watching those Chapters employees milling around at the front, and they seem to be upset about something."

One of the men wearing a blue Chapters shirt stepped forward and cleared his throat. "I'm sorry. I'm afraid we're going to have to postpone the reading for tonight. Mr. de Lint has been unavoidably delayed, but he's promised to make it here as soon as he can. If you'd like to leave your number at customer services, we'll contact you with the time of the next reading. Again, I apologize for the inconvenience."

Terry and Jan looked at each other as the murmuring crowd slowly dispersed.

"Did you want to go home, then, or would you like to stay and finish your coffee, maybe do a little browsing afterwards?" Terry asked.

"I'd hate to interrupt the men when they're deep in their game. Rob might never forgive me if I prevented him from thrashing Donny." Jan raised her cappuccino. "Why don't we find a better spot to relax and drink these? It's not too often that I'm out for an evening, so I might as well take advantage of it."

Terry followed her to a couch between shelves labelled psychology and political affairs. "Judging by your library, you probably already own half these books."

"Oh, nothing as deep as this," Jan said. "When it comes to books, I'm strictly an escapist reader. I like to keep up on world events through the newspapers, but when it comes to leisure reading, I want to be swept off into fantastic worlds, with fascinating people doing incredible things. Rob's never really understood that. He prefers military techno-thrillers like Tom Clancy that are solidly grounded in politics and realism. He sometimes accuses me of having my head in the clouds, but as I told him, the real world is harsh enough — why wouldn't I want to leave it now and then?"

"I know what you mean. I like nothing better than to lose complete track of time when I'm reading or watching a movie. If I'm that absorbed in someone else's vision, then I emerge at the end feeling like I've taken a trip without ever leaving home."

"Are you quite a movie buff?" Jan asked.

"I used to be. My mom always knew that if she couldn't find me on Saturday afternoon, odds were that I was at the theatre. Lately though, I mostly rely on videos to keep up as I never get to the movies I want to see before they've left town. I always make mental notes about which ones I might like. Then I'm shocked when I finally have time and they've long since departed the theatre. My life's too darned busy at the moment." Terry shook her head. "I think the last film I actually saw in a theatre was the final *Lord of the Rings*."

"Rob and I went to see that one, too. Even my thoroughly

hard-headed husband enjoyed it, though I should've known anything with sweeping battle scenes would engross him."

"It was good, though I'm not one of those who went back to see it twenty times in a row."

Jan smiled. "Do you mean to say you weren't swept away by Orlando's elfish charms?"

"Hardly." Terry shook her head.

"So are you more a Viggo Mortensen type? I'm assuming you're single by lack of a ring, not that that necessarily indicates anything."

Terry hesitated. It was always difficult to know the right timing for coming out to new people in her life.

"Hello, Terry." The voice came from behind her. "What a lovely surprise running into you here." Marika stepped around in front of them. "Aren't you going to introduce me to your friend?"

Terry groaned inwardly. *Jesus, of all the people to run into tonight. Coincidence? I doubt it.* "Marika, this is Mrs. Jan Spencer. Jan, this is Marika Havers, and I'm sure that she was just leaving."

Marika raised an eyebrow. "*Mrs.* Spencer, is it? It's so nice to meet you. Of course, it's always nice to meet one of Terry's friends."

Terry glowered at her.

Marika took a step back. "I'm sorry I can't stop and chat. It was nice meeting you, Mrs. Spencer. Terry, I'll see you again soon." She walked away.

"Not if I see you first." Terry hadn't thought Marika would hear her muttered words, but her pace faltered before picking up as she walked to the exit.

Jan gazed at Terry. "Do you want to tell me what just happened?"

Not really. "Marika and I dated for about a month before I broke it off. That was several weeks ago, but she keeps turning up wherever I am. I feel like she's stalking me, but she doesn't do anything overt that I can pin her on. She's always just there."

"That answers my question about your type, then." Jan drained her glass.

"Is that a problem?" Terry held her breath.

Jan smiled. "It's no problem at all. I'm glad you were open with me."

Terry sighed. *Thank God. Marika didn't ruin things after all.*

Jan set her empty cup aside. "I think the next round is on me. Do you want another of the same?"

Terry nodded, and Jan walked over to the corner coffee bar. *I hope Rob is as open-minded as his wife.*

Jan returned with their drinks, and they settled into the ends of the couch, half-facing each other.

"So you told me a little about your roommates. Do you have family in the city?" Jan asked.

"And how. My parents had five kids, so I've got three older brothers and one younger. Alex is married with nine-month-old twin girls, and Duncan is engaged. Jordy's got one more year of high school. What about you?"

"Family? Other than Rob I have an older sister, Kate, and her family here, and my mom lives back east."

"Are you close to your sister?"

Jan nodded. "Pretty close, but of course she's busy with work and raising her son, so we don't see a lot of each other. What about you? Do you get along well with all your siblings?"

"With Alex and Duncan, yes. And Jordy is my favourite. He's eight years younger than me, but sometimes it seems like he's twenty years older than me. He's a really special kid."

"You left one out, didn't you?"

Terry frowned. "I did."

Jan waited quietly.

Terry blew out a breath. "Matt and me, we don't really get along all that well. Never have. We're the closest in age. Maybe that's part of the problem. Matty had big dreams when he was younger. He was a helluva hockey player, and he might've made it to the NHL."

"But?"

"But the dumbass was hot-dogging with some friends out of bounds on the ski hill, and he somersaulted off a cliff and into some trees. Busted himself up so bad that it ended his pro hockey dreams." Terry shook her head. "He got mean after that. One time he so thoroughly convinced Jordy that he'd been adopted that the little guy was going to run away. Luckily, I came on him packing his ball mitt and GI Joe and found out what was going on."

"Why did Jordy believe he was adopted?"

"Because all the rest of us look like me and he doesn't."

"So he's not tall and lean with dark hair and eyes?"

Huh, she noticed. "No, Jordy's stocky, and he's got sandy hair and blue eyes."

"So how'd you convince him to stay?"

"I showed him some old childhood photos of our maternal grandfather. Jordy is his spitting image. Then I smuggled some of Mom's chocolate chip cookies downstairs before dinner and reminded him if he ran away he wouldn't get any more cookies. It worked."

Jan laughed. "Rob can be manipulated with homemade cookies, too."

"They do say that the way to a man's heart, even a little man, is through his stomach." Terry set her empty cup aside. "Anyway, I was so pissed off at Matt that when I found him, I punched his lights out. I got grounded for a month, but it was worth it."

"So you have previous experience being a knight in shining armour, then." Jan's eyes sparkled.

Terry blushed. "I suppose so. But enough about me. Tell me about you and Rob. Where did you two meet?"

"We were both posted in Ottawa many years ago. I arrived there as a young corporal in air traffic control, and we both worked out of base operations," Jan said. "He and his wife had split up not long before. Rob was still pretty devastated."

"It's hard to imagine anyone leaving him. He's so … charismatic."

Jan nodded. "He is. Wheelchair or not, he attracted people to him like bees to honey. But she couldn't handle the fact that MS had left him disabled. It was a bitter split, to say the least."

"So you started dating soon after?"

"Not exactly," Jan said. "There was the small issue of him being an officer and I wasn't, not to mention he's quite a bit older than me. He told me later that he fought his attraction to me, but when we were both on duty, we got along so well that he finally asked if I'd be interested in extra work cleaning his condo."

Terry blinked. "Really? He just wanted a cleaning lady?"

"No, he had two really good cleaning ladies at the time." Jan laughed. "He fired them so he could hire me."

Terry chuckled. "Did you know what was on his mind?"

"Not in the least. I was used to working second jobs, and it seemed like a good opportunity." Jan shrugged. "But once I was around him outside of work, we grew closer and closer until we fell in love."

Terry whistled. "That must've gone over well at work."

"We kept it from them as long as possible. I even rented

an apartment with a friend for a year and never stayed there once. My buddy redirected all my mail and covered for me while I lived with Rob."

"So what happened? Did you get caught?"

"Yes and no. Eventually, I received a posting to Edmonton. We were both distraught at the thought of being separated." A distant look dawned in Jan's eyes. "Even so, you could've knocked me over with a feather the night he proposed. He was so sweet about it. He said he'd understand if I didn't want to throw my lot in with him since he was coming up on retirement and had been in declining condition, so he knew it was unlikely he'd be able to get another job."

"But you said yes." Terry rolled her eyes. "Obviously."

"I did, and the next day I put in for my release. We've never looked back. We had some really good years seeing the country after he retired, until travelling became too much to handle."

"How did you end up out here in Calgary?" Terry asked.

"Rob's dad passed away, and he wanted me to be close to Kate so I would have support close by if his health worsens, so we moved west."

"I'm glad you did."

Jan nodded. "So am I."

An hour later, after they'd finished their cappuccinos and done a bit of browsing and buying, they returned to Terry's car.

Terry gestured at the bag of books on Jan's lap. "Aren't you going to run out of space for books one of these days?"

"That's what Rob says, too, but there's always room for more books. I've only begun putting bookcases downstairs, so I'm good for at least another few years. Besides, it could be worse. I could be hooked on diamonds and furs instead of books."

Terry steered her car into the light traffic. "I suppose if you're going to have an addiction, books are pretty benign. How come you don't just go to the library?"

"When I was younger, I practically lived in libraries, but after I married Rob and we had some spare money, I found that I really enjoyed owning books. I find a great sense of peace in being surrounded by them. I know that if I'm upset or feeling out of sorts, all I have to do is walk into a bookstore and I feel calmer. I suppose that sounds a bit strange."

Terry shook her head. "Not at all. Everyone takes comfort in something different. My mom had to forcibly remove my favourite blankie from my arms when I was about ten, just because it had fallen to shreds and was leaving pieces of itself all over the house. My brother Jordy had an old stuffed horse that he slept with up until our older brothers tormented him so unmercifully about it that he hid it. But I happen to know that he's still got it tucked away in his closet. I think we all need some kind of security blanket. Books are as good as, if not better than, anything else."

When Terry pulled up in front of the Spencer home, she turned to Jan. "Do you think you and Rob might like to go for Sunday brunch sometime? I know a really nice restaurant that overlooks the river. It's kind of small and not very well known, but the food is great."

"I'd like that, and I'm sure Rob would, too. Is the restaurant accessible?"

Terry's brow furrowed. "I think so. I don't remember there being any stairs to get in, but I can call and confirm. When would you like to go?"

"Is this Sunday too soon? We can leave it for a few weeks if you'd rather."

"No, this Sunday is great. Do you mind if I ask my little brother to join us?"

"Not at all. I'm sure we'd both enjoy meeting him. I'll talk to Rob and call you, all right? I'll have to get directions from you on how to get there."

"No problem. I am a direction-giver par excellence."

Jan chuckled. "That may be so, but I generally leave the map-reading up to my co-pilot and he once got us lost in the wilds of northern Minnesota, not that he'll admit it. Listen, thanks very much for the invitation tonight. I'm sorry that the reading was cancelled, but I had fun anyway. Maybe when de Lint does make it to town, we could try again."

"It's a date." *Damn it.* Terry flushed. "I don't mean a *date* date—"

Jan put her hand on Terry's arm. "Relax. I didn't take it the wrong way. Anyway, have a good night, and I'll give you a call about Sunday."

Terry waited until Jan went inside, then smacked herself on the forehead. "Dumbass. Could you possibly have made things any more awkward?" She started the car. *Oh well. It was still a great evening. And Sunday's only a couple of days away.*

CHAPTER 5

S UNDAY MORNING, TERRY PULLED UP in front of her parents' home and got out of her car. *Wonder if I gave Jordy enough time to drag himself out of bed.*

In the yard, Emily was working in her tiered rock garden.

"Hi, Mom. Is that lazy brother of mine up yet?"

Emily sat back on her heels. "I did try, Terry. I called him at nine and nine thirty and finally had your father drag him bodily out of bed about fifteen minutes ago. Last I heard, he was being directed toward the shower, so if you give him a few more minutes, I'm sure he'll be ready."

"Aw, I knew he wouldn't be ready in time anyway. That's why I told him we had to be there at ten thirty, but we're really meeting them at eleven."

Emily rose to her feet and brushed the dirt off her knees. "Have I met this couple you're having brunch with? I don't remember you mentioning them before."

"No, though I'd like you and Dad to meet them sometime. I think you'd really like them. You have a lot in common with Jan. She's a garden-loving bookworm just like you. Rob's a former fighter pilot. He has MS now, so he's in a wheelchair, but he's got a terrific sense of humour. I'll bet he and Dad would get along like a house on fire."

"Bring them over for Sunday dinner, then, dear. You know we always have room at the table for more." Emily's brow furrowed. "It might be best for them to come when we're barbequing because he could come directly in from the back alley. If we were in the house, I'm not sure how we'd get the wheelchair inside. Could we just lift it up the stairs?"

"I think Jordy and I could probably handle it fine between us. For that matter, I'm guessing Jan has wrestled him up a stair or two. She's been looking after him all these years, so I assume she's gotten him in and out of lots of tight spots. Actually, that was the way I met them. Remember I told you about the man I helped rescue on my route?"

"That's right, I remember now." Emily smiled. "My daughter, the good Samaritan."

They turned as the front door banged open.

A dishevelled Jordy burst through the doorway and ran down the steps. "I'm ready." He tried to tuck his shirt in his pants while he stumbled over untied shoelaces.

Terry put her hands on his shoulders. "Slow down. We've got lots of time." She ran a hand over his cheek. "In fact, we have more than enough time for you to go back and shave."

"Aw, Terry, it's the weekend," Jordy said. "I hate shaving on weekends."

"You hate shaving period, but I'm not taking you out to brunch looking like a porcupine, so go run the shaver over that stubble."

Jordy's shoulders drooped, but he climbed back up the stairs and went into the house.

Terry shook her head. "Remember when he first grew a couple of hairs on his face? He could hardly wait to start shaving."

Emily nodded. "The novelty quickly wore off, but I'm glad you said that. He looks so nice when he's cleaned up. I wish he listened as well to your father and me as he does to you."

"He listens to you, especially about the important stuff. He just can't let you think you run him, that's all. I'm sure I was just as bad when I was young."

"Oh yes, Methuselah, you were just as bad. Do you remember the battle I had dressing you for school?"

Terry snickered.

"Honestly, I should've had a clue then." Emily shook her head. "If I put a dress on you, it inevitably got ripped on the playground, but if I sent you in jeans, your clothes came home in decent condition."

"Did you have a clue? You didn't really seem surprised when I came out to you."

"I wasn't all that shocked, no. I don't think any of us were."

"You were all decent about it." Terry scowled. "Except Matt, but no surprise there."

"Terry —"

Terry shook her head. "Forget it. It doesn't matter anymore." She looked away from her mother's penetrating gaze.

Jordy bounced out of the house and down the stairs and drew himself up into a mock salute in front of Terry. "Present for inspection, sir!"

"That's ma'am to you, soldier, and don't you forget it, or you'll be giving me fifty of your best." Terry circled her brother. "Okay, you'll pass this time, although you could have used a little more spit and polish on those shoes."

Jordy looked at his feet. "They're runners, for crying out loud. Why would I spit on them?"

"Details, details." Terry waved airily. "I don't make the regulations, I just enforce them." She wrapped an arm around his shoulders. "Okay, let's get going. See you later, Mom. I'll ask Jan and Rob about coming for Sunday dinner and let you know what they say."

"Are we meeting the king and queen of Sheba today?" Jordy asked as they walked to the car.

"No, just people I'd like us to be friends with, so behave yourself. And no telling any of those gross jokes you were swapping with Gary the other night either, or you and I will be having words."

Jordy glanced at her. "Oh, um, you heard those, did you? Mom didn't, did she?"

"Not that I know of, but I'd be careful if I was you. She hears you and it doesn't matter how old you are. You'll find your mouth full of soap before you know it." She grinned at his blush. *Mom's ways might be old-fashioned, but they still work.*

Terry rounded a curve and pulled into a small gravelled parking lot in front of the River Garden restaurant. The parking lot was filled almost to capacity, but she found a spot and turned off the car. "We're a few minutes early. I think we'll wait here so we can give Jan a hand if she needs it."

Jordy followed her to sit in the shade of a tall, old willow tree. "Are you treating today?"

She snorted. "Now you ask? What happens if I say no? Are you planning on doing dishes to cover your part?"

Jordy elbowed her, and she toppled over on the lawn.

She laughed and sat upright. "I suppose I could be persuaded, but it'll cost you."

"Cost me what?"

"Oh, a little sweat and manual labour. My car is seriously in need of a good cleaning out, not to mention a wash and wax. You can even hang on to it for a couple of days." *If I don't have wheels for a few days, I'll spend more time writing.*

Jordy grinned. "You've got a deal. When do you want it done?"

"You can take it after brunch today. Just drop me off at my place and have it back to me by Wednesday, all clean and polished. But make sure you have it to me by five, because I'm going out that night."

"Oh, yeah? Got a hot date?"

Terry shook her head. "You're as bad as Michael. Actually, it's just the ball team's end-of-season bash at Oly's. I wasn't sure if I should go because I missed so many games when I threw my shoulder out, but Lisa and Robyn said they'd hog-tie me and drag me along if I tried to bow out."

"If Robyn said that, you'd better go, because she could hog-tie you with one hand behind her back."

Terry laughed. "She's got the muscles for it, all right. But then you'd have biceps like hers if you spent all day every day handling luggage and cargo, too."

A van pulled into the parking lot and parked in the handicap zone.

Terry stood and pulled Jordy up with her. "I think that's them."

As they walked toward the van, the rear door opened upward and a ramp lowered to reveal Rob's chair. Jan hopped out of the driver's seat and came around to the back. She waved at them. "Good morning. Isn't it a beautiful day?"

"Good morning, Jan." Terry leaned into the van. "Hi, Rob."

"Hey, Terry, how's it going?" Rob waited for Jan to unlock his chair.

"Great. Guys, this is my baby brother, Jordy."

He shot her an indignant glance.

"Jordy, this is Jan and Rob Spencer."

After shaking hands with Jan, Jordy poked his head around the corner of the van. "Hi, Rob."

"Hi, Jordy," Rob said. "I'd shake hands, but I'm a little tied up at the moment."

"Give me a moment to spring him," Jan said.

"Can I help in any way?" Terry asked.

"No, thanks, it just takes a second." Jan unlocked the tie-downs and the chair's brakes and began to roll the chair down the ramp. Backing away from the van, she activated a remote control latched over the chair's frame, and the door began to close.

Jordy whistled. "That's quite the set-up you have there."

Jan nodded. "It makes it so much easier to get around than if we had to depend on handi-cabs all the time. Shall we go in, then?"

Terry pointed at a path leading around the restaurant to the backyard. "Is the outdoor patio okay, or would you rather be inside?"

"Outdoors is fine as long as there's some shade for Rob. Otherwise, he'll last longer if he's inside out of the sun."

Rob rolled his eyes. "Geez, you make me sound like crab salad at a picnic."

"You and I both know what happens when you get overheated. You turn into a limp noodle." Jan glanced at Terry, who walked beside her as she steered Rob's chair. "He'll try and push it if he can, but he's really better off if he can stay cool."

"No problem at all. I know the waiters here pretty well, and I'm sure we can find a shady spot." Terry led them around to a stone patio set with tables and chairs. At least three quarters of the tables were filled, but there was a table in the corner under overhanging trees.

"Terry!" Aaron, decked out in his crisp black-and-white waiter's garb, swept up to her and gave her a quick hug. "I haven't seen you in forever. Don't tell me you didn't bring that delicious roommate of yours with you this time."

"Hi, Aaron. No, sorry. Last I saw, that delicious roommate of mine was stumbling out to the backyard hammock with an ice pack. He was moaning something about not moving for the next three days." Terry laughed. "I think the boy may have partied too well last night."

"I heard Trey had his annual summer blast last night, but of all the lousy luck, I had to work the late shift and missed all the fun." Aaron pouted. "But where are my manners? Let me get you seated."

"Can we have that table over there?" Terry pointed at the shaded corner table.

"For you, fair lady, anything." Aaron led them past other customers to the desired table. After he removed a chair to make space for Rob, he placed menus in front of each place and promised to return with coffee.

"Is this all right?" Terry asked.

Jan and Rob nodded.

"Great. I hope you brought your appetites with you, because they don't stint on portions and everything is made from the freshest ingredients they can find. The owners run a small farm not too far from here, and they use a lot of their own produce in the restaurant."

"Well, considering that my wife has been starving me all morning in anticipation, I'm more than ready to chow down." Rob perused the menu that Jan opened and placed in his lap.

"Excuse me?" Jan raised an eyebrow. "I was starving you? Who wouldn't even eat his toast this morning because he was so excited about going out?"

Rob grinned. "I guess that would be me. So, Terry, what do you recommend?"

"Depends if you feel like breakfast or lunch." Terry scanned her menu even though she knew most of it by heart. "Jordy will order their hamburger, home fries, and giant chocolate sundae, because they give you enough to choke a horse."

Jordy, who had been uncharacteristically quiet, blushed. "I'm a growing boy." He glanced at Rob. "If you don't want lunch, they make terrific eggs Benedict here."

"You've stumbled on my husband's weakness," Jan said. "He loves eggs Benedict, and he claims I never make them as well as restaurants do. Rob?"

"Sounds good."

Jan turned to Terry. "Do you have any favourites?"

"Well, like I said, you can't go wrong with anything here, but I'm partial to their Belgian waffles with Saskatoon berries and real whipped cream."

"That's sounds great. I think I'll go with that."

"Me too." Terry motioned Aaron over.

After he left with their orders, Jan took a short straw from her purse, put it in Rob's coffee, and held the cup for him to take a sip. "Careful, love. Don't burn yourself." She gazed around at their surroundings. "What a beautiful spot. I'm amazed I've never heard of it before."

"The owners are deliberately low-key," Terry said. "They're more interested in catering to an appreciative clientele than becoming the 'hot new place to be' in town. They've actually been here three years, and they do a steady business. I often see the same people, and I try to come back at least every month or so. You should see it in the winter. The patio's closed then, of course, but from the dining room after a fresh snowfall, it's like you're looking out over a faerie kingdom."

Jan glanced back at the restaurant. Floor-to-ceiling

windows enclosed an interior dining area. "We'll have to try it sometime in the winter, then, don't you think, Rob?"

"Yes, if we can get access, that would be great." Rob looked at Jordy. "So what do you do? Are you still in school?"

Jordy nodded. "I start my last year of high school in September, and then it's on to the real world."

"And what are you planning to do in the real world?" Rob smiled at Jan. "It seems like only yesterday that I was making those sorts of plans myself."

Jordy glanced at Terry.

My gut says to trust him, buddy. She nodded. "Go ahead."

Jordy drew a breath. "I want to become a pediatrician. Unfortunately, my dad has other plans, but Mom and Terry think they can persuade him to see the light."

"We will," Terry said. "Don't doubt it. You're going to be the best pediatrician ever." *Even if I have to pay your way through med school myself.*

Jordy flashed a smile at her. "Rob, I hear you and Jan used to be in the military. That must have been an interesting life."

Jan and Rob chuckled.

"I guess that's one way of putting it," Rob said. "It was kind of like the ancient Chinese proverb about living in interesting times, but yes, I loved flying and I had a great time until this bloody disease grounded me."

"I thought about learning to fly in my younger years." Jordy ignored Terry's stifled laugh. "But I was never sure if I could handle it or not. I've never even flown in a big passenger jet, so I'm not sure how I'd feel on a fighter. I always liked the wild rides at the Stampede, though, and they never bothered my stomach much, so I think I'd be okay. Heck, I went on the Skyscraper ride this year with no problems, and they say you're pulling at least 4 Gs on that, so I think I could handle fighters okay."

Rob tilted his head. "Would you like to get a taste of real flying?"

Jordy's brow furrowed. "Um, I didn't think you could fly anymore."

"No, I can't. But I do have a very good friend who will be participating in the Springbank air show on Labour Day, and I think I could persuade him to take you up. He's an old Air Force buddy of mine who flies for Air Canada out of Vancouver now, but in his spare time, he has an air demonstration team that performs at air shows all over North America. If you're interested, I'll give him a call. It's just a little bi-wing prop job, but he'll do a few loops and circuits and give you a taste of what flying is all about."

Jordy's eyes widened. "Are you serious? That would be better than the Skyscraper."

God, that's nice of Rob. Terry ruffled his hair. "What do you say?"

"Thank you, thank you, thank you!"

Rob grinned. "I hope you feel the same way when you've got your feet back on the ground afterwards."

"I will, I swear." Jordy leaned forward. "Did you ever fly air shows?"

Rob and Jordy began to talk air shows, past and upcoming.

Terry listened for a moment, then turned to Jan. "That's an incredible offer. Do you think Rob's friend will agree?"

Jan nodded. "Eric's one of the nicest guys you could ever hope to meet, and he's got a real soft spot for Rob. They flew together over in Europe and got into trouble off-duty all the time, usually with the local Fräuleins. Eric stuck by Rob through thick and thin. He'll jump at the chance to do him a favour, especially one like this where they both get to show off their love of airplanes. We were going out to the air show as Eric's guests anyway, so Jordy is more than welcome to come along, as are you, if you're interested."

"I've never been to an air show, but I'd love to see Jordy's first ride. I'll be sure to bring along my camera and some brown paper bags."

Jordy glared at Terry. "I'm not going to need any bags."

"Don't be too hasty," Rob said. "I know of even the occasional experienced pilot who's had to clean his cockpit after a wild flight. Not that it ever happened to me, of course."

"Really?" Jan's eyes twinkled. "Not even the time you got lost?"

Both Terry and Jordy leaned forward, but Aaron interrupted with their meals.

C'mon, c'mon, Aaron. I just know Rob's got a story on-deck.
Once everyone was served, Terry asked, "Okay, so what happened when you got lost?"

Rob's gaze was fixed on his plate as Jan cut up his eggs Benedict. "Oh, you don't really want to hear any of those old stories."

Terry and Jordy grinned at each other. "Yes, we do."

Rob sighed and looked at Jan. "I'm going to get you for this, you know." He turned to the other two. "She loves to embarrass me about this story, but okay, if you insist. I'd flown out of our base in France on a training mission. I hadn't been in Europe long, so I wasn't all that familiar with the route I was to take. I thought I was on-course, and I was sitting back enjoying the flight when I noticed a very built-up area on the ground. According to my maps, there shouldn't have been any large towns where I was, so I looked around, trying to recognize some landmarks. That's when I saw it."

Jan laughed.

"You saw what?" Jordy asked.

"Only one of the most recognizable landmarks in the world." Rob shook his head. "I was flying low-level, Mach one, directly at the Eiffel Tower. Somehow, I'd gotten turned around and was heading right over Paris in controlled airspace, which wasn't on my flight plan. I pulled away hard, and the next thing you know, I'm over Orly, panicked because the controllers had to have picked up this unidentified aircraft right in the middle of one of the busiest airspaces in the world."

"Oh my God!" Jordy stared at him. "What did you do?"

"I lit my afterburner, stood my 104 on its tail, and prayed I wouldn't intersect with some passenger jet coming in to land. I flew back to base, convinced that the moment I landed I was going to be arrested. At the very least, I figured I'd be busted to flight cadet and sent back to Canada in disgrace. But nothing happened. No one ever said anything to me, so I guess the French never figured out what idiot crashed their airspace and flew over Paris like it was a village green. To this day, I can't believe I did such a dumb thing and, even more so, that I got away with it."

"Too cool." Jordy's eyes gleamed. "You must've had so many adventures while you were over there."

Terry smiled at him. *I do believe my baby brother just developed a serious case of hero worship.*

"Yes, and most of them aren't repeatable." Jan shook her head. "Rob was not exactly the poster boy for model behaviour when he served overseas."

"But I had fun." Rob canted his head. "And after all, it's only natural to sow your wild oats when you're young."

"You, my love, sowed enough wild oats to cover half of Europe."

"Rumours and lies. Half of the stories my buddies told about me weren't true."

Jan snorted. "Even the half that was true was more than enough to cement your reputation as a wild man."

"You should meet our dad," Jordy said. "He served in the military too for a few years, though I think he was Army, not Air Force."

Perfect opening, little brother. "You should. My mom said to ask you to come over for a barbeque whenever it's convenient. They have family and friends over every Sunday, and you'd be more than welcome to join us. Would you like to?"

Jordy grabbed Terry's arm. "I know. Two weeks from today is your birthday." He turned to Jan and Rob. "Why don't you plan to come over then?"

"Wouldn't we be intruding on a family birthday party?" Jan asked.

Terry shook her head. "Not at all. I'd love for you to be there, and, really, it's no big deal. Mom just adds a birthday cake to her usual Sunday dinner, and the victim of the day gets lots of razzing from the rest of the clan. I'll have Mom give you a call this week to confirm the date. How's that?"

Jan glanced at Rob, and he nodded. "That sounds wonderful. We'd love to join you. May I bring something?"

"You and Mom can work that out, but she usually takes care of everything," Terry said. "She really likes putting on big family dinners and always has extra places for friends to drop by."

Conversation flowed easily during the rest of the brunch, and Jan convinced Rob to tell a couple more stories from his European flying days.

Terry was fascinated by how deftly Jan fed herself and Rob and never missed a beat. When Rob was ready for a bite or sip of coffee, it was there for him. *It's sort of like watching a ballet – perfect timing and no moves wasted.*

They were nursing coffees after they finished eating when Aaron came up behind Terry and wrapped his arms around her shoulders. "Do tell, beautiful. What happened with you and that divine blonde I last saw you with? Are you two still an item, or did she kick you out of her bed?"

Terry rolled her eyes. When she was last here, she and Marika had only been dating a week and couldn't keep their hands off each other. *I should've known Aaron would remember given how much he teased us that night. Damn it.* "Yesterday's news." She glared at Aaron. "Marika and I didn't work out."

Aaron laughed and stood with his hands on Terry's shoulders. "You sure looked like you were working out well when I saw you." He waved his hand. "Well, it's not like there won't be another lovely woman along shortly. You seem to have an endless stream of them. Don't know where you find them, darling, but if any of them have twin brothers, you be sure to send them my way, 'kay?"

God, open up the ground and swallow me now. Terry slouched in her chair and stared at the table.

Someone from another table summoned Aaron. He patted her shoulder and ambled off.

Terry looked up.

The others stared at her, Jordy with barely suppressed hilarity, Jan with amused sympathy, and Rob with frank curiosity.

Terry blinked at Rob. "Sorry about that. He talks too much."

"It's okay. I already knew that my masculine wiles are wasted on you." Rob batted his eyes. "And here I thought no woman could resist me."

Jan and Jordy burst out laughing.

Terry laid her hand on his arm. "Rob, no one could possibly resist you."

He grinned. "Ain't it the truth. I must say, though, I'm positively in awe. I don't remember having half your success when I was after beautiful blondes."

"Then your memory has slipped a few links," Jan said. "As I recall, you didn't limit yourself to blondes, and you cut a pretty wide swath through Europe yourself."

Rob winked at her. "But now I'm focused exclusively on redheads."

Jan raised an eyebrow. "Would that be redheads plural, husband of mine?"

He shook his head. "Nope, I'm strictly a one-woman man now."

"Uh-huh. That's only because I'd have to drive you to any assignations, so it'd be a bit difficult carrying on with other redheads...or blondes or brunettes."

"You wound me deeply, o wife of mine. I'm as faithful as an old hound dog and just about as wrinkled, too." Affection shone in Rob's eyes.

Jan lifted a hand to caress his cheek.

Terry smiled. *I'll bet you were a ladies' man in your day. You probably still would be, wheelchair or not, if you weren't so crazy about your wife.*

They drained the last of multiple coffees, paid the check, and walked back to the parking lot.

As they approached the van, Jan activated the remote control to open the rear door.

After saying their goodbyes to Rob, Terry and Jordy stood out of Jan's way as she pushed him into the van and locked his chair down. She stepped out and pressed the button to close the van door.

"Thank you both, so much," Jan said. "We really enjoyed ourselves today, and I appreciate your invitation for the barbeque, too."

"It was our pleasure." Terry had rarely meant the words more. "I'll have Mom give you a call, okay?"

"That's sound great. I'll look forward to hearing from her." Jan walked to the front of the van and got in. A few moments later, she backed up, waving at Terry and Jordy as she pulled out of the lot.

"So did you have a good time?" Terry asked.

Jordy nodded. "Yeah, I really did. Thanks for inviting me. They're very nice people, and that Rob is a riot. What a rotten thing, though, to go from flying fighters to riding a wheelchair, eh?"

"It is, but you'd never know it to listen to him, would you? He doesn't seem to have a smidgen of bitterness over how his life's turned out."

"You know, in his place, I don't think I could be nearly as calm about it. Did you see how Jan had to do everything for him, even wipe his nose?"

"I did, but I don't think they think twice about it. It seems as natural to them as breathing. They really seem to be two halves of a whole in a sense. You have to admire the way they handle things, that's for sure."

"No kidding. I just hope I never find out what it's like to be in his shoes."

"Amen, brother."

CHAPTER 6

T HE NEXT MORNING, JAN MET Terry at the door, and they chatted for a few moments before Terry moved on with her route.

The following day, the drapes were drawn, and there was no sign of Jan or Rob.

Wednesday, Jan was again at the front door to accept the mail, but her face was drawn and her weary eyes were shadowed by dark circles.

Terry stared. "Are you okay? Is everything all right with Rob?"

Jan shook her head. "No, Rob's having a bit of a tough time right now. He came down with another bladder infection, and it's hit him harder than usual."

"But he seemed fine on Sunday," Terry said. "How'd this happen so fast?"

"His immune system is very weak. He doesn't have the strength to fight infections off, so they come on fast and knock him down flat." Jan rubbed her eyes, worry etched deep in the lines of her face. "It started Monday afternoon, and it's just got to run its course now. It's nothing we haven't handled before, and he's already on the medication he needs, so it's a matter of waiting it out."

"You know, if you need me for anything, and I do mean anything, you can call me, right? I'm serious, Jan. You don't have to do this alone. Even if it's only to bring you some takeout so you don't have to cook, I don't mind a bit." Terry hesitated. "Can I see him, just for a moment to say hi? Or is he sleeping right now?"

"He sleeps off and on, but I think he's awake right now."

Terry stepped over the threshold and set her bags down. She expected to see Rob in his customary spot in the recliner, but he was stretched out on the couch. His eyes were closed, and he was covered with a blanket. His breathing rattled in the quiet, darkened room.

Swallowing, Terry crossed to his side and knelt. She laid a hand on his arm and touched his forehead. "Hey, big guy. What are you doing just lying around all day?"

Rob's eyelids fluttered open. His eyes were glazed and bleary, but he struggled to say something.

Terry laid her fingers over his lips. "Shhh, it's okay. I just wanted to say hi and check to see how you were doing. You go back to sleep now, and I'll stop by again tomorrow."

Rob closed his eyes.

Terry stood and steered Jan into the kitchen. In a hushed voice, she asked, "Is he all right staying at home? Shouldn't he be in the hospital or something? He felt so hot to me."

Jan pulled back, and resentment flashed in her eyes. "This isn't the first time we've been through this. I know what I'm doing and how to handle it." She half turned away. "Rob hates going into the hospital, and it would just make things worse. Besides, they'd never care for him as well as I can, and he's on the usual antibiotics to beat this."

Jesus, I'm an idiot. Open mouth, insert foot. Terry gently tugged Jan so they were face to face again. "I'm so sorry. I'm not questioning you. I was just surprised to see him like this, and I overreacted. You're the expert; you know what you're doing."

Jan nodded, though her body was rigid.

Terry took a deep breath. "I'm also worried about you. You don't look like you've slept a wink in days, and this has to be hard on you. Would you like me to come back after work and pull a relief shift so you can catch up on some sleep?"

"I, uh, no, thanks, but we'll be okay." Jan wrapped her sweater more tightly around herself.

"Are you sure, because I wouldn't mind a bit and I could wake you up immediately if he seemed to be in any distress." *Please let me help.*

Jan mustered a weak but genuine smile. "I really appreciate the offer, but we'll be okay. We've handled these infections many times. By the weekend, he'll be almost back to normal. I don't want to impose."

"It's not an imposition. Not in the least." Terry didn't want to leave matters on the sour note she'd inadvertently struck. "Look, how about I give you a call toward the end of the week, and if Rob's up to it, I'll bring Chinese and some DVDs over on Saturday night."

"I'd like that," Jan said. "But I'll have to see how he's doing, okay?"

Terry nodded. "I guess I'd better get back to work." Impulsively, she pulled Jan into a quick hug. "You take care of yourself, too, you hear me?"

"I will...and thanks."

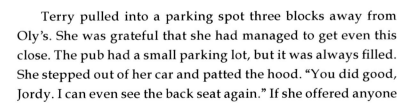

Terry pulled into a parking spot three blocks away from Oly's. She was grateful that she had managed to get even this close. The pub had a small parking lot, but it was always filled. She stepped out of her car and patted the hood. "You did good, Jordy. I can even see the back seat again." If she offered anyone a ride home tonight, she wouldn't be embarrassed to let them in her car.

When she approached Oly's, Lisa and Robyn were lounging outside.

"Hi, guys." Terry smiled. "All ready to party?"

They flanked her walking toward the entrance.

Terry looked from one to the other. "What's up? Why the escort?"

Lisa and Robyn exchanged glances.

"It's possible," Lisa said. "Maybe...not for sure but likely — "

"What?" Terry frowned. "What's going on?"

"We really wanted you to be at the party tonight," Robyn said. "After all, you were a big part of the team until you wrecked your shoulder."

"And — ?"

Lisa took a deep breath. "Well, as I was saying, it's entirely possible that Marikamightbeheretonight." She and Robyn each grabbed one of Terry's arms.

Terry stopped. "What? You didn't tell me that before."

"Obviously," Lisa said, "or you would have cancelled out on us." They tried to pull Terry forward, but she resisted.

"How'd she get in on this anyway? She doesn't play ball. God knows she wouldn't want to risk breaking a fingernail."

Lisa heaved a sigh. "You know, the whole world doesn't revolve around you. Marika being here tonight has absolutely nothing to do with you."

Terry snorted. "Sure it doesn't. And it doesn't snow in winter either."

"Well, it doesn't if you live in Florida." Lisa tugged on Terry's arm. "Besides, she's here with Val, and I'm sure she couldn't care less whether you're here or not."

"With Val? Our first baseman? That Val?"

"That would be the Val in question, yes." Lisa grinned. "So you see, you're perfectly safe, and besides, Robyn will keep away any predatory blondes."

"But not too far away," Robyn said.

Terry glared at Robyn but started to move forward. "So when did this happen? I thought Val was going out with Liz."

"Old news, my friend." Lisa reached for the door handle. "You really need to get out more."

Terry shook her head but followed them into the pub.

They made their way through the Wednesday crowd and heard their teammates long before they saw them. The team had spread out over several tables. They found chairs and sat down.

Half-empty pitchers of beer and scattered pretzels, peanuts, and popcorn testified that the party had been underway for a while.

As they anteed up for beer, Terry glanced around. Marika sat farther down the line of tables beside Val. *Has she really moved on? God, I hope so.* She'd been flattered at first when Marika was so persistent, but her attentions had quickly become burdensome.

Marika looked up from her drink and met Terry's gaze.

Terry ducked her head and eased back so Robyn's bulk blocked Marika's view. She turned to Gale on her left. "So I hear I'm going to have some stiff competition for third base next year."

Gale shook her head. "Not a chance. It's all yours. I'm going back to right field, where I can listen to the dandelions grow. Now that I know why they call it the hot corner, I don't want any part of it."

"I dunno. You did a helluva job while I was out." Terry

poured herself a draft. "Are you sure you want to go back to Sleepy Hollow again next year?"

Gale drained her own glass and held it out for Terry to refill. "Yup, I'm not the least bit interested in standing in the way of women rounding my base headed for home. Do you know one idiot even came in at me with her spikes flying? I had to dive out of the way just to avoid a mortal wound."

"I remember that play," Robyn said. "No worries, though. Did you see her take a header when I blasted one right over her head the next inning?"

Gale laughed. "Oh yeah, and I loved every second of her picking gravel out of her teeth. I knew I could depend on you to uphold the team's honour, Robyn."

Nods went around the table.

Robyn blushed. Then she smiled at Terry. "Did Lisa tell you that we finally found the one?"

"You mean a house? You found your house? That's great. Where? What's it like? When do you move in?"

"It's up in Ranchlands. It's only a two-bedroom, but the basement has a lot of potential for development, and the yard is terrific. We take possession on the thirtieth. We're planning on doing the move that weekend." Robyn elbowed Terry. "I don't suppose you could lend us a hand, could you?"

Terry nodded. "Not only will I help, I'll recruit my brothers and roommates to pitch in. With all of us, we should have you moved in a day. Pizza and beer are on you, of course."

"Of course." Robyn lowered her voice. "Once we're in the house, we're going to go ahead with that other project, too." She glanced at Lisa, who was deep in an argument with their manager, Patrick.

Terry put her arm around Robyn's shoulders and hugged

her. "That's great. You two are going to make the best parents I know, other than my own, I mean."

They picked up their glasses and clinked them together.

Nursing her first beer, Terry listened to the buzz of conversation. Several more pitchers were drained, and a round of shooters was ordered. She passed. *Not this year. I've got to work tomorrow.* After last year's party, she'd woken up in a stranger's bed, uncertain how she had even gotten there. She hadn't remembered the woman's name and made a rapid and graceless exit. *I'm not doing that again.*

Terry drifted mentally and mused over her encounter at the Spencer house that morning.

Robyn tapped her shoulder. "Hey, where'd you go? You haven't heard a word I said."

"Oh, sorry. I just have a few things on my mind tonight." Terry stretched. "I think I'll make it an early evening."

"I can't say I blame you. Natalie has been making ominous comments about firing up the karaoke machine."

They laughed. Gale and Natalie had a well-deserved reputation for getting up and singing when they had been into the suds. Neither could carry a tune, but that never seemed to deter them.

Terry stood to make her goodbyes. After she brushed off a chorus of protests at her early exit, she headed for the front door.

Marika stood between her and the exit.

Terry scowled. "Excuse me."

"Please." Marika held up a hand. "May I just talk to you for a moment?"

"Jesus Christ! What the hell does it take to get through to you? We're over. I don't want to see you. I don't want to talk to you. And I sure as hell don't want to sleep with you. I'd rather have a goddamned porcupine in my bed. Now leave me the hell alone!"

Marika froze, and tears welled up in her eyes.

Terry brushed by her and stomped out of the bar. On the walk back to her car, she began to cool down. "Shit. I didn't have to humiliate her. Or make such an ass of myself." She sighed. "Oh well, at least she'll keep her distance now." *Damn it, damn it, damn it.*

CHAPTER 7

AFTER SHE ARRIVED HOME FROM Oly's, Terry sat on the steps of the back porch and watched the long summer evening fade into darkness. She had been there twenty minutes when the screen door behind her opened and closed again.

Claire sat beside her. "Do you mind the company?"

"Not at all."

Silently, they absorbed the warmth of the air and the sounds of the oncoming night.

Finally, Terry glanced at Claire. "So what have you been up to this evening?"

Claire picked up an envelope she'd set beside her. "I was just writing Maman, to let her know that I'm still alive in this den of Anglo iniquity."

"Mmm. Did you ever tell your mother the truth about Michael and me?"

"I've told her many things about my friends," Claire said. "But no, not that. I think it's better to let some things go, yes?"

"She really wouldn't be cool with it, would she?"

"No. You have to understand. My mother is a very good woman, but the Church and her family, these are her two loves. She is a little provincial, I know, but that's how she has lived her life."

Terry nodded. Claire came from a very large family in

the Eastern Townships and was the first one of her family to travel beyond Quebec's borders, let alone go to school in an English environment. "I don't know if I ever told you, but I really admire the courage it took for you to leave home. Not to mention how hard you work."

"My family sacrificed a lot to give me this opportunity." Claire shrugged. "It would be wrong to squander it."

"Like Michael, you mean?"

Claire shook her head. "You cannot compare us. He comes from old money. I come from the Eastern Townships. He can afford to focus on having fun. I cannot. I owe my parents too much."

"Do you — ?" Terry paused. *I stuck my foot in it once tonight.* Claire looked at her. "Do I what?"

"Do you still have a problem with us? With Michael and me? Is that why you don't tell your family about us?"

Claire was quiet for a long moment. "You know that I consider you both my very dear friends, oui? But it's true that in the beginning, I didn't know if I would stay here long. I didn't even unpack all my suitcases for the first month. I'd never met anyone like you before, and I only knew what the Church taught me. Now I know that you are good people, even if I don't quite understand your ways. Maman, though, she hasn't seen how Michael sneaks extra money into the grocery kitty and thinks I don't know. Or how you miraculously found a friend who was selling the textbooks I needed for half the going price last semester. She could not judge you based on who you really are."

Terry scuffed at the ground and avoided Claire's gaze. "You knew about that?" She had been certain their altruism had gone undetected.

"And what kind of a business major would I be if you two

slipped such matters by me?" Claire nudged her. "I know you were trying to protect my pride, and I accept your generosity in the spirit in which it was given. Thank you, Terry. Someday, I'll have other means to show my gratitude, but for now, thank you."

"You're welcome. It really was our pleasure to help, you know."

"Oui, I know this."

They sat quietly for several more minutes.

"Wasn't your team party tonight? Why are you sitting out here in our backyard instead of at Oly's?"

"I've been thinking of a friend of mine. Actually, two friends of mine. I kind of stuck my foot in it this morning, and I'm hoping I didn't do anything too stupid." Terry told Claire about the incident at the Spencers' that morning. "I mean where did I get off telling Jan how to look after Rob, for crying out loud? I've known them for a few weeks, and she's been caring for him for years."

Claire patted Terry's leg. "I'm sure she realizes you were just concerned for his well-being. You must have been startled to see how ill he was."

"That's it exactly. I was shocked at how they both looked. I never thought of Rob as really sick. I know that sounds stupid when he's a quadriplegic, but he's always so cheerful and funny that I didn't see it. I really don't know a damned thing about MS or what he's going through."

"It shouldn't be that difficult to find out about it. Mon oncle Jean-Guy had MS. But he wasn't badly afflicted and only walked with a cane for many years."

"I don't even know if it eventually kills people." Terry's breath caught.

"You can always do research or... It may not be the most

scientific way, but when I was at the video store last weekend, I was looking at an older movie called *Hilary and Jackie*. It was about two sisters, both musicians, and the one who had MS became very famous. It looked very interesting, but my friend wanted to rent *Cold Mountain* for the fiftieth time, so I didn't get it." Claire rose to her feet. "Why don't we walk down there and see if it's available? I have to mail my letter anyway, and the box is en route."

Terry jumped up, eager to take action, any action. *It's a place to start. Maybe by the next time I see them, there'll be less chance of me making a fool of myself.*

———⟨≡⟩———

Terry and Claire turned their heads as Michael clattered down the stairs. When he saw them, he stopped abruptly and bounced over to lean on the couch. "Whatcha watching? Some weepy chick flick?"

Weepy chick flick? Terry looked at Claire with a raised eyebrow.

She nodded, and they each grabbed an arm and pulled Michael over the back of the couch. They dropped him in a sprawl at their feet, knocking a large, half-empty bowl of popcorn off the coffee table.

"Hey! What did I do?"

Terry glared at him, then returned her attention to the movie. *God, this is breaking my heart.*

On the TV screen, a slender, dark-haired woman walked away from the open door of a car, along the side of a country road. She stumbled, tears rolling down her face.

Terry took another tissue and passed the box to Claire. The pile of used tissues had grown significantly in the last half hour.

The credits began to roll. Michael pulled himself up from

the floor and plopped down between them. "So what were you watching?"

Terry stopped the film, and Claire answered, "*Hilary and Jackie.*"

"Oh yeah, I've heard about that one. Wasn't there some kind of kinky thing going on between the sisters?" Michael flinched and rubbed his pummelled shoulders. "Ow."

Terry huffed. "Did anyone ever tell you that you have the sensitivity of a rhino?" *Not that I can really argue with you this time.*

"What? What'd I say?" Michael looked from one to the other. "I thought that's what I'd heard about it, but it's been so long ago now. So what was it about, then?"

"Well, actually," Claire said, "there was a sort of strange relationship between the two sisters."

"You've got that right," Terry said. "Made me glad I only have brothers. That's taking sibling sharing just a little too far if you ask me."

"Uh-huh, so I was right." Michael wilted when they glared at him again.

Claire shook her head. "That was only a small part. Really, it was a very moving show about the bonds of sisterhood and the demands of the artistic temperament. Jackie was a very complex person. Besides, we were watching mostly for research purposes."

"Research of what? The mating habits of mad English-women?" Michael asked.

Claire looked across him at Terry. "We wanted to find out more about MS and thought this might be a good first step."

"It was very sad at the end, don't you think?" Terry sighed and shook her head. "She seemed so terribly alone, once she couldn't play the cello anymore. It was like that was her whole identity, and with it gone, she was hollow. Even her beloved sister wasn't with her at the end."

Claire leaned across Michael and squeezed Terry's hand. "Rob isn't alone. You know that. And from what you've told me, he's not nearly as bad as Jackie was. Just because she died doesn't mean that he will, too."

Terry nodded, but Claire's words did little to ease the ache in her chest. *Doesn't mean he won't, either.*

"If you want to learn about MS," Michael said. "Why don't you go online and see what information you can find there?"

Terry rose to her feet. "That's the next step." She winked at Claire. "I think Michael should have to clean up the mess, don't you? After all, he caused it."

"Oh, absolument."

They climbed the staircase to the sound of Michael's protests.

Terry chuckled as they closed the basement door.

Claire smiled. "That really wasn't very nice of us, you know."

"It wasn't, but you know as well as I do that we'll probably find every bit of popcorn in the same place in the morning. Besides, it's my turn to clean the party room, so I'll get to it after work tomorrow. Right now, I want to see what I can find online."

As she reached the second-floor landing, Terry paused. "Thanks, Claire. It was a good idea, even if it did scare me a bit."

"Just remember, it doesn't necessarily mean that the same thing is going to happen in Rob's case."

"I know. See you in the morning."

Terry climbed to her garret and turned on the computer. "All right. Let's see what I can find out."

An hour later, she leaned back in her chair and clasped her hands behind her head. MS appeared to be such an unpredictable disease. No two victims necessarily had identical symptoms. There was such a diversity of complications. Fatigue seemed to be a constant at any stage of the disease, but the number of other potential problems appeared endless. Her research hadn't eliminated the roiling in her stomach. She was haunted by the vision of Jackie DuPre's condition at the end of the movie. *How do Rob and Jan deal with the awful uncertainty?*

With a sigh, she pushed away from her desk. She was in bed within minutes, but it would be hours before she slept and days before the movie's impact faded.

The following Saturday, Terry spent all day at her computer. She had woken in the morning, driven by the need to write, and hadn't stopped to shower or eat. In a tattered pair of shorts and a T-shirt that had seen better days, she had been pecking away at her keyboard for hours. A bag of Pirate cookies was her sole sustenance. Now, satisfied with two new chapters she had roughed out, she glanced at the time.

"Damn. How did it get to be four thirty already?"

Jan had confirmed their arrangements the previous night as Rob was doing much better, so she was expected at the Spencers' by six.

Terry saved her work and shut down her computer. *Time for a quick shower and I'm off.*

An hour later, her hair still damp but her clothes more presentable, she stood in front of shelves of movies at her favourite video store. *I wish I'd asked Jan for some ideas on what they might like. Rob's probably a* Master and Commander *kind of guy, but I can't see Jan being too interested in that.* She picked up the last available copy of *Hellboy*. *This will do.* Scanning shelves as she headed to the checkout, she stopped in front of a romantic comedy. *I'll bet that's more to Jan's taste.* She took it, too.

Terry swung by her favourite Chinese takeout place and picked up the order she'd called in. By six o'clock, she was parked in front of the Spencers'.

Jan walked down the path toward her.

Terry's brow furrowed. *Uh-oh. Has Rob relapsed? Is she going to cancel?*

Jan's smile eased her concerns. "I thought you might need a hand." She reached for one of the bags.

Terry followed her up the walk. When she entered their living room, she was delighted to see Rob back in his recliner.

Jan took the other bag. "Why don't you say hi, and I'll get this all set out in the kitchen."

Terry crossed to Rob's side and knelt. "I'm so glad to see you doing better."

His eyes were bright and clear again. "Me too. It was a bit rough there for a couple of days."

"But you weren't going to let some little old bug beat you, were you?"

"Not in the least. So, what did you bring us to watch tonight?"

Several hours later, as the first movie drew to a close in a climactic battle scene, Terry glanced over from the couch. Rob was sound asleep in his chair. "He can sleep through this?"

"He's still easily tired." Jan smiled at her husband. "It will take a week or so before he's back to normal again."

Terry sat up. "I'd better go, then, and let you two get some sleep."

"You don't have to do that. He's perfectly comfortable

where he is, and he'll probably wake up after he has a nap. Why don't we put the other movie in?" Jan hesitated. "Unless you have to get going?"

Terry shook her head. "Are you sure, though? I don't want to intrude."

"Positive, but I wouldn't want to interfere if you have a date tonight. You certainly don't have to spend your Saturday night with a pair of old fogies, even if we do enjoy your company."

Terry relaxed back on the couch. "I really can't think of any place I'd rather be at the moment. Besides, there's a distinct dearth of dates in my life at the moment."

"Aw, poor Terry." Jan went to change the DVD. "Has Calgary run out of tall, blonde beauties, then?"

Terry threw a small cushion at her. She ducked when Jan picked it up and tossed it back at her. "I think you've gotten entirely the wrong idea of my love life."

"Interesting." Jan tilted her head. "So Aaron was just making all that up last Sunday?"

Terry groaned and pulled the pillow over her face. "I'm never going to live that down, am I?"

Jan smiled. "No, I'm pretty sure you never will." She started the next movie.

CHAPTER 8

J AN JAMMED ON THE BRAKES as foot traffic crossed her path against the light. Battling downtown traffic and a multitude of oblivious pedestrians was not her favourite activity. *Oh well. There's no hurry. It's not like Kate will be ready when I get there anyway.*

After she parked under the office tower, she took the elevator to Kate's floor. The security guard waved her past, and she walked down the hall to Kate's office.

Kate's assistant looked up from her computer. "Hello, Mrs. Spencer. I'm afraid your sister is tied up with a client for a few more minutes."

Jan patted her purse. "That's fine. I brought my book."

The assistant smiled. "I knew you would."

Jan settled into a padded chair and eyed the dark wood and lush burgundy carpet. *Katie's done all right for herself.* Her sister had started years ago in the accounting department of a local oil company and had risen to a position as senior vice-president of the company's financial branch.

Jan took a novel out of her purse. She'd only turned a couple of pages before Kate emerged from her office with a client and bade him farewell.

Jan stood for Kate's hug.

"Just give me a minute to grab my purse, and we'll be on our way, okay?" Kate went back to her office and returned with a large purse slung over her shoulder. She took Jan's arm as they left the office. "I thought the Green Apple today, if that's all right?"

"Sure."

They arrived at the restaurant and gave Kate's name to the hostess. She led them up a curving flight of stairs to a glassed-in dining room overlooking an inner-city park. The first time Kate brought her here for lunch, Jan had been amazed that this park existed. It was completely hidden from the busy city streets and a favourite of brown baggers from surrounding office towers.

After settling into their chairs, they asked for coffees and scanned their menus. Then they looked up and laughed.

"Why do we even bother?" Kate shook her head. "We always get exactly the same thing."

Jan nodded. "You're going to get that rabbit food."

"And you're going to get red meat dripping in calories and cholesterol." Kate sighed. "Why couldn't I have gotten Dad's metabolism, too?"

"At least we both got his hair."

"Yes, we could have ended up with Mother's."

Kate signalled the waitress, and they placed their orders.

Jan added cream to her coffee. "So is Kevin excited about going into a new school this year?"

"He's a little nervous about being low man on the totem pole after being a senior in his old school. But at least his best friend is going to be in the same class, and he's happy about that. So how's Rob feeling? Is he recovered from last week?"

"He is, but you know how this goes. It's only a matter of time until the next one. It's just the way it is."

"And there's nothing his doctors can do about it?"

"No. We've tried all sorts of non-medical remedies, but

ultimately, it's a consequence of using the catheter. We just have to deal with the infections as they arise. At least I've gotten quicker at recognizing them when they start. That helps. And his GP trusts me, so she doesn't wait for the lab results before she starts him on antibiotics."

Kate fiddled with her cutlery.

Jan eyed her sister. "What's on your mind?"

"Do you ever regret it? Marrying Rob? You know I think the world of him, but this wasn't the life I imagined for you."

"You didn't imagine me going into the military either."

"No, but I understood your desire to leave home. I just always thought you'd eventually discover your true calling and leave the Forces to follow it."

"In essence, I did. I can't imagine my life without Rob. And it hurts to even think of what could've happened to him if we hadn't met." Jan shivered. "You know he didn't force me into this life. He told me he'd manage with hired caregivers if I wanted to continue working. It was always my choice."

"I do respect that, I just... It doesn't matter. Listen, I forgot to tell you that Mother is coming for a visit next month."

"Let me guess, she's decided to stay with you and John." Given that their mother had never stayed with her and Rob, it was an obvious assumption. "It's all right, Katie. After all, she wants to see her only grandchild, so it's natural that she wants to stay with you. Besides, we'll arrange to get together sometime while she's here. Maybe you can come up for dinner one night."

"Damn it." Kate scowled. "I argue with her every time she's here, but she's so convinced that Rob ruined your life that she won't give him a chance."

"Well, even after eighteen years you have your doubts,"

Jan said. "And you know him much better than Mother ever will."

"I don't have my doubts. I only asked if you ever did."

Jan raised an eyebrow. "Splitting hairs, are we?"

Kate winced.

"No, it's okay. I know you're behind us one hundred per cent," Jan said. "Believe me, I haven't forgotten what happened the day before our wedding. I'll always be grateful for that."

"All part of being a big sister."

"Mmm-hmm, your epic screaming match with Mother will forever be a part of our family history. Kevin's great-grandchildren will speak of that day in awe."

"Oh, hush. It wasn't that bad. Was it?"

Jan leaned forward and laid her hand on Kate's. "It was that good. It reminded me of all the times you stood up for me when we were young."

Kate squeezed Jan's hand. "You didn't need my help all that much. You certainly didn't need it against that one boy in fifth grade... What was his name?"

"Mackie Cunningham."

Kate chuckled. "I'm sure he thought just because you were such a quiet little bookworm that he could take your pocket money with impunity. I'm not sure who was more surprised when you whacked him on the head with your book rather than handing it over."

"He never bothered me again." Jan smiled. "It taught me a good lesson."

"Don't back down from bullies?"

"Never be without a book."

Kate laughed. "Well, you certainly mastered that one. Listen, before I forget, do you want to come over for dinner on Sunday? John volunteered to host his company's summer wrap-up barbeque this year, so we're going to have a ton of food."

"Thanks, but we'll have to take a rain check this time. We've been invited to a friend's place for Sunday dinner."

"You have?" Kate blinked. "Where are you going? What friends are these? Where did you meet them?"

The waitress returned with their orders, and Jan took a perverse pleasure in making Kate wait while their plates were set before them. "It's a birthday party for Terry Sanderson. Remember the woman I told you about who helped me out the day Rob and I ended up on the floor? The barbeque is over at her parents' place in Varsity Estates."

Kate stopped poking at her salad. "She invited you over after just one meeting?"

"No, actually we've gone out with her a couple of times. Well, at least I have, and Rob and I went to brunch last Sunday with her and her brother." *Terry has eased so naturally into our lives.* "They're good people, Kate. I know you'd like them. On Saturday, she brought Chinese food and DVDs over, and we had a great time together. She and Rob have really hit it off, and I'm looking forward to meeting her family."

"I'm so glad you've made new friends," Kate said. "Don't you worry about missing dinner at our place. We'll just make it for the Sunday after, all right?"

"That's sound fine." Jan chuckled. "Rob and I are becoming quite the social butterflies. If this keeps up, I may have to start keeping an engagement calendar."

"Good. I worry about you two being so alone most of the time. It's not healthy."

"I don't mind it, but I do worry about Rob. He was always the life of the party, and it's been hard on him to see old friends drift away. I know it makes him sad to remember the days when buddies and beer were plentiful and parties went on for days."

Kate nabbed a couple of fries off Jan's plate. "Then he's thinking of a time long before you, because I can't even imagine you partying for days on end."

"True, but we were pretty social until we moved here." Jan batted Kate's hand away when she reached for more fries. "It's just hard to replace old friends with new when we don't get out much. That's one of the reasons Terry is such a godsend to both of us."

After lunch they walked back to Kate's office. "Where are you off to now?"

"Rob needs a couple of fall shirts, and then I'm going to the bookstore."

"Now there's a surprise," Kate said. "I'd never have guessed that."

"I guess I am a little predictable."

"And lovably so. Well, I'd better get back to work. Have a great afternoon off. I'll call you on the weekend." Kate hugged Jan and entered her building.

An hour later, Jan had bought three shirts for Rob and five books for herself. She returned to the van, set her purchases on the passenger's seat, and glanced at her watch. "Only three o'clock. I could go to the park or library. Or...no, it's stupid." She took out her cell phone and studied it for a moment. Then she looked up a number in her address book and started to dial. But before she finished, she closed it up again. *Oh, for heaven's sake. She's not going to bite.* She opened her phone and dialled. Her heartbeat sped up and her fingers trembled as she waited.

A familiar voice came on the line, and Jan took a deep breath. *What was I nervous for?* "Hi, Terry. It's Jan."

"Hey, Jan, whatcha up to?"

"Um, I was wondering... Well, I'm on my afternoon off, and I thought you might've finished work by now —"

"I am," Terry said. "Why don't you drop over for coffee? I should warn you, though, that I haven't gotten to the house cleaning yet, so be prepared. Have you got a pencil? I'll give you the address."

Jan cradled the phone on her shoulder and grabbed a pen and paper from her purse. "Go ahead."

"Okay, you know where Charleswood is? We're in that area, closer to the university but still on the opposite side of Crowchild. The address is 2917 Chisholm Drive. Got that?"

"Yes, I've got it. I have a city map in the van, so there shouldn't be any problems. I'll see you in about twenty minutes, then?"

"Sounds great. I'll be looking forward to it."

Thirty-five minutes later, after one wrong turn, one cul-de-sac, and one lengthy backtrack, Jan drove down a lovely, tree-lined street of older homes. Terry sat on the steps of a tall, narrow brick house. Jan pulled up in front, and Terry jumped to her feet.

Jan left the van, reassured by Terry's welcoming smile.

"Did you have any problems finding the place?"

"Not a one," Jan said. "So this is where you hang your hat, is it? What a nice neighbourhood."

"Thanks, we like it. Come on in, and I'll give you the nickel tour." Terry led her up the stairs to the front door.

They entered through an arched doorway into a dark, narrow hall. Another flight of stairs ran up the right side of the hallway, and wide French doors opened into a spacious room on the left.

Terry steered her into that room. "We might as well start at the beginning. This is our living room. Uncle Lou always calls it the drawing room, but I don't think our furniture is classy enough to call it that."

An eclectic assortment of furniture was scattered about the room. The oddly coloured and motley collection did little to complement the high ceiling, solid wood paneling, and luxurious old crown mouldings. *But it suits her.*

Terry grinned. "We call it the College School of Decorating."

"Who's Uncle Lou?" Jan asked.

"He's the owner and my mother's brother. He's let me live here for six years at a very reasonable rent. I just had to promise not to let my roommates destroy the place, and so far, I've been really lucky with the people who've lived here with me."

Terry led her into a small dining room that opened into a large, messy kitchen. Pots were piled on an old gas stove, and worn wooden cupboards hung open haphazardly. Dishes were stacked in the sink and on the table. A fridge that had seen better days was covered with notes, pictures, and bus schedules.

Jan scanned the room. *Uncle Lou obviously doesn't believe in replacing appliances if they have any life left in them.* The only modern thing in the room was a small microwave oven in one corner. Even the table was an old Formica model, which wouldn't have been out of place in June Cleaver's kitchen.

Terry surveyed the mess with a frown. "Well, I did warn you that I hadn't cleaned up yet."

Jan laughed. She had never been to college, but this was exactly what she imagined a student residence would look like—cluttered, messy, and well lived-in. "That's okay. There are days my kitchen doesn't look much better."

"Why do I have problems believing that?" Terry jerked a

thumb over her shoulder. "C'mon, since this didn't scare you off, it'll be safe to take you down to the party room."

Jan followed her out of the kitchen and back down the hall to a door set in under the stairwell.

Terry flipped on a light switch and opened the door to reveal a narrow set of steps descending to the basement. "Watch your step."

When they got to the bottom of the stairs, Terry pointed to an enclosed area on their left. "That's Michael's apartment, and the laundry room is off in that corner." She led Jan forward into a large room that ran the width of the basement and was outfitted with a big-screen TV, an impressive stereo array, several couches, a large easy chair, and a fridge that was decades younger than the kitchen model. "This is the most popular room in the house."

The contrast between the expensive electronics, the comfortable quality furniture and what she had seen in the upstairs living room was startling. Jan looked at Terry.

"It's all Michael's equipment and furniture," Terry said. "He wanted a nice place to have friends over, and we all benefit from his generosity."

"Michael is well-off, then?" *How does a university student afford this set-up?*

Terry nodded. "Very, but he doesn't like to talk about it, and he's not one to flaunt it either. He just saw no reason why he shouldn't be comfortable even if he footed the whole bill. We've had some great times down here. One party last winter to celebrate the end of the semester, we must have had over a hundred people. It took us almost two days to clean up afterwards, but it was worth it. Come on, I'll show you the upstairs now."

Terry led the way up to the second floor. "This is Claire's

apartment. She has a bedroom and sitting room, and we share the main bathroom."

They passed the second-floor landing and continued upwards. Jan focused on her breathing. *I'm glad I live in a bungalow.* She looked at Terry's long legs and clearly defined muscles. *Still, there are some benefits to living on the top floor. She looks like she could climb a mountain and never break a sweat.*

They reached the top and walked down the short hall to a door. "This used to be the attic, but Uncle Lou turned it into a garret room just for me. I really like having the top of the house, though it has its drawbacks temperaturewise." Terry pushed open the door and stood back for Jan to get by.

Jan entered a spacious room under an angular and wide-beamed ceiling. It was painted in a pale cream and trimmed with maple woodwork, which lent an airy feel to the garret. There were three windows in the room: one over a large bed in the corner, a bay with a padded window seat by an old but sturdy wooden desk, and the third in the far corner, obscured by a noisily humming air conditioner. A thick cinnamon-coloured carpet covered the floor.

The walls were surprisingly bare, with only a large watercolour seascape on one side of the room. It was peaceful and inviting, albeit littered with stacks of books and piles of clothes.

Jan stifled a grin as Terry furtively kicked something under her bed and swept a mound of clothes off a large padded rocking chair into a neglected laundry basket. "I guess the maid didn't quite make it up here either?"

Terry stopped and sighed. "Well, actually, we're responsible for our own rooms, so this mess is all mine. I was going to clean up tonight...really."

Jan laughed.

Terry dropped into the chair. "Next time you come over, you'll have to give me more warning so I can clean up first."

Next time, eh? I like that. Jan wandered over to the desk and looked at the pile of printouts. "Are you working on something right now?" There was no answer. She turned around. "Is something wrong?"

"No, it's just—" Terry stared at her hands, her brow furrowed.

Jan studied her expression and waited.

Finally, Terry's face cleared. "I haven't told anyone but Jordy about this. I guess I don't want to jinx it, or maybe I just don't want to get anyone's expectations up or be laughed at."

Jan tilted her head but still said nothing.

"What I want—what I've wanted for a long time now... is to be a writer. I always wrote articles for school papers, but I've had this idea for a couple of years and I finally decided to try a novel."

A writer? Jan nodded. *I bet anything you'll be a good one.*

"That's why I took the post office job when I graduated, but I didn't want to tell my parents in case it didn't work out. I let them think I was just tired of school and wanted to take some time off."

Jan crossed to Terry's side and knelt beside her. "I think that's a wonderful ambition, and I'm so proud of you for following your dream rather than finding all sorts of reasons why you shouldn't even try." She squeezed Terry's hand. "I won't say anything to anyone if you don't want me to, but I'm honoured that you trusted me enough to tell me."

Relief shone in Terry's eyes, and she turned her hand to grasp Jan's. "Thank you. Would you like to read it sometime? It's far from done, but I'd really value your opinion. You've certainly read enough that you can tell me whether it's dreck or not."

"I'd be happy to provide some feedback, and I have no doubt it'll be far from dreck. Whenever you're ready for me to read it, just let me know."

"Hey, you want something to drink? We can grab something downstairs and go out to the porch for a bit."

Jan smiled. *Someone's changing the subject.* "That sounds good. I'd love some iced tea, if you have it." *She's too cute.*

They clattered down to the kitchen. Terry poured Jan an iced tea and grabbed herself a beer. She led the way out of the back door onto a wide porch and gestured at the scattered chairs on the porch. "Take your pick."

Jan headed for a double swing chair. Terry joined her, propped her legs on the banister, and pushed to move the chair slowly back and forth. They sat for several minutes before Jan broke the comfortable silence. "Haven't any of your roommates noticed you working on your book?"

"No, we all honour each other's space, especially once school starts again. Ever since Claire threw a book at Michael's head when he interrupted her studying for an exam, we generally respect closed doors."

"But you've finished school now. Do you still get the solitude you need to write?"

Terry blushed. "Uh, they don't... Well, they know I might — um, they didn't necessarily think I was studying if my door was closed."

"Oh...got it." Jan smiled. "What happened to hanging a necktie on the doorknob when you're entertaining?"

Terry pressed the beer bottle to her flushed cheeks. "It's not that I have someone over all that often."

"If you say so."

Terry elbowed her.

"Hey, can I help it if your reputation precedes you?"

"Lies, all lies. Well, mostly lies anyway. Actually, the biggest problem is that I'm easily distracted by everything that goes on. When Michael has friends over, it's hard to fight the temptation to join in the fun when I should be writing." Terry shook her head. "I'm severely lacking in the self-discipline department, and at the rate I'm going, it'll be five years before I have a first draft complete."

I wonder — No, I'd better talk to Rob first. Jan was enjoying the growing rapport between them. *It's been so long. I forgot the pleasure of making a new friend. And it's so much fun to tease her.* She was flattered by Terry's apparent interest in her own life. She was also warmed by Terry's trust. *We've known each other for such a short time, but it's so easy with her.* Their mutual love of books had eased the early stages, but they were beyond that foundation now. *Rob, my love, it was definitely one of our luckier days when you took that tumble.*

Jan tucked Rob's coffee cup into his hand and held it in place on his chest with a ring of towels. After ensuring he could reach the straw, she took his dinner tray away. When she returned from the kitchen, she sat down in his wheelchair and idly pushed back and forth a few inches.

Rob smiled. "What's on your mind?"

"How do you know something's on my mind?"

"Because you always do that to the chair when you want to talk about something. What's up?"

"You know how I was telling you about Terry's problem with finding quiet time to work on her writing?"

Rob nodded.

Lois Cloarec Hart

"I was thinking that we might be in a position to help her out, if you think it's a good idea."

Rob listened as she laid out her idea. "Sure, why not? Why don't you give her a call and ask her to drop over?"

Jan leaned out of the wheelchair and wrapped her arm around his shoulders. "You really are the sweetest man."

Rob darted his gaze around the room. "Shhh. Don't tell anyone."

Jan laughed and ran her hand over his hair. "Right. I forgot that you're my toughie." She grabbed the phone and dialled Terry's number. When a man's voice answered, she asked for Terry.

He yelled, "Yo, Terry, a conquest awaits."

There was a clatter of footsteps. "Hello?"

"Hi, Terry. Sorry to disappoint, but it's just Jan."

"Hey, Jan. No, I'm glad it's you. Michael was just being his usual swinish self. Don't mind him."

"Oh, I don't. I know you have a reputation to uphold. Listen, Rob and I were wondering, if you had a few minutes to spare sometime, would you drop by?"

"Of course. Is everything okay? Do you need help with anything?"

"No, everything's fine, but we had a little something we thought you might be interested in. There's no hurry or anything. Whenever it's convenient."

"I'm free right now. Why don't I come around in half an hour or so?"

"That would be great. We'll see you then." Jan hung up and turned to Rob, who had been listening to her half of the conversation. "She'll be over in half an hour. I think I'll go check and make sure everything's tidy."

86

Twenty minutes later, Terry arrived at the Spencers'. Since Jan's enigmatic phone call, she had been trying to figure out what Jan and Rob were up to. *Whatever it is, it must be something good. Jan sounded pretty happy.* She rang the bell, and Jan opened the door. "Hi, Jan. You know, we have to stop meeting like this."

"You're right. Whatever will the neighbours say? Come in. Would you like a cup of coffee?" She motioned Terry to have a seat and went over to perch on the arm of Rob's chair.

"No, thanks." They were looking very pleased with themselves. "Okay you two, time to 'fess up. What are you up to, and why do you resemble a pair of Cheshire cats?"

Jan and Rob looked at each other, then back at her.

"Who, us?" Rob asked. "Would we be up to something?"

"Definitely," Terry said. Picking up one of couch pillows, she shook it at the grinning couple. "C'mon, guys. What's going on? Are you going to make me beat it out of you?"

Jan winked at Rob. "I was thinking about something you said this afternoon, and we think we may have a solution to your problem."

Terry's brow furrowed. "What problem is that?"

"Well, I hope you don't mind, but I told Rob what you were working on and that you had problems with too many distractions in your house." Jan glanced at Rob. "You know, this might be easier if I just showed her. Will you excuse us a moment, love?"

He nodded, and Jan motioned Terry to follow. They walked through the kitchen, down a short hall and arrived at the top of stairs Terry hadn't noticed before.

"I should have given you the nickel tour when you were here last weekend, but I didn't think of it. Come downstairs, and you'll see what Rob and I are talking about."

Jan led her down a flight of stairs and through a small alcove that opened into a large room. Bright throw rugs over the laminate floor differentiated between a sitting area near the gas fireplace and a compact kitchen with a butcher block island. Three doors opened off the far end of the room.

"Go ahead, and look around."

Terry walked to the back of the main living area and peered into the other rooms. Two fully furnished bedrooms, done in complementary colours of greens and white faced her, each with pretty patchwork quilts covering large beds. A tiled washroom separated the bedrooms.

She turned back to Jan, who was watching her explore. Terry spread her arms to encompass the living area. "I don't understand."

"You need a writer's retreat. We have the space for you. Rob and I would like you to feel free to come over here whenever you need peace and quiet to write. We're not a noisy pair, and while I do use that fridge to store extra groceries, I'm only usually down here to do laundry. It's on the far side of the basement, so I'd try not to bother you at all."

Terry gaped at her. "Are you...? I mean, do you know...? Are you sure you want to do this?"

Jan dug in her pocket, then walked over to Terry and took her hand. She pressed a key into Terry's palm and closed her fingers over it. "Yes, we're very sure. You've been so kind to us. If we can return that, we'd like to. Besides, it'll be nice to have someone else around the place, even if we only see you coming and going."

Terry stared at the key in her hand. *I wouldn't have expected this in a million years.* "Thank you. You have no idea what this means to me."

Jan smiled. "Yes, I do. C'mon, let's go tell Rob there's a new part-time tenant moving in."

When they reached the living room, Terry stuffed the key in her pocket and walked over to Rob. She stopped in front of him and shook her head. "You guys are too much, you know that?"

Rob chuckled, and she leaned over to hug him. "If I'm ever in the way, you have to promise to let me know, okay?"

"You won't be in the way," Rob said. "We'll probably barely know you're there."

Jan nodded. "And please feel free to use it at any time. We don't have to be here, not that we go out that much. We want you to consider the basement suite yours as long as you want it, all right?"

"I feel like a kid on Christmas. I got exactly what I wanted, without even having told Santa my wish. I will never be able to thank you adequately, but this definitely calls for a celebration. How about I go get ice cream?"

Rob's eyes brightened. "Fabulous idea. If you're going to Bertie's, I'll have a double chocolate toffee crunch."

"Then that's where I'm going." Terry looked at Jan. "And what can I bring you, madam?"

"I'll have what he's having." Jan walked her to the door.

Terry's cheeks ached from her wide smile. Impulsively, she turned and hugged Jan. Then she jumped for joy over the single step at the entrance and bounded down the walkway to the sounds of Jan's soft laughter. "Back in half an hour."

Once in the car, Terry pulled the house key out of her pocket again. She studied it for a moment and added it to her key ring. "Unbelievable. Absolutely friggin' unbelievable. Talk about an awesome early birthday present."

CHAPTER 9

E MILY CHECKED THE BACKYARD TO ensure nothing had been overlooked. *Though after two days, I should think I have everything ready.*

Gordon hovered over one grill and monitored the slow-roasting chickens. Duncan and Karen had brought their grill over the day before to cook the steaks, which were currently marinating in Emily's secret recipe. Alex was setting up his large, folding picnic table, while Diane kept a close watch on their daughters. Jordy had tied a multitude of large blue and silver balloons to the trees, bushes, and fence to add a festive air to the yard.

Looks like everything's under control.

"How many are we expecting, Em?" Gord asked.

"Could be about twenty people, if Matt shows up." They exchanged glances.

"Did he say he'd come? I mean with it being Terry's birthday and all?"

Emily sighed. "Well, you know Matt. He did promise, and he even asked if he could bring a date—"

"But that doesn't necessarily write it in stone." Gord nodded. "Whether he comes or not, you've got enough here to feed an army. As always."

Emily slapped his arm. "You know, if you keep staring at the chickens, you'll let all the heat out."

Coming Home

Gord closed the lid and backed away with upraised hands.

Emily chuckled. "Why don't you go finish your punch now, and tell Jordy he can start bringing out everything that's piled on the kitchen table." She started unfolding chairs and set them around the two long picnic tables.

Alex joined her and started to put one at the end.

She shook her head. "No, son. Leave that open for the wheelchair."

"Okay, Mom. Have you met these new friends of Terry's? What are their names again?"

"Rob and Jan Spencer, and no, I haven't met them yet, but Terry is eager to have them here. She even asked me to make sure I had Bertie's double chocolate toffee crunch ice cream on hand to go with her cake because it's their favourite. I swear I haven't seen Terry this excited about making new friends since she started kindergarten."

Alex rolled his eyes. "Terry and kindergarten…not my favourite memories. How many times did you guys make me babysit her when you got summoned to another parent-teacher meeting?"

"Oh, it wasn't that bad."

"Mom…how often did Dad leave the house grumbling about how one tiny girl could be so much more of a handful than her three big brothers?"

"Well, she's all grown up now."

Alex laughed. "Yup, you survived her childhood. I think the party should be for you, not her."

"Just be glad she wasn't the first-born, Alexander, because then she'd probably have been an only child."

Chuckling, Alex walked over to where Diane swung on an old playground set, holding a twin in each arm.

Emily watched them for a moment. *C'mon, old girl. Guests*

will be arriving any moment and you still have work to do. She returned to the kitchen, where Jordy was trying to balance a large stack of plates and glasses. "Set some of those down. You don't have to do it all in one trip, you know."

"Sorry, Mom." Jordy set some of his load on the table and took the remainder outside.

Emily returned to cleaning and slicing raw vegetables for the salad. She glanced out her window as Gordon emerged from the basement walkout, carrying a large covered bowl of his secret punch, a staple of their family dinners.

Michael's Pathfinder parked behind the fence, and he, Terry, and Claire piled out. Lisa and Robyn's pickup pulled in next to them.

Emily dried her hands on a dishtowel and went outside to greet her guests.

When Terry and her friends came through the back gate, Jordy and Alex mobbed their sister with bear hugs and birthday greetings. Gordon waded into the fray, swung his laughing daughter in a circle, and planted a big kiss on her cheek. Terry turned to Emily with open arms.

"Happy Birthday, little one."

Terry grinned and looked down into her mother's eyes. "Not much little about me anymore."

"You'll always be little to me. Now go make sure everyone has something to drink. Beer and pop are in the fridge. Your father's made his punch. You know where everything is."

Terry started to amble away but looked up as a van pulled in beside the Pathfinder and the pickup. Her face lit up, and she hurried to meet the new arrivals.

Emily followed at a slower pace and leaned against the gatepost as the rear of the van opened.

A woman hopped out of the driver's seat and came around to the back.

Emily studied her. She was a head shorter than Terry, with a sturdy build. Her large, dark eyes and straight, freckled nose were framed by wavy, auburn hair cut to shoulder length.

"Hi, Jan. Hey, Rob." Terry hugged her and stepped back out of the way.

Jan unsnapped the wheelchair restraints, backed the chair down the ramp, and pulled it around so Rob could face Terry. She reached in the back and pulled out a gift-wrapped parcel, which she handed to Terry. "Happy birthday."

Rob grinned. "Yeah, happy birthday, Terry. I'd give you a birthday kiss, but you're going to have to help me out here."

Laughing, Terry bent down and offered her cheek to Rob for a kiss. "You guys didn't have to bring me anything." She began to unwrap her present.

"We know," Jan said. "But I ran across this last week and thought you'd enjoy it. I know I did, very much."

Terry tore the wrapping and grinned at Jan as she uncovered a book. "Hmm, Stevenson. I don't think I know his work."

"Actually, it's *her* debut novel. It's been getting excellent reviews, and I picked one up for myself, too. I couldn't put it down once I started and read it right through until two in the morning. It's a historical romance, set in medieval England."

Terry flipped open the cover to read an inscription. When she looked at Jan, an unspoken communication seemed to fly between them.

Terry beckoned to Emily. "Come here, Mom. I want you to meet my friends. This is Jan, and this handsome hound dog is Rob. This is my mom, Emily Sanderson."

Emily and Jan shook hands. "It's nice to meet you, Jan, and

you too, Rob." She laid a hand on Rob's arm. "I've heard so much about you both. I'm so glad you could make it today."

"We've been looking forward to it," Rob said. "Thank you for inviting us."

Emily was struck by the vitality of the man. Despite his weak, immobile limbs and a head that canted continually to one side as if he lacked the strength to hold it upright, Rob's eyes shone with intelligence and humour. Thick, brown hair threatened to fall over his eyes, and Jan absentmindedly pushed it back as she must have done a thousand times. His long legs slumped to the right, and Emily estimated he would be as tall as Gord if he could stand. With his engaging grin, it was easy to see how Terry was so taken with him.

"Why don't we join the others?" Emily motioned them ahead of her. "Terry, grab the gate."

As they entered the yard, Duncan and Karen came around the house from the front, and Terry was quickly drawn into introducing Jan and Rob to the rest of her friends and family.

Matt was the only one missing now, but he would arrive, or not, in his own time.

Terry hovered over her newest friends. She pulled up a chair for Jan to sit beside Rob and ensured they both had punch before dragging up her own chair to sit close to them.

With a quick glance over the noisy assembly, Emily made certain that everyone had settled in with a drink in hand and five different conversations going on at once. "If you'll excuse me for a few minutes, I have a couple of more things to do."

"If you're going in, would you put this on top of the fridge? I'll pick it up later." Terry handed Emily the book she'd been given.

After taking the book, Emily walked back to the kitchen.

She yielded to her curiosity and opened the book to read the inscription.

Dreams do come true
Love, Rob and Jan.

Emily re-read the words. *Now, what on earth is that all about? It obviously means something to Terry…and it's none of my business.*

She was busy at the counter when the back door opened.

"May I give you a hand with anything?"

Emily glanced over her shoulder. "Oh, hi, Jan. Sure, if you want to grab the steaks and take them out to Gordon. Tell him I'll have everything ready in fifteen minutes, so he can plan from there, depending on how people want their steaks."

Jan crossed the kitchen and opened the door to the refrigerator.

"Wait!" Emily was too late.

A bowl of precariously balanced potato salad began to topple out. Jan deftly snatched it from mid-air, but two bottles of salad dressing crashed down, followed in quick succession by a large tomato, a block of cheese, and a plastic container of noodles.

"I'm so sorry." Jan tried to push things back inside.

"Don't worry about it. It wasn't your fault. I should have warned you; my fridge is a danger zone." Emily knelt to help. "Everyone always approaches it with extreme caution." She pulled out a large container from the lowest shelf and handed it to Jan. "Here are the steaks, and if you wouldn't mind, tell Gord to move the potatoes to the upper rack now."

Jan took the steaks and left the kitchen.

When she glanced out the window, Emily saw Terry

jump up to take the steaks. They exchanged words, and Terry laughed. She nudged Jan back to her chair and took the steaks to her father.

Emily walked back outside. She stopped short when Matt came around the corner of the house with a thin, blonde woman on his arm and a smirk on his face. She hurried to intercept him.

Her son once had the same rangy build and curly, dark hair of his two older brothers, but the edges of his once lean, athletic body had blurred by the past few years of self-indulgence. His features had coarsened, and he was prematurely acquiring his father's burliness. Where Alex and Duncan were cheerful, amiable men, Matt's sharp features were usually sullen. But he smiled at her approach, and for a moment, Emily saw the boy he'd once been.

"Hi, Mom. I want you to meet a friend of mine. This is Jenna. Jenna, this is my mom."

Jenna held out her hand. "Pleased ta meetcha."

Emily shook her hand. "Nice to meet you, too. Welcome to our home." She regarded Matt sternly. "No fights today, got it?"

"Of course not." He tugged his date over to the tables.

Less than reassured, Emily followed in his wake. *Lord, I hope that Terry's good mood will prevent any hostilities from breaking out.* To her surprise, Terry, who normally reacted to Matt's arrival with raised hackles, barely glanced at the newcomers before returning her attention to Rob, who was telling a story.

Matt frowned and strode around the table, Jenna trailing in his wake. "Hey, little sister, are you going to introduce me to your friends?"

Terry looked up. "Jan and Rob Spencer, this is my brother Matt and his friend...?"

Matt pulled Jenna closer. "This is Jenna. So, you alone today?"

Terry raised an eyebrow. "Hardly. Look around, Matt." Then she urged Rob to go on with his story.

Matt shifted feet and stared at her.

Emily shot a glance at Alex, who nodded and beckoned Matt and Jenna to the other end of the table near him.

Emily dropped into a chair beside Gord, who had been listening to Rob spin his story. At her husband's sympathetic glance, she leaned toward him and whispered, "Sometimes I feel like Switzerland between those two."

Gord wrapped his arm around her shoulders. "Well, at least she's not giving him a rise today." He nodded his head toward Rob. "You should listen to this guy. He's got a million stories." He handed Emily a glass of punch. "Here, relax for a few minutes. I'm not putting the steaks on until I hear what happens."

Emily took the punch and settled back to listen.

Rob picked up where he left off. "So there we are, four young pilots out on a Parisian night, and we've had maybe one or two drinks."

Jan coughed, and Rob grinned. "Whose story is this, love? Okay, let's just say, we were feeling no pain. We'd finished dinner and we wanted to go to Pigalle — "

"And why were you so intent on going there, husband of mine?"

"French wine, French music — " Rob waggled his eyebrows. "French women."

Everyone, including Jan, laughed.

"Anyway, there was a line of cabs waiting outside the

restaurant, so me and a couple of the guys climbed in the back of one and Eric got in the front. But our driver kept talking to the cabbie behind us, and we got tired of waiting."

Jan shot Rob a droll look. "What a shock."

Rob winked at her. "So I suggested Eric could drive us, and being a fine, young pilot, he took control."

"Being an inebriated young pilot, you mean," Jan said.

"That, too. We're motoring down the street, having a fine old time, when this other cab pulls up beside us, honking his horn. Our cabbie was hanging out the passenger window screaming and waving his arms at us, so Eric pulled over."

Jan snickered.

Emily glanced at her. *I'll bet she could tell this story by heart.*

"You should know I wasn't present for the rest of what happened, but Eric told us all about it later," Rob said. "We bailed before Eric even brought the cab to a full halt. He said he turned around to talk to us and couldn't believe it when we weren't there. We were probably halfway back to the base before the gendarmes arrived."

Jordy looked at Terry and mouthed, "Gendarmes?"

"French police, buddy." Terry leaned forward. "So Eric was busted?"

"And how. The cab driver hauled him out from behind the wheel and slammed Eric against the side of the car. Fortunately, he was so...uh, loose-limbed, that he barely got a bruise, but it probably was a good thing that the police came when they did. They took everyone to the nearest gendarmerie to sort things out. Once they checked Eric's military ID they pretty much ignored him."

"Did he have immunity?" Jordy asked.

Rob laughed. "No, but they figured he was just a harmless drunk so they were trying to calm the two cabbies down."

Emily glanced at Gord. "Why do I get the feeling he wasn't nearly as harmless as they thought?"

Rob grinned at her. "You'd be right, but I have to say what happened next wasn't with malice aforethought. Eric's got the softest heart you could imagine, and when he saw all the caged dogs —"

"Caged dogs?" Emily asked. "Why were there caged dogs in a police station? Were they police dogs?"

Rob shook his head. "No, the station also served as an interim pound for lost dogs. Eric was just being his usual sweet self when he decided to open all the cages so he could pet the dogs. The next thing he knew, there were dogs running all over the station house and everyone — cabbies and gendarmes — was yelling at him."

Rob's audience roared with laughter.

"Eric's French wasn't all that fluent, but like he told us later, he had no difficulty figuring out that what they were saying about the *pilote Canadien* was less than complimentary."

Emily wiped at the tears in her eyes as she pictured a scene right out of the Keystone Kops.

"As you can imagine, the Royal Canadian Air Force had done little that night to cover itself with glory. When they called the base duty officer to come pick Eric up, the BDO was not happy with him to say the least." Rob paused to take another drink. "But you know, when they took Eric back and questioned him on who he'd been with, he never ratted us out, even though he ended up getting six months extra duties for it. Coincidentally, de Gaulle kicked NATO out of France shortly after that, and our squadron moved to Germany. Now, I'm not saying it was all Eric's fault that international relations broke down, but we were always suspicious about the timing."

"Is that the same Eric that we're going to see at the air show on Labour Day?" Jordy asked.

Rob nodded. "The very same. Mind you, he's settled down a lot. He hasn't caused an international incident in years now, though he was on the Canada-Europe run in late '89 when the Iron Curtain started to crumble, so maybe our government's been using him as a secret weapon." He grinned at Jordy, who was drinking in every word.

Emily nudged Gord toward the abandoned steaks. "Time to get those going, love."

He did as she asked but turned the grill so he could watch and listen.

Emily tapped Karen on the shoulder. "Would you mind giving me a hand with the rest of the stuff? Terry has the day off since it's her birthday."

Karen stood and followed Emily. "He's really got some stories, doesn't he?"

"That he does. Jordy told me he was quite the storyteller, and he was right. Personally, I think Jordy's developed a severe case of hero worship." Emily glanced back. Jordy was nearly leaning on the arm of Rob's wheelchair.

"I think you might just be right about that," Karen said. "Rob certainly knows how to keep a party lively. Even Matt's behaving himself tonight." She glanced at Emily. "Uh, I mean — "

"It's okay." Emily sighed. "I know what you mean, and yes, he is being more restrained than usual."

"Who's the whippet dipped in peroxide he has on his arm this time?"

Emily cocked her head. "Was it Jeannie? No, that doesn't sound right. I'm sorry. I can't remember."

Karen shrugged. "That's okay. We'd just have to forget

when the next one came along. Actually, I'm a bit surprised Terry doesn't have one of those adornments with her tonight. It's not like her to let Matt have the upper hand uncontested."

Emily began to extract things from her fridge and pass them to Karen. "I think Terry was more interested in introducing her new friends and making sure they had a good time than competing with her brother."

Karen glanced out the window. "She is sticking pretty close to them. Hey, does this mean we're not going to have the traditional Sanderson grudge match this year? And I had such fun nursing Duncan's bloody nose last year."

Emily shook her head. Terry's twenty-sixth birthday had ended in a virtual free-for-all, precipitated by a quarrel between her and Matt, with everyone else trying to pull them apart.

"No, no fights this year, and bless the Spencers for that. Besides, after last year, I threatened to banish both of them from all future family dinners if they pulled that stunt again."

Karen's eyes widened. "Wow, that would do it. You might as well have threatened to exile them to Siberia."

Emily smiled wryly. "That was next up."

They gathered their load and returned to the backyard, making several trips before everything was laid out to Emily's satisfaction. With Gord serving up steaks and Alex carving the chickens, everyone soon dug into the feast.

Once dinner was done and dishes cleared, Emily brought out a three-layer cake, with twenty-seven candles blazing among silver and blue roses. She set it down in front of Terry and winced while her mostly tone-deaf progeny bellowed the traditional song. "Go on, Terry. Make a wish."

Terry caught Jan's eye and smiled before blowing out all but one candle. This brought the expected ripostes from her brothers, roommates, and friends. Terry grinned, snuffed out the last stubborn candle, and started slicing and handing around pieces. "This looks like one of your masterpieces, Robyn."

Robyn nodded and ducked her head. "Your mom asked me if I'd make one." She blushed as the other guests complimented her on the cake.

Long after the cake, ice cream, and coffee were gone, the guests sat around the tables, arguing, gossiping, and generally having a great time.

Emily surveyed her family and guests, completely content. *Even Matt's been on his best behaviour. It may only be a temporary detente, but I'm going to enjoy it while it lasts.*

CHAPTER 10

T ERRY GLANCED OVER HER SHOULDER at Jordy, who hung over the middle seat, talking to Rob. She turned back to Jan. "He's so excited. I sure appreciate you taking us with you."

Jan eased the van into heavy highway traffic. "It's our pleasure. Rob's been looking forward to showing Jordy around the static displays before handing him off to Eric for a flight."

They drove west along the TransCanada highway toward the small Springbank airport that would be hosting the weekend's air show. Terry looked at the long line of vehicles. "Seems like a lot of people are going to the same place we are. Do you think we'll have any problems finding parking?"

Jan tapped the blue and white handicap-parking placard hanging off the mirror. "Don't worry. Between this and Eric's VIP pass, we'll have no difficulties. He said he'd leave it for us at the front gate."

"You haven't seen him yet?"

"No, he got in late last night and called us to set things up. He's staying with his wingman at a hotel but promised to come for dinner before he flies out. When Rob asked him about Jordy, he said it'd be no problem taking him on a flight as long as we got out there early enough for his practice run, since he didn't want to take him during the actual show."

"Ah, that would explain this crack-of-dawn expedition."

Jordy better appreciate me getting up on a Saturday at six a.m.
Terry took a deep swallow of her coffee and smiled. *Like I'm not almost as excited as he is.*

It was a smaller air show than the big international ones at Lethbridge and Red Deer, but according to Rob, there would be a good selection of new and vintage aircraft.

"Do you think we'll get to see the Snowbirds?"

Jan shot her a glance. "I don't know. They're not scheduled until this afternoon. Rob might wear down before that, and I'd have to take him home. I'm sorry."

"Not a problem, believe me. I'm just thrilled that Jordy's going to get a chance to fly."

Forty-five minutes later, they reached the head of a slow-moving line of traffic turning off at the Springbank exit. Jan pointed to a small, fenced-off parking enclosure. "That's where Eric said to meet him." She pulled out of the row and drove up to the enclosure, where she gave the traffic controller her name.

He checked his list, handed her a pass, and pointed toward the front of the lot.

Jan winked at Terry. "Aren't you glad you're travelling with a VIP?"

"Absolutely. I'd hate to be fighting that mess back there." Terry gestured at the vehicles still inching their way toward the open parking field.

Jan broke into a big grin and pointed ahead of them. "Rob, there's Eric!"

A stocky man in a dark blue flight suit with a bright red baseball cap waved at them as Jan drove up to him. She threw the van in park and jumped out.

Eric grabbed her in a bear hug and whirled her in a circle.

"Eric, you old coot, put me down before I get sick." Jan

laughed down at him as Terry got out and came around the front of the van.

He set her on her feet but left his arm around her shoulders. "So have you finally seen the light? Are you ready to leave that old reprobate and marry me?"

Jan elbowed him. "Oh sure, and what exactly would Anne have to say about that?"

"Probably 'thank you.' I think she could use the break." Eric grinned. "So are you going to introduce me to your lovely friend here, or is Rob keeping her all to himself, too?"

Jan rolled her eyes. "Pilots. You're all incorrigible."

"That we are and proud of it. Hi, I'm Eric."

"Eric, this is Terry."

Terry shook his hand. "Nice to meet you."

"You, too."

"Come on, let's spring Rob. I know he'll be chomping at the bit back there." Jan tugged him to the back of the van

Terry trailed behind, grinning at Jan's unusual exuberance.

Jordy carefully backed Rob's chair down the ramp. He turned Rob to face Eric and threw the switch to raise the ramp and close the door.

"Boomer!" Eric pounced on Rob and wrapped him in a gentle hug. An expression of sadness crossed his face as he held Rob, but it cleared before he stood back.

"Buzzard, you haven't changed a bit."

"Neither have you, you old jet jockey. You still have the most beautiful women in the country at your side." Eric's gaze flicked from Jan to Terry. "I've never understood what you have that I don't."

Rob's eyes twinkled. "Hair."

Eric groaned and clutched his chest. "Oh, ya got me." He pushed back his ball cap and ran a hand over his shining, bald pate, then held out his hand to Jordy. "You must be my co-pilot for the day. Eric Landon."

"Jordy Sanderson. I'm pleased to meet you, and I really want to thank you for offering to take me up."

If Jordy's smile gets any bigger, his face is going to split. It was worth getting up with the roosters for this. Terry instinctively liked Eric, and it was clear he was special to Rob and Jan.

"My pleasure. Any friend of my old wingman is a friend of mine. C'mon, let's go up to the line. We have to get our practice flights in before noon, so the official show can start, and I've booked us for nine, which gives us half an hour or so." Eric took the handles of Rob's chair and pushed him toward the sidewalk leading out of the parking lot.

Jordy trotted along beside while Jan and Terry followed at a more sedate pace.

"Boomer and Buzzard? There has to be a story behind those nicknames."

Jan nodded. "There is. Rob got his nickname when he and Eric participated in a NATO competition for reconnaissance pilots. They were flying from their base in Germany to the base in Holland, where the competition was to take place." Her pace slowed, and Terry matched her, content to let the men get farther ahead. "There were another two Canadians on the team, but they were flying up later. All the commanding officers and most of the other competitors from the other countries had already arrived. The COs and a bunch of brass were gathered in the briefing hut on the hangar line. Rob and Eric were never ones to arrive anywhere quietly or inconspicuously, and this time was no different."

Terry watched Jan's face as they strolled along the path. "I'll bet they were hell on wings in their day."

"That they were. Anyway, Rob was flying lead, and he

told Eric to stay with him because they were going to wake people up. They received clearance to do a fly past, but then they came in fifty feet off the deck, right over the briefing hut. From what I understand, there was a near sonic boom when they went overhead, and everyone in the hut dived for the floor and under tables...except for the Canadian CO, who stood there, calmly surveying his NATO colleagues, and announced, 'Gentlemen, the Canadians have arrived.' That's how Rob became 'Boomer.'"

Terry laughed at the thought of all those exalted military men scrambling for cover. It was never hard to picture Rob as an incorrigible prankster. "So how'd Eric become 'Buzzard'?"

"He had this habit of taking up with his buddies' ex-girlfriends, so one very miffed ex-boyfriend accused Eric of being a vulture. I believe Eric came out of that discussion with two black eyes, but the ex had a broken nose and Eric had the girl, so he claimed he won. Ever since, though, he's been Buzzard."

"They have quite the colourful past, don't they?"

Ahead of them the men navigated around service vans and onto the hangar line.

"Yes, they have." Jan sighed. "You know, a lot of Rob's old friends couldn't handle it when he started to deteriorate, but Eric and Anne have been staunch in their support and affection. I don't think there's anything Eric wouldn't do for Rob. They were roommates and squadron mates in Europe. I really think they regard each other as brothers more than anything else. Eric always stops by when he's on a layover in town, and he calls Rob every couple of weeks to tell him what's going on with all their old buddies."

"Friends like that are treasures."

Jan met her gaze. "Yes. They are."

They had drifted to a stop and stood for a moment, looking at each other.

Jan shook her head. "I guess we'd better hurry up. They're going to start wondering if we got lost."

"C'mon, you two," Jordy called. "What's taking so long? Eric's almost ready to strap in, for crying out loud."

"I believe we've been summoned," Terry said.

They caught up to where the men waited for them.

Rob looked up at them. "Get lost?"

"No, just filling Terry in on some of your and Eric's youthful escapades," Jan said. "So, Eric, which one of these beasts is yours?"

Eric pointed at two red and black bi-wings parked on the tarmac. "Those Pitts Special S-2Bs. Tom's probably in the hangar right now, but we'll go take a look." He wheeled Rob across the tarmac to the aircraft as Jordy, Jan, and Terry tagged along.

"Weren't you guys going to Yak-55s this year?" Rob asked.

"Nah, we looked into it, but we got a real deal on these babies, and they do everything we want and more. I haven't had this much fun flying since you and I were beating up Europe."

Rob smiled. "What's the climb rate on one of these?"

"Specs say twenty-seven hundred feet per minute, but we've pushed the envelope a bit further, though not during shows."

While Eric and Rob discussed the plane's capabilities, the other three walked around the aircraft and admired the small but nimble-looking bird.

"Do you think he'd be insulted if I told him it was cute?" Terry whispered.

Jan winked. "I don't think they like to hear that about their toys."

They laughed.

Jordy scowled, which only made them laugh harder. He huffed and returned to where Eric and Rob were deep in conversation.

"Do you think we bruised his male ego?" Jan asked with a smile.

"If we did, it'll heal. He's young and resilient and so excited nothing could ruin this day for him." Terry nudged her and pointed toward a tall man coming in their direction, wearing the same blue flight suit and red baseball cap that Eric wore. "Is that his partner?"

"Yes, that's Tom. Looks like Jordy's adventure is about to begin."

Twenty minutes later, the two Pitts taxied by to the button of the runway. Jordy sat in the back seat of the lead aircraft, helmet on his head, eyes forward.

Terry waved, though she doubted he had an awareness of anything outside the cockpit.

Moments later, they took off and angled westward as she stared after them.

Jan touched her arm. "You don't have to worry about him. Eric's a terrific pilot, and he won't let anything happen to Jordy, other than maybe an upset stomach."

"Oh, I know. I'm not worried. I just hope this lives up to his expectations." She turned away. "Hey, I wonder if we can get a cup of coffee?"

"Of course," Rob said. "What's the good of being VIPs if you can't even get a decent cup of coffee?"

They moved off to the enclosed pavilion half-covered with a brightly striped tent. Jan showed their pass to the attendant, and he pulled back the velvet rope for them to enter. After securing coffee and pastries, they found a table close to the flight line and sat down facing the airfield.

While they awaited Jordy's return, Rob entertained them with tales of air shows past when he had flown with demonstration teams all over Canada and the States.

Just before ten, Terry spotted the red and black biplanes returning. "Let's go meet them. I want to see how he did."

By the time they made their way back through the growing crowds swarming over the tarmac to the Pitts' parking spots, the aircraft were taxiing into position.

When the planes coasted to a stop, both pilots pushed back their canopies.

Jordy clambered out of the cockpit after Eric. As soon as Terry reached him, he threw his arms around her. "You should have seen us! We did rolls and loops and passes, and Eric even let me take the controls once their routine was done. I did a hammerhead stall and recovery, almost on my own, and Eric said I could fly with him any day."

Terry ran her knuckles over his cheek. "I don't know, little brother. You look a little pale to me. You sure you brought back that brown bag empty?"

"Of course I did. I was way too busy to get sick. Oh, Terry, it was awesome!"

The older men smiled indulgently.

I wonder if he reminds them of when they were his age. Terry knuckled Jordy's head and grinned at him.

Eric had replaced his helmet with his ball cap, but he took it off and put it on a beaming Jordy. "There you go. Now you're officially one of the team."

Terry leaned down and whispered in Rob's ear, "Thank you. I so owe you one."

Rob shook his head. "No debt. It was entirely my pleasure."

A lump rose in Terry's throat. It would have been so easy for Rob to become embittered at what life had done to him, but there wasn't a trace of that. She blinked and straightened.

Jan watched their exchange with a smile.

Terry was very glad she had been delivering mail on that particular route, on that particular day.

It was almost noon, and the small party, minus Tom, who headed back to the hangar, had returned to the VIP enclosure for lunch. Terry was discussing the upcoming Snowbird aerobatic show with Eric and Jordy when Jan touched her arm. She turned.

Rob's head was slumped to his chest, and his eyes were half-closed.

"I'm sorry," Jan said. "But I'm going to have to take him home. It's been a long morning, and he's worn out."

Disappointment flashed in Terry but was quickly overridden. "Of course. We'll leave as soon as you're ready."

Jan studied her for a moment and then turned to Eric. "Are you still coming over for dinner tonight?"

"Yeah, we were going to cut out of here after our show around four, and I should be at your place about five, depending on traffic."

"You have your own transportation, then?"

"We do. We rented a car for the weekend, and I'm going to drop Tom off at his cousin's on the way. Why, do you need something?"

Jan nodded. "Would you mind giving Terry and Jordy a ride? I know they were looking forward to the Snowbirds, but Rob's got to get home now."

When Terry started to protest, Jan shook her head. "You

know you were, and there's no reason you have to miss them. We've seen them many times, so don't worry about it."

"I don't mind at all," Eric said. "Besides, it'll give Jordy more time to pick my brain on the military." Jordy had been peppering him with questions since their return. "I think he may just be considering a career as a flyboy."

Terry raised an eyebrow at Jordy.

"It's settled, then," Jan said. "Terry, why don't you and Jordy stay for dinner with us, and I'll run you home afterwards."

Terry blinked. "Okay, sure." *Though I wish you could stay.*

Jan unlocked Rob's brakes and pulled him back from the table. He was too tired to protest their premature departure. As everyone bid them goodbye, Jan pushed him out of the VIP enclosure and soon disappeared into the crowds milling around the tarmac.

Eric stared after them. "Do you know, there was a time that man could party all night and fly all day, and nothing ever slowed him down?"

"I wish I could have known him then," Terry said. "I'll bet he was the life of the party when you two were over there."

"He was. He was also the most loyal friend you could ask for. There was nothing he wouldn't do for you. Even if it ended up getting us all in trouble. Did he ever tell you about the checkerboard and the commandant's desk?"

Terry leaned forward. "No, I don't think he's mentioned that one. What was it all about?"

"Well, a good buddy of ours got a speeding ticket on the base from the military police. He was only going five kilometres over the limit, but the meatheads didn't have anything better to do than play traffic cop." Eric paused, drained his coffee cup, and signalled the waiter for another coffee. "Our buddy was complaining about it in the squadron room, and Rob decided the meatheads needed a lesson on priorities. Our squadron emblem was a checkerboard, so Rob got a couple of cans of black and white paint, and that night, he led half a dozen of us on a raid."

"What did you guys do?" Jordy asked.

"We broke into the base commander's office, painted a huge checkerboard all over his oak desk, and left a note pointing out how lax base security was and suggesting that something be done about it."

Terry's eyes widened. "No way!"

"Yes, ma'am, we did so. And when the base commander came in the next morning, he hit the roof. He called the meatheads' section head in and went up one side and down the other. 'Course then the head went back to his section and raked them over the coals. Hell, those meatheads were so mad they were spitting bullets. They'd been publicly humiliated, and within hours, the entire base was laughing at them. They spent months conducting an inquiry into that stunt."

"Did they ever catch you guys?" Jordy asked.

Eric's eyes twinkled. "No, they never did, but it sure wasn't for lack of trying. They investigated their asses off, but no one cracked. A year later when the base commander was being posted out and we had a farewell mess dinner for him, he brought the subject up himself. Said he couldn't prove it, but he knew Spencer and Landon had to be behind it. He was looking right at us, but we just sat there, looking like choir boys."

"I'll bet that was believable." Terry chuckled, imagining Rob and Eric's attempts to look innocent.

"Maybe not," Eric said. "But no way were we going to confess. We both wanted long careers, and we knew we'd run into the base commander somewhere along the line."

"Did you?" asked Jordy. "I mean, run into him again?"

"Uh-huh. About five years later, he was promoted and appointed head of the Air Force. But you know, he was one of the guys that helped keep Rob in when his health started to go downhill. They could've easily kicked him out after he couldn't fly anymore, but he'd made so many friends and admirers over the years that they reassigned him to a desk job and let him stay in as long as he could handle it."

"I'd wondered," Terry said. "I guess that answers that."

"I think it would have killed Rob to lose the Air Force, especially after his first wife left him. It kept him going until he met Jan, and that lady literally saved his life." Eric's expression darkened. "He came within a couple of hours of dying one time, you know. She wouldn't let him. Never seen anything like it. Just stubborn as a mule, she was. Told him he'd promised her sixty years, and he wasn't going to welsh on her or she'd haunt him for eternity. She sat there and held his hand and talked to him day after day. Doctors couldn't believe it, but he recovered because she told him to."

Terry's eyes misted. "They're quite a pair."

Eric nodded. "You don't know the half of it."

CHAPTER 11

TERRY PLODDED UP THE STEPS to her house. The endless workweek was finally finished. With a week to go until October, the weather had turned cool, and sullen grey skies threatened early snow. When Terry pulled open the front door, she had to fight the wind to close it behind her.

She kicked off unlaced shoes and tossed her uniform jacket into the hall closet, then slouched into the living room and collapsed on the nearest couch. She closed her eyes. *Wild horses couldn't drag me out again.* Even her nightly trek to the Spencers' was out of the question.

Someone bounced down beside her on the couch.

Terry opened an eye and cast a jaundiced glance at Michael. "No. Whatever it is, no."

"Aw, c'mon, you haven't even heard what I was going to say. Besides, you're not allowed to say no this time, because we've decided you've been playing hermit too long."

"Who's 'we'?" Terry opened both eyes and glared at him.

"Lisa, Robyn, Randy, and I. We were talking this week and couldn't even remember the last time you came out with us. So we're kidnapping you to Oly's for TGIF. We intend to get you wined, dined, and bedded tonight."

Terry groaned. Her big plans included a long, hot bubble bath and a trashy novel. "Maybe I don't want to be wined, dined, and bedded."

Michael gasped and clutched his chest. He tumbled off the couch in an exaggerated pratfall. "You don't want to be bedded? Did the sun rise in the west today? Is our dollar actually worth a dollar? Are the Flames going to make the playoffs?"

Terry couldn't stifle a laugh.

Michael sat up and leaned against her legs. "Seriously, you have to come out with us. Your Doña Juanita credentials are in imminent danger of being revoked by the Lesbian Collective. All you do anymore is hang around here or go over to the Spencers'. What's gotten into you anyway?" He rested his arms on her lap and studied her.

"Nothing's gotten into me. I just haven't felt like going out lately."

"C'mon, Ter. Just think of all those lovely ladies you're depriving of the pleasure of your company. You have a duty to get out there and circulate."

Terry pushed him over with her knee. He sprawled on the floor with a triumphant grin.

"Oh, all right. Far be it from me to deprive all those lonely women. What time?"

"Randy's coming over around seven, and Lisa and Robyn are going to pick us up about eight." Michael stood up and tweaked his trousers. "I want you to wear those new black jeans and the boots I gave you."

Terry threw a pillow after him as he ducked through the door. "Do I at least get to choose my shirt?"

"Yes, but I'll be by at seven thirty to approve it."

Terry resigned herself to going out that evening but toyed with a plan to make an early exit. *Forget it. They won't let me get away with it.* She sank deeper into the couch, intent on a nap because the night promised to be long and the morning after even longer.

Terry followed Randy and Michael through Oly's door, Lisa and Robyn hard on her heels. A blast of noise and smoke greeted them as they burrowed into the crowd and found a spot to stand by the bar.

The pub was bursting with the usual Friday night revellers.

"Think we'll be able to find a free table?" Terry asked.

Lisa craned her neck to study the crowd. "No worries. We'll be seated in five." As always, her uncanny ability to spot an opening had them worming their way through the crowd a few minutes later, glasses of beer held high to protect them. Lisa pounced on a table just as the occupants were getting ready to leave. She glared at a couple attempting to claim the same territory. With Robyn's and Randy's solid presence at her back, Lisa carried the day and the table was theirs.

They settled around the table. Randy inched his chair close to Michael's and rested one arm around his shoulders. Terry liked the large, quiet man whose muscular, rough looks contrasted so sharply with Michael's slender, urbane appearance. Randy looked exactly like what he was, a rigger who spent as much time in the oil patch as he did in the city.

She'd been surprised when they started dating on Labour Day after meeting in Oly's. She hadn't expected it to last even this long. Since his disastrous relationship with Owen, Michael had refused to be pinned down. *It might end when Randy goes back north. I can't see Michael staying faithful to an absentee lover.*

Randy tugged Michael to his feet and pulled him toward an open dartboard. Terry's gaze followed them. *Still, I can't remember the last time I've seen him this happy.* She sipped her beer and surveyed the mix of Oly's regulars and a good many strangers. Her gaze drifted over the people clustered at the bar and settled on an attractive, older woman sitting at the far end of the bar, nursing a drink.

The woman's pale blonde hair was cut in a bob, and her expensive, well-tailored suit draped over generous curves. She turned on her stool and surveyed the room. When she noticed Terry watching her, she smiled and dropped her gaze before turning back to her drink.

Terry didn't know if she'd pursue the invitation, but she was intrigued nonetheless. She looked back at her friends.

Lisa and Robyn grinned at her.

Terry's brow furrowed. "What?"

"It's just good to see you getting back in the game." Lisa looked at Robyn. "Hon, would you mind getting us another round?"

Robyn stood. "Another of the same, Ter?"

Terry nodded.

Robyn disappeared into the crowd.

Lisa regarded Terry seriously. "I'm really glad you decided to come out with us tonight. Frankly, we were considering running an intervention on you."

"What are you talking about?"

"It seems like every time Robyn or I call for you lately, you're over at the Spencer house."

"I like them, and I like going over there. They're really great people. You met them at my birthday; you know that."

"They are good people, but I can't help worrying about why you're spending so much time with them to the exclusion of all your other friends. I ran into Jordy the other day, and he said even he hadn't seen much of you lately."

Terry didn't want to go into why she spent almost every night at the Spencers'. *Maybe I've been a little obsessed, but I'm writing like a house on fire right now. At this rate, I'll have the first draft completed by Christmas. Why is everyone making such a big deal out of it? It's not like I started skydiving or bungee jumping. But...maybe they're feeling neglected?*

"You're not doing something dumb, like falling for a straight, married woman, are you?"

Terry gaped at Lisa. "Where in the hell did you get an idea like that? They're my friends...both of them."

"We all saw the way you looked at Jan at your birthday party. You couldn't keep your eyes off her. I know it's not your style, and I know Rob's your friend, too, but I think you may be getting into deep waters here."

Terry jumped up. "You're frigging crazy if you think I would ever do anything to hurt either one of them." She spun, almost running into Robyn coming back with three beers in her hand. After grabbing one, Terry stalked off to the bar. With only a moment of hesitation, she angled toward the blonde and slid in next to her. "Hi, would you like some company?"

When the woman nodded, Terry motioned the bartender over. "Can I get you another of those?"

"Yes, please. Chivas on the rocks."

Terry held out her hand. "My name's Terry Sanderson."

"Patricia Wilson. Trish for short."

"Hi, Trish. I don't think I've seen you around here before. Are you new to Oly's?"

"Actually, I'm new to Calgary, and I'm only here for another couple of weeks. I'm on a contract assignment from my head office in Toronto to straighten out a mess with our local branch office. Are you from around here?"

"I'm a Calgarian, born and raised." Pushing the distasteful conversation with Lisa from her mind, Terry settled in to get to know Trish.

The next couple of hours flew by as they talked about jobs, families, and the differences between their cities.

Terry liked Trish's casual confidence and easy conversation. The woman was intelligent, well-travelled, and a good conversationalist. Plus Trish found many opportunities to lay her hand on Terry's arm.

Partway through the evening, Michael came up and wrapped his arms around Terry's waist. "Randy and I are cutting out to Harlequin's, and Lisa and Robyn are heading to the Arc. Did you want to come, or can you find your own way home?"

Terry glanced over to their table, where Lisa, Robyn, and Randy were getting ready to go.

"I've got a rental car," Trish said. "I could drop you off at your place later if you'd like."

"Are you sure you don't mind?"

"No, not at all. Besides, I'd hate to lose such charming company so early." Trish smiled at her, with a veiled promise in her gaze.

Terry patted Michael's arm. "You guys go on, then. I'll catch you later. And tell Lisa no hard feelings, okay?"

Michael gave her a quick hug and returned to the waiting trio. He spoke to Lisa, who looked Terry's way and smiled.

She returned the smile, relieved that Lisa's ridiculous theory hadn't created a rift between them. Lisa was seeing chimera, but she hated to argue with her old friend.

"Are you hungry at all, Trish? Would you like to drop over to Pieder's for a bite to eat?"

"That sounds like a wonderful idea. I haven't eaten in ages." Trish gathered up her purse and followed Terry's lead as she threaded her way through the boisterous crowd and out into the cool fall night.

Terry smiled as she held the door for Trish. *The night is young.*

Terry surged upward in one last spasm of pleasure and settled back onto the dishevelled sheets. She brought her breathing under control and caressed Trish's hair. They lay quietly, until Terry reached down and urged Trish higher on the bed.

She tugged a sheet over their cooling bodies just as her door burst open and Michael staggered inside.

Trish shrieked and dove under the covers.

"Michael! What the hell are you doing?"

Michael swayed in the doorway. "How kin ya tell 's me? I'm in disguise."

Terry picked up one of her pillows and threw it at him. She nailed the lampshade that covered his head. It was enough to offset his precarious balance, and he landed on his butt with a thud.

Randy skidded into the room. Wearing only jeans and an appalled expression, he glared at Michael. "Aw shit, Terry. I'm sorry. He got away from me. I was trying to convince him to pack it in for the night, and while I was in the washroom, he disappeared, along with the lampshade."

"It's okay. But could you drag him out of here? He's not exactly what I had in mind for tonight."

"Yeah, this wasn't exactly what I had in mind either." Randy bent down to help Michael up.

Michael looked at him blearily and hung an arm around his neck.

Randy lifted him and tossed the lampshade aside. "I'll pick that up in the morning, okay?"

"No problem. But when the lush wakes up, tell him I want to have a word about his timing."

Randy hooked his foot around the door to close it as they left.

The room quieted, and Trish stirred beside her. Terry peeled the covers back far enough to slide an arm around her shoulders. "I'm sorry about that. Michael has a weird sense of humour at the best of times, and when he's been drinking, it goes right off the wall. Are you okay?"

"Yes, I just wasn't expecting company. You have quite the exciting household."

"It can be at times, but I wouldn't trade my roommates for anything."

Trish eased up enough to put her head on Terry's shoulder as she settled in.

The exhaustion Terry had held at bay all evening resurged, and this time she yielded to it.

———◆———

When Terry finally opened her eyes to a room lit with morning sunshine, she was mildly surprised, but not displeased to find herself alone.

Trish had left a note on her pillow. *Thanks for a wonderful night, lampshade man and all. I'm in town until mid-October at the Sheraton, if you feel like giving me a call.* She had signed it with her name and hotel room number.

Terry tossed the note on her bedside table, pushed back the covers, and stood up. *It was fun. Trish was nice. But I doubt that I'll call her.* She gathered what she needed for her shower.

An hour later, showered and dressed, she shared a pot of coffee in the kitchen with Claire.

They turned their heads as the basement door creaked open and Michael staggered into the kitchen.

Coming Home

Claire smothered a smile.

Terry grinned. "Geez, you look like something the cat dragged in. What the hell did you do to yourself last night?"

Michael stared at her with bloodshot eyes, winced at the brilliant morning light, and groped his way along the counter toward the coffee maker. He grabbed it like a drowning man reaching for a life preserver and stared at the dregs barely coating the bottom of the pot. "How could you do this to me? I thought you loved me."

Terry and Claire looked at him cradling the pot in his arms and then at each other as they broke out in laughter.

Michael clapped his hands over his ears. He hit himself with the pot, which only made them laugh harder.

Terry took pity on him and pried the pot out of his fingers. She replaced it with her own coffee mug and turned to make a fresh pot.

He staggered to the table and took deep swallows of the coffee. Then he grimaced. "What'd you do, put a little coffee in your cream?"

Terry frowned. "Beggars cannot be choosers. Besides, after what you did last night, you're lucky I even let you near my coffee."

"What I did? What did I do that you would be so cruel as to deny me the fluid of life in my hour of need?" Michael propped his face on one hand.

Before she could answer, a knock sounded on their back door, and Terry opened it. "Good morning, Robyn. Where's your better half today?"

"Lisa had to run some errands, so she's going to swing by later. You know how much I love shopping, so I decided to drop in for a cup of your world-famous coffee instead."

Robyn tossed her coat over the back of a chair and joined the roommates around the table.

"Good luck on the coffee." Michael scowled. "And I have dibs on the first cup when the pot's ready."

"What's with Little Mary Sunshine?"

Claire smiled. "Our suave and debonair friend managed to get rather inebriated last night and now he's paying his penance and not very graciously at that."

"Never again." Michael lowered his head to the table. "I'm never again doing Jell-O shooters with Randy. That man could put Babe the Blue Ox under the table. Hell, I think he *is* the Blue Ox."

"Well, you would know more about that than we would," Claire said. "But we'll take your word for it."

Michael punched her arm. "Ha ha. You're such a funny lady."

"Where is that man of yours?" Terry sat down next to Robyn.

"Still asleep. Exactly where I'd be if I had any sense at all." Michael rolled his head and peered at Terry. "What were you talking about that I did to you last night?"

"So you don't remember staggering into my room while I was in flagrante delicto, wearing a lampshade on your head and giggling like a mad schoolboy?"

Michael's face was blank for a moment. Then a look of horror washed over it, and he jerked upright. "Ohmigawd. I didn't dream that?"

"No, you sure didn't. You know, for someone who was determined to see me bedded last night, you weren't exactly helping things along."

Michael blushed. "Oh, shit." He extended a hand to Terry.

"I'm so, so sorry. I can't believe I did that. Was your date really upset?"

Terry shook her head. "Lucky for you, all you disturbed was the afterglow."

Claire raised an eyebrow. "There was no doubt about that. Your guest was so loud that if we'd had any crystal in the house last night, I'm sure it would have shattered."

Terry polished her fingernails on her shirt. "What can I say? When ya got it, ya got it."

A chorus of groans met her boasts, and Terry grinned. "Hey, you two were the ones insisting on me being bedded last night." She poked Michael and Robyn. "I was only following instructions. Can I help it if the lady appreciated my efforts?"

Claire shook her head. "Next time, I think you should either gag your guest or issue us all ear protectors."

"If there is a next time, I'll keep that in mind."

"If? What do you mean, 'if'? Did something go wrong last night?" Michael's brow furrowed. "I didn't really screw things up for you, did I?"

"No, everything was fine. I mean Trish was fun, you know. She's a nice lady, and we had a good time, but..." Terry trailed off, unsure how to define what was missing. She shrugged. "I don't know. Maybe I was just more tired than I thought."

"I know what it was," Michael said. "She failed the Terry Test, right?"

"What's the Terry Test?" Claire asked.

"As I understand it, the lady in question has to enjoy sharing ice cream but despise lima beans, know who scored the winning goal in the '72 Canada-Russia series, love Tolkien, and hate Danielle Steel. If she fails in any of those crucial categories, she's history, right, Ter?"

"I'm not that bad." Terry grinned. "I can cut them a little

slack if they miss the hockey question, but I am inflexible on the ice cream issue."

"Did last night's date fail the ice cream test?" Claire asked.

"We never actually got around to talking ice cream, but I doubt she knows Tolkien from Tolstoy. She doesn't like to read, not even trashy novels. Can you believe that?"

Robyn tilted her head. "I didn't know that was so high on your list of priorities."

"Well, not for a casual date of course," Terry said. "But I figure if you're going to hook up with a person long-term, those are vital areas of compatibility. Not that I thought Trish was going to be long-term. She's not even going to be in town much longer." She nudged Michael. "Besides, until he coerced me into going out, my big plan was to spend my Friday night in a bubble bath." When the others snickered, she rolled her eyes. "By myself."

"It would have been much quieter if you had." Claire stood. "I have a paper to work on, so I'm off to the library."

Michael squinted at her. "You're not talking about Crowley's assignment, are you?"

When Claire nodded, he groaned. "That thing's not due for months yet."

"It is due in four weeks. And unlike some people I could mention, I prefer not to leave everything to the last minute and then pull an all-nighter." She left the kitchen.

Michael shook his head. "I don't know how she does it. That woman is the most organized person I've ever met."

"Next to you, everyone looks organized," Terry said. "So, party boy, is your conscience going to bother you? Are you going to hit the books early this time?"

Michael drew himself up. "Don't be silly. I have a reputation to preserve. If I started a paper more than seventy-two hours before it was due, people would think I was actually serious about my grades."

"God forbid."

He yawned, then stood and poured himself another cup. "I'm heading back to the bed I should never have left this morning. Are you going to be around later, Ter?"

"I don't know. I was thinking of going over to Jan and Rob's this afternoon, and I'm not sure what time I'll get back. Did you need something?"

"Nothing important. I'll catch you later." Michael fluttered his fingers and departed.

Robyn regarded Terry with a creased brow.

"Oh, God, not you, too." Terry glowered at her. "They're just friends, period, end of sentence."

"I didn't say anything. Your business is your own, and I'm not going to butt in."

"I just don't understand why everyone's acting so weird lately. You'd think I'd done a Jekyll and Hyde or something. I haven't changed. I made some new friends, and they're terrific people. It's not like I'm abandoning all of you, for crying out loud."

"Shhhh, I know that. So does Lisa. She's just worried about you."

Terry leaned back in her chair. "And what about you? Are you worried, too? Do you think I'm getting into some kind of a mess?"

Robyn stared at the table. "I think that you've reached the point where you want more than casual dates, and that makes you vulnerable. You told me once that someday you want what your parents have, that you want the love and commitment you've seen between them every day of your life. Do you remember that?"

Terry nodded.

"I don't for one minute think you'd consciously hurt your friends, but I also don't think you'll be as careful about protecting yourself. And that's what concerns me because you have a big heart, and I can easily see you losing it in a hopeless cause. I've known you since fifth grade, and I've never really seen you in love before. I've seen you in lust more times than I can count, but you've always held back part of yourself. I think the first time you give that part of yourself will also be the last, so I want you to give it to the right woman, a woman who's free to love you back. So yeah, I worry about you."

Terry stared. That was more words than Robyn usually spoke in a month. "Robyn." She stopped, uncertain what to say.

"No, it's all right. Just don't get mad at us for caring, okay?"

"I won't. You guys are worrying for nothing, but I do appreciate that you care."

CHAPTER 12

T ERRY BASKED IN SUNSHINE ON the short drive to Jan and Rob's. It was a welcome change after the dull, windy week just past. Windows down, she inhaled the crisp fall air permeated with the scents of a world going to sleep for another winter.

When she turned onto the Spencers' street, Jan was in her front yard, raking up leaves. She turned to wave as Terry got out of her car and crossed the lawn.

"Hey, Jan. How's it going this glorious day?"

"It is a gorgeous day, isn't it? Though I'm beginning to think I should conduct a midnight raid to chop down my neighbour's tree. I swear he waits until the fall winds have blown most of his leaves into our yard before he even thinks of raking his own." Jan shook her head and gazed at the thick mat of dead leaves.

"You've sure got a good crop on your hands. Want some help raking?"

"Don't you want to get to work?" Jan asked. "I don't want to cut into your writing time."

"Nah, it's too nice a day to be cooped up in the basement all afternoon. I'll give you a hand if you have another rake. It has to go better than when we tried to fix the fence."

"Oh, the fence didn't turn out that bad. It's keeping the neighbourhood dogs out, and that's all that matters. But sure, if you don't mind helping, there's another rake hanging in the garage. It's not as good as this one, but then it all depends on the skill of the user, of course. Think you can keep up?"

Terry chuckled. "Are you challenging me?"

Jan gave her a gentle push in the direction of the garage. "I am. Let's see what you can do with all those youthful muscles."

Terry ambled off but then turned with her hands on her hips. "You're not trying to pull a Tom Sawyer on me, are you?"

Jan smiled and resumed raking leaves. "No, I promise I won't trick you into raking the whole yard by yourself."

Terry stood for a moment. The sun illuminated Jan's hair like a bronze flame, and she fell into a graceful rhythm as she drew the rake repeatedly over the lawn.

Jan looked up, and her rake slowed.

Terry shook herself out of her reverie and started toward the garage. She swung by the front door and stopped for a moment to call a greeting to Rob. After a brief exchange of friendly insults, she went around to the garage and found the other rake. It looked as if it had been through a lawnmower, sporting missing and bent prongs and a taped-up handle. She shook her head. *I think I'm starting at a distinct disadvantage.*

When she returned to the front yard, Jan looked up. "Do you want to swap?"

"No, I'm good." Terry started raking.

"I know you are, but your equipment is somewhat inferior." Jan wrinkled her nose. "It really wasn't my intention to put you to work today."

Terry snorted. "After all you and Rob have done for me? This is little enough."

Jan stopped to pull some leaves off her rake. "You know how much we enjoy having you here."

"And I love being here. But I still feel guilty sometimes about infringing on your time."

"Phsst. Most of the time we barely know you're downstairs. You're not infringing in the least."

"Uh-huh. I'm pretty sure you know I'm there when dinnertime rolls around."

Jan leaned on her rake and eyed her. "Considering you supply dinner half the time, we have no complaints. Especially Rob. You spoil him rotten. He didn't get Chinese half as much before you came into our lives."

"He does love his Kung Pao chicken."

"He'd eat it every second night if he had his way. I think the only thing he loves as much is a good steak and a glass of red wine."

Terry smiled. *And you.* "Well, just remember if there's anything else I can do, you only have to ask."

They raked for the next half hour and built an ever-increasing pile in the centre of the yard. Finally, satisfied that they had collected all the errant leaves they could find, they stopped to survey the results.

"You sure you're not descended from some ole plantation boss?" Terry asked.

"Oh, like you were working so hard. Don't think I didn't see you kicking them around."

"I do like the sound of them when they're all dry and crunchy."

"Me too. I really like the smell of them, too. It's sort of earthy, like a harvest smell. This is, without doubt, my favourite time of year." Jan closed her eyes and sucked in a deep lungful of the air.

Terry hip-checked her into the large pile.

Sputtering and pushing leaves out of her face, Jan sat up with an indignant expression.

Terry laughed and backed away, her hands raised. "I'm sorry, I couldn't resist. That pile was just screaming for someone to land in it."

"Uh-huh, and you figured that someone should be me, eh?" Jan jumped to her feet and stalked after her. "You do realize you've ruined an hour's work and that you will pay, right?"

Without waiting for an answer, she wrestled Terry into the now scattered pile of leaves. Screams of laughter erupted from a flailing mass of arms and legs as they rolled around. Each tried to bury the other in the disintegrating pile as they threw leaves with both hands. Finally, out of breath, they flopped back on a bed of fragrant, crushed leaves.

Terry grinned at the brilliant blue sky. *God, that felt good. I haven't done that in...I don't remember the last time.*

Jan pushed herself up on one elbow and leaned over. She brushed a few stray leaves off Terry's forehead and tucked her dishevelled hair back behind an ear.

Terry froze. Unable to move, unwilling to breathe for fear Jan would retreat, she was overcome with a longing to wrap her arms around Jan and bury her face in her hair.

Jan drew back but left her hand on Terry's shoulder. "Thanks to you, I think I've got leaves in places leaves have no business being." She pushed back on her heels, rose to her feet, and extended a hand. "Come on. You helped make the mess; you get to help clean it up."

Terry allowed herself to be pulled upright. As Jan searched for her rake, Terry's mind echoed with one thought. *Oh God, Lisa was right!*

Terry stared at her screen. She hadn't typed a word since

sitting down. Finally, she rubbed her forehead and glanced up at the clock on the wall. Was it really only an hour since all the pieces had fallen into place, and she discovered that place could never be hers? *Maybe I'm just imagining things...because of what Lisa and Robyn said.*

She closed her eyes and recalled the feeling of Jan's body squirming under hers as they wrestled in the leaves and how those sparkling, laughing eyes enraptured her.

No, I didn't imagine it. Maybe it's just lust? Jan was an attractive woman. Not her usual type, certainly, but perhaps she was reacting with a heightened libido because of her encounter with Trish.

Terry covered her face with her hands. *Don't lie to yourself. Sex with Trish was nothing. This...this is so much more I can't begin to deal with it. Aren't Robyn and Lisa going to have the last laugh. Talk about a fucking impossible situation.*

She stood and began to pace. *It is impossible, right? Of course it is. Jan is happily married and devoted to Rob. She'd be shocked if she knew what I'm feeling.* Besides, whatever she felt for Jan, she would never step between her and Rob. *No way would I hurt him like that. His whole world revolves around Jan.* Without her, he would be condemned to the unimaginable loneliness of a permanent care facility.

Terry drew in a deep breath. *Okay, so how to handle it?* Well, she certainly wasn't going to act on it or let Jan know; that much was for sure. She couldn't order her heart to stop caring, but maybe by ignoring it as much as possible, this fresh new love would wither from neglect.

She groaned softly. The only way this was ever going to vanish was if she moved to the other side of the country for the next three decades. *I wonder if they take Protestant nuns. Oh yeah, throw me in a community of women; that'll help.*

A laugh came from the doorway, and Terry's head jerked up.

Jan leaned against the doorframe.

Terry's heart rate doubled, and her breath caught.

"Do you always go through such agonies when you're writing?"

"Uh, I was just, um, thinking," Terry said. *Shit, how long has she been watching me?*

"Yes, I could tell. You seemed lost in a world of your own."

Terry blushed. "Just working out some details before I start the next chapter. Saves a lot of rewriting that way."

"Uh-huh. Well judging by that very attractive shade of pink you're sporting, I'm guessing this must be one of 'those' scenes." Jan crossed the room and peeked at the uninformative screen. "Care to share the details?"

"No, nothing like that." Terry fought to stop herself from reaching for Jan. "Was there something you needed?"

"Yes. I just wanted to see if you'd have dinner with us tonight. After all, feeding you is the least I can do after I worked you so hard this afternoon, even if you did create a lot of that work yourself."

"I made work?" Terry fell gratefully into their familiar banter. "May I remind you who was right there scattering leaves with the best of them?"

"Yes, well, who started it? You didn't really think I'd just let you get away with that, did you?"

"I didn't think you could tackle like a defensive back, either. You should come with a warning label attached. You play rough."

"Uh-huh. I distinctly remember being pushed into that pile when I was most vulnerable. There I am, eyes closed as I enjoyed the fall air, and wham! The next thing I know, I've got a face full of dead foliage." Jan touched Terry's shoulder and laughed. "Hold still. You've still got a few strays in your hair." She tilted Terry's head to the side and pulled some leftover bits of leaf out of her hair.

Terry absorbed her nearness and the gentle industriousness of her fingers as she removed the last remnants of their play. *Oh God! It's too soon.* "Um, thanks. I'll just go run a brush through and get the rest out. Why don't you give me a shout whenever dinner's ready, okay?"

She beat a quick retreat to the washroom, painfully aware of Jan's puzzled expression and terrified that if she'd stayed there a moment longer, she'd have pulled Jan into her arms. After closing the door, she leaned on the sink and looked in the mirror. Wide, frantic eyes stared back at her.

"Get a grip! You cannot do this." Terry breathed deeply and began to pace within the confines of the small room. "Okay, you'll be fine as long as you're not alone with her. That's the key. I'll stick close to Rob when I'm not down here writing. And no more solo outings with Jan."

Maybe I shouldn't come over here anymore. The thought almost doubled her over in pain. They would never understand if she abruptly vanished from their lives. She refused to hurt them when they had done nothing but offer her unqualified friendship.

She leaned against the nearest wall. *Am I being selfish? Maybe. Probably.* Slowly, she slid down the wall until she sat on the floor, knees drawn up to her chest and head buried in her arms.

Terry didn't know how long she'd sat there, but her butt was numb. She pulled herself up, turned on the cold water, and washed her face. *I just need to act like nothing's changed so that no one knows that everything has.* She closed her eyes.

"Okay, early resolution. You can stay in Jan's life as long as you don't hurt either of them. If it looks like that's happening, you'll have to withdraw. You'll have to." Her stomach roiled. She clenched the edge of the sink and looked in the mirror. "Then it's up to you to make sure it doesn't come to that."

She returned to her computer, though she'd never felt less like writing. She longed to scurry home to the refuge of her garret, but she'd already agreed to have dinner. *I can't begin operation "Above Suspicion" by running from the first challenge, but I have to buy myself some time. I need to get some perspective on this mess.*

Terry passed a couple of hours puttering and accomplished nothing productive before Jan called her for dinner.

When Terry emerged in the kitchen, Jan glanced up. "Everything all right?"

"Mmm-hmm. I think I'm running into writer's block after all, though." Terry avoided meeting Jan's gaze. "In fact, I've been pushing it pretty hard these last few weeks. I need to recharge my batteries for a while and not think about the book at all, you know?"

"So what's your plan?"

Terry took Rob's lap tray out of the cupboard and arranged his dishes and napkin on it. "I think I'll just set it aside for a week or two, let the ideas percolate a bit before I get back to it."

"I guess we won't have the pleasure of your company every night for a while, then."

Terry fiddled with Rob's cutlery. "Well you're probably pretty sick of me hanging around all the time anyway. You might find you've missed your peace and privacy."

Jan stopped ladling the homemade clam chowder into bowls. "I thought I'd made it clear, Terry. We enjoy having you here, and that's not going to change. But if you need to go do other things for a while, we have no claim on your time. When you're ready to come back, we'll be here. We're certainly not going anywhere." She added thick slices of freshly baked bread to the tray and took it from Terry. "Your mom called while you were downstairs and asked us over for Sunday dinner next week, so maybe we'll see you then."

Uh-huh. This is going to work really well. Wish I could tell Mom what a big help she's not being. Picking up her own bowl and a couple of slices of bread, Terry stiffened her resolve and went to join her friends for dinner.

CHAPTER 13

J AN PUSHED ROB UP THE walkway to the bottom of the
stairs. Terry, Gord, and Jordy hurried down to carry the
wheelchair into the house.

"Thanks, guys." Jan relinquished Rob's chair to Gord and
Jordy and smiled at Terry. "Hey, you. Did you manage to get
rid of all the leaves yet?"

Terry's gaze avoided her, and she said nothing as she took
hold of one wheel and lifted.

Uh-oh. What did I say? The absence of Terry's usual
affectionate greeting was disconcerting, particularly when
she'd missed her so much. Their home had been far too quiet
the past week without Terry around, and she'd been looking
forward to seeing her again.

Jordy took the other wheel, chattering to Rob a mile a
minute. Gord manhandled the back of the wheelchair up the
stairs, and they all spilled into the front hallway.

Jan's stomach began to churn as the evening wore on. Terry
didn't sit by her, found excuses to leave the room, and gave
short, unresponsive answers to any conversational gambits.
She was equally evasive with Rob. *Why is she mad at us? Did I
do something wrong?* She and Rob exchanged puzzled glances
on several occasions.

After Jan helped clear the table, she and Jordy encountered
Terry on the way to the kitchen. Terry scuttled backwards to

get away. When Jan reached out a hand to calm her, Terry flinched. Jan drew back and tried to give her as much space as possible in the narrow hallway.

Jordy balanced a stack of dishes in his hands. "What the hell has gotten into you tonight? If you were going to be such a jerk, you bloody well should have stayed home. Mom and Dad did not raise you to be such an ill-mannered bitch."

Jan almost dropped her dishes. She fought her instinctive reaction to defend Terry and took a deep breath. *Okay, I don't know what's happening here, but Jordy worships Terry. If anyone has the right to call her out, he does. It's not your business.*

Terry mumbled some inanity and made her escape.

When Jan returned to the dining room, she lowered her mouth to Rob's ear. "I think we should go, love. We may have overstayed our welcome."

Rob nodded.

Jan turned to Emily and Gord. "Thank you so much for dinner. It was lovely."

Emily frowned. "Do you have to leave so soon?"

Jan glanced at Terry and nodded. "I think it's best. Rob… he's a bit tired today." She shot Rob an apologetic look for using him as an excuse.

He gave her a small smile.

Emily walked them to the door and wrapped each in a hug. "Please come again soon. We so enjoy having you join us, and you're always welcome."

"Thank you, Emily. We really appreciate your hospitality."

Jan put Rob's coat on and tucked his arms securely inside the chair before Jordy and Gord picked it up.

Terry trailed behind them and muttered goodbye before she hastened to her own car.

Terry slammed the door as she entered her home. Dinner at her parents' had been the first time she'd seen Jan and Rob in a week, and she'd failed miserably at operation "Above Suspicion." She tossed her keys on the side table and ran her fingers through her hair. *No point in trying to write.* The muse seemed to have temporarily—at least she hoped it was just temporarily—flown the coop. *Ugh, mindless distraction it is.*

When she opened the door to the basement, the television blared from below. Not in the mood for company, she almost changed her mind. *No, goddamn it. I have as much right to be down there as Michael and Claire.* She stomped down the stairs.

Michael looked up as she entered the room and threw herself on the couch beside him. He regarded her for a moment. "What's got your tail in a knot?"

"Nothing." Terry slouched down in the cushions and refused to look at him.

"Uh-huh."

Terry glowered at the TV for long moments, then threw back her head and screamed.

"Feel better now?"

Terry nodded. "Sorry. I didn't mean to take it out on you."

"What are friends for? Want to tell me what's bugging you?"

"Nothing, really. Just been one of those weeks, you know? And then tonight at Mom and Dad's, I couldn't seem to do anything right. Now I've got everyone mad at me."

"I'm not mad at you."

"Thank you for that. Dunno what I'd do if I was in your bad books, too." Terry rested her head against his shoulder.

Michael put his arm around her. "If you do want to talk about anything, you know I'm always here for you, right?"

"I know. Thanks." *In a really shitty week, it's nice to have at least one port in the storm.* Michael would listen without judgement if she told him of her newly discovered feelings for Jan. But he would also try to talk her out of them, which was looking more and more like a hopeless proposition.

Terry had done little else over the last week. She had reasoned and argued with herself endlessly while she walked her route each day and in the quiet of her garret each night. No amount of logic made a dent, nor had her absence from the Spencer household dimmed her feelings in the slightest.

When she had seen Jan tonight at her parents' house, her chest had tightened, quivers wracked her knees, and dizziness swept over her. She had covered by bolting to the kitchen on some pretext until she got her rebellious body under control. *At this rate, I'm going to have to start carrying smelling salts.*

Terry and Michael watched TV until the phone rang beside them and they both jumped.

Michael grabbed the receiver. "Hello." He sat upright and assumed a more formal tone. "Oh, hello, Dad. It's nice to hear from you. How's Mother?"

Terry grinned at the contrast to his usual easy-going slouch, but then her smile faded as Michael turned pale.

"Of course. I'll be delighted to see you both. Shall I pick you up at the airport, or will you take a limo to your hotel?" Michael listened for a moment. "That's fine. I'll see you once you're settled in, and we can go out for dinner. I'll look forward to your call." His hand shook as he hung the phone up.

Terry waited for him to say something, and when he didn't, she nudged him. "Folks coming for a visit?"

Michael turned an anguished face toward her, then jumped up and started pacing. "Oh God. What am I going to do? Dad's got a two-day conference here this week, and they're flying in from Toronto on Wednesday evening. Mother's coming along so they can both have a visit with me. Why would they do that? They never come to Calgary. Ever! Ohgodohgodohgod!"

If Michael hadn't been so upset, Terry would've laughed, but she'd never seen him so agitated. He was making her dizzy. She finally grabbed his arm and hauled him back to the couch. "Get a hold of yourself. What's the big deal? So your parents are going to drop in for a visit. So what? It's only for a couple of days. I'm looking forward to meeting them."

Michael stared at her. "Are you insane? The Seatons never leave Toronto except on vacations and errands of doom. If they're coming to see me, disaster is imminent."

"Now you're being neurotic. Your father has a business trip, and your mom's coming along to see her son. What's so ominous about that?"

"Dad does not do business trips to anywhere other than New York or London. He leaves national trips to his minions. If they're coming here, it's to drop some kind of bomb on me." Michael gasped. "I know what it is. They're going to pressure me to get engaged."

"They're what?" Terry's eyes widened. "Are you telling me that they don't know you're not the, um, marrying kind? You never told me that."

Michael covered his face with his hands. "I know. It's embarrassing to confess that I'm too gutless to come out to them. They expect me to carry on the family name, and they think I've sort of got an arrangement with an old friend of the family."

Terry gaped at him. "Are you sure they don't know? You're not exactly...I mean you're—"

Michael eyed her between his fingers. "I'm hiding in plain sight. Parents tend to see only what they want to see, and when I'm around them, I do try to live up to their image of me. Besides, there was always Patsy around to divert suspicion."

"Patsy? Who's she? Your beard?"

"I suppose in a way, but really she's just an old friend. Our fathers are business associates, our mothers are friends, we lived in the same neighbourhood, and we've been pals for as long as I can remember."

"Well, surely she must know, then. She's not expecting a proposal, is she?"

Michael winced. "Patsy's lived a very cloistered life. I'm not sure she even knows there are alternative lifestyles. It was just easier to let everyone assume we had an understanding. I knew she wouldn't push me while I was in school, and it took the pressure off me not seeing other women, you know?"

"If that's why your parents are coming out here, you're going to have to do some fancy dancing, my friend." Terry blinked. "Good God, you're not going to do something stupid like go through with this, are you?"

When dead silence met her question, Terry's eyes widened. "You can't do that...not to yourself and not to Patsy. It's not fair to either of you."

Michael hung his head. "Wouldn't be the first time it happened."

Terry's problems were now forgotten in the midst of Michael's startling revelations. "Jesus, what a predicament. I can't believe your parents would pressure you into a loveless marriage."

Michael froze. "Ohmigawd! What if they want to see my room while they're here?" He jumped over the couch and dashed for his bedroom.

Paper ripped from his walls.

Terry winced. *There goes Brad Pitt.* A second long rip. *Aw, not the James Dean poster, too.*

He reappeared in his doorway, holding the remains of two large posters.

Terry shook her head. "I don't suppose you could've taken them down carefully and let me store them for you until they left?"

Michael looked down at the paper hanging in strips from his hands. "Aw, shit."

At the look of stunned desolation on his face, Terry couldn't maintain a poker face. Despite the looming family crisis, it was a relief to release the strain of the past week.

After a moment, Michael joined her amid gales of laughter. "You don't think they'll inspect my underwear drawer, do you?"

"You mean the pink silk boxers? I don't know. You might want to invest in some butch flannels for the occasion." Terry looked at Michael, then howled with renewed laughter. Helplessly, they leaned against each other until Michael quieted.

"God, Ter. What am I going to do?"

Sobering, Terry sat up and took his hand. "Why don't we wait until we see what exactly they want and take it from there, okay?"

Michael nodded, but his shoulders slumped and his grip on Terry's hand was so tight that it hurt.

Jan and Rob said little to each other on the way home.

When Jan called Terry later in the evening and on successive days, her calls were ducked.

She hung up the last time and looked at Rob, her heart heavy. *Why? I just don't get it.*

He raised an eyebrow. "She still won't talk to us?"

"No." *I miss her.* Troubled, Jan sat in his wheelchair and rolled back and forth. "Did we do something to anger her, love?"

"Nothing I can think of," Rob said. "I thought we were all getting along fine."

"So did I. I don't think I'll try calling her again. Whatever's bothering her may have nothing to do with us. We'll just give her some time, and hopefully, she'll be back to normal soon."

"What time are they supposed to be here?" Terry asked.

Michael continued to pace. "Their flight arrives at six thirty. By the time they get to their hotel, it'll probably be close to eight or so."

"Then you've got lots of time. Why don't you sit down before you wear a hole in the rug?"

Michael stopped and sat in the nearest chair. He adjusted his dark blue pants until they hung properly and flicked bits of lint off his grey tweed blazer. His hands drifted to his muted silk tie, tugging its perfect knot.

Terry shook her head. *Who needs oil wells? He's putting out enough nervous energy to power the entire province all on his own.* "So how much have you told your parents about your life out here?"

"Oh you know, stuff about sharing a house with you and Claire, how my studies are going, shows I've seen, and concerts I've gone to." Michael smiled. "Mom used to take me to Roy Thompson and Massey Hall all the time when I was a kid, and we had season tickets for the Toronto Symphony Orchestra. I miss that, you know?"

Terry nodded. Michael rarely spoke of his life in Toronto and even less of his family. "Didn't your dad go along with you?"

"No. Dad was only interested in business and golf. I think he was glad when I was old enough to go with Mom so she stopped trying to drag him with her. But Mom and I used to make a big deal of it. We'd go out for dinner, all dressed to the nines, and she'd always talk to me like another adult. Once we got to the Hall, we'd both get lost in the music, and when we got home, we'd spend hours talking about what we'd heard."

"She sounds pretty special."

Michael nodded, studying his hands. "She is. Actually, in his own way, my dad's a decent fellow, too."

"Are you sure they wouldn't understand?" Terry asked. "Maybe you should just—"

Michael shook his head. "No, you don't get it. My father's views are very, very conservative. I remember sitting at the dinner table, listening to him rave about 'those damned Liberals' in Ottawa and how the Charter of Rights was going to be the ruin of the country. Shortly after I figured out for myself that I was gay, there was a scandal at his company when a senior VP was found to be cheating on his wife with a man." He shuddered. "You'd have thought the world was going to crumble the way he ranted and railed. It was all he talked about for a whole month, and I'm almost certain he was instrumental in getting the man to retire for the good of the company."

"Okay, maybe your father wouldn't be receptive, but what about your mother?"

"Mom's no doormat. She'd never let Dad dictate her decisions about anything, but I think in this case, she'd probably agree with him. I'm sure she looks forward to grandchildren one day." Michael's shoulders slumped. "We were really close when I was growing up. I don't want to sound like a cliché, but Mom and I were the best of friends back then."

"So what happened?" Terry asked.

"When I was sixteen, I fell in love for the first time. He was a classmate at my private school. Once I accepted my feelings for him, I understood that a divide had opened between me and my parents—one that couldn't be crossed. I knew that what I felt, what I was, wouldn't be acceptable to them at all, so I just withdrew. I doubt Dad even noticed, but Mom did, not that she understood why. I'd catch her looking at me, like she was trying to figure me out, but I'm sure she wrote it off to normal teenage angst. It became easier to stay in our separate worlds and only meet on neutral ground."

"That's really sad. I wish it had been easier for you."

He laughed with no hint of humour. "Yes, well, we can't all have Emily and Gord for parents, can we?"

Terry glanced over his shoulders out the front window. "Did you say you were expecting them around eight?"

"Yes." Michael examined his highly polished shoes. "Why?"

"Because a black limo just pulled up in front of our house, and I don't think it's Claire."

Michael blanched and whirled to look out the window. "It's them. They're early. I'm not ready. I can't do this. Maybe you could tell them—"

Terry grabbed Michael and pulled him into a tight hug until he calmed down. Then she ran a quick hand over his hair, smoothed it into place, and nudged him toward the front door.

He glanced over his shoulder. "You'll hang around, won't you?"

Terry nodded, and the front doorbell rang.

He straightened and reached for the doorknob.

Michael's father was a tall, burly man with a monk-like fringe of incongruously curly hair. He shook Michael's hand and clapped him on the shoulder.

A slender woman stepped in behind him and waited for her turn to greet their son.

Terry smiled. There was certainly no doubt which parent

Michael took after. Mrs. Seaton's slight build, delicate features, and intelligent, deep blue eyes were the feminine incarnation of her son. Unlike her husband, she cast formality aside and wrapped Michael in a hug. She released him to arm's length and looked him over. "I'm relieved to see you're not wasting away out here," she said, in the time-honoured fashion of mothers convinced their offspring will starve once they fly the nest.

"Aw, Mom, you know I can cook. I can even sew a button on if I have to."

Terry stifled a laugh as she remembered the previous Halloween when Michael had created hand-sewn costumes for both of them from original patterns. *He can definitely sew, but I'm guessing he'd rather I didn't bring that up right now.*

Mrs. Seaton glanced over her son's shoulder. "Michael, where are your manners? Aren't you going to make introductions?"

Terry stepped forward.

"Mom, Dad, this is one of my very best friends and roommates, Terry Sanderson. Terry, these are my parents, James and Elizabeth Seaton."

Terry held out her hand. "I'm pleased to finally meet you, Mr. and Mrs. Seaton."

James Seaton enveloped her hand in a firm grip and gave it a quick shake.

Elizabeth Seaton smiled and took Terry's hand in both of hers. "We've heard so much about you. I've always been very glad that my son has such a good friend here." She turned to Michael, took his arm, and steered him into the living room. "Why don't we make ourselves comfortable, dear?"

James and Terry followed and sat in chairs flanking the couch, where mother and son had settled.

"I thought you weren't getting in until later," Michael said, his gaze focused on his mother.

"We hadn't planned to, darling, but then an opportunity came up for us to catch a ride with Edward in his private plane. You remember Edward Bell, your father's senior partner, don't you?"

Michael nodded.

"Ed's daughter is having some kind of problem out in Vancouver," James said. "He had to fly out to straighten matters around, so he offered to drop us off en route. It was a lot more convenient and got us here early enough that I was able to arrange an advance meeting with a client. I'll have to leave for that in an hour or so."

Michael's brow furrowed. "Are you talking about Christy Bell, Dad? I knew her. She was a couple of years ahead of me. What kind of trouble is she in? I hope it's not serious."

James snorted. "If it is, Ed will get it cleared up. He didn't want to go into it, but from what I understood, the silly girl went and got in with a bad crowd. He's going to bring her back to Toronto as quickly as he can wrap up her affairs there. Should never have let her go to that crackpot university in the first place."

Terry and Michael exchanged glances.

Elizabeth watched their byplay with interest.

"May I offer you some coffee, Mrs. Seaton?" Terry asked.

"Tea would be lovely, if you have some," Elizabeth said. "But please don't go to any trouble."

"No trouble at all." Terry stood.

Michael jumped up, too. "I think I'd better give her a hand. Terry's not allowed in the kitchen alone for all of our sakes." He grinned at Terry's look of chagrin. "You know it's true, Ter.

Who was responsible for half the fire department showing up at our door the last time she attempted to cook dinner?"

"But that wasn't my fault."

Michael propelled her down the hall.

"Who knew you had to peel the stupid things before you put them in the oven? You'd think they'd put clearer instructions on the package." Terry lowered her voice. "Besides, I didn't see you complaining about men in uniform showing up at our door." She dodged his elbow and leaned against the counter as he fussed over the kettle, teapot, and cups. "I could have handled it, you know."

"Uh-huh. Sure you could." Michael smirked. "Why don't you get down the tea bags?"

Terry eyed the multitude of cupboards. "Okay…"

Michael snickered, and she frowned at him. "I can find them, just give me a minute."

"By the time you find them, my parents will be back in Ontario." Michael reached high into a corner cupboard and pulled down a brightly coloured tin.

"Well, if you're going to hide them like they were buried treasure, no wonder I didn't know where they were." Terry was glad that his mood had lightened. "Your folks seem like decent people. I don't know what you were so worried about."

Michael glanced at her as he continued his preparations. "If I wasn't carrying the weight of parental expectations, I'd probably think they were lovely folks, too. Come on, grab the cups and we'll head back into the lion's den."

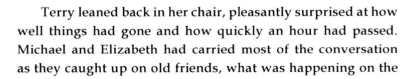

Terry leaned back in her chair, pleasantly surprised at how well things had gone and how quickly an hour had passed. Michael and Elizabeth had carried most of the conversation as they caught up on old friends, what was happening on the

Toronto concert scene, eastern politics, and Michael's activities in Calgary.

Michael adroitly steered the conversation away from potential trouble areas and back into the safer waters of tales from school and of his roommates. His back straight and shoulders square, he was the image of an up-and-coming young businessman. One hand rested on his knee, while the other wielded a teacup as if he had been raised in fine salons. *Which he probably was.*

Drifting mentally from the current discussion of the Seatons' upcoming Mediterranean vacation, Terry considered Michael's chameleon-like veneer in his parents' presence. Rather than the amiable, often profane party boy she lived with, a sophisticated, socially adept young man sat in front of her, conversing in perfect diction with the elegant woman who had raised him. She now understood how Michael could carry off a double life right under his parents' noses. *He would've been a terrific actor if he'd wanted to be.*

James stood. "I have to go if I'm going to make my meeting. Michael, why don't you come along with me? It'll be good preparation for you to meet our clients and see the way we do things."

Michael glanced at Terry. "But, Dad, I can't just leave Mother by herself."

"Nonsense, I'll have the driver drop her at the hotel, and once we're done, we'll all meet for dinner."

Elizabeth smiled. "Actually, James, if Terry doesn't mind, I'll stay here until you two are finished. I'd certainly rather enjoy such lovely company than look at four dreary walls in a hotel room."

"You're booked into a suite in the Four Seasons, Mother.

I'd hardly call it dreary, and besides, Terry probably has her own plans." There was a note of desperation in Michael's voice.

Elizabeth looked at Terry. "Would you mind keeping me company for a while, or did you have other matters you needed to attend to?"

Uh-oh. I don't like the sound of this. Terry forced a smile. "Of course, Mrs. Seaton. You're more than welcome to wait here."

"There, that's settled, then. Come on, we don't want to keep the client waiting." James and Michael crossed the room and opened the front door to find Randy on the doorstep, hand raised to ring the bell.

"Hey, Mikey," Randy said. "Since when did you get such fancy wheels?"

Terry bolted out of her chair and dashed by a startled James and a frozen Michael. Flinging her arms around Randy, she planted an enthusiastic kiss on his lips. "Sweetie, I forgot all about our date tonight. I'm so sorry, something's come up. Can I have a rain check?" She spun Randy around, locked her arm around his, and marched him back down the path to his truck.

By the time he'd gotten his bearings, he was standing beside the driver's door, staring at Terry.

She pulled Randy's head down toward hers and pretended to nuzzle his ear. "I'm sorry. It was an emergency. I'll have Michael call you when he gets home later, okay? His parents are in from Toronto, and he has to go out to dinner with them."

"Okay, darlin'." Randy grinned and opened his door. "Tell him from me that he's an idiot for not cancelling our date, but I'll forgive him under the circumstances. Although I'm thinking seriously about changing teams after that greeting."

Terry blushed.

As Randy slid behind his wheel, he looked up and winked.

"And tell him he did a damn fine deer-in-the-headlights bit. I think that boy of mine owes you big time."

Terry groaned and leaned her head against the truck door. "God, you don't know the half of it. I have to entertain his mother while he goes off with his dad. I think I'll be busting into that new bottle of CC later tonight."

Randy laughed, started his truck, and pulled away, waving at Terry as he went.

Terry started back up the walk, drained by ebbing adrenaline and the prospect of spending the next couple of hours in Elizabeth's formidable company.

Michael shot her an expression of pathetic gratitude.

James put out a hand to stop her. "I hope we didn't mess up your plans, young lady. Was your boyfriend upset?"

"Not at all, Mr. Seaton. Randy's a very understanding guy, and I'll make it up to him tomorrow." The false implication fell glibly from her tongue. *Sheesh, maybe Michael's not the only one who could've been an actor.*

Elizabeth stood in the doorway with her arms crossed and a smile on her face.

Terry stopped short. *God, it's like she's looking right through me.* She shook off her nerves, climbed the rest of the stairs, and followed Elizabeth back into the house.

Terry was about to resume her seat in the living room when Elizabeth gestured her to Michael's vacated spot on the couch beside her. *Aw, geez.* She settled uneasily on the old couch.

After reaching for the teapot, Elizabeth poured what was left into her cup.

"Would you like some more?" Terry asked. "It'll only take a few minutes."

"From what my son says, that's a pretty dangerous offer,

but thank you, this will be enough." Elizabeth sipped from her cup, and the silence built between them.

Terry couldn't think of a conversational gambit to save her life. *Damn, her dress probably cost more than my entire wardrobe put together.*

Elizabeth Seaton was the image of a Rosedale socialite. She exuded grace and controlled her environment without lifting so much as one well-manicured finger, yet Terry didn't sense any hostility or arrogance from her.

After what felt like a year to Terry, Elizabeth set her cup on the coffee table and leaned back. "That was your boyfriend, then, was it? I do hope that he doesn't mind me stealing you away for a little while."

Terry's gaze darted away. "Randy's a great guy. He didn't mind me putting off our date until tomorrow."

"That was very considerate of him considering the short notice. It's always nice when our significant others understand, don't you think?"

Terry was afraid to open her mouth for fear of incriminating herself.

Elizabeth raised one perfect eyebrow. "Have you two been seeing each other for very long?"

God damn it, Michael! You are going to owe me so big. "Not that long really. We met earlier this year." *Well, that part's true anyway.*

"Interesting." Elizabeth studied her. "I was under the impression from Michael that you were gay. Perhaps I misunderstood him?"

Shit, now what? You won't tell them about yourself, but you tell them about me? Terry shot mental daggers at her absent friend. "Umm, what exactly did he say to give you that impression?"

Elizabeth smiled. "I believe his exact words were, 'Terry's gay.'"

Damnit, damnit, damnit! Terry slouched farther into the couch.

Elizabeth chuckled.

Terry lifted her gaze from an intense study of the faded carpet to find eyes bright with merriment focused on her.

"My son certainly left you in quite a pickle, didn't he?"

"I'm going to kill him when he comes home."

Elizabeth canted her head. "So why the charade?"

Terry was unable to come up with a single, plausible reason on the spur of the moment.

"I want to tell you a little story. Will you listen, please?" Elizabeth's voice was iron velvet.

Terry nodded.

"I realize you don't know me," Elizabeth said. "And I have a hunch my son doesn't speak much about us either."

Terry shot her a guilty glance.

Elizabeth sighed. "You have no reason to think I'm anything but an idle, rich woman living on Glen Road and meeting other 'ladies who lunch' at Prego every Friday, but I assure you that's not the entire picture."

"I didn't think it was. Michael never gave me that impression about you at all."

Elizabeth smiled. "Thank you. I won't say I don't enjoy the fruits of my husband's labours, but I've also tried over the years to find more satisfactory uses of my time than lunching and shopping. One of the things I've been involved with for quite a number of years is fundraising for such organizations as the AIDS Committee of Toronto and hospices like Casey House and Trinity Home."

Elizabeth paused. Her eyes reflected an unspoken pain.

"I've met some wonderful people through my work, but I've also seen far too many beautiful young men die long before their natural time."

Terry tensed.

"I'm not a fool. Nor am I blind to my son's nature, no matter how deluded he is about me. I'd say Randy was here today to pick up Michael, not you. Isn't that so?"

Terry tugged on the collar of her shirt. "Don't you think you should be talking to Michael about this?"

Elizabeth sighed. "It's not like I haven't tried, but he can be the most evasive creature on this earth when he doesn't want to be pinned down on something."

"Boy, don't I know it."

"It's quite all right. You haven't told me anything, and really it's not that I need the confirmation anyway. I think I've known almost as long as he has, though I was in denial for a few years." Elizabeth pinched the bridge of her nose. "I've been so afraid for him, so afraid he'd end up like those young men I see at the hospices." She brushed at the corner of her eye. "Please, Terry. Just tell me if he's happy and if he's safe. I'm not asking you to reveal any confidences."

Terry hesitated, unwilling to break faith with Michael. *How would Mom feel in Elizabeth's shoes?* Her back stiffened. "I think Michael's happy, and he's assured me he's being careful."

Elizabeth studied her.

"He thinks you guys are here to pressure him about getting married." Terry clapped a hand over her mouth.

Elizabeth laughed long and hard.

Terry joined in the laughter, and the tension lifted.

"Exactly who did Michael think we wanted him to marry?"

"Some old friend of his named Patsy?"

"Good lord. Does he think we're total idiots? Even James thinks that girl is the dimmest bulb in the box. She's a sweet thing, mind you, but living proof of the dangers of social inbreeding."

"So I take it she isn't exactly daughter-in-law material?"

Elizabeth raised an eyebrow. "She isn't exactly dog-walker material."

A thought occurred to Terry. "Does Mr. Seaton know about Michael?"

Elizabeth shook her head. "No. James is not stupid, but he is utterly focused, to the exclusion of anything outside the normal parameters of his world. It would no more occur to him that Michael's gay than it would that he's a communist." She sighed. "James loves his son, but I think he would have great difficulty with this, and Michael's probably wise to keep it quiet for now."

They sat quietly for a few moments.

Finally, Elizabeth asked, "Is Randy a good man? Do you think it's serious?"

Terry waggled her hand. "Yes and no. Randy's definitely a good guy, there's no question about that. And he really does seem to care about Michael, but—"

"But my son isn't one for monogamy?"

"That's part of it, I suppose, but it's also that Michael got badly burned last year, and he's been leery of relationships ever since. Still, I think if anyone can get him to settle down, it'd be Randy. I don't think I've ever seen Michael as relaxed and contented with anyone as with that oversized oil rigger, and Randy seems just as happy to be with him."

"I'm glad. Michael's young yet, but I'd love to see him settle down permanently at some point, though God knows how we'd ever break it to James."

Terry thought of her own mom. Eastern socialite or western matriarch, mothers weren't all that different in their aspirations for their children.

CHAPTER 14

THE FAMILIAR NOISES OF THE old house offered slight comfort to Terry — the creak as Claire mounted the stairs to her suite, the ancient furnace kicking in to counter a cool fall night, and the sound of water flowing through pipes. Her mind wandered over the hours she had spent with Elizabeth Seaton and the promise the woman had extracted from her.

"Please, Terry. Don't tell my son what we've spoken of tonight. I need him to tell me himself when he's ready."

Michael would interrogate her on their conversation, and Terry wasn't sure if it would be disloyal if she omitted telling him that his mother knew he was gay. But she understood Elizabeth's position, and she had promised to keep her trust. She just hoped Michael wouldn't find out that she was keeping a secret from him.

Terry pulled a pillow over her face and groaned into it. *How do I get into these situations?* She threw the pillow aside and stared again at the garret's ceiling. *Don't I have enough complications in my life right now?*

She tossed about the bed, achy and unable to get comfortable. Finding a cool spot, she tried to settle down, but the stairs squeaked as someone climbed past the second floor.

Michael's home. Terry smirked. *Well, in the absence of truth, I can always yank his chain a little. He certainly deserves it for what he did to me.*

A soft knock came at her door, and Michael's head poked around the edge. "Are you awake?"

"Well, if I wasn't before, I am now. Come on in."

Michael flopped down beside her on the bed, and Terry rolled over to face him. He had discarded his blazer, his tie hung loosely, and the top buttons of his shirt were undone. With his wide happy smile and dishevelled blond hair, he looked like a little boy just out of school for the day.

"So," Terry asked. "How did it go?"

"Actually, not too badly. We were all astonishingly civil to one another, and I even got Dad to admit that Calgary wasn't the armpit of civilization he'd assumed it to be."

"Uh-huh. Any mention of marital prodding?"

Michael sat up and wriggled backwards until he leaned against the headboard. "Not a word, oddly enough. I wonder what was going on."

"Gee, you don't suppose they really only wanted to visit their son, do you?" The sarcasm was wasted.

Michael shook his head. "No, I'm sure there's something else going on. I just don't know what it is."

Terry bit her tongue, picked up a pillow, and belted Michael with it.

He teetered on the edge of the bed. "Hey, what's that for? What did I do?"

"You're an idiot, but I love you." Terry sat up and leaned against him. "Do you remember that little incident with Randy's arrival at the house?"

"Well, yeah." Michael rolled his eyes. "You really saved my life there. I owe you a big one."

"Uh-huh. Well, my dear dim-witted friend, do you also recall a conversation you had with your mother once, telling her all about your roommates and the fact that one of them was gay?"

Michael stared at her blankly for a moment, then comprehension dawned and an expression of horror crossed his face. "Oh shit! I told her you were gay!"

"No fooling, Einstein."

"Ohmigawd." Michael grabbed her arm. "What did you tell her? Did she remember me telling her that? Of course she did. That damn elephant brain of hers never forgets anything!"

Terry cuffed him.

"Ow! What did you do that for?" Michael rubbed his head.

"Because I don't want a hysterical queen in my bed, waking the neighbours. Besides, I handled everything, so there's nothing to worry about." *Okay, not quite the truth, but there really isn't anything to worry about.*

"What did you say? What did she say?"

"Well, no thanks to you for the advance warning." Terry glared at him. "But I sorta, um, kind of…I told her I was bi and that Randy was just too good to pass up."

Michael stared at her, and then he started to giggle. He reached a full-fledged belly laugh, and Terry hammered at him with her pillow. He toppled to the floor with an indignant squawk.

Laughing, Terry crawled to the edge and peered down at him. The light from the half-open door fell across his relaxed face. She extended her hand and pulled him back on the bed.

Stretching out beside each other, they were quiet for a while until Michael nudged her. "Seriously, I really do appreciate what you did for me tonight. Anything I can do for you, just name it."

Terry elbowed him back. "Aw, you'd have done the same for me, but if you really want to pay me back…"

"I do. Just name it."

"You can take my laundry detail for the next couple of weeks."

Michael groaned. "All right, I guess I owe you that much. Consider it taken."

"And no turning my underwear pink for revenge."

"Hey, that was an accident. I didn't notice Randy's red flannels had gotten in with the rest of the stuff, honest."

She snorted. "Sure, you didn't. Got a bridge you want to sell me, too?"

Michael laughed.

Terry resigned herself to getting her underwear back in flamboyant shades. *Oh well, it's worth it to get out of my chores for the next couple of weeks.*

He was quiet so long that Terry wondered if he had dropped off to sleep. It wouldn't be the first time that had happened. They often talked long into the night and were too tired to move when conversation tapered off. She was at that hazy state between wakefulness and slumber herself when Michael nudged her again.

"You know I don't like to pry — "

Terry yawned. "Yes, you do. It's one of your favourite hobbies."

"Okay, well maybe, but I've been pretty good recently, haven't I?"

"I suppose. What's on your mind?"

"I'm worried about you."

"About me?" Terry's eyes widened. "Why me? I thought you were the one with the problem."

Michael pulled himself up and faced her. "Something's wrong, and we all know it. The girls and I were talking about it the other day. You're not yourself. You're moody and surly, and it's like you've done a complete about-face. You were flying high up until a week or so ago, and now you're this sullen, miserable person that none of us has seen before. Even Jordy is pissed at you. C'mon, talk to me. What's going on?"

Terry sat up, her knees touching his. Her head was bent, and her shoulders slumped.

Michael took her hand. "You'll feel better for getting it out. Maybe I can help."

"No one can help." Terry was torn between wanting to shut down this turn of conversation, and desperately needing to talk to someone. "I'm sorry. I know I've been an asshole lately. It's nothing you or anyone else has done."

Michael waited for a long moment, then he squeezed her hand. "Please, let me help."

Those simple words broke the dam. "I've done something incredibly stupid. I can't believe it myself. I mean I never, ever thought it would happen to me in a million years." She tried to push more words past the lump in her throat, but they stuck.

Michael caressed her hand and waited.

"I think, I mean I'm pretty sure..." Terry drew a deep breath. "I've fallen in love with Jan."

He didn't flinch. "Are you sure? That it's love and not just a crush?"

Tears filled Terry's eyes, and she nodded. "I'm sure. I didn't want this, I swear I didn't. They're both friends of mine, you know?"

Michael took both her hands in his.

Terry rocked back and forth. "She's in my mind constantly, waking and sleeping. I can't be in the same room with her without wanting to pull her into my arms. It's like I'm a magnet and she's true north. I have to literally fight with myself not to touch her. You want to know something really weird? It's not even about sex. I mean, yes, I dream about making love to her, but it's so much more than that, too. Just to be in her presence, to listen to her voice, and to make her laugh…God, Michael, I've got it so bad." She pulled her hands away and angrily dashed tears from her eyes. They were falling faster now, obscuring her vision and dampening the sheets. "I'm so fucking stupid. I finally find the woman I want to spend the rest of my life with, and not only is she straight, she's married to a terrific guy, whom I happen to think the world of. Could I have made any bigger mess of things?"

Michael sighed. "Well, that explains why you've been over at their house every night."

Terry shook her head. "No, you don't understand. I, well, I've been trying to write a novel."

"You have?" Michael stared at her. "You never said anything about that."

"I know. I didn't want to jinx it, I guess. Anyway, Jan and Rob found out, and they offered me the use of their basement suite as a writing retreat anytime I wanted it."

"That was nice of them."

"I know, right? They've taken me in, both of them, and treated me as if I were a member of their family. They've been incredibly kind to me, and how do I repay them?" Terry slapped the bed. "I go and fall in love with Jan. I'm such a rotten bitch."

"Shhhh, you're no such thing."

Terry searched his expression. She could almost see the wheels turning in his mind. "Talk to me."

Michael sighed and cradled her hand in his. "First off, I'm not all that surprised. We've all picked up on the fact that Jan is special to you. The way you talk about her all the time; the way you can hardly wait to head over to her place almost as soon as you're in the door from work; the way you look at her when she's around. You practically glow in her presence."

Terry's eyes widened. She'd been sure she'd concealed her feelings. *I hid them so well from myself that I wasn't even aware of them until the leaf fight.*

"Don't worry. I'm sure neither Jan nor Rob knows. It's just your old friends, who've never seen this in you, who got suspicious."

Terry hung her head. "What am I going to do? It's killing me to stay away from her, but I can't let her know. It'd ruin our friendship, and then I'd never get to see her. And Rob... Oh God, how could I even think of hurting him by wanting his wife? I'm such a traitor."

"No," Michael said. "You're not a traitor. You're simply a woman who's fallen in love. It's not like you planned this, and I know you'd never intentionally hurt anyone, especially a friend. Okay, we need to think this out clearly."

"What's to think out? I love her. She's his, and she couldn't even love me if she was free. Jesus, how could I be so dumb?"

Michael tilted her chin up. "I want you to listen to me. I'm not so sure you're right about the hopelessness of this situation."

Terry stared at him.

"It's clear to me that Jan's very fond of you, too." Michael held up a hand. "Wait, I know what you're going to say, that it's just friendship on her part. Maybe that's true, but I noticed something at the barbeque. Her eyes rarely left you. Even when Rob told his story about Paris, she was watching you react."

"Yeah, well, she's probably heard that story a dozen times before."

Michael sighed. "You are so mulish. Listen to me. She was looking at you the way you were looking at her. I'm not imagining things here. I know what I saw. And when I mentioned it to Lisa later, she'd seen it, too. Where do you think we all got the idea that something might be going on?"

"No, that's impossible."

"It's really not. If we proceed on the premise that there is a possibility she could feel the same for you as you feel for her, we come to the overwhelming factor—Rob. I don't know Jan as well as you do, but my impression is that she'll stand by him for life."

Terry nodded.

"Okay, so we're agreed there," Michael said. "But, Ter, without being harsh, Rob isn't exactly in great shape. I'd guess his life expectancy isn't that long."

Terry recoiled. "Jesus, that's morbid."

"Yes, it is, but it's also realistic. And there's another matter to consider. There really isn't any way to be delicate about this—"

"Like you've been delicate up to now?"

"No, but I think you need to hear these things, and I'm going to be the one to say them. Rob's a quadriplegic, isn't he?"

"Yeah, so?"

"So I'm assuming he isn't exactly…fully functional, if you catch my meaning."

"I suppose not, but what's that got to do with anything?"

Michael leaned forward. "It's a lousy situation you've found yourself in. There's no noble way out for anyone that I can see, but what if there is a way for at least two out of three of you to find some happiness without really hurting Rob?"

Terry's brow furrowed. "What are you talking about?"

Michael blew out an extended breath. "Have you ever talked to Jan about, well, about how she handles things?"

"Things?"

"Jesus, Terry. What she does about sex."

"Oh. Ohhh…" Terry blushed. "Um, no, the topic's never come up. But I suppose in that movie's immortal words, 'It is the age of electronics.'"

"Well, you'd know about that. You've practically got your own toy store in that drawer of yours."

Terry grinned sheepishly.

"What I'm getting at though is if Jan feels the same as you do, and even if she wouldn't leave Rob—"

"I would never ask her to." *I couldn't.*

"I know," Michael said. "But what I'm saying is that maybe you and she could work out a discreet arrangement that allows you two to be together sometimes but doesn't take her away from him while he still needs her."

Terry gaped. "You're talking about me having an affair with a married woman."

"Yes, I am, and I wouldn't normally do that, but this situation is so complex that normal logic doesn't apply. If you found out that she wanted and needed you as much as you want and need her, is it fair to deny both of you a chance at happiness?"

Terry scowled. "You're dreaming in Technicolor. She's straight. For God's sake, she adores Rob. Anyone can see that."

"Uh-huh. And never in the history of the world have married, so-called straight women switched sides in mid-stream."

"But even if you're right, and I still think you're out in left field here, we couldn't take our happiness at Rob's expense." *If she loves me… Is it even possible?* Terry shook her head. *Doesn't matter. We couldn't. We just…couldn't. It would be wrong on so many levels.*

"It wouldn't be at his expense if he didn't know. And if nothing in his world changes because of it, where's the harm?"

"Damn it, you should have been a lawyer." There had to

be flaws in Michael's reasoning, but Terry couldn't pick them out right now.

"Just playing devil's advocate. Someone has to."

"I was sure you'd tell me to stop being so stupid and forget about Jan."

"Would it have helped?"

Terry shook her head. "I've tried. I've failed."

"That's pretty much what I thought."

Does he have a point? Is he right about Jan? Terry shot him a troubled glance as he watched her. *She's so devoted to him. She couldn't possibly feel anything but friendship for me – could she?* "I don't know. I don't know what to say or what to think."

"Then just relax. You're driving yourself crazy over this. At this rate, you'll end up with ulcers. Nobody's going anywhere, and there's no time limit on your heart. Why not try to get things back to normal as much as possible and then let things fall where they may?"

Terry sank back into her pillows.

Michael got off the bed and bent to kiss her forehead, only to pull back. "Hey, you're pretty warm. Are you feeling all right?"

"Hmm? Yeah, I'm fine. Go to bed, Michael. It's late."

Michael padded out the door, and Terry turned over his words in an endless loop. *An affair? With Jan? That's crazy…isn't it?*

CHAPTER 15

J AN RE-READ THE SAME PARAGRAPH for fifteen minutes and didn't absorb a single syllable. *This is useless.* She closed her book and stared at the shelves of books. She was spending her respite afternoon in one of her favourite haunts, the bookstore she and Terry had come to on their first outing. *We were getting along so well. I was certain we were building a strong friendship until last weekend.* She sighed. *What happened? What went wrong?*

After weeks of coming to their house virtually every night, Terry stopped dropping by either to use her downstairs retreat or simply to visit. She never rang the doorbell anymore to say hi when she dropped their mail off. Rob felt Terry's absence almost as keenly as Jan did. The worst part was that she couldn't find any reason for the sudden change. There was no falling out that she was aware of, but nothing accounted for Terry's behaviour at her parents' place either.

When Emily called a couple of days ago to invite her and Rob to Thanksgiving dinner, Jan had accepted the invitation. *That might've been a mistake. If Terry's retreating from our friendship, I don't want to intrude on her space.* Jan's irritation rose. *Damn it. If she isn't interested in being friends, the least she could do is say something rather than leaving us to wonder what the hell we did.*

Jan glanced at her watch. She still had several hours left

before she had to be back to Rob. *I can sit here and stew or try to do something about it. Terry might not be home from work yet, but I'll wait for her. It's time to have this out. Either I find out what the burr under her saddle is and remove it, or…or I have to accept this friendship wasn't meant to be.* She closed her eyes against the ache of that possibility, then took a deep breath and put her book away.

There were lights on at Terry's house when Jan arrived, but as she walked up the path, her resolve weakened. *What if Terry pushes me away?* Terry wouldn't be mean. She didn't have a nasty bone in her body, but that wouldn't soften the blow much. *It's not like I have so many friends that I can afford to lose one.* Jan braced her shoulders. *Whatever she says, I'll accept it. At the very least maybe I can solve the mystery of what on earth is going on.*

After ringing the bell, she drew her coat more tightly around her and thrust her hands in her pockets.

Michael opened the door.

She drew a deep breath. "Hi. I know it's early, but I wondered if Terry's home from work yet?"

"Actually, she's been off work for most of the week. She's had a really bad case of the flu."

Jan's aggravation vanished. "Is she all right?"

"She's a bit better today. I think it's pretty much run its course, but she's as weak as a baby. I don't think she'll be up dancing for a week or so."

"May I see her?"

"I'm sure she'd like that, though she may be dozy. I just made her some tea. Why don't you take it up? Make sure she drinks it all, because she hasn't kept anything down in days."

Jan shrugged off her coat and tossed it over the hallway chair.

Michael handed her a steaming cup. "Just holler if she needs anything, okay? I've got to get another load of laundry in."

Jan carried the cup upstairs and quietly pushed Terry's door open, not wanting to wake her if she was asleep. The room had a musty, stale odour, as if it had been closed off for months.

Terry was burrowed into a nest of dishevelled bedding. Matted, unwashed hair framed the sharp lines of her pale face. Her body undulated restlessly from one side to the other and back again.

Jan watched her for a moment, then set the tea on the bedside table and perched on the edge of the bed. She brushed the hair back off Terry's forehead and trailed her hand down the side of her face.

Terry opened her eyes. Wriggling closer, she curled her body around Jan's and rested her head against Jan's thigh.

Jan stroked her hair.

"I'm sick."

Jan smiled. "I know, sweetie. I wish I'd known sooner."

"Wish you had, too." Terry's eyes fluttered shut, and she seemed content to stay where she was.

A fierce protectiveness and deep affection rose inside Jan. *There's no way I can stay mad at you, is there?* She would have been happy to let Terry cuddle against her for as long as she liked, until she remembered Michael's admonition and the forgotten cup of tea. Gently, she shook Terry's shoulder. "Come on, sweetie. I need to get some tea into you."

Terry snuggled closer.

"Come on, you. Over you go." Jan eased Terry onto her back and propped several pillows under her head. She pressed the tea into Terry's shaky grasp and closed her hands around Terry's to guide the cup to her lips. She coaxed her into drinking the whole thing, then took the empty cup and set it aside.

Terry reached out, and Jan took her hand, frowning at how weak her grasp was. *At least there's more alertness in her eyes. Good call on the tea, Michael.*

"I've missed you." Terry's raspy voice warmed Jan's heart.

"I've missed you too," Jan said. She was rewarded with a sweet smile and a tightening of the fingers interlocked with her own.

Terry wrinkled her nose. "I think I stink."

Jan laughed but couldn't disagree. "Well, I imagine it's been a few days since you were able to shower."

"I'd kill for a bath about now."

"That could be arranged, and you won't even have to commit homicide. Give me a couple minutes, okay?" Jan disentangled their hands and left the room.

On the second-floor landing, she met Michael with an armload of folded laundry.

He looked over his stack of towels. "How's she doing?"

"Better, I think. She wants a bath, so I'm going to run one for her. Will you give me a hand to make sure she gets down the stairs safely?"

"Sure. Just call when you're ready."

"And could you change the sheets and open the window to air out the room while she's in the tub?"

Michael nodded. "It is getting a little ripe in there, but I didn't want to disturb her before. I'll take care of it."

"Thanks. You're a good man."

Once the bathtub was filled and fresh towels set out, Jan called Michael and ran back up the stairs to find that Terry had drifted off to sleep again. For a moment, Jan contemplated letting her sleep but decided bathing was more of a priority.

She'll feel better once she's cleaned up. "Hey, Terry. Your bath's ready." Jan pulled back the covers. "Come on, sweetie. Let's sit up." She helped Terry swing her legs over the edge of the bed. Terry swayed and almost fell back, so Jan sat down next to her and wrapped an arm around her waist. Michael entered the room and positioned himself at Terry's other side. Together they pulled Terry to her feet and supported her as they descended the stairs to the second floor. When they reached the bathroom, they lowered her to the edge of tub.

"Holler if you need me for anything else." Michael closed the door behind him.

Jan kept a steadying hand on Terry's shoulder and began to unbutton her sleep shirt.

Terry looked up at her. "Um, I have to use...you know."

"Can you manage on your own?"

"Uh-huh, but don't go too far."

"I'll be just outside." Jan stood in the hall with the door slightly ajar. Hearing the telltale flush, she pushed the door open again and caught a faltering Terry as she stood. Jan finished unbuttoning the long shirt, pushed it off her shoulders, and helped her into the bathtub.

Terry slid into the warm water with an ecstatic sigh.

"Why don't we get you washed up, and then you can relax for a while?"

"'Kay." Terry never opened her eyes and didn't move an inch.

Jan waited for a moment and then picked up a bar of soap. "Come on, Terry. Sit up for me, and I'll get your back."

Terry grumbled but pulled herself into a sitting position and rested her arms on bent knees.

Jan lathered up her hands and began to wash her back.

Terry sighed and buried her head in her arms.

Jan sluiced off the soap with handfuls of water. When she finished, she eased Terry back.

Terry made no move to take the soap, and Jan hesitated. She was accustomed to bathing Rob on a daily basis, but this... this was different. Terry was not her helpless charge. Jan's gaze drifted over the long body with its small breasts and lean hips. She frowned. Too prominent ribs bracketed a concave belly. Terry could ill afford the weight she had lost over the week. *A few days of Michael's cooking should fix that.*

Jan pressed the soap into Terry's hand and tucked her fingers around it. "C'mon, sweetie. Time to get the rest of you clean, and then you can soak for a bit."

Terry's eyes half-opened, and she held the soap out to Jan. "No, that's up to you."

Terry made a half-hearted effort to finish the bath, then sank back as if it had used up all her reserves.

Jan picked up the shampoo from the side of the tub. Supporting Terry's neck, she worked the soap through her hair.

Terry sighed. "God, that feels good."

"You're just a pleasure hound, lady." Jan tapped a soapy finger on Terry's nose.

"Mmm-hmm." Terry brushed the soap off.

Jan rinsed out the shampoo, and long after all the soap disappeared, she ran her fingers through Terry's hair. Finally, conceding that she couldn't get her hair much cleaner, she leaned against the tub and studied Terry's serene face.

The humid, scented air cradled them in a world of their own, content in companionable silence. Whatever had come between them in weeks past vanished as surely as soap bubbles subsiding into the water.

Sometime later, Jan looked up from where her hand had been lazily drawing circles in the water, to meet Terry's gaze. She said nothing, feeling—but not understanding—the unspoken energy emanating from Terry.

She would soon have to return home, but she was reluctant to disturb the re-established rapport between them.

Terry snagged Jan's fingers and gave them a soft squeeze. "I guess I should get out of here before I turn into a prune."

Jan turned Terry's hand over and touched her fingertips. "I think you may be too late. You're well on your way to raisin status. You probably don't want to put that nightshirt back on, do you? Give me a minute, and I'll grab you a fresh one."

"Thanks. There should be some clean T-shirts in the right side of the bureau."

Jan returned to the garret. The room, flooded with crisp, cool outside air, was now fresh. After lowering the wide-open window, she turned down the clean bedding, and fluffed the pillows. Searching for a change of clothes, she opened the top right-hand drawer of the bureau, but promptly closed it and flushed. "Okay, not that one." She found a clean, oversized T-shirt in the next drawer down and returned to the bathroom.

Jan draped one towel over Terry's shoulders and rubbed her wet hair with another. Once Terry was dry and dressed, Jan wrapped an arm around her waist and helped her back to the bedroom.

Terry sank into the clean bed.

Jan pulled the sheets and comforter up and tucked them close. She sat down beside her and brushed some damp curls back. "I'm going to have to get going soon. Donny's only there for another half hour."

"Thanks for coming over. I really do feel much better for having gotten cleaned up." Terry moved an arm from under the covers to take Jan's hand.

Jan squeezed her hand, then leaned over and kissed

Terry's forehead. "I'll give you a call tomorrow to see how you are, okay?"

"I'd like that." Terry hesitated. "Would it be all right if I drop around next weekend? I'd like to get back to work."

Relief surged through Jan. "Of course. You know you don't have to ask. Rob will be thrilled to see you, too. He's missed you."

Terry dropped her gaze. "I'm sorry. I've been a jerk these last couple of weeks. Forgive me?"

"Always. But what happened? Did I do something to upset you?"

"No, absolutely not. You didn't do a thing wrong." Terry stopped and closed her eyes for a long moment. "I had to work some things out, and I'm really sorry that you got caught in the fall-out. You guys have been nothing but kind to me, and you didn't deserve that at all."

"So we're okay now?"

Terry grimaced. "As long as you'll overlook my adolescent behaviour."

"Done. We'll just write it off to an extended case of PMS." With a quick squeeze of Terry's hand, Jan left. Back in her van, she pondered their encounter. *I still don't know what happened, but as long as she's okay again...as long as we're okay, I'll leave it alone.*

Jan was startled at how right it felt to care for Terry. *I was just doing for her what I do for Rob every day.* But there had been more between them than the simple concern of one friend for another, and she knew it.

She closed her eyes, only to have them shoot open when she realized where her mind had drifted. She tried to shake the mental image of Terry lounging half-submerged, her sleek nakedness a magnet for Jan's disobedient gaze.

What the hell is going on with me? Jan drew in several deep breaths in an attempt to calm her racing heart. She certainly wasn't unfamiliar with the concept of women being attracted to other women, but it had never happened to her before. *Well, okay, there was that once after we won the softball championship, but the whole team was drunk and having a good time, right? It didn't mean anything.*

Her fingers beat an unconscious rhythm on the steering wheel. *You cannot possibly be reacting to Terry that way. You're imagining things.*

Her erratic mental gymnastics didn't calm her rapid pulse, so Jan shook her head and started up the van. *It's just been too long, that's all.*

CHAPTER 16

MILY WIPED HER HANDS ON her apron and surveyed the kitchen. Karen and Jan were busy peeling a huge mound of potatoes. In consideration of her convalescent status, Terry was sitting at the table, folding napkins and quartering tomatoes. *Even Terry can't ruin that.*

Jordy, Diane, and Michael were assigned to set the two long tables that extended the length of the dining room and into the living room. Gord, Alex, and Duncan were dragging up chairs from every corner of the house and garage. Rob and the twins watched the organized chaos flow around them, and Matt hadn't made an appearance yet.

Emily gave a contented sigh. It was shaping up to be a wonderful Thanksgiving. She'd been up at five a.m. to get the huge bird into the oven for a noon meal, and the aroma had her family drooling for the past couple of hours.

Terry still looked a little wan, but whatever had bothered her the last time she was over for dinner was obviously no longer a factor. She chatted and laughed with everyone, including Jan and Rob. *Must've been the early stages of the flu that had made her so dippy.*

Jordy poked his head around the kitchen door. "Hey, Rob, are you going to let us take you downstairs to the family room after dinner for the game? We won't drop you, I promise."

Terry grinned at Rob. "Trust me. If you have the Y-chromosome, that's where the action will be."

Rob turned big puppy dog eyes on Jan.

"Go ahead, love, but don't expect me to endure a minute-by-minute replay on the ride home."

Emily glanced out the window. Matt was coming up the back walk. She studied his face. For today at least, his usual expression of perpetual discontent was absent. He had called earlier in the week and, during the course of their conversation, inquired if Terry would be bringing a date for Thanksgiving. When she had told him no, he said that he would be solo himself this year, so not to set an extra plate.

Please, God, let that mean that the destructive competition between them is finally coming to an end. Emily busied herself making the gravy base. *And thank you, too for bringing the Spencers into our lives.* Terry seemed happier and more settled than ever, and Emily gave the Spencers much of the credit.

Emily never commented on any of her children's affairs, but Matt's and Terry's wild social lives had been distressing. *Some of the women those two dated...* Despite her open-door policy for all her children's friends, she wished they'd adhered to the old adage about the type of women you shouldn't bring home to meet Mother.

Matt came through the back door and slung his jacket into the hall closet. He entered the kitchen and sniffed appreciatively. He hugged Emily, greeted the other workers, and nodded at Terry. "I heard you were pretty sick this week. Hope you're feeling better now."

Terry's eyebrows rose. "Thanks. Yeah, I'm okay now. Just a little tired still."

"That's good." Matt looked around the kitchen and down the hall to the living room. "Did Claire come over with you?"

Terry shook her head. "No, not this time. She's working with her church group today. They're putting together Thanksgiving dinner for street people. They figure they'll feed up to five hundred people before they're done."

"Oh." Matt's shoulders slumped, but he nodded amiably before going in search of his brothers.

Terry stared after him. "Okay, who was that man, and what has he done with Matt?"

Emily stifled her grin. "What? Did you think you were the only one who could grow up around here?"

Jan leaned over Terry's shoulder and snagged a quartered tomato.

"Hey, hands off!" Terry tried to slap Jan's hand.

Jan danced out of range and popped the ill-gotten fruit into her mouth. Karen slipped in from the other side and stole another piece before ducking away.

"Ack! Mom! They're stealing your salad." Terry held up her small knife in defence of the diminishing pile of ripe red wedges.

Emily snapped a dishtowel at the miscreants. "Are you troublemakers all finished with the spuds?"

"Uh-huh," Karen said. "Between the two of us, we have officially peeled PEI's entire yearly output."

"Oh hush, like you won't be coming back for seconds." Emily looked at the pile of potatoes. "Okay, get them started, and as soon as they're done, we're ready to eat."

Jan and Karen looked at the crowded stove stop, at each other, and then at Emily. Simultaneously, they asked, "Where?"

"Oh for heaven's sake, you just have to shuffle things around a bit." Emily moved pots and slid covered serving dishes into the hot oven. After lifting the large roaster out, she carried it to the table. "Karen, will you call Gord and tell him I'll need him to carve shortly?"

Karen left the kitchen, and Jan assisted Emily in moving the bird to the carving board. Terry's eyes widened at the size of the turkey in front of her.

When Emily turned to get tin foil to cover it, Terry pulled a piece of crisp skin from the side of the bird. Just as she was about to pop it into her mouth, Jan's hand seized hers and her lips snatched the delicious morsel away.

Emily caught the last of the byplay and laughed at the outrage on Terry's face. "All right, you two. Stay out of the turkey until it's carved and on the table."

"But, Mom —"

"No buts," Emily said.

"But she — I didn't — No fair..." Terry scowled.

Jan wrapped an arm around Terry's shoulders. "Let's get out of your mom's hair for now and go see if the table's ready."

Emily covered the turkey as they departed the kitchen.

"Look at all the trouble you're getting me in," Terry said.

Emily couldn't hear Jan's low-pitched response, but she heard Terry laugh.

Emily glanced around the table. Steady inroads had been made on the Thanksgiving feast, and her family was starting to slow down.

Diane was already sitting back in her chair, groaning at the amount she had consumed. Terry, handicapped by a week that shrunk her stomach, was also finished. The twins were having their own meal, with as much strained turkey and peas on their beaming faces as on the towels prudently placed under their high chairs. Jan fed Rob and herself while carrying on a conversation with Terry and Jordy, who sat beside them.

Gord and Matt were in serious debate about a problem at work, and Alex, Duncan, Karen, and Michael were in an animated argument, though about what, Emily couldn't determine. However, they seemed to be enjoying themselves, and that was all that mattered to her.

Emily was content to preside over her small kingdom as she ensured that no one went without and emptied bowls were swiftly replenished.

Soon, only Jordy was still cleaning his plate while the others loosened belts and buttons. Even the once lively conversation had become desultory as post-turkey syndrome set in.

Emily went to make coffee. As she filled the pot, Jan stacked dirty dishes on the table.

"Thanks, Jan."

"You're welcome. Do you want me to start loading the dishwasher?"

"Good idea, but could you get the dessert plates first?"

Jan opened a cupboard and took down a stack of small plates. She then arranged dirty dishes in the dishwasher. "I really appreciate you asking us over. I can't remember the last time I've enjoyed Thanksgiving so much."

Emily measured coffee into the filter. "It was our pleasure to have you. You and Rob are always welcome, you know that." She tilted her head at the furrow in Jan's forehead. "Is something wrong?"

"You don't think Karen felt pressured to ask us, do you?"

Emily shook her head. During dinner, conversation turned to Karen and Duncan's upcoming nuptials. Karen had leaned across the table to invite Jan and Rob to the wedding. Emily was certain that the invitation hadn't been expected. "Trust me, Karen invited you two because she likes you and considers you part of the family. Karen isn't one to let social niceties dictate her actions. If she asked you, she wants you there."

"I haven't been to a wedding in years. I don't think I even have anything suitable to wear."

"Suitable for what?" Terry arrived with a stack of dirty dishes, trailed by Jordy with his own load.

"Suitable to wear to the wedding," Jan said.

"Guess you're going have to go shopping, then."

"I haven't picked out my outfit yet either, Jan. Why don't we go shopping together next weekend?" Emily took the dirty dishes from Terry. "We can make a day of it and have lunch while we're out."

"I'd like that, but I'll have to make some arrangements for Rob. I know he wouldn't be thrilled to shop for a whole day. But yes, if I can set something up, I'd love to go with you."

Jordy set his pile of dishes on the counter. "I could keep him company if you like. I don't have any shifts at work until Sunday."

"Are you sure?" Jan asked. "You really wouldn't mind? I'd pay you the same as I pay Donny."

Terry snorted. "Are you kidding? A chance to spend a day with his idol? He'd probably pay you."

Jordy flushed. "Terrrrrry!"

"Huh, you know it's true." Terry punched his shoulder. "You worship the ground he rolls on."

"Stop it, you're embarrassing your brother," Emily said. "That's a lovely offer, Jordy, and I'm sure Rob will enjoy your company."

Jordy stuck his tongue out at Terry and scampered out of the kitchen as she tried to cuff him. Terry turned to her mother and Jan. "Hey, can I come along, too?"

Emily's jaw dropped. "You want to go shopping with us? I haven't been able to get you shopping since the first grade."

Terry scuffed at the floor tile. "Well, Duncan won't let me wear a tux, so I need something for the wedding."

Jan smiled. "We'd love to have you come with us, wouldn't we?"

Still stunned, Emily nodded.

"It's settled, then," Jan said. "Next Saturday, the three of us will go find the most beautiful dresses in town."

Terry's eyes widened. "Whoa, who said anything about a dress? I'm not wearing a dress."

"Why don't you wait and see what we find?" Jan said. "You never know. You might actually want to try it for a change."

"Nuh-uh, no way are you getting me into a dress." Terry glared at them.

Jan winked at Emily and dragged a still protesting Terry back to the dining room to retrieve another load.

Emily grinned. *If anyone can talk that stubborn daughter of mine into a dress, it will be Jan.*

———◆———

"How come the guys always end up in front of the TV and we always end up in here?" Karen was elbow-deep in suds.

Emily tried to find room in her fridge for leftovers. "Because they're convinced they've done their part if they set up chairs and carve the turkey. Besides, you know darned well that if we made them help with dishes, half my china would 'accidentally' break. I don't mind, though. After all, how often do I get all of you to myself at the same time?"

"Thanksgiving, Christmas, Easter…" Terry reached to put dishes away on an upper shelf. She swayed and clutched the edge of the counter.

"Whoa, girl." Jan took Terry's arm, guided her to a chair, and rested a hand on her shoulder.

Emily frowned. "You, young lady, are pushing yourself too much. You can't expect to be one hundred per cent after the week you had. Now you just sit there and rest. We're almost done here anyway."

One twin on her hip, Diane brought a glass of water to Terry, and she drained it in three gulps.

Karen eyed Terry. "Maybe you should call it a day. You really do look washed out."

Emily nodded. "Why don't you go lie down in your old room for a while?"

"I think I'll just go home if you don't mind, Mom. It'll be a lot quieter there. Would you call Michael for me?"

Emily touched the back of her hand to Terry's forehead. "I'll take you home, dear. We'll let Michael have some male bonding time."

Terry glanced up at her wryly. "In case you hadn't noticed, Michael gets lots of male bonding."

There was an outburst of laughter, and Emily rolled her eyes.

"But Rob doesn't," Jan said. "Why don't you let me take you home, and we'll leave the guys to do their thing for the afternoon?"

A smile lit up Terry's face. "Are you sure you wouldn't mind?"

Jan squeezed her shoulder. "Not at all. Just give me a moment to let Rob know I'll be back in a while, okay?"

A few minutes later, Emily walked Terry and Jan to the front door and, amidst farewells, made plans for the following weekend's shopping trip.

Terry hugged Emily. "Thanks, Mom. Dinner was great as always. I'll give you a call later on."

Emily watched them descend the stairs. Jan kept a precautionary grip on Terry's arm and steered her toward the large van. She made sure Terry was settled before going around to her own door.

Emily waved and closed the door. *I'm so glad Terry has such a good friend.*

———◆———

Terry dozed on the drive home. Jan woke her when they arrived, and she blinked open her eyes.

"Hey, sleepyhead, we're here."

Terry opened her door and was not surprised when Jan met her and again took her arm. She was feeling stronger now but didn't feel it necessary to mention that.

When they reached the garret, Jan helped her to her bed.

Terry slumped back into the pillows.

Jan stepped back and looked around. "I guess I should go and let you get some rest."

Terry sat up. "No, don't go yet. I'm feeling much better. Why don't you stay and visit for a bit?" *Oh, that's subtle, doofus.*

Jan peeled off her coat and kicked her shoes away. She dragged the old chair close to the bed and settled into it, then propped her feet on the bed. "I'd ask if you mind, but having seen the state of your bedroom, I don't think feet on your bed will faze you."

"Hey," Terry said. "Are you calling me a slob?"

"If the label fits, dear."

Terry glanced around her room and frowned. "Yeah, well, I've got an excuse this week."

"Uh-huh, and the reason for the other fifty-one weeks would be?"

Terry tossed a pillow at her.

Jan took it with a smile and tucked it behind her back.

"Speaking of this week, I really do appreciate you coming over on Thursday. If I forgot to say it then, thank you."

"You're very welcome. I was glad to help." Jan grinned. "Of course, if I'd known what I was going to find when I went hunting for a clean T-shirt..."

Terry blushed. "I...I don't suppose you'd believe I was hiding them for Michael, would you?"

Jan laughed. "Not for a second. That's a pretty impressive collection you have there, not that I stopped to inspect it or anything."

Terry ran a hand over her flushed face. "Michael teases me I could start my own electronics store. He said he just didn't get it, but I explained it to him."

"What did you tell him?"

"I told him my toys don't get PMS, they're always ready when I am, they don't cause carpal tunnel syndrome, and they work...every single time."

"I'll have to take your word for it."

Terry raised an eyebrow. "You don't like toys?"

It was Jan's turn to blush. "I really can't say. I've never tried them."

"Oh, so you prefer a hands-on solution?" Terry didn't want to embarrass Jan, but the echo of Michael's words was compelling.

The silence dragged on for long moments, and Jan refused to meet her gaze.

Idiot! Let her off the hook. "I'm sorry," Terry said. "It's none of my business."

"It's just that I've never spoken to anyone about this."

"Not even Kate?" *You really have to stop this. It's not fair to her.*

Jan shook her head. "No. I love my sister, but I think she'd have a heart attack if I ever brought up this subject."

"It's up to you. We can talk about it or not, whatever you prefer. I want you to know that as far as I'm concerned, you can talk to me about anything."

"I do know that, and I appreciate it." Jan's hands twisted in her lap. "Actually, I think I would like to talk it out. I guess I just don't know where to start."

"Would it help if I started?" Terry asked. When Jan nodded, she considered her options. "Is Rob able to...? Well, you know."

"Not for quite a few years now. It's been a difficult adjustment for him, and I know he misses it."

Terry rolled on her side so that her thighs pressed against Jan's feet. "What about you? Don't you miss it, too?"

Jan was quiet again for a long moment. "You can't miss what you've never had."

"What you've never had? Weren't you lovers in the early years, before things got so bad for him physically?"

"But it never worked for me, you know?" Jan's voice was so low Terry had to strain to hear it.

"Oh! Okay, I get it." Terry chewed her lip a moment, uncertain how to offer comfort. "Well, maybe there's a medical reason why you can't—"

"It's not that I can't. I've woken from dreams on the tail end of marvellous orgasms. I just can't in the waking world."

"Um, maybe Rob wasn't doing it right?"

"No, Rob was a very considerate lover. We had to make allowances for his disability, of course, but he really tried to take care of me. I think it always bothered him more than me that I couldn't find satisfaction in our bed. He even encouraged me to try it on my own when we were making love."

"I take it that didn't work out well?"

"No. I think I was just too aware of disappointing him or too tense or something."

"What about when you weren't with him? Did you ever try it when you were by yourself?"

Jan raised an eyebrow. "Do you have any idea how rarely I'm by myself at home? It's a little hard to get comfortable when I might be summoned at any second."

"I don't suppose you could tell him that you were taking a half hour off and not to call you for the duration?"

Jan laughed. "I can just see handing Rob my masturbation schedule for the week and informing him he's not to have any problems during the designated periods."

Terry giggled, and her mind strayed to the possibility of posting her own events calendar on the outside of her door.

"In reality, there are times I could have the privacy I need. It's more a case of feeling like I'm not being fair to Rob by indulging in something he enjoyed but can't have anymore, so I don't even try."

Terry sat upright and wrapped a hand around Jan's foot. "That doesn't make any sense at all. You know damned well that Rob wouldn't begrudge you this. For crying out loud, I've heard his stories. That man had more than his fair share of conquests in his younger years. He loves you. He wouldn't want you to live like a nun on his account." She squeezed Jan's toes.

Jan squirmed.

Terry watched her closely. "That's not all, is it?"

"Well, that's a big part of it, but... It just doesn't work when I try it for myself." Jan blushed.

Terry leaned forward and took Jan's hand. "Hey, it's nothing to be ashamed about." Growing up in her exuberant family, she'd never been shy about sex. Her parents had treated the subject candidly from the beginning. She hadn't even disconcerted her parents when she came out to them.

Now, conscious of the pleasure that her body gave her, Terry was saddened that Jan was missing that in her life. She was hesitant to intrude on such personal matters, but an aggrieved sense that Jan was being deprived — for whatever reason — of something wonderful, overrode her caution. "Can I ask you something?" She waited for Jan's nod. "Do you want to do this? Because there are ways and means that are almost one hundred per cent guaranteed."

"Well, I hear it's a great stress relief...and I did enjoy those dreams. Besides, sometimes I feel like the only one on the outside of the window watching the rest of the world party."

"There you go. And I can definitely vouch for the stress relief part."

"But I don't think I could ever bring myself to go into one of those stores."

"Ah, but that's the glory of the Internet age." Terry stood and pulled Jan up with her. She hit the power button on her laptop and offered her usual chair to Jan.

Jan glanced at her. "I don't have my credit card with me."

Terry pulled up another chair. "Not a problem. We'll use mine, and you can pay me back later. I know you're good for it."

"I don't know. If this works out, you may never see me out of the house again. I've got a lot of years to make up for."

Terry entered a few commands, then clicked on a bookmark that took them to her favourite online sex shop.

When the somewhat lurid website came up, Jan covered

her eyes before she peeked through her fingers at Terry. "You're having way too much fun with this."

"It's not every day I get to introduce an older woman to the joys of 'mastering her domain.' Okay, I think we'll start with the basics. You're probably not ready for the more exotic stuff."

Jan stared at the page. "These are the basics? I'm not even sure what all these are for."

"Fear not, I am, and I'm willing to share the fruits of my in-depth studies and hard-earned knowledge with you."

They spent the next half hour scrolling through the selections while Terry extolled the virtues and drawbacks of various items.

Occasionally, Jan burrowed a very red face in her hands, but overall, she was attentive. Finally, she followed Terry's suggestions, and they sent her choices to checkout.

Jan thumped her forehead on Terry's shoulder. "I cannot believe you've talked me into this."

Terry laughed but kept on typing. "Do you want this to go to your house or mine?"

"Might as well send them here since they know the route so well. Besides, it'll save explanations at home."

Terry entered the final details, and her finger poised above "enter." "Are you sure?"

"Now you ask me?"

"It's not too late to back out."

Jan pushed Terry's finger down. A window popped up, thanking them for their business. "You are such a bad influence."

Terry winked. "You're welcome."

They collapsed in helpless laughter.

CHAPTER 17

"OKAY, MOM, I'LL BE READY." Terry hung up the phone and glanced at her faded jeans and sweatshirt. *Guess I'm sort of underdressed. Remind me again why I agreed to this…why I actually volunteered for it? I need to have my head examined.*

After returning to her bedroom, she surveyed her closet, then spun on her heel and went to her door. "Michael, help!"

By the time Michael dashed into the room, she was throwing discards over her shoulder onto a growing pile of clothes.

"What?" Michael doubled over panting. "What's the emergency?"

"I don't know what to wear today."

Michael straightened and sucked in gulps of air. "You made me run up all those stairs for fashion advice? Do you realize I could have expired on the second landing?"

"Sorry," Terry said. "But I really do need your help here. We're going to Cilantro's for lunch and then shopping for wedding clothes. What I've got on isn't going to cut it."

His jaw dropped. "You're going shopping? Clothes shopping?"

Terry put her hands on her hips and glared at him.

Michael went into action.

Almost before Terry could turn around, she was outfitted

in charcoal grey wool pants and a peach-coloured blouse Claire allowed them to liberate from her closet. She also contributed a matching pair of earrings.

"Your selection of footwear is abysmal." Michael frowned at Terry's shoes, jumbled together on the floor of the closet. He picked up a pair of old black loafers and held them at arm's length. "These are the best of a very sorry lot."

Terry dusted them off on her bedspread and slipped them on.

As Michael surveyed the final results, the doorbell sounded from below.

"Oh, gotta go. Thanks for the help." Terry grabbed her leather jacket and ran downstairs to join her mother.

———————◆◇◆————————

Terry dug the toe of her shoe into the plush carpet and scowled at her mother and Jan, who waxed ecstatic over yet another dress. *Five friggin' stores. They've hit five stores and still haven't found Jan the perfect dress.* She'd been so optimistic when in the first store they entered, her mom picked out a tailored coral suit with a cream silk blouse for herself. Terry even suggested that Grandma's pearls would match the pearl suit buttons.

Emily was still recovering from the shock of her daughter offering a fashion suggestion.

Three hours ago, Terry had been proud of being a good sport and contributing to their girls' afternoon out. *But that was four stores ago. And I can't even duck out since Mom's driving. I'm in hell.*

Terry hadn't found something to wear, not that she'd looked very hard. By the third store, she'd decided to send Michael out with her credit card and orders to bring back something decent for the wedding. *He's the only reason I'm not completely a duck out of water here.* She contemplated the swanky interior of Giorgio's, convinced that the elegant clerks were looking down their noses at her. *Ugh, think how bad it would've been if I'd come in my jeans and boots.*

"She's pouting." Jan's amused voice came from the direction of the changing rooms.

"She is. You wouldn't happen to have a sucker in your purse, would you?" Emily asked. "That always worked to distract her when I took her shopping as a little girl."

Terry scowled. "I was not pouting."

"You were definitely pouting." Jan crossed the store, knelt beside Terry, and laid one hand on her knee. "I'm sorry, sweetie. Is this really driving you crazy?"

Terry blinked. *What was the question?* Her brain couldn't focus on anything but the warmth of Jan's hand on her leg. "Uh, no, I'm fine. You guys go ahead. I'll just wait here."

Jan gave her knee a gentle squeeze. "Tell you what. The clerk has one more outfit for me to try and then we'll go for a coffee break, all right? There's a wonderful café that makes the best chocolate pastries right around the corner."

"Chocolate?" Terry perked up.

Jan laughed and rose to her feet. "Uh-huh, chocolate. Give me a few more minutes, and we'll go."

The clerk returned with something green draped over her arm. Jan took it from the woman and whispered something to her as she glanced back in Terry's direction. The clerk disappeared to the back of the store.

Emily took the seat beside Terry and patted her hand. "I've enjoyed having you along today. It's quite the rare treat."

"Don't get used to it, Mom. This is really not my thing. But I did enjoy lunch with you guys, and if you ever want to do that again, I'd love to come along. Just leave me out of the shopping part."

"I hope Jan gets lucky with this dress." Emily glanced at Terry. "She's a very nice woman, isn't she?"

Terry didn't meet her mother's gaze. *Mom couldn't know, could she?* She reviewed her behaviour that afternoon. *No. I didn't stare at Jan over lunch, and I paid equal attention to both of them. It's just my conscience talking.* "She's great. Both she and Rob are terrific people." She cast about for a change of subject. "Are you sure we should be here, though? I mean I'm not sure she can afford Giorgio's. They're on a fixed income, you know."

"Have you ever listened to Rob discussing investment strategies with your father? Trust me, she can afford to shop here or any other place in town she takes a fancy to."

"Oh. Okay." Jan and Rob owned their house outright, but it was just a modest bungalow. *It's not like they live ostentatiously. I'll bet their biggest expense is Jan's books.* "I'm not sure if I could afford to buy in here. It'd blow my yearly clothing budget in one shot."

"What clothing budget?" Emily asked. "Your biggest expenditure is a new pair of runners once a year."

"Hey — " Terry was about to defend her wardrobe when Jan stepped out of the change room and twirled in front of them.

Terry gaped.

Jan wore a dark green silk dress that clung in all the right places and floated down to a mid-calf length. It wrapped around her waist, crossed in the front, and framed her curves with a pronounced V-neck.

"That's beautiful," Emily said. "Terry, don't you think it's perfect?"

Terry was silent.

Emily looked at her. "Terry?"

"Perfect. Uh, yeah, it's perfect." Terry stuttered on her words.

Jan looked at her exposed cleavage and frowned. "Are you sure it's not too revealing?"

"No! No, it's perfect, really. You look great. I definitely think you should get that dress." Terry slunk down in her chair as Emily stared at her.

Jan nodded. "I think I will. I even have a pair of shoes that would match perfectly."

The clerk returned with another dress. "You look gorgeous, madam."

Jan took the new garment from the clerk. She tugged Terry to her feet and led her to a changing room, where she hung the dress on a hook. "Your mom and I have outfits for the wedding, and you've barely looked at anything. I want you to try this on." She closed the door, shutting Terry inside.

Stunned, Terry looked at the short black dress. "But, but — "

"Uh-uh. Just put it on and come out so we can see it," Jan said sternly from outside the cubicle.

Aw, fuck. I hate dresses. Terry stripped off her clothes and slid the form-fitting sheath over her head. She smoothed it down and straightened the spaghetti straps. *Huh. How did Jan know what size to ask for?* Cut straight across, the dress had a less revealing bodice than Jan's, but it still clung to her smaller curves. She tugged at it, but it remained inches above her knees. Shaking her head, she opened the door and exited the change room.

Emily saw her first. "Oh, my, don't you look wonderful."

Jan turned and drew in a sharp breath. "My God. You look incredible."

They circled Terry while she tried again to tug down the hem.

"She'd need a good pair of black heels," Jan said.

Emily nodded. "And black hose, of course. I know. There's a shoe store one street over we can check out. I'm sure she won't have anything suitable in her closet."

"Whoa, slow down." Terry backed away. "I haven't even decided if I'm going to get it yet. Besides, isn't black inappropriate for a wedding?"

"Don't be silly, dear." Emily's gaze was glued to Terry. "Their theme is black and white, so you'll fit in perfectly."

Eyes wide, Terry looked at Jan, who had stopped in front of her. "Heels?"

Jan nodded. "Heels." Then she met Terry's gaze and tilted her head. "Does that really bother you? Even if it's only for one night?"

Terry shivered, already feeling the pain in her feet.

Jan touched Terry's arm. "Maybe this isn't for you after all. You don't have to make a decision right now. Why don't you take a few days and think about it?"

Terry heaved a sigh of relief and ignored the disappointed clucks from Emily. She made her escape to the change rooms, where she shucked the dress and got back into her clothes and comfortable shoes.

By the time Terry returned the rejected garment to the hovering clerk, Jan had paid for her dress. "Let me drop this in the car, and we can go get some coffee."

Once the new outfit was stashed, they walked to the café Jan recommended and settled at a table by the window with coffee and pastries.

Terry bit into her almond chocolate croissant, closed her eyes, and hummed with delight. She opened her eyes.

Jan and Emily grinned at her.

"What?"

Jan brushed crumbs from Terry's face. "Can't dress you up and take you out anywhere, can we?"

Terry's skin tingled from Jan's touch. Her resolve was weakening with each moment she spent in Jan's presence. She glanced at her mother.

Emily observed them quietly while she sipped her coffee.

Terry finished her croissant in three bites and scrubbed at her face with a napkin.

Jan dug her cell phone out of her purse. "I apologize, but I want to check in with Jordy and make sure everything's okay. It'll only take a minute."

"Oh good, could I talk to him for a moment when you're done?" Emily asked. "I forgot to give him a message from his dad this morning."

"Sure." Jan activated the speed dial. After a brief conversation with Jordy to confirm he and Rob were fine, she passed the phone to Emily.

"Hi, son. I forgot to tell you that your dad asked if you want to pick up some work hours on the Krieger project. He said it's up to you, but he has to know right away because if you don't want it, he's going to have to hire some part-time help." Emily listened and shook her head. "No, he just thought you might want to make some extra Christmas spending money. You don't have to if you don't want to. All right. Let him know, then. Okay, I'll see you later." She ended the call and returned the phone to Jan.

"Everything okay?" Terry asked.

"Oh yes. It's just that Jordy's convinced that every time your dad offers him some part-time work, he's trying to trap him into the family business." Emily frowned. "Gord thought he was doing Jordy a favour, and Jordy's being paranoid about it."

Jan looked from Emily to Terry.

Terry shot her a half-smile. "Remember? Dad is sure that Jordy is going to join the company just like Alex, Duncan, and Matt did, and Jordy is hell-bent that he's not going to end up in construction just because it's the family trade."

Jan nodded. "I remember now."

"Jordy's going to be a terrific doctor," Emily said. "He's had his mind made up since he was a little boy."

"But that's such a wonderful ambition." Jan's brow furrowed. "Won't Gord be proud of him?"

"Dad's pretty set on Sanderson and Sons including all four of his sons," Terry said. "The trouble is that the older boys were fine about joining him, so he's got tunnel vision about Jordy. Mom and I have tried to talk to him about it, but it's like he listens and doesn't hear. I think it goes in one ear and out the other."

"Jordy *is* going to medical school," Emily said. "But it would make it a lot easier if Gord were onside."

Jan bit her lip. "I don't want to step in where I shouldn't, but I know Rob and Gord get along well. Would it help to have an outsider present Jordy's case? I'm sure Rob wouldn't mind. He thinks the world of that boy."

Emily eyed her for a long moment. "It might. Let me think about it for a bit, will you?"

"Of course. I'll talk to Rob in the meantime and see what he thinks. I know he'd do it, though. Jordy is practically the son he never had."

"You two couldn't have kids?" Terry asked before she could stop herself.

"Terry." Emily scowled at her.

Terry flushed. "Sorry. None of my business." She stared at the table.

Jan's hand covered hers. "It's okay. You can ask me anything. Actually, knowing what Rob's prognosis was, we chose not to have children. He was afraid he wouldn't be able to be a real father to them, and he thought it would be too much for me to handle, caring for him and raising children at the same time."

Terry studied her. "You didn't agree, did you?"

"No, I didn't. But if he didn't want children, I didn't feel it was right to pressure him into it or get pregnant by 'accident.' He had enough to deal with as it was." A wistful expression flashed over Jan's face. "Still, in the balance, I think he'd have found our children would've added to our life. But that's long behind us, and there's no point rehashing old decisions. I have to say, though, Jordy sure has been a bright spot in his life."

"Yeah, well, it's not exactly a hardship for Jordy to hang around so much. He's there almost as much as I am."

"And I worry about both of you taking advantage of them." Emily shook a finger at Terry.

"No, your kids are great," Jan said. "Rob and I both look forward to their visits. Besides, we're over at your place for Sunday dinner so often that it's only fair that we return the favour." She smiled. "It's hard to remember a time before we knew you all because it feels like we've known you forever."

Terry smirked at her mother, vindicated for the moment but sure she hadn't heard the last of it. *Good thing she doesn't know exactly how often I'm over there.* Her mother had cast several speculative glances her way, and Terry didn't want to give rise to unfounded suspicions. *All right, so they aren't entirely unfounded, but they are one-sided.* She just didn't want to be scolded for something that was never going to happen anyway.

CHAPTER 18

T ERRY OPENED THE FRONT DOOR and beckoned Jan inside. "Come in for a few minutes, okay?"

"Sure, but I thought we were going for a hike today."

"We are, but there's something I want to show you first."

Terry led the way up the stairs. "You know, I'm really glad that Rob switched Donny to Saturdays. I'm having so much fun on our outings."

Close at Terry's heels, Jan chuckled. "I don't think you thought horseback riding was all that much fun."

Terry glanced over her shoulder. "Well, if a certain someone had mentioned that she was an expert rider, it might've made a difference."

"I'm not an expert. I just spent a lot of time at my grandparents' farm when I was a kid. Besides, it was my turn to pick. Can I help it if you ended up so bowlegged that they could drive cattle between your legs?"

"Considering how sore I was, there certainly wasn't going to be anything else between my legs for a long time." Terry rubbed her buttocks. She'd spent hours soaking in the tub after that excursion.

Jan laughed. "Poor baby. Did the mean horsies ruin your love life?"

Terry snorted. "What love life?" She reached her bedroom and opened the door for Jan.

"Wow, you actually picked up in here." Jan turned to her. "Was that what you wanted to show me?"

"No, of course not." Terry picked up a box from her desk and put it in Jan's hands. "This arrived yesterday."

Jan looked at the parcel and hid her face behind the box.

Terry grinned. "C'mon, open it up. You know you want to." She steered Jan over to sit on the bed.

Jan stared at the box, then at Terry.

"Don't worry. I don't expect you to demonstrate their use." Terry dodged the cuff aimed at her head.

Jan opened the box and burrowed tentatively through the packing.

"They're not going to bite, you know."

"Then what did I buy them for?" Jan pulled out a long, slender white box and emptied the rest of the contents onto the bed.

They were silent for a moment, examining the selections.

Terry took out the package she had hidden behind her pillow and passed it over. "Consider this an aid to the aides."

Jan tore the paper off, revealing a thick blue paperback with a stylized naked woman on the front. "Herotica?"

"It's all the inspiration you'll ever need. Written by women, for women, with lots of stories from all over the spectrum, gay and straight."

Jan thumbed through the book. "Guess I'd better take the laundry downstairs tonight, eh?"

"I don't know. Do you have a lot to do?"

"Definitely. I think it may take me at least an hour to sort, wash, and fold."

"After thirty-nine years?" Terry shook her head. "I'm thinking this first load of laundry might take the short cycle."

Jan stared at her and started to laugh.

It was contagious. Within moments, they were rolling on the bed, laughing so hard that tears streamed from their eyes.

They had worn themselves down to the odd guffaw when Terry grimaced and pulled a bright pink toy from under her back.

Their eyes met, and they convulsed in laughter all over again.

Terry was late for supper at her parents' the following night. By the time she arrived, Jan was helping Emily and Diane in the kitchen and Rob was nowhere in sight.

Terry stopped to kiss her mother and hug Jan and Diane. "Where's Rob?"

Jan and Emily exchanged glances.

"What's up?" Terry stole a carrot and went back for a radish.

Emily slapped her hand. "Rob is having a private conversation with your father."

Terry swallowed hurriedly. "Are they talking about Jordy?"

"Your mom okayed it," Jan said. "So Rob decided there was no time to waste."

"Excellent. Does Jordy know?"

"We didn't want to say anything until we found out how Gord reacts." Emily cast a glance down the hallway. "They've been in the den almost an hour. I hope everything is all right."

Jan laid a hand on Emily's arm. "Please don't worry. I can vouch for Rob's powers of persuasion."

Terry smiled. *I'll bet you can.* She turned to Diane. "So what does Alex think? Is he okay with Jordy taking a different path?"

"Are you kidding? He and Duncan are thrilled at the prospect of having a pediatrician in the family. Our kids will be first in line when he opens his office."

Terry leaned against the counter. "What about Matt?"

Emily shot her a glance. "I'm sure he's fine with whatever Jordy wants."

"He is, actually," Diane said. "I think all the boys are proud of their kid brother and look forward to the day he graduates med school."

"From your mouth to God's ear." Emily put her hands on her hips. "Well, we can't wait any longer, or this roast is going to be like old shoe leather. Terry, call the boys and Karen from the basement. Gord and Rob will just have to join us when they're ready. Ladies, will you give me a hand getting things on the table?"

Gord and Rob emerged from the den as everyone was sitting down. Gord pushed Rob into his customary spot beside Jan.

Jan leaned over to murmur something to him, and he nodded. He looked from Emily to Terry and smiled.

Terry grinned. *I knew he could do it.*

Emily beamed and mouthed "thank you" at Rob.

Gord passed the potatoes to Jordy. "So I hear you're going into pre-med, son. Have you submitted your application yet?"

Jordy gaped at his father, then his gaze flashed to Emily, who nodded. He grinned. "Not yet. It doesn't have to be in until January, though I've got most of it filled out."

"Show it to me later," Gord said. "I might be able to help."

"Sure." Jordy shot a gleeful glance at Terry.

She winked at him and turned her attention to Jan. "So did you get your laundry done last night?"

Jan choked on her water and coughed at length.

Jordy patted her on the back. "Are you okay?"

Jan muffled her laughter with her napkin and nodded. "Fine, thank you."

Fighting to keep a straight face, Terry accepted the green beans from Duncan. Then she made a mistake and met Jan's gaze. They both exploded into laughter.

Everyone stopped and stared at them until they subsided.

Terry's cheeks hurt. She focused on her plate as conversation resumed around her.

"Laundry went very well," Jan said, her chuckles barely diminished. "Thank you ever so much for asking."

Terry almost fell off her chair laughing.

Jordy reached across the table, picked up Terry's water glass, and sniffed it. "What exactly did you put in here, Mom?"

For the rest of the meal, Terry kept her head down. When at last she snuck a glance at Jan, she had to excuse herself and leave the table. Safely in the washroom, she buried her face in a towel and laughed until her sides ached. By the time she returned to the table, her mother was bringing out the pie.

Emily cut a huge slab of lemon meringue and set it front of Rob.

He raised an eyebrow at her.

"If you can't eat it all, you can take some home with you." Emily cut smaller slices for everyone else.

Rob looked at Jan. "Want to share?"

"Sure." Jan began to feed Rob and herself. When everyone was occupied with their dessert, she leaned toward Terry and whispered, "You are so dead."

Terry focused on her pie. It was safer that way.

***

Terry snuggled deeper into her bed, drowsily grateful that

she didn't have to get up for work. Then her eyes flew open. *It's Saturday.*

As she swung her feet over the edge of the bed, she shivered at the coolness of the early December morning. She darted to the space heater, turned it on high, and dove back under her covers to wait until the chill came off the room. *I hope Rob's cold won't cancel our afternoon out.* She looked forward to these afternoons all week.

When the room was warm enough to emerge from her cocoon, Terry pushed back her covers and grabbed her robe. She glanced at the bedside clock. It was just past eight. *Hmm, Saturday morning. That means blueberry pancakes with maple syrup. Wonder if they've eaten yet.* Terry smiled. Even if Rob and Jan had eaten already, Jan would save enough batter to make her pancakes.

Twenty minutes later, she grabbed her skates and hurried out to her car. Today they were going skating on the frozen lagoon by the river. *I have to remember to talk Jan into bringing a thermos of hot chocolate.*

Terry drove over streets still icy and rutted from the week's snowstorms as she recalled the wonderful Saturdays that she and Jan had shared all through the fall. They'd gone to local farmers markets, taken long lunches and hikes along the river paths, browsed old bookstores, and attended a pre-Christmas craft show the previous weekend. At the end of the day, they usually picked Rob up and went to dinner and a movie, often with Jordy accompanying them.

Jan had even taken Terry to do her Christmas shopping early, and, for the first time in her life, Terry finished before the twenty-fourth of December.

She had purchased one Christmas gift on her own. With

Duncan and Karen's wedding next weekend, she planned to give Jan her present today.

Thoughts of the times they'd spent together didn't sadden Terry. To her surprise, since their reconciliation, she'd found it easier to relax and enjoy Jan's company without letting her latent feelings interfere. It wasn't that she'd fallen out of love with Jan. If anything, her love had deepened to a steady undercurrent of her life. Jan was constantly in her thoughts, but she had tamped her desire down to manageable levels.

Only in the privacy of midnight thoughts did the longing to hold Jan in her arms, to make love to her, and to see that love reflected back in Jan's eyes overwhelm her.

When daylight returned, Terry could again rejoice in their friendship. Jan had become her best friend, and the brief moments of conversation when she dropped off mail, the evening visits with both her and Rob after writing was done, their Saturday afternoons together, and long talks on the telephone made up the fabric of her days.

After she had finished the first draft of her book last week, Jan and Rob had insisted on taking her out to dinner to celebrate. She and Rob had gotten giddy on wine while Jan laughed at how both of them were going to pay for their indulgence in the morning.

Terry grimaced as she remembered how right Jan had been. She wasn't even able to make it over to her parents' place for Sunday dinner that night.

All in all, she'd never been more contented, and even if fantasies about sharing a life with Jan lingered, she wasn't hurting anyone. Jan couldn't be hers. Terry knew that. She'd never been one to worship from afar or pursue a hopeless situation, but this…this was different. This was Jan, and she could no longer contemplate life without her friendship.

The car went into a fishtail as Terry turned onto the Spencers' street, and she quickly countered the spin. With a sigh of relief, she navigated to a stop in front of their house.

The curtains were still drawn. Terry frowned. She rang the doorbell and waited, but there was no answer. *Maybe she's downstairs doing laundry.* Terry unlocked the door. *Get your mind out of the gutter, Sanderson.*

The house was quiet. Not even a radio played in the back rooms, and the covering was still on the birdcage. *What the hell…?* Jan always uncovered the budgies as soon as she woke up. A shiver rippled down her spine.

"Jan, are you here? Rob?" Terry kicked off her boots and dropped her skates by the door. "Hey, guys? Are you up?" She walked down the hall to the master bedroom and stopped short. "Jesus, what the hell happened here?"

Sheets and pillows were thrown on the floor, bits of plastic and paper were scattered on the dishevelled bed, and closet doors were half-open.

Something's wrong. Terry backed out of the room, her heartbeat accelerating. *Damn it, I wish I knew Kate's number.*

She returned to the living room and uncovered the birds. They chirped at her. "I know, guys. Your family seems to have gone somewhere in a hurry. The question is where…and why?"

Terry checked the answering machine, but it was turned off. She bit her lip and tried to ignore the gnawing worry in her belly. On the pad next to the phone she wrote, "Came early, but you were gone. Please give me a call when you get home. Love, Terry." She left her skates in the hallway when she went out the door.

Jan and Rob's neighbour was shovelling his walk. As

she walked over to his house, the elderly man looked up and smiled.

"Hi, Mr. Leibowitz."

"Hi, Terry. What are you doing in these parts on your day off?"

"I was just going to visit with the Spencers —"

"Is he back from the hospital, then?" Mr. Leibowitz leaned on his shovel. "I thought when the ambulance took him —"

Terry gasped. "The ambulance? When? What happened? Where'd they take him?"

The old man blinked. "Well, I'm not sure where they took him, but it must have been around six thirty this morning. I don't sleep so well anymore, you know, and I was up, prowling about, when I heard all the ruckus."

Terry quelled her impatience.

"I looked out the window, and there was an ambulance with the lights going 'round and a bunch of boys in blue pouring into the house. Then a couple of 'em came back for a stretcher, and the next thing you know, they're taking somebody out. I figure it had to be Rob, since Jan was right behind them."

Terry sucked in a breath. "Foothills, it has to be Foothills they took him to. Thanks." She ran back to her car.

Mr. Leibowitz waved. "If you see them, you give them my best now. Such a nice couple they are."

Terry burst through the emergency room doors and looked around the waiting room. She didn't see Jan in the crowd so she went to the window, where a frazzled triage nurse was processing a long line of people. She shifted from foot to foot, wanting to rush the window and demand information, but she knew all that would get her was a rude dismissal.

Ten minutes later, Terry was curtly informed that they

didn't give out patient information and directed to the processing desk. Again she stood in line, the roiling in her belly becoming worse by the moment. "Excuse me, could you tell me if a Rob Spencer was brought in this morning by ambulance?"

"I'm sorry, ma'am. We're not allowed to give out patient information."

Terry closed her eyes and damned all regulations to everlasting hell. "Would it be breaking any rules to tell me if you've seen a redheaded, probably distraught woman waiting around here?"

A nurse passing behind Terry paused. "Are you looking for Mrs. Spencer?"

Terry whirled around. "Yes. Do you know where she is?"

"I put her in the private waiting room when they brought her husband in. It's the first door on the right past the double doors."

"Thank you." Terry hurried down the hall. She paused before a door unmarked except for a room number. She pushed the door open.

Jan paced in a small, softly lit room, her eyes red and swollen. Another woman perched on a couch. Jan looked up with fear on her drawn face.

Terry wasn't sure who moved first, but a second later, Jan was wrapped in her embrace. She burrowed past Terry's open parka and buried her head against Terry's neck.

Terry murmured meaningless words into Jan's hair and rocked her. They stood together for long moments.

Terry looked over Jan's head. The woman on the couch bore an unmistakable family resemblance to Jan. She nodded to Kate.

Kate nodded back.

When Jan stirred, Terry eased her back until she could see her face. "Hey, are you all right?"

Jan blinked away tears and gave a shaky smile. "I've had better days."

Terry brushed her thumbs over wet eyes and pushed Jan's hair back behind her ears. "Come on, let's sit down and you can fill me in." She steered her to the nearest couch, shucked her coat, and they settled down.

Jan closed the tiny space between them and nestled against her.

Terry took Jan's hand. "Why don't you tell me what happened and how Rob is?"

"I don't know how he is yet. They're still working on him." Jan's eyes filled again.

"The doctor was in once, but he didn't have much information for us yet. I'm Kate, by the way."

"Oh, I'm sorry," Jan said. "Terry, this is my sister, Kate. Kate, this is my best friend, Terry."

"Hi, Kate. It's nice to finally meet you, though I wish it wasn't under these circumstances."

"It's nice to meet you too," Kate said. "I've heard so much about you and your family."

"She's been telling tales out of school, has she?" Her gentle tease coaxed a small smile out of Jan.

"I'm going to get some coffee. Terry, would you like some?"

"Yes, please. Double cream."

Kate left the room.

Jan rested her head on Terry's shoulder. "How did you know we were here?"

"I went to your place, hoping for blueberry pancakes, and Mr. Leibowitz told me about the ambulance. I guessed it was going to Foothills since it's the closest hospital, but I was on my way to Rockyview next if I couldn't find you here. What happened this morning? When I talked to you last night, I thought he just had a bad cold."

"That's what I thought, too." Jan looked down at their interlocked hands. "He's had a rough week and hasn't been getting much sleep with coughing and all. We were awake until about two this morning when he finally fell asleep. When I woke up, I decided to grab a shower and let him sleep some more. When I did try to wake him, he wouldn't open his eyes. I shook him and shook him, but I couldn't wake him up."

Jan choked back a sob, and Terry raised their hands to her lips. "It's okay. It'll be all right." *God, I hope that's the truth.*

Jan tightened her grip on Terry's hand. "I called 911, and they were there so fast. They swarmed all over and loaded him into an ambulance, and we came here. All we've heard so far is that he's in serious condition, but that they've stabilized him. That was about a half hour ago, and we're still waiting for more information." She looked up with anguish in her eyes. "His breathing was so raspy, like he was working for every breath. How could I have slept through that? Maybe if I'd woken up sooner and noticed something was wrong, he wouldn't be in such bad condition now."

"This is not your fault. You were exhausted; no one blames you for getting what sleep you could. Even if you'd woken up sooner, you would've thought it was just the cold making him raspy and let him sleep." *Please listen to me, love. Believe me.* "He's going to be fine. He's in the best place he can be right now. You know that."

Jan nodded, but there was uncertainty on her face.

"Why didn't you call me once you were here?"

Jan ducked her head and mumbled something.

Terry released Jan's hand and tilted her face up. "What was that?"

"I wanted to, but I didn't think I should bother you that early. I called Kate, and she came right over. I was going to call later, honest."

"You can call me anytime, for anything. Don't you know that by now?"

Jan bit her lip and looked away.

Terry pulled her into a hug. "Don't you ever doubt that. I'm here for you...and Rob, too. Always."

Jan leaned into her embrace and wrapped her arms tightly around Terry.

They were still locked together when Kate pushed through the door. She balanced three coffee cups and was followed by a doctor in blue scrubs.

Jan stiffened and sat upright.

Kate set two Styrofoam cups in front of them and took her place in a chair as the doctor sat opposite Jan.

The doctor leaned forward. "Mrs. Spencer, we're going to be moving your husband to intensive care in a few moments, and once he's set up in there, you can see him."

"Is he going to be all right?"

"He's in serious condition, and he's going to be in the ICU for a few days before we can move him onto a regular ward. He has viral pneumonia with a probable bladder infection to complicate matters. As you know, the MS has radically reduced his lung capacity and ability to breathe, and with his compromised immune system, we have to be careful not to overlook any potential complications. I'm afraid you're looking at a couple weeks in the hospital, at least."

"But he will recover, right?" Jan's voice shook.

"We've started him on a full course of IV antibiotics, and

we're confident that we'll get the pneumonia under control. But I think you have to accept that your husband's health is very precarious. Each time he deals with a crisis like this, it leaves him weaker and more susceptible to opportunistic infections, which in turn deprive him of even more of his limited strength. There are some further issues that will have to be addressed, but for now, we'll deal with the immediate dangers."

Jan shivered in Terry's arms.

With a quick glance at her sister, Kate asked, "Are we talking about a life-threatening situation with Rob right now, Doctor?"

Jan looked gratefully at her sister.

You were afraid to ask that, weren't you, love? Terry's heart ached for Jan.

"I don't think I'm telling you anything you don't know when I say that Mr. Spencer has already beaten the odds by living as long as he has, given the acute nature of his MS. It isn't my area of specialty, and I certainly wouldn't try to put an exact time frame on it, but to answer your question…yes, I would say that every time he has to deal with a crisis like this, his life hangs in the balance. Have you and Mr. Spencer ever discussed issues such as directed care and living wills? Do you know what his wishes are in such situations?"

Jan nodded. "He doesn't want extraordinary measures. He always said if it came to that, I wasn't to keep him hanging around on machines. I was to let him go."

"Then you should be prepared that they'll ask you about putting a DNR on his records once he's set up in the ICU." The doctor stood. "Now if you'll excuse me, I have to get back. If you want to move to the ICU waiting room down the hall, they'll let you know when you can see him. I should warn you that he'll be unaware of you or his surroundings for probably the next day or so, but he should start responding to the antibiotics fairly quickly and you should see a marked improvement."

The doctor left, and they sat quietly.

Terry was stunned. Rob always exuded such vitality despite his physical condition that it was hard to accept the doctor had spoken in such imminent terms of his death.

Tears rolled unchecked down Jan's cheeks.

Terry grabbed tissues from the box beside her and gently wiped Jan's face.

Kate came over and knelt in front of her sister. "Hey, Jannie. You know the doctors have written that stubborn husband of yours off before. They were wrong then; in all likelihood they're wrong now. Why don't we go down to the ICU waiting room? You'll feel much better once you see him."

Jan and Terry stood up together.

They found the ICU waiting area down the hall. It was a large room with separate seat groupings and four smaller rooms set off the main area. A huge fish tank was opposite the door, and pillows and blankets were scattered haphazardly around the room.

There were a dozen people in the room already, and the air of controlled anxiety was palpable. Terry saw a phone on the wall. "I'm just going to give Mom a call. I'll be with you in a minute." She left Jan and Kate to find their seats in the corner of the sun-lit room and dialled an outside line. When her mother answered, all Terry could choke out was, "Mom."

"Terry? Terry, what's wrong?" Emily's worried voice rang in her ear.

Terry tried to bring her emotions under control.

"Sweetheart, please. What's wrong? Where are you?"

"I'm at Foothills."

Emily gasped.

"No, Mom, I'm okay. It's Rob."

"What's wrong with Rob? Are you there with Jan? Is she all right?"

Emily's voice steadied her, and Terry filled her mother in. She could hear Jordy in the background, demanding to know what was going on. When she'd brought her mother up to date, a wave of relief surged through her. *Mom will know what to do.*

"Jordy and I are leaving right now," Emily said. "We'll meet you all as quickly as we can get there."

"Thanks, Mom." Terry hung up and returned to her companions. She sat beside Jan, who was curled up in the corner of a couch. "I talked to Mom. She and Jordy are on their way."

"That's so nice of them. You didn't have to ask them to do that." Jan extended her hand to Terry.

Terry took it. "Ask them? Like a herd of elephants could've stopped Mom once she heard what was going on. Besides, you know Jordy will want to see Rob, too."

Emily and Jordy arrived within twenty minutes. Emily marched up to Jan and swept her into a hug along with murmured words of comfort and reassurance. Jordy awkwardly patted Jan's hand, his youthful uncertainty evident.

Introductions were made as the newcomers met Kate, and the small party settled back to wait.

Half an hour later, a nurse entered and called out, "Spencer?"

Jan stood, and the nurse walked over to her. "Mrs. Spencer? Mr. Spencer is in the ICU now, and you can go in to see him. We'd prefer you keep your visit short however, and only two people at a time."

"Kate, why don't you go with Jan, and we'll wait our turn here," Terry said. She was loath to leave Jan's side but acutely aware that Kate was family and she wasn't.

Kate followed Jan, who was close on the nurse's heels.

Once they were out of the room, Emily turned to Terry. "How's she doing?"

"She's scared. I get the feeling that not being able to wake him up this morning terrified her, and it's not helping matters that the doctors can't give her a more optimistic outlook."

Jordy stared at her. "He's not dying, is he?"

Terry regarded her brother. His only exposure to death was the usual childhood trauma of short-lived hamsters and an old black alley cat that had chosen their yard in which to expire. Now he was faced with the mortality of a man he idolized. She chose her words carefully. "You know Rob isn't in very good health, right?"

Jordy nodded.

"We all tend to overlook the truth of his condition because he's such a vital man in other ways, but Rob is close to the end of a very long battle. He's fought this disease longer than you've been alive, but ultimately, he can't win."

Jordy's eyes began to fill.

Terry looked helplessly at her mother.

Emily leaned forward to place a hand on Jordy's knee. "It's okay, son. It's not fair what's happening to him, and it's all right to be sad and angry about that, but they'll do the best they can for him here, and we'll just pray that he'll be all right this time. In the meantime, you can best honour him by being strong for Jan, because she's going to need our support."

Jordy scrubbed at his eyes and tried to pretend he wasn't crying.

Terry nudged a box of tissues across the coffee table, and he grabbed a handful. She watched him, filled with love for her brother. Jordy's big heart would cause him endless grief once he became a pediatrician, but it would make him an outstanding doctor. She was certain that he would remember the unspoken lessons Rob had taught him these past months about facing adversity with courage and grace.

Kate came back into the waiting room and joined them. "Terry, could you give Jan a ride home when she's ready to go? She insists she can take a cab. I'm committed to taking my son and his friends to a school basketball tournament in Edmonton today, so I can't stay."

"Sure, no problem. I was planning to keep her company anyway."

Emily stood. "Why don't I go in next and then Jordy, if you're going to remain here?"

"Sure, Mom. You guys go ahead."

After Emily and Jordy returned from their brief visits with Rob, visibly upset by what they had seen, Terry went down the short hall and through the double doors into the ICU. She stopped at the desk, asked for Rob's bed number, and was directed to the far end of the room by the window. She passed a dozen cubicles and stopped at the end of Rob's bed.

Jan leaned over Rob, stroked his hair, and spoke softly to him. His eyes were closed, and tubes ran into his mouth and nose. More lines were attached to his arms, and wires ran from flat circles pasted to his chest to wall monitors where ominous red lines and numbers flashed continuously.

A large lump rose in Terry's throat. Rob was so pale, but it was his stillness that overwhelmed her. He always bubbled with jokes, stories, and friendly insults. His eyes sparkled as he confronted life head-on and dared it to get the better of him. For the first time, Terry comprehended how vulnerable he was to the damned disease that was stealing his life away.

A nurse sat at a station nearby. She entered a command on her computer and looked up at Terry.

"Is he all right?" Terry asked, embarrassed at posing such an obvious question.

"We've got him stabilized. And he's already had a full course of IV antibiotics. He woke up briefly when we moved him to his bed, but he's pretty exhausted. I wouldn't expect much awareness out of him before tomorrow at the earliest, but I doubt that he'll have to be in here more than a couple of days before we can move him to a regular ward."

Terry nodded and moved behind Jan.

Jan glanced up at her with a quick smile before returning her attention to Rob.

For a long time, Terry listened as Jan spoke to Rob about everything and nothing while the nurse periodically entered the cubicle to check monitors and adjust settings.

Finally, the nurse turned to Jan. "Mrs. Spencer, he'll be out of it for the rest of the day. Why don't you go home and get some rest? Come back tomorrow, and he'll know you're here then."

Jan frowned.

Terry rested her hands on Jan's shoulders. "Let me take you home. He'll be fine, and you're not going to be any good to him if you pass out from exhaustion yourself."

Jan studied Terry's face for a moment. She leaned over and kissed Rob's forehead, caressed his hair one last time, and allowed Terry to lead her away.

———⋙⋘———

Terry stared up at the ceiling of the guest room and listened to Jan move around the house. In the hours since they came from the hospital, Jan hadn't been able to settle in one place for more than ten minutes at a time. Terry had gotten tired just watching her.

Jan resisted her urgings to nap, and when Terry ordered a

pizza for their dinner, Jan barely picked at it. She hadn't protested when Terry announced she would be staying overnight.

She's running on automatic pilot. It's all going to hit her sooner or later, and she's going to crash.

The bedside clock read one a.m. With a sigh, Terry pushed back her covers and stood up. *If she's going to wander all night, the least I can do is keep her company.*

She found Jan at the kitchen window, watching the falling snow.

Terry came up behind her and whispered a soft "hey."

Jan glanced back and gave her a weary smile.

Terry rubbed the knotted muscles of Jan's neck and shoulders until Jan exhaled softly and leaned back. She wrapped her arms around Jan's shoulders as she relaxed against her body. They stood in silence and watched the soft glow of the white landscape.

"Looks like I'm going to have to do some shovelling tomorrow," Terry said.

"Mmm-hmm. I've always loved the light reflected off the snow at night. It's like the whole world has been scrubbed clean and all the ugliness hidden under a beautiful blanket."

Terry rubbed her cheek against Jan's hair as she nestled against her chest. She was content to hold Jan and give her a safe place to talk, or not, as she desired.

Jan was quiet for long moments. "I thought I was ready, you know? All these years, I've tried to condition myself to his death. I hoped it would make it easier when the time came. It hasn't."

Terry tightened her embrace. "It's not necessarily his time. They said he should only be in there for a few weeks."

Jan uttered a short, bitter laugh. "Not this time, no, but what about next time or the time after that? I'm not stupid. I can see how he's deteriorated over the last year. No one comes right out and says it, but we all know his time is limited."

Terry had no answer for that, no bland reassurances to rebut the truth of Jan's words, so she rocked her gently. *You're not alone, love.*

Jan brushed her fingertips over Terry's arms. "I can't tell you how many times I've woken up in the middle of the night and listened for his breathing, desperately afraid to move until I heard him. Or the times when I couldn't hear him and I'd reach out to touch him, sure that his skin would be cold and that he'd slipped away from me in the night. Do you know what I've always prayed for?" She choked back a sob. "Two things...that I'd stay healthy at least one day longer than he lived so I could always care for him at home, and that he'd have an easy death, that he'd die peacefully in his sleep rather than plugged into tubes and machines."

Terry turned Jan in her arms. Jan's arms went around her, and she laid her head against Terry's shoulder.

They stood together for a long time. Terry stared out the window and stroked Jan's hair and back.

Eventually, Jan pulled back and patted the shoulder she'd rested on. "I seem to be making a habit of crying all over you today."

"That's okay. It's Rob's shirt anyways."

Jan chuckled.

"Do you think you might be able to sleep now?"

When Jan nodded, Terry led her down the hall to the master bedroom. She had remade the bed earlier with fresh sheets, and now she turned back the quilt and fluffed the pillows.

"Are you going to tuck me in, too?"

Terry nodded. "Uh-huh, and I might even throw in a bedtime story."

Jan kicked off her slippers and tossed her robe at the foot of the bed, then slid between the sheets.

Terry pulled the quilt up and tucked it around her before she sat on the edge of the bed. "So what'll it be? Goldilocks? Billy Goats Gruff? Rumpelstiltskin?"

Jan rolled over to face her. "I've always liked 'The Selfish Giant.'"

"Ah, yes, Oscar Wilde and the redeeming power of love. Good choice. Okay, so once upon a time, in a land far, far away, children loved to play in a beautiful garden. But one day the mean, selfish giant who owned the garden came back from a trip and saw the children playing there..." Terry lightly rubbed Jan's back as she continued with the story, her voice low.

Jan's eyelids fluttered and closed. Before the end of the story, deep, regular breathing signalled that she had finally ended a very long day.

Terry continued to stroke Jan's back until a big yawn reminded her that her own day had also been wearisome. With a final caress to Jan's face, she turned and left the room, never looking back at the empty expanse on the other side of the bed.

CHAPTER 19

J AN PROPPED THE NEWSPAPER ON Rob's lap and put his reading glasses on his nose. "There you go, love. Now you can catch up on what the world's been up to." She smiled, watching him scan the headlines. *Who'd ever guess you were at death's door just a few days ago?* She looked up from Rob's bedside as Terry and Jordy entered the room. "Hey, you two. Look who has improved enough to be in a regular ward."

"That's what they told us at the nurses' station. Most excellent." Terry dragged another chair close to the bed. "You look a million times better, Rob."

Jordy stood behind her. "You really do look better."

Rob smiled. "Thank you, both. I feel almost human, though I doubt I'll be up dancing anytime soon."

Jan glanced at Terry. "Speaking of dancing, would you mind taking our gift for Duncan and Karen to the wedding with you?"

"Sure. They're going to be awfully sorry you can't make it, though. We all are."

"Whoa." Rob's gaze flicked from Terry to Jan. "Just because I can't go doesn't mean you shouldn't."

Jan shook her head. "No, love. It's okay. I'd rather stay with you, anyway."

"And do what? Watch me sleep? That's crazy." Rob looked at Jordy. "Would you do me a favour?"

Coming Home

"Anything, just name it."

"Would you escort my wife to the wedding?"

Oh, for heaven's sake. Jan shook his arm. "You can't ask that. What if he's already taking a date?"

"I'm not taking anyone," Jordy said. "And I'd be pleased to, if you'd like to go."

Jan glared at Rob, but he just grinned.

Jordy waited for her answer, his expression solemn.

Then she glanced at Terry, who hadn't said anything. There was a hopeful expression in her eyes. Throwing up her hands, Jan surrendered. "All right, I'll go."

"Good. That's what I wanted to hear." Rob cocked his head at Jordy, who was frowning. "What's the matter, buddy?"

"I...I don't know how to dance," Jordy said.

Rob chuckled.

Jordy stared at his feet.

"Hey, it's okay. I'm sorry. I'm a pretty bad dancer myself," Rob said. "I wasn't laughing at you."

"Yes, you were." Jordy refused to look up.

"Jordy, look at me." Rob's voice was quiet but compelling. "I don't give a damn if you can't dance. There's no other man in the world that I'd rather have escorting my wife if I can't be there myself, got that?"

Jordy drew his shoulders back. "Got it. You can count on me."

"I knew that from the first time I met you."

Jordy beamed.

Jan smiled. Rob's relationship with Jordy reminded her of how he had handled people as an officer and why he had been so popular with both peers and subordinates. *You've still got it, love.*

223

"C'mon, little brother. Let's go home, and I'll teach you how to dance so you don't crush Jan's toes on Saturday."

"Okay, but you have to let me lead."

Terry sighed as the others laughed. "Oh, all right, but only for you." She slung her arm over his shoulders and winked at Jan and Rob. "Honestly, the sacrifices I make for you."

The sounds of the siblings teasing each other faded down the hall, and Jan turned back to Rob. "Are you sure, hon? I really don't mind missing it, you know."

"You miss too much already. I'm feeling much better now. All I'm going to do is sleep or watch TV, so there's no point in you sitting here when you could be having a good time."

Jan's eyes glistened as she picked up Rob's thin, inert hand and cradled it between her palms. "First you scare me half to death and now you want me to go out and have fun. You're too much, you know."

"Hmm, too much what...too handsome, too witty, too light on my feet?"

Jan raised Rob's hand and kissed his knuckles. "All of the above. Definitely all of the above."

———◆———

Jan and Jordy left the packed dance floor and made their way through the crowd to their table.

"Would you like some punch, Jan?"

Jordy's earnest concern for her every whim amused her, but she tried to conceal it. She nodded, and Jordy disappeared into the mass of wedding guests. Wincing, she kicked off her shoes and rubbed her right foot with her left. *Jordy wasn't kidding when he warned Rob that he couldn't dance.*

Terry dropped into the chair beside her. "Where's your date?"

"He's off finding us something to drink. Dancing is hard work, you know."

"How's he doing anyway? Did any of my lessons take?"

"Depends, did your lessons include how to tenderize your partner's feet?"

Terry rolled her eyes. "I tried, really I did. I swear my baby brother was born with two left feet."

Jan laughed. "Don't worry about it. He's so sweet, and he's trying very hard. I'm actually having a lot of fun. He keeps apologizing and telling me how you're the dancer in the family."

"Well, I do enjoy it. Always have."

"Maybe I'll have to drag you out there sometime tonight, then." Jan was only half-teasing.

"It would be my honour to dance with the loveliest lady here."

Jan was suffused with warmth. She fingered the fine gold chain around her neck. "I want to thank you again for the beautiful gifts. They match my dress perfectly."

"I'm glad you like them. They set off your eyes really well, too."

Jan traced the oval ammonite cradled in a delicate gold setting. Matching earrings reflected the deep green and gold depths of the stones. Terry had given them to her when she and Jordy picked her up for the wedding earlier that day. "You have exquisite taste, but then I guess you've had lots of practice picking out jewellery."

"Actually, no, though I've bought the odd thing over the years for Mom."

Jan hadn't expected such a serious response, and she was even more touched at Terry's thoughtfulness.

Terry's eyes widened, and she bolted upright. "Damn!

Here he comes again. I've got to get out of here. I'll see you later."

Jan's jaw dropped as Terry scrambled away and disappeared into the crowd.

Jordy returned with two overfilled glasses of punch and set one in front of Jan.

"What in heaven's name has gotten into your sister? She took off like a bat out of hell."

Jordy glanced up to where a tall, heavy man with thinning blond hair and a droopy moustache was lumbering after his rapidly escaping sister. "Oh, no. I was really hoping he wouldn't show up. Damn, he's going to ruin Terry's whole night."

The man caught up with Terry when she was blocked by a group of inebriated celebrants. He grabbed hold of her arm and dragged her onto the dance floor.

Jan frowned. "Who is he? And why is he manhandling Terry?"

"That's Karen's cousin, Roy. We all met at Duncan and Karen's engagement party this summer, and for some reason he fixated on Terry and decided she was perfect wife material." Jordy shook his head. "Geez, she wouldn't give him the time of day, and we all thought he'd forget about it."

Jan stared at him. "Didn't anyone tell him that Terry doesn't play for his team?"

Jordy snorted. "Everyone told him that, but for one thing, Roy isn't the sharpest tack in the box, and for another thing, he didn't believe it. Terry had just broken up with Marika and didn't bring a date to the party, so he thought it was just an excuse to get rid of him."

"I'm surprised she didn't bring a date to the wedding." *Though I'm glad she didn't.* "Maybe if he saw her with a woman first-hand, he'd leave her alone."

"You're probably right, but Terry hasn't brought anyone home for Sunday dinner in months now. Even Michael mentioned that she's been flying solo for ages." Jordy scowled as Roy pulled Terry close even though she argued with him. "That's it. I've had enough. I'm going to grab Alex and Matt, and we're going to convince Roy that Terry's off limits." He started to get to his feet.

Jan put her hand on his arm. "I don't think Terry wants a fuss on Duncan and Karen's big day. Why don't you let me handle this?"

"You can't take him on. He's a man-mountain."

"Well I don't intend to punch his lights out. I have a better idea." Jan slipped her wedding ring off and pressed it into his hand. "Here, hold this for me. I'll be back for it later." She wriggled her feet back into her shoes and set out to rescue Terry. After wending her way through the dancers, she tapped Roy on a massive shoulder. When he turned with an inquisitive look on his face, she asked, "May I cut in?"

Roy grinned and let go of Terry. As he extended his hand to Jan, she slipped around him and into Terry's arms.

"Darling, I've been wondering where you were. Honestly, you invite me to the wedding and then you abandon me to your brother. It's time you made up for your neglect." Jan almost laughed aloud at the bewildered look on Terry's face. She stepped closer and settled one arm over Terry's shoulder.

They started to waltz, and a grin spread across Terry's face. She glanced over Jan's shoulder at Roy. "He looks like someone pole-axed him."

Jan smiled. *Smooth as clockwork.*

Terry took control, and Jan revelled in a long-lost pleasure. She hadn't really danced since she'd met Rob, but there was a time that she couldn't be pried off the dance floor until the last song ended. She leaned back in Terry's arms. "You look really good tonight. Not as good as you'd have looked in that little black dress, but Michael did well by you."

He had outfitted Terry in a classically tailored, pewter grey silk pantsuit, with a charcoal grey camisole peeking out from under the jacket. Black demi-boots and simple silver earrings finished off her ensemble.

"I really can't blame Roy for wanting to get up close and personal with you."

Terry ducked her head. "I clean up all right, then, do I?"

"Oh yes," Jan said. "You most certainly do."

When the music ended, Terry started to lead her off the floor, but Jan resisted. When Terry looked back in surprise, Jan tilted her head. "Another, please?" Terry glanced around the crowded hall, but Jan shook her head. "I don't care. I'm having fun dancing with my best friend, and if she's having fun, too, why should anyone else's opinion matter?"

A slow smile crossed Terry's face as she stepped closer and drew Jan back into her arms. "Why indeed?"

Jan's thoughts whirled in chaotic turmoil. It was a pleasure dancing with Terry, but she marvelled at her lack of self-consciousness. Jordy and one of his cousins danced past them, bumping into couples as they went. *I'm just protecting my feet. Besides, I've sat on the sidelines for so many years that this is just plain fun.* A part of her rejected that simplistic rationalization. *No, be honest. Roy was only a convenient excuse for doing exactly what you wanted to.*

As Jordy and his partner intruded on their space again, Terry pulled her closer and spun them away from imminent collision.

Jan made no effort to draw back from the heat of Terry's body, but she fought the urge to lay her head against Terry's shoulder. She was quite willing to spend the rest of the night dancing with Terry, but when the music ended, the DJ announced that it was time for the bouquet to be thrown and Jan turned back to her table.

When Terry trailed after her, she stopped and, with her hands on her hips, turned and eyed her.

"What?"

"Exactly what do you think you're doing?" Jan raised an eyebrow and tapped her foot.

"Um…walking you to our table?"

"No, you're not. You're going to march your cute butt back out on that floor with the rest of the single women and catch the bouquet."

Terry sighed but then brightened. "You think I have a cute butt?"

Jan broke out laughing. With a slap on the subject body part, she pushed Terry back toward the gathering crowd of women.

Terry looked over her shoulder beseechingly, but Jan pointed at the centre of the floor. She grinned at Terry's adorable pout and returned to her table. Emily and Gord had joined Jordy there.

"I can't believe you talked her into going out there," Emily said. "When Alex and Diane got married, she did a five-minute rant on why such ridiculous rituals demeaned everyone taking part in them."

"I suppose it is a little silly, but I couldn't resist."

Jordy grimaced. "Roy's probably been up there rigging the bouquet to land right in Terry's hands."

Karen tossed her flowers high and far over the heads of the women. The flowers hit Terry in the chest and slid to the floor. Karen's young niece scrambled to pick up the bouquet while Terry retreated as if it were a live grenade.

Hoots and cheers went up from the crowd. Blushing, Terry returned to their table.

Jan pulled out a chair for her. "No hard feelings?"

"I am so going to pay you back for this." The threat was undercut by the amusement in Terry's eyes.

Jan leaned close to whisper in her ear. "Uh-uh. I already owed you one from our last Sunday dinner. Now we're even."

Terry laughed. "I guess we are."

Gord claimed everyone's attention with his story of ending up at the wrong church earlier in the afternoon and only barely getting to the right one on time for the ceremony.

Jan glanced away from Gord. Emily was watching her intently. Startled, she focused on Emily, who immediately tapped Gord on the shoulder and asked him for a dance.

I wonder what that was all about. Jan's musings were interrupted when Jordy requested a dance.

For the rest of the evening, Jan alternated dances between Jordy and Terry, always managing to stay out on the floor longer with her best friend.

Roy spent most of the evening downing beer at the bar and glaring at Terry, but Jordy enlisted the rest of the family to help run interference.

The Sanderson clan threw up a protective cordon around Terry, and even Matt left his date long enough to dance once with his sister. Terry was never alone, even—much to her exasperation—when she went to the ladies' room.

Jan strove to make her claim on Terry clear to Roy, leaning close, whispering intimately in Terry's ear, and leading her to the dance floor at every opportunity.

A couple of hours after the newlyweds departed to the cheers and catcalls of their guests, the party began to wind down. Most of the guests were gone when Jan pitched in with the remaining Sandersons to help clear away the detritus of the celebration.

Streamers and balloons were pulled off walls and pillars. Dirty plates and glasses were packed off to the kitchen, where Emily loaded the dishwasher. Jordy and Alex grabbed brooms and began pushing piles of litter to the centre of the room while Gord and Terry filled large garbage bags.

On her sixth trip into the kitchen, Jan gratefully accepted a proffered cup of coffee and sank down in a chair beside Emily. "It was a wonderful wedding, Em. I had a marvellous time, and I haven't danced like that in more years than I can remember."

Emily glanced at the piles of dirty dishes stacked on every available surface. "It did go well, didn't it? Now if only we had our own personal genie to wink this mess all away."

"Maybe if we leave it all overnight, the cleaning elves will take care of it."

"No such luck, I'm afraid. I tried that theory on the boys' rooms, but the mess never once disappeared overnight."

"What about Terry's room?" Jan was curious if her sloppiness was a lifelong trait.

"Hah! Terry was worse than all three of the older boys put together, but she had a knack for hiding things in the strangest places when she knew I was on a cleaning binge. All the kids were supposed to bring their laundry down to the basement for washday, but that daughter of mine... Do you know I once found a week's worth of dirty socks and underwear stuffed down the heating register in her room? Honestly, if I hadn't smelled something funny when I was changing her sheets, she might have burnt the whole house down. Another time, I found a half-eaten sandwich stuffed in the toe of a dirty old sneaker. When I asked her why, she looked up at me with these big innocent eyes and said she knew I wouldn't want her to waste food, so she was saving it for when she was really hungry."

Jan burst out laughing as she pictured Terry as a curly-haired urchin with mischievous dark eyes, getting in trouble every time she turned around.

Terry stood in the doorway. "Mother. You are not telling tales on me, are you?"

Emily smiled and finished her coffee.

Terry spun a chair around and straddled it. "Got any more?"

"Depends. Did you finish getting the hall tidied up?" Emily poured her a cup and pushed it across the table.

"For the most part. Dad, Alex, and Jordy are piling the bags out by the dumpster. I think we can leave the rest of the cleanup until tomorrow. If we come back in the morning, we'll have it all done by noon and still have lots of time to see Duncan and Karen off at the airport."

"Where are they going on their honeymoon?" The last Jan had heard, they were trying to decide between Cancun and Costa Rica.

"Believe it or not," Emily said. "They got a fabulous last-minute deal on a Mediterranean cruise. As soon as Karen heard about it, she put down their deposit. She said she was tired of waiting for Duncan to make up his mind and if she left it to him, they'd end up ice-fishing for their honeymoon."

"Sounds like ole Dunc has the ball and chain firmly attached to his ankle now," Terry said.

Emily shook a finger at her. "Don't laugh at your brother. Your turn will come. Besides, Karen is exactly what Duncan needs. That boy would daydream his way through life, given half a chance."

"I can't argue with that. He always did have his head in the clouds, but as for my turn coming someday…not likely. I'm never getting tied down."

"Just you wait, Terry. Someday, some woman is going to wrap you right around her little finger, and you're going to be just as helpless with her as your brothers are with their wives."

Jordy poked his head through the kitchen's swinging doors. "Hey, you two. Alex's battery died, so I'm going with Dad to help him boost it. Then I'll warm up the car and bring it around by the back door. How 'bout I pick you up there in ten minutes or so?"

"Thanks," Jan said. "You're such a sweetheart. We'll be ready to go when you are."

"I take it Jordy is your designated driver tonight?" Emily asked.

Terry stood and stretched. "Yeah, he figured he wouldn't get away with swiping beer under your nose anyway, so he volunteered. Anything more we can do here, Mom?"

Emily surveyed the kitchen and shook her head. "I'm going to put in one more load of dishes before your father and I leave, but everything else can be left until the morning. You two go ahead, and I'll see you later."

Terry kissed her mother's cheek and held the kitchen door open for Jan, who bade Emily good night.

They went to the cloakroom; Terry held Jan's overcoat while she slipped into it.

Terry pulled a bright multi-coloured scarf out of her coat sleeve and wrapped it several times around her neck.

Jan smiled. The scarf evoked the little girl who had hidden her sandwiches and dirty laundry, and she felt a rush of affection.

"What?" Terry glanced at her. "Don't you like my scarf? I'll have you know my great-aunt knitted this for me."

"It's lovely. No, I was just thinking about what a wonderful night it's been."

Terry smiled the half cocky, half shy smile that Jan found so endearing. "It was great, wasn't it? You really are a good dancer."

"Once I shook the rust off you mean. Actually, it's just that you can make any partner look good."

They argued good-naturedly about who made whom look good, as they left the hall and stood outside on the back landing.

When Jan shivered, Terry looked at her with a concerned expression. "Would you rather wait inside? I'm sure Jordy will honk the horn when he comes around."

Jan tilted her head back to stare at the clear black sky spotted with brilliant diamonds. "No, it's too seldom I get to see the sky like this. Let's wait out here, all right?"

"Sure," Terry said. "But if it gets too cold, let me know."

Jan inhaled deeply, and the inside of her nose crinkled from the frigid air. It had been a glorious evening. *Thanks to Terry.* She had been touched by Jordy's sweet attentiveness, but dancing with Terry made her feel alive in a very unaccustomed way. She couldn't remember the last time she felt so exhilarated. She would have to examine that more closely later, but for now she was content to bask in the afterglow.

The night was so silent that Jan started at the roar of an engine being gunned. Puzzled, she looked down the road leading to the front parking lot.

An orange pickup truck barrelled along the icy road toward them.

Terry groaned. "Damn it! Why won't that idiot just go home?"

Roy leered at them over the steering wheel as he slammed

to a sliding stop in front of the landing, stumbled out of the door, and slipped on the snow-covered pavement.

Jan retreated and grabbed for the handle of the door behind her, but it had locked automatically behind them.

Terry stepped in front of her. "Why don't you just leave? Haven't you caused enough trouble for one night?"

Roy raised the beer bottle in his hand and drained it. "You think you're so good. S'pose a bitch like you wouldn't be caught dead with a guy like me."

"You just don't get it, do you? I wouldn't be caught dead with any guy. Not that I'd go out with you if I were the straightest woman in the world."

Roy hawked up a wad of phlegm and spat it in their direction. "Like I bought that for one minute. Bet you've spread your legs for half the guys in the city, but I just ain't good enough for you, ya slag!"

Terry tensed.

Jan stepped forward and turned Terry to face her. She cupped her neck and drew her head down. The last thing she was aware of before cold lips met her own was dark eyes regarding her with amazement. Then the rest of the world melted away.

Distantly, Jan heard Roy curse and the sound of glass breaking as his beer bottle hit the wall not far from them. She was vaguely aware of his truck starting up and roaring away, but her whole world focused on the soft lips possessing her own, the warm tongue exploring her mouth, and the way it turned her entire body to liquid.

Long after the pickup screamed out of the lot, they stood, pressed together, deep in an ardent kiss.

Finally, Terry pulled back, long streams of hot vapour steaming into the winter night as she tried to catch her breath.

Jan had equal difficulty breathing, sucking in icy air that

did nothing to cool the fire in her body. Locked in each other's arms, Terry lowered her head again. Jan could have kissed her all night, but all too soon Terry pulled back. "Jordy."

Jan closed her eyes and nodded.

Terry feathered light kisses over her brow and stepped back to a respectable distance.

Jan swayed as if something vital had been ripped away. She didn't speak, unwilling to fracture the crystalline moment between them. She wrenched her gaze from Terry's and turned away. Fearful that her emotional turmoil was written on every line of her being, she waited for Jordy to pull up.

When Jordy clambered from the car and held the passenger door open, Jan slipped in and nodded her thanks.

Terry climbed in the back.

Jordy conducted a solo chat about the reception all the way to the Spencer home. When he stopped, he rushed around to open the door and offered Jan his arm. She stepped out, as did Terry.

Jan murmured good night and allowed Jordy to escort her to the door, where she leaned forward and kissed his cheek. "Thank you for a lovely evening. I'll tell Rob what a wonderful escort you were."

Jordy beamed. "I'm glad you had fun. Good night."

Terry stood beside the car and watched Jan as Jordy trotted back down the walk. For a long moment, their gazes locked, then Terry turned to get into the front seat.

Jan entered her home and slid down against the foyer wall until she sat on the floor. With her arms wrapped around her knees, she bent her head low and soundlessly rocked back and forth as the birds chirped a welcome home.

CHAPTER 20

J AN RUBBED HER HAIR DRY and tossed the towel on the bathroom counter. The hot shower hadn't done much to repair the evidence of a sleepless night. She picked up her brush and started drawing it through the wet tangles. Mechanically, she coaxed her hair into place, then stopped and regarded her hand in the mirror.

She dropped the brush and sat down heavily on the edge of the bathtub, cradling her left hand in her right as she stared at her naked ring finger. She hadn't taken that simple gold band off since the day Rob placed it there.

It's all right. Jordy has it. I'll call him and get it back today. Jan lifted her hand as if testing the weight of it. *Oh God. What the hell am I going to do?* It was the same question that was responsible for the deep shadows under her eyes, the question that plagued her through the long hours of the night, and the question for which she had absolutely no answer.

Closing her eyes, she replayed those moments in Terry's embrace, lost in the sweetest kiss of her life. A small shudder ran through her body, and she wrenched herself out of that prohibited train of thought.

Desperately, she focused on one thing as she got dressed and ready to go. *Rob's waiting for me.*

Terry stared into the dregs of her coffee. Her housemates had gone east to spend Christmas with their families. She longed for Michael's comforting shoulder and had even considered calling him last night before remembering that it was past three a.m. in Toronto. He wouldn't mind, but his parents wouldn't have been impressed.

She shook her head. The woman she was in love with had kissed her last night. *She kissed me.* And any charade to convince Roy evaporated the instant their lips met.

When she pulled back, there was shock in Jan's eyes, but also desire...and love. Even if they never spoke of that moment again, in that instant, Jan felt for her what Terry had been feeling for months.

She rubbed the bridge of her nose and tried to ease the incipient headache. *What do I do?* She had been able to cap her feelings when she was sure they were one-sided. *God help me now.*

A part of her wished last night had never happened, but a stronger part exulted in the memory. Her body remembered the heat of Jan's pressed close as they danced, and she shivered.

Terry ran a thumb over her lips. She had kissed her first girl when she was fifteen and long ago stopped keeping track of the number of partners who had drifted in and out of her orbit, but never had a simple kiss affected her as Jan's.

Simple, sure. The only simple thing about it was your brain for letting it go on the way it did. You couldn't just step back after a quick kiss. If you had, you could have laughed it off as old Roy burned out of there. No, you had to let your feelings out. Fucking idiot. But for all her self-castigation, she was only one side of the equation. *Jan was in it as deep as I was. She didn't want to stop any more than I did.*

Terry dropped her head into her hands. *What if Jordy*

hadn't been with us? What if Jan had invited me in? What if Rob – ?
Angrily, she shoved her cup across the table and scowled as
the cold coffee spilled.

The front door opened. "Hey, Terry. Are you ready to go?"

"In here, Jordy." *I can't think about it now.* She mopped up
the spilt coffee and rinsed her cup in the sink. *Time to clean up
last night's mess.* She grimaced. *At least part of it.*

———◆———

Terry waved as Duncan and Karen disappeared into the
airport customs enclosure. The Sandersons and Karen's family
shouted goodbyes while Jordy tossed some leftover confetti
after them.

The large group of well-wishers began to disperse, and
Terry trailed her family down the concourse.

Emily turned and eyed her. "You've been awfully quiet."

"Um, I…I'm just tired from last night, that's all. I had such
a good time I couldn't get to sleep when I got home."

Emily studied her.

"Shoot, Terry, I forgot to tell you," Jordy said. "Rob asked
if you'd drop by around five tonight. Jan's going to her sister's
for dinner, and he wants to talk to you."

Terry swallowed hard against the surge of nausea.

Jordy canted his head. "Hey, are you okay? You're kinda
pale."

"No, no, I'm fine. Uh, you saw Rob already today?" Terry
couldn't stop her voice from trembling.

"Yeah, I forgot to give Jan her ring back last night. I knew
she'd be up at the hospital today, so I swung by to leave it with
Rob before I picked you up. I told him all about Roy and what
a jerk he was and how Jan rescued you."

Breathe, just breathe. "Oh."

"Yup, he thought it was pretty funny how Roy chased

you all over, and Jan snuck you away right under his nose."
Jordy chuckled. "I told him that you rescued Jan from my
dancing, too."

"Did, ah, did he say what he wanted tonight?"

"Nope. He just said to make sure you came by when Jan
wasn't there."

Terry's queasy stomach did flip-flops. She glanced
from Jordy's cheerfully oblivious face to the unreadable but
penetrating gaze her mother fixed on her.

"Are you coming by the house, dear?"

The last thing Terry wanted was to be alone with her
mother. "No, thanks. I'm going over to Lisa and Robyn's for
a while. I'll see you all later, okay?" She strode away without
waiting for an answer.

⋖◆⋗

Lisa opened the door. "Hey, stranger. You do know where
we live after all."

"I know. I suck. I'm a terrible friend." Terry held out a
bucket of chicken wings and a case of beer. "Forgive me?"

A long arm reached over Lisa's shoulder, and Robyn
grabbed the bucket. "Hell, yeah. For hot wings, we forgive
anything. Get in here."

In short order, they were sprawled in the living room,
consuming wings, drinking beer, and catching up.

"So what's happening on the stork front?" Terry asked.

Lisa rolled her eyes. "We're having problems agreeing on
the donor. I think we should go the anonymous route, and
Robyn wants to ask a friend, someone we know and like. I'm
afraid of complications if he wants to get involved after the
baby's born, but she doesn't like the idea of not knowing much
about the father."

"Huh." Terry sucked the last of the meat off a wing and picked up her beer. "Did you have anyone in mind?"

"I was kind of hoping that Michael might agree," Robyn said.

Terry choked on her beer. "Michael?"

"Why not?" Robyn asked. "He's smart, funny, nice, and good-looking."

"Yeah, but—but—Michael?" Terry imagined Michael outfitting his offspring in designer diapers and tiny Armani suits and laughed.

Lisa scowled. "I told her that there was no way Michael was going to allow the precious Seaton genes to be wasted on people like us—"

"Whoa." Terry held up a hand. "Stop right there. Michael doesn't have an arrogant bone in his body. I happen to know he thinks very highly of you two. The only reason I hesitated is because I have trouble picturing him changing diapers."

Robyn shook her head. "But that's just it. We wouldn't expect him to change diapers or contribute anything else but his sperm."

"Michael's not the kind of man to ignore his own child, guys. I think if you did ask him and he agreed, he'd want to have some sort of visitation privileges."

Lisa stood and grabbed another beer from the open case. "We still have to work out a few things between ourselves before we decide if we even want to ask him." She pushed the case across the coffee table.

Robyn shook her head, and Terry indicated her half-full bottle.

"So what have you been up to?" Robyn asked. "We were starting to think we were going to have to send out a St. Bernard to look for you."

Terry studied her bottle and peeled little strips off the label. A lump welled up in her throat, and her eyes filled.

Robyn set her beer aside and slid closer on the couch. "Terry? Hey, what's the matter?"

The question was Terry's undoing. The tears she had fought back since last night flooded free.

Robyn took the bottle from Terry's listless grasp and set it on the table. She drew her into an embrace and murmured wordless sounds of comfort into Terry's hair.

Lisa sat behind Terry and rubbed her back as Robyn rocked her.

When Terry finally ran out of tears, she pulled back and scrubbed at her face. Lisa pressed a napkin into her hand. "I'm sorry. I didn't mean to do that."

"Like you haven't always been there for us." Robyn sighed. "You did it, didn't you? You gave away that one part of your heart you never have before."

When she nodded, Robyn and Lisa exchanged glances. Terry sat up straighter. "You knew?"

Lisa shrugged. "Told you before what we were seeing between you two, so yeah, we strongly suspected. You're a lousy poker player, my friend. Everything you feel is written all over your face."

Horrified, Terry flashed on Rob's summons for this evening. She dreaded their meeting because of her guilty conscience, but she hadn't thought Rob could possibly be aware of the whole picture. *Jordy wouldn't have been so casual if Rob was upset, right?* But what if her face had long ago given away her feelings for his wife? *Does he know? Could he know?*

Robyn kept one arm draped around Terry's shoulders. "Why don't you tell us what's going on?"

Haltingly, Terry began to tell them of the events of the

past few months. By the time she reached the wedding, words were spilling over as she unburdened herself. She hadn't told anyone, not even Michael, the extent to which she had become emotionally involved with Jan. When Terry reached the end of her narrative, she slumped in exhaustion.

Lisa and Robyn were silent as they contemplated her story. Finally, Lisa asked, "What are you going to do?"

Terry grabbed her abandoned beer and took a long drink. She rubbed burning eyes and grimaced. "What the hell can I do?" The words were as acrid on her tongue as the flat beer. "She's married, and there's not a chance in the world she'll leave him. I...I couldn't ask her to anyway." It was an acknowledgment of the truth she'd known from the first moment she realized that she had fallen in love with Jan.

Lisa and Robyn exchanged looks again before Robyn asked, "Are you sure? From what you said about last night, it doesn't sound like it's one-sided."

"It's not." And that, too, was an undeniable and agonizing truth, like putting a banquet one inch beyond the reach of a starving woman. "God, what kind of person would I be if I stepped on Rob's toes? For crying out loud, he's helpless. More importantly, he's a friend." Terry looked at Lisa. "You couldn't do that to someone, could you?"

"For Robyn, I'd move heaven and earth, and God help anyone that stood in my way."

Terry blinked.

"Shhh, love," Robyn said. "Terry has to make up her own mind and live with whatever she decides. In the meantime, don't you forget that we're here for you, okay?"

Terry nodded. They didn't have answers, but she was grateful for their unqualified support.

———◄◆►———

Why do they paint the walls such a putrid shade of green? Rob's room was at the end of the long hall, across from the sunroom. Terry trod the route with all the enthusiasm of a condemned woman walking the last mile.

The light of the short winter day was fading, and the window at the end of the hall was almost dark. Terry tried to remember if she had turned off her headlights when she parked the car. *Maybe I should go check. A dead battery is no laughing matter in winter.*

One of Rob's nurses was at the nurses' station. "Oh, there you are. He mentioned that you'd probably be by."

Terry forced a smile. She had gotten to know Rob's nursing rotation by sight, if not name. This woman was the most gregarious of his caregivers and would be sure to ask Rob how their visit had gone. Her avenue of escape closed, Terry walked the last few yards and paused at Rob's doorway.

"Hey, come on in. Pull up a chair and make yourself comfortable."

Terry dragged the chair up beside the bed and slung her coat over the back. "Hey, Rob. How's it going?"

"Good. I really appreciate your coming by. I was hoping I could ask you for a favour."

"What did you have in mind?"

A nurse's aide bustled in and placed a covered tray on Rob's table. "Do you need help here, sir, or will your friend be assisting you?"

Rob glanced at Terry. "Do you mind? Jan normally does it, but the aide will help if you'd rather not."

"No, no that's okay. I don't mind." Terry removed the tray top to expose the interior and wrinkled her nose at the unappetizing contents.

Rob chuckled. "It sure isn't my wife's cooking, but it's marginally edible."

"If you say so." Terry unrolled the cutlery from the napkin and cut up the mystery meat before offering a forkful to Rob.

He took it, and they settled into a feeding routine.

"I was wondering if you'd pick up Jan's Christmas present for me. I did a bunch of research with Donny, so I know what I want, but our plans to go out and get it last weekend kind of fell through...obviously."

Her present? He wants me to pick up her present for him? Terry almost laughed in sheer relief. "So what are you getting her?"

Rob's eyes shone. "A laptop computer. She's really impressed with yours, and she talks about getting one all the time. I know exactly what I want, and I had her leave me a cheque made out to you. Just fill in the amount, and I'll tell her after Christmas next week so she can record it in her chequebook. She's going to be so surprised."

Terry shovelled another spoonful of mashed potatoes into his mouth.

He chewed hastily. "Don't you think it's a good idea? I was thinking of a digital camera, but I think she'll get more use out of a computer."

"No, I think it's a great idea. She's going to love it."

Between bites, Rob outlined the specifications he had in mind. He finally turned his head away from the empty spoon Terry extended.

"Oh, sorry." Terry had been feeding him by rote with her mind a hundred miles away.

Rob peered at her. "Are you okay? I mean if you don't have time or something, I'm sure I could get Jordy to pick it up for me."

"No, I'd be happy to go get it for you." Terry dabbed a

napkin at a stray pea on his chin. "Sorry, I'm a bit tired after last night."

"I heard it was a wonderful party. Jordy was telling me about your not-so-secret admirer. Sounds like a real pain in the ass."

"Was he ever." Terry peeled the paper off a straw for Rob's juice but was unable to look him in the eyes. "Did Jan get her ring back all right?" She raised the glass to his lips.

"Yes, she got here shortly after Jordy dropped it off, so it's back where it belongs."

"Good." Terry held the glass up for another sip.

"It sounds like Jan really enjoyed herself last night. I'm glad. She loves to dance, and I'm not exactly Fred Astaire."

"Neither is Jordy."

Rob chuckled. "So I heard. However, rumour is that you are."

"Ah, well…" Terry squirmed.

"Thank you."

Terry froze. "For what?"

"For taking such good care of my wife. For tripping the light fantastic with her and seeing that she had a great time."

Terry desperately wanted to be anywhere else but in this room.

"Terry?"

She met Rob's gaze.

He gave her a half-smile. "It's all right."

Terry stared at him, her heart beating in double time. "You know?" She could barely hear her own words.

Rob nodded.

"How long?"

"How long have I known my wife was otherwise orientated, or how long have I known that you two were falling in love?"

Rob's melancholy question seared, and Terry hung her head. *I'm lower than pond scum.*

"I don't actually sit on my brain, you know." Rob sighed. "Jan is my whole world. I notice everything about her. It's not like there are a lot of other distractions in my life. I see how she lights up when you're walking up the front path. I hear how her voice sparkles when she's talking to you on the phone. On Saturday mornings, she glows with excitement because she's going to spend the afternoon with you. She can hardly stop talking about all the things you do together. It wasn't exactly hard to add two plus two, though I did hope for a long time that it was just the pleasure of having a new friend rather than the alternative."

"But it was your idea for her to change to Saturdays so we could do things together."

Rob's gaze sharpened. "Do you have such a low opinion of me that you think I'd take away something that makes her so happy? Damn it, Terry. Do you think I don't know what she gave up by marrying me? Don't you know I'd give her the world if I could? Well, I can't. This body dies a little more each year, and all I can do is watch as she tries her best to keep the pieces together."

The utter frustration on Rob's face and his tear-filled eyes shook Terry to the core as he fought for breath. Alarmed, she half-rose from her chair to summon help.

Rob shook his head and whispered, "Juice."

She raised the glass to his lips and let him take a long pull through the straw. Setting it back down, she grabbed a tissue and dried his eyes and cheeks.

His chest rose and fell in rapid, shallow succession. He closed his eyes, and any semblance of vitality disappeared.

"Would you like me to go?"

Rob opened his eyes. "No. Just give me a few minutes."

They remained silent as Terry periodically offered the juice until Rob drained the glass.

He again focused his intense gaze on her. "I won't give her up." Even in Rob's weakened voice, the words were absolute. "I need her...far more than you."

Terry couldn't help herself. "What about what she needs?" At the instant anguish on Rob's face, she wished she could retract the words.

"Maybe if I was a better man, I could put her happiness first and let her go, but I can't do it. If I lose her, I lose my life. And the thing is, I know her. I know that whatever she feels for you, she'll stay with me. She does love me, and she's too honourable to leave."

I know that.

Rob's expression softened. "I also know that whatever you're feeling right now, ultimately, you're not going to tear her apart by asking her to make an impossible choice. You're too damned honourable yourself."

I'm not going to cry. I'm not going to cry. I'm not going to... Terry grabbed several tissues and mopped at her eyes.

"She's never taken that ring off before, you know. It was odd to see her hand bare today, even if it was just for a few minutes."

"She was just trying to fool Roy. She didn't mean anything by it."

"Mmm, maybe."

"You said something earlier about how long you've known Jan was, um—" Terry's voice trailed off as it occurred to her how sensitive a subject this would be for him.

"Differently orientated?" A note of humour returned to Rob's wispy voice. "Probably a lot longer than she has, though to be honest, I wasn't absolutely sure until you came into our lives."

"Uh, how did you—?" Terry was distressed at her inability to complete a sentence.

Rob tilted his head and was quiet for a long moment. "As far as I know, Jan's never been with anyone but me. It used to disturb me that I couldn't bring her satisfaction back when we were lovers, but she always assured me that it was just the way she was and not to worry about it. I finally evolved a theory that my wife lived so much in the realm of make-believe, she had a hard time reorienting to the real world in some respects. But she didn't seem unhappy, and she willingly made adjustments as this disease progressed. I got the feeling, though, that she didn't mind a bit when that part of our life became impossible."

Terry was fascinated at the insight into the woman she loved.

"Then you entered our lives…" The words were mild, but Terry still flinched. "And my wife came alive like I'd never seen her before."

"But, we're not—" Terry couldn't finish that statement as the tactile memory of Jan's soft lips under hers flashed through her.

"Not lovers? I know. But every Saturday when she returns home, she's alive with the passion of living and the excitement of being with you. As I told you, I may not be able to scratch my nose, but I do have eyes and ears. The irony is, I know Jan had no clue what was happening."

"Neither did I for a long time."

"No, I guess you didn't." Rob sighed. "I know you two never meant for this to happen, but it did, and now we have to deal with it."

Terry's chest hurt. "How?"

His eyes were stern. "She was very unhappy when she was here this afternoon, even though she tried not to let me see it. As I said, I won't allow her to be torn between us. So you're going to have to fix things."

Terry walked over to his window and stared out across the parking lot many floors below. "What do you want me to do? Just walk away?"

There was a long silence, and Terry wondered if he was gathering himself to tell her exactly that. She half-hoped, half-feared that was what he would say.

"No, she needs her 'friend,' now more than ever."

Terry heard his emphasis on the word and turned. "I don't understand. What exactly do you want me to do?"

Rob's gaze was unyielding. "She has to know that you're unavailable as anything other than a friend."

Bitterness filled Terry's mouth like ashes. "Why? You already said she'd never choose me."

"She wouldn't, but Jan's a dreamer, always has been. She'll stay with me and dream of being with you until it rips her apart. We can't do that to her."

An iron vise clamped over Terry's heart. "She has to see me with another woman."

"She has to know you're romantically involved elsewhere."

Terry had never felt such pain. "Do you have any idea what you're asking?"

His sombre reply would echo in her ears forever.

"Yes."

CHAPTER 21

ERRY WADDED UP HER UNIFORM and tossed it in the general direction of the laundry basket. She wouldn't need it for the next five days. Weeks ago, she had booked off Christmas Eve. The plan had been to spend it cross-country skiing with Jan before they joined Rob for a pre-Christmas feast. Jan and Rob were spending Christmas day with Kate's family, and Terry would be with her family, so tomorrow was to have been their own personal celebration.

She donned a ragged pair of sweatpants and a thick sweater, threw herself back on the bed, and stared at the ceiling. *Guess I'm free tomorrow now.* Their plans hadn't been formally cancelled, but Terry hadn't heard from Jan since they parted after the wedding several days before. *It's not like I've called her either.*

She had picked up Rob's gift for Jan earlier in the week, but before dropping it off, she checked the hospital parking lot for the Spencer van. Once she was sure Jan had gone home for the day, she took the wrapped box in.

Terry covered her eyes with her arm and bitterly recalled writing out the tag for Rob. *For Jan – Forever Love, Rob.* Her hand shook as she wrote out the words he dictated. When she finished, she mumbled an excuse and fled. She hadn't been back since.

Terry pushed off the bed and plodded downstairs to the

kitchen. She put on a pot of coffee, opened the fridge, and eyed the sparse contents. With Michael gone, her eating habits had deteriorated. She grabbed the egg carton, milk, and butter and took them over to the counter. She was poking through the stack of dirty dishes in the sink, trying to find a frying pan when the doorbell rang.

When she answered the door, Jan stood there.

It took everything Terry had not to pull her into an embrace.

"May I come in?"

Terry stepped back and held the door open. Her hands trembled, and she tucked them in her pockets.

Jan entered, hung up her coat, took off her boots, and followed Terry to the living room.

Terry waited for her to take a seat on the couch and chose the chair opposite. "Can I get you some coffee? I just made a fresh pot."

"No, thank you. I was just coming home from the hospital, and I thought I'd stop and see how you were doing."

Terry's gaze drifted to Jan's lips, and her chest felt heavy. "Fine, thanks. How's Rob doing?"

"Much better." Jan's smile didn't reach her eyes. "I get to bring him home tomorrow."

"Good. He'll be home for Christmas, then."

The stilted conversation stuttered to a stop.

Jan shifted and stared at her hands. "I want to apologize for the other night. I was out of line."

Terry's head drooped. "No, it's all right. I mean, you were just saving me from Roy. I know you didn't mean anything by it." *She's not going to buy that. How could she? I know she felt what I did. I know it.* The air was thick with tension. *God, I hate this!*

"Why didn't you bring a date to the wedding?"

Startled, Terry looked up to find Jan studying her. "I...well,

I thought about it actually." She stood, walked to the window, and stared out at the fading daylight. *Time to tell Rob's fairy tale.* "I've been seeing someone recently, and I almost asked her to come."

In the silence that followed her announcement, Terry turned. For a split second, she saw the naked anguish in Jan's eyes.

Jan's shoulders slumped. "Oh? You hadn't mentioned that. Anyone I know?"

The forced lightness in her tone pierced Terry like a blade. She dug her fingernails into her palms. "She's a friend of Lisa's. Her name is Jesse Harrison. She and Lisa work together, and Lisa's been trying to get us together for ages."

The lie had a grain of truth. Lisa had tried to set her up with her friend months ago, insisting they were perfect for each other, but Terry had refused.

"Is it serious?"

Terry almost crumbled at the poorly disguised pain in Jan's voice. "It might be. We get along really well, you know? Actually, one of the reasons I didn't ask her to the wedding was because I didn't want my family and friends getting on my case about my romantic history in front of her. I want to give this relationship a chance to grow without any pressure." Terry couldn't believe how glibly the untruths spilled from her lips.

Jan stood and offered a wan smile. "I hope it works out for you. You deserve someone special in your life."

I have someone special in my life. Agony almost overwhelmed Terry's resolve. She took a step toward Jan but stopped.

Jan fumbled in her purse and withdrew a small, brightly wrapped box. She thrust it at Terry with a trembling hand. "This is from Rob and me. Just something we thought you could use." When Terry made no move to accept it, Jan set it on the couch and began to back up. "I'd better go. I've got to get Rob's things ready to take to the hospital tomorrow. I guess we won't see you until after the holidays, so I hope you have a nice Christmas. Please tell your family we sent our best wishes."

Terry took another step toward her, but Jan shook her head. "No, that's okay. I know my way out."

Terry allowed her a dignified escape without saying a word. She didn't move when the door opened and shut. She didn't move as Jan passed under the streetlight and paused to look back. She didn't move until the van had driven off, and then she moved.

She shot the interior bolt on the front door and turned off the lights in the living room and hallway. She unplugged the phone and returned the eggs, milk, and butter to the fridge. She switched off the coffee pot and turned off the light in the kitchen. She bolted the back door and found her way in the dark to the basement door.

Terry descended the stairs and went to the fridge in the TV room, which Michael had restocked before he left for Toronto. She grabbed a couple of beers and wrenched the top off the first. By the time she crossed to the bookcase full of DVDs, she'd drained one bottle. Tossing it aside, she started on the next as she perused the selections.

She trailed a finger over dusty cases and paused at *Fried Green Tomatoes.* She shook her head. *Cop-out.* She tapped a finger on *Basic Instinct* but passed that by, too. After she took another deep swallow, she seized on *Terminator 2* and managed to pull out *Bound* at the same time.

"Oh, I'll be back for you later, Gina. Right now, Linda and I have a date. Don't be jealous, babe. I've got all the time in the world." Terry tossed another empty bottle in the general direction of the first. "At least as long as the beer holds out."

Terry inserted the DVD and picked up the remote and two more beers. She settled on the couch and slung her feet up on the coffee table. Turning on the TV, she cracked another beer and advanced through the opening sequences. When she reached an image of a leanly muscled woman doing pull-ups on the legs of an upturned bed, she settled back and tipped the bottle to the screen. "You were so wasted on that mutant, muscle-bound cyborg."

———— ◆ ————

"Hello?"

"Jan, it's Emily."

"Oh, hi, Emily. Merry Christmas."

"Merry Christmas to you and Rob, too. Look, I hate to bother you this early..."

"Don't worry about it. We've been up for a while. What can I do for you?"

"I'm not sure. By any chance is Terry at your house?"

There was silence for a moment. "No, I haven't seen her since the night before last. Isn't she there?"

Emily sighed. "No. She was supposed to be here an hour ago. We always have a huge family breakfast and open presents. I've tried calling, and there's no answer. I even sent Jordy over to get her. He said her car's there, but the doors are locked and no one answered the bell."

"Maybe she just slept in?"

"That's not like her. Not on Christmas. Heavens, she's usually the one rousting all of the rest of us out at the crack of dawn. She loves Christmas."

"When I talked to her, she mentioned she's seeing someone new." Jan swallowed hard. "Maybe she spent the night at her place?"

"She is? Well, for heaven's sake. She never told me that. You wouldn't happen to know who it is, would you?"

"It's a friend of Lisa's. I think her name was Jesse something." Jan barely got the words out past the lump in her throat. "I'm sorry, I don't know more than that."

"Thanks, Jan. I'll give Lisa a call and see if I can get a phone number."

"Emily, I... Would you let me know when you find her?"

"Sure. I'll have her give you a call —"

"No! No, don't bother her. Just if...when you find her, I'd really appreciate if *you* 'd let me know, okay?"

Emily was slow to respond. "Okay. I'm sure she just got tied up with a friend or something."

"I'm sure you're right. I'll talk to you later."

"Definitely."

Jan set the receiver back in the cradle. Rob called, so she wiped her eyes and left the room.

———————⟨⟨⟨⟩⟩⟩———————

"Morning." Lisa held out her cup for Robyn to fill.

"Lisa? It's Emily Sanderson."

"Oh, hi, Mrs. Sanderson. Merry Christmas."

"Thank you, and merry Christmas to you and Robyn. Look, is Terry with you by any chance?"

Lisa frowned. "Terry? No, she hasn't been by since last Sunday. Did you try Jan's place?"

"Yes, I just called there, and they haven't seen her for a couple of days either. Listen, Jan told me that Terry's been dating a friend of yours, a Jesse something? Would you have her number?"

"Uh, Jesse Harrison?" She shot Robyn a puzzled glance.

"Jan wasn't sure about the last name, but if she's a friend of yours, she's probably the one. Do you have her number?"

"Why don't you let me give Jesse a call, and I'll call you right back, okay?"

"Would you? Thanks very much, Lisa. This just isn't like Terry, and I'm starting to get worried."

"Sure, no problem. I'll call you right back." Lisa ended the call and looked at Robyn. "Something is very strange. Did Terry or Jesse mention anything to you about getting together?"

Robyn's brow furrowed. "That's crazy. You know as well as I do that Terry's completely hung up on Jan."

"I know, but according to Mrs. Sanderson, Terry told Jan she's seeing Jesse. I'm gonna give Jess a quick call and find out what's going on."

———◈———

Lisa took a deep breath and dialled. *Okay, how do I finesse this?*

"Hello?"

"Hi, Mrs. Sanderson. It's Lisa. I talked to Jesse and…uh, she hasn't seen Terry recently." Lisa frowned as Robyn rolled her eyes.

"Oh. You wouldn't have any ideas where else I might check, would you?" Emily's voice trembled.

Damn, she sounds upset. "No, but Robyn and I are going to her dad's place, and we've got a key to Terry's house. We'll swing by there on the way and check things out. It could be she just slept in or something. We'll give you a call from there, okay?"

"Thanks, Lisa. I really appreciate it. I'm beginning to wonder if I should call the police."

Lisa could tell that Mrs. Sanderson was on the verge of

tears. She hung up and scowled. "Goddamnit. I'm gonna kick Terry's ass."

Robyn grabbed her coat. "Let's find her first, then we can all stand in line to kick butt."

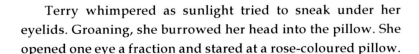

"Jesus Christ. Look at this place." Lisa spun slowly and took in the mess. Empty beer bottles littered the floor. DVDs and empty cases were strewn over every surface. Wads of used tissues were piled by one end of the couch, which had lost its cushions to various corners of the room. A giant bag of chips had been ripped apart and half the contents crushed underfoot in the carpet.

"Do you think she had a party?"

"Without calling us?" Lisa shook her head. "We'd have heard one way or another. No, I have a hunch this is all Terry's doing."

"Then where the hell is she? We've searched this house from top to bottom, and she sure isn't here." Robyn turned to Lisa, dread dawning in her eyes. "You don't think she'd do anything stupid, do you?"

"No. Not Terry. She can be thoughtless at times, but she'd never hurt her family like that. Knowing her, she's shacked up with some bimbo and forgot what day it is."

"You're probably right," Robyn said. "Still, I've never seen her as broken up as she was about Jan."

"I am so going to kill her." Lisa picked up the phone to report in to Mrs. Sanderson.

Terry whimpered as sunlight tried to sneak under her eyelids. Groaning, she burrowed her head into the pillow. She opened one eye a fraction and stared at a rose-coloured pillow.

Pink? Since when do I have pink pillows? She bolted upwards. Her mutinous stomach threatened to unload all over the pink sheets falling in folds around her naked body. *Naked? I'm naked in pink sheets?* She sucked in deep, slow breaths as she examined the room.

It looked vaguely familiar, but for the life of her, she couldn't remember where she was or how she had gotten there. The last thing she remembered clearly was sobbing with Idgie when Ruth died. Everything since then was a jumble of broken images.

I think I ran out of beer. I'm pretty sure I was going to go to Oly's when it opened in the morning, wasn't I? This morning?

Laughter sounded from across the room.

Terry's mouth dropped open.

Marika leaned against the doorframe with a glass of water in her hand.

"Marika?" Terry grabbed for the sheet and pulled it up over her breasts.

Marika smiled and brought her the glass. "You needn't bother. I've seen it all, remember?"

"Uh, no, actually, I don't." Terry drained the water and handed the glass back. Her head a little clearer, she studied Marika. "Did we…um, you know, um…?"

Marika cocked her head. "Did we what? Make cookies? Go shopping? Decorate the Christmas tree?"

Terry flushed. "Forget it."

There was silence for a long moment.

Marika regarded her sadly. "No, I prefer my lovers sober enough to know up from down. I also prefer that they actually want to be with me, and you've made it amply clear that you'd rather sleep with a porcupine."

Terry dropped her head. Remorse flooded her as she

recalled her harsh words in Oly's. She'd felt justified at the time, but she'd been unable to forget the hurt in Marika's eyes when she lashed out. "I'm sorry." She reached for Marika's hand.

Marika flinched but allowed Terry to take her hand.

"I was cruel, and I hurt you. It was churlish of me, and I apologize."

"Maybe it was necessary." Marika's eyes glistened, and she looked away. "I certainly wasn't getting the message until then."

Terry couldn't believe she was having this conversation, but then she couldn't believe she was naked in Marika's bed, wrapped in pink sheets either. *Might as well seize the opportunity.* "You know, I never really figured that out. Why the heck were you so set on me anyway? It wasn't like you couldn't have just about anyone you wanted."

Their gazes met. "I wanted you. I'd never had what I had with you for that month, and I couldn't bear to give it up without a fight."

"But I don't remember one real conversation we had. Hell, we barely knew each other."

"And here I thought we knew each other pretty well." Marika shook her head. "No, you're right. We really didn't know each other at all. How could we, when every time we were together, we were looking for the nearest horizontal surface?"

"Oh, I can remember finding some pretty interesting vertical surfaces, too." They laughed together, and Terry's tension eased. She plucked at the sheet. "Seriously though, how did I end up here?"

"You really don't remember?"

"No, I really don't."

"I'd just left a Christmas gathering with some colleagues when I noticed you stumbling out of Oly's with some pretty, young thing. It was only about two in the afternoon, but you were already blasted. I was too far away to hear what was going on, but you were having a heated argument. She slapped you so hard you almost fell in the snow. She took off, and you went back into the bar."

Terry grimaced and raised a hand to her cheek.

"I was curious, so I slipped inside and took a seat in the back corner. You were so out of it that you wouldn't have noticed if a herd of elephants had marched in. I spent the next couple of hours watching you outdrink everyone in the bar." Marika paused and studied Terry. "What's going on with you? I've seen you have enough to be feeling no pain, but I've never seen you completely out of it."

Terry hugged her knees and buried her head in her arms.

"Anyway, when Megan called closing at five, you were really pissed off and didn't want to leave. She was trying to reason with you, telling you it was Christmas Eve and she wanted to be home with her family — "

Terry's head snapped up. "Christmas Eve? Isn't today Christmas Eve?"

"No, today's Christmas."

"Shit! What time is it?" Terry scrambled out of bed.

Marika glanced at her watch. "Eleven o'clock."

"Oh, God! I'm so screwed." Terry spun around and looked for her clothes.

Marika's nose wrinkled. "They're in the dryer. You puked all over them last night, not to mention my carpet and my cat, too."

Terry shot Marika an apologetic glance and scrambled for the bedside phone. Hastily, she dialled home. "I'm sorry, Mom." She winced. "Yeah, I know. I'm an irresponsible idiot. I'm really, really sorry. Mom…Mom…MOTHER!" It came at the cost of a split cranium, but at least Emily stopped chewing her out long enough for Terry to get a word in edgewise. "Go ahead and open the presents without me. I'm at a friend's place, and I'll be over later this afternoon, all right?"

After several more abject apologies, Terry hung up. She sank down on the edge of the bed and cradled her aching head in her hands.

Marika held out a faded pink robe. "Here, try this. Not that I mind the view."

Terry blushed and accepted the robe. "What's with you and all this pink?"

"I like it. What can I say? It's been my favourite colour for as long as I can remember." Marika shrugged. "Anyway, if you feel up to it, come to the kitchen. You look like you could use toast and coffee."

Terry stood and trailed Marika from the room. "Coffee, yes, but I'm not so sure about anything else."

Marika glanced over her shoulder. "I doubt you've had anything but liquid sustenance for quite a while. You probably should start on something easy like toast, though I can heat up some soup if you'd like."

Terry stared at Marika as she followed her down the hall. *I don't think I'd be half as nice if our positions were reversed.*

After a light brunch, they took their coffee to the living room. A pillow and blanket were stacked on one end of the couch. *She must've slept out here last night. Damn, giving up your bed to an antagonistic drunk... There's more to her than meets the eye.*

They took seats on either end of the couch. A grey and white cat stalked into the room and stopped. He stared at Terry, and his tail swished angrily. He marched past her and jumped up on Marika's lap.

Marika stroked the cat as he stretched and settled onto her legs. "I don't think the Spookmeister likes you very much."

Terry winced. "Did I really…uh, you know?"

"Puke all over him? Oh yes. Poor Spooky scrambled for cover, but he wasn't fast enough. I had to bathe him even before I bathed you. And he'd been thinking you made such a nice cushion, too."

Terry covered her eyes. "God, I cannot believe I did that." She peeked through her fingers. Marika was smiling, her demeanour warm and relaxed. "I'm really sorry. I mean, for everything."

"Spooky will survive, and as for rescuing you…" Marika focused on the cat. "It's not the first time I've dragged a drunk home and dried her out."

"No?" Marika never volunteered anything about her past, but then, Terry had never asked either.

"No. I started bringing my mother home from the bars when I was twelve." Marika's tone was flat, as if all emotion had been excised many years ago.

Terry didn't know what to say, and Marika clearly didn't want to go any further down memory lane. She glanced around. "No Christmas tree this year?"

"No Christmas tree any year. I may not be able to avoid the season outside my home, but I don't have to import it in here." Marika shot her a wry look. "I guess that sounds rather Scrooge-like, doesn't it?"

"A little. Any particular reason you don't like the season?"

"What's to like?"

The cryptic answer shook Terry, who loved everything associated with Christmas. "Family, food, presents…what's not to like?"

Marika concentrated on stroking Spooky and said nothing.

Terry looked at her surroundings. Elegantly decorated, the

room was bare of any hint of the season, but more tellingly, it was devoid of any photographs of anyone. "You don't see your family at Christmas, do you?"

Marika's eyes were bleak. "I don't see my family at any time. I've been persona non grata since they found me in bed with the maid when I was sixteen."

"I'm so sorry."

Terry's soft words were met by a shrug. "It doesn't matter. Dad and his wife made sure I was well educated...in boarding schools as far away from the family as possible. Dad hired the shrinks who tried to cure me of my deviance, and when I failed to rehabilitate, paid my way through law school. He was quite generous, actually. I just had to stay far away from him and his new family."

Terry edged closer on the couch. "God, that sucks."

"There are worse things than being a remittance woman."

Spooky spat at Terry, and Marika tried to soothe him. When Terry rested a hand on Marika's shoulder, Spooky jumped off and disappeared around a corner.

"Do you think he'll ever forgive me?" Terry asked with amusement.

"Bribe him with catnip. The boy can be bought."

Terry grinned and rubbed Marika's thin shoulder. Then she sat bolt upright. "You know what? You are going to have a proper Christmas dinner this year."

Marika's expression turned to alarm. "Oh no, I couldn't."

"Yes, you could. Mom always has space for one more at her table, and with Duncan and Karen gone on their honeymoon there'll be lots of room."

"No, thank you. I usually have Christmas dinner with some friends, but they went south for a winter vacation this year. I'll be fine on my own." Marika edged away. "Your family doesn't like me, and I don't want to make anyone uncomfortable."

"They don't know you. Besides, I like you, and I'm taking you home for dinner."

"You don't owe me anything, Terry."

"Yes, I do, but that's not what this is about. I know our relationship has been kind of—"

"Unconventional? Irritating? Aggravating?" Marika ducked her head. "That's my fault, and I do want to apologize."

"No, you can't take all the responsibility," Terry said. "I handled things poorly, and I'd give anything to take back what I said to you in Oly's. Do you think we can forget that night and try to begin again as friends?"

Marika studied her, then slowly nodded. "If you like."

"I do. And you can start by accepting my invitation for Christmas dinner, okay?"

"I don't know... I really don't think I'd be welcome. I'm fine here, honest. I have some work to do, and I promised Spooky extra tuna for his dinner."

"You can feed him when you get home. Trust me, Mom won't mind in the least." *You could've walked away and you didn't. I do owe you... my friend.* Terry grinned. "Besides, if you're there, I'm a whole lot less likely to get chewed apart for missing this morning."

"Are you sure?"

"I am."

Marika took a deep breath. "Then I accept, and thank you."

"Hello?"

"Hi, Jan. It's Emily again. Good news, the prodigal daughter called in. She wasn't with Jesse, but she stayed overnight with a friend and slept in. She'll be over for dinner."

Relief flooded through Jan. "That's great, Em. I'm glad she's all right."

"Well, she may be missing a few strips of skin right about now." They both laughed. "So what time are you heading down to Kate's?"

"Actually, our Christmas will be delayed a few days. My brother-in-law and nephew both came down with the flu yesterday, but we'll have our celebration once John and Kevin are healthy again."

"Oh, that's too bad. Well then, you and Rob must come and have dinner with us."

"That's awfully nice of you, but I don't want to impose at this short notice."

"Oh pish. You two are virtually part of the family, and I'd have invited you in the first place if I hadn't known you were going to Kate's for dinner. I'm not taking no for an answer."

Jan chuckled. "All right, if you're sure—?"

"It's settled," Emily said. "We'll eat about six, but you come over whenever you're ready."

CHAPTER 22

DEEP IN THOUGHT, JAN DIDN'T hear her name called until Jordy's voice penetrated her fog. Startled, she looked up. "Sorry, what were you saying?"

Jordy was being overrun by two giggling toddlers. One of the twins tackled him around the neck while her sister tried to scramble up his body. Laughing, he wrapped his arms around the two and dangled them over his shoulders. Amidst squeals of glee, he nodded his head at Rob. "I think your husband wants more coffee. I'd get it, but I'm a little tied up at the moment."

Embarrassed to be caught woolgathering, Jan turned to Rob, who regarded her with mild reproach. "Did you want more coffee, love?"

"Yes, please."

Jan stood and took the cup from his hands. She glanced around the room. Most of the Sanderson clan was gathered around a large, brightly decorated Christmas tree. The opened boxes and scraps of wrapping paper littering the floor testified to the orgy of gift giving that had gone on earlier. "Can I get anyone else some while I'm up?"

Sprawled in an easy chair flanking the tree, Matt held out his cup. "If you wouldn't mind, I'll take another."

Jan picked her way across the room between bodies and gifts. Stepping over an excited toddler who was trying to scuttle around to launch a rear attack on Jordy, Jan couldn't help smiling. Despite her less-than-festive mood, this was her idea of Christmas, bubbling over with family, exuberance, and cheerful noise.

She had been unsure about accepting Emily's invitation to dinner, uncertain of how she would deal with seeing Terry. Rob's recent sojourn in the hospital would've been a reasonable excuse to decline, but she didn't want to deny him a chance at a boisterous family Christmas. Nor did she want to raise any questions over her own reluctance to attend.

Relieved that Terry wasn't already there when they'd arrived an hour ago, she nevertheless caught herself listening for her entrance.

Gord raised a hand. "Hey, Jan, could you ask Em when she wants me to have the punch ready?"

Jan nodded and took the cups to the kitchen. She was halfway down the hall leading to the kitchen when the rear door opened. She froze.

"Hi, Mom. I hope you don't mind setting an extra place. I brought a friend home for dinner."

Jan's heart sank. *Stop being so foolish. You were going to meet the mysterious Jesse sooner or later.*

"Hello, Marika. I haven't seen you around in a while." Emily's voice was cool.

Jan blinked. *Marika? What happened to Jesse?*

"Thank you for letting me join all of you, Mrs. Sanderson. I hope I'm not imposing."

"Of course you're not imposing." There was a hint of a challenge in Terry's voice. "Mom always has room for one more at her table...don't you, Mom?"

"Yes. There's always room for more. Now if you'll excuse me, I have some things to bring up from the basement."

Whatever Emily's opinion on the unexpected guest, she was obviously not about to violate her own standards of hospitality.

Jan drew a deep breath and prepared to make her presence known but stopped again.

"I don't think this is a good idea," Marika said. "Your mom really doesn't like me. Maybe I should just go home."

"No, I told you. I like you, and that's all that counts."

"But I don't want to make anyone uncomfortable. I really don't mind. Spooky and I are used to dining alone together."

"No way. I'm not letting you out of here until you're stuffed with turkey and Christmas pudding." Terry's voice took on a teasing note. "Besides, after last night, I owe you one."

Their shared laughter cut through Jan like a blade. She closed her eyes and fought the urge to run down the hall and out of the house. *I can't face her. I can't face them.* She took a step backwards.

"Hey, Jan. What's taking so long? Are you picking the coffee beans?"

Jordy's call left Jan little choice, so she forced herself to advance into the kitchen.

Terry was lifting a long coat off the shoulders of the tall, slender woman Jan remembered from months earlier at Chapters. *She doesn't exactly have a face you forget.* Summoning every bit of her resolve, she nodded. "Merry Christmas, Terry. It's nice to see you."

Terry stopped dead with the coat halfway down Marika's arms.

Jan almost smiled at the stunned expression on Terry's face. She moved to the coffee maker and filled the two cups.

Terry cleared her throat. "Umm, hi. I thought you were going to Kate's for Christmas."

Jan set the pot back and turned. "We were, but unfortunately, Kevin and John came down with the flu, so your mother was kind enough to invite us here."

"Oh...uh, that's good. I mean not that they're sick or anything—"

Jan had never seen Terry so at a loss.

Terry still hadn't moved, and Marika glanced at her before she stepped forward so the coat slid off her arms. Then she crossed to offer her hand. "Hi, I don't think we've met. My name is Marika Havers. I'm a friend of Terry's."

Jan shook her hand. "Hello, Marika. Jan Spencer. We actually did meet once at Chapters."

"Oh, of course. Please forgive my memory."

"No problem."

Jan picked up the cups and returned to the living room. She set one coffee beside Rob and carried the other to Matt.

"Thanks, Jan." Matt reached to take it, then stopped and stared past her.

Jan glanced over her shoulder.

Terry led Marika into the room by the hand.

Jan looked back at Matt and was surprised to see anger in his eyes, but when Terry made introductions, he stood and extended his hand.

By the time Terry worked her way around the room, Jan had resumed her seat beside Rob and held the cup for him to sip from.

Terry led Marika over to them. "Marika, you've met Jan, and this is Jan's husband, Rob. Rob, this is a friend of mine, Marika Havers."

Marika automatically extended her hand, then flushed.

Rob smiled at her. "Nice to meet you. I'm glad you're joining us for dinner."

Marika returned his smile and pressed his hand in

greeting. "It was kind of spur of the moment, but Terry talked me into it."

Terry slid an arm around Marika's waist as they walked away.

Jan focused on Rob's cup and tried to ignore the sight of Terry and Marika sitting closely on the couch. At a peal of laughter, she glanced up to see Terry slip an arm around Marika's shoulders as she grinned at her.

Jan set the almost empty cup on the table. "I'm going to go give Emily a hand." She escaped to the kitchen where Emily welcomed her assistance.

When everyone was summoned to the table, Jan was dismayed to find that she and Rob were right across from Terry and Marika. She divided her attention between feeding Rob to her right and talking to Alex on her left.

"So, Jan, are you and Terry going to ski that cross-country route I was telling you about in K-country?" Gord asked. "It'd take you about four hours, but it's well worth it for the view alone."

Jan glanced across the table.

Terry watched her.

Turning to Gord, Jan forced a smile. "Actually, I'll be cancelling my afternoons off for a few months. With Rob just out of the hospital, I'd rather not take a chance."

Gord nodded. "You can always hike that trail in the summer, and it's just as beautiful. Helluva lot warmer, too."

Rob's eyebrows rose almost to his hairline, but before he could protest, Jan pressed a forkful of turkey to his mouth. He glared at her but accepted the offering. They would discuss this later, but although the words had been spontaneous, she had no intention of backing away from them.

The buzz of conversation swept around Jan. She ignored

it and stoically fed Rob and herself. Emily's festive dinner was like ashes in her mouth, but she ate enough to deter any attention before she pushed her plate aside.

By the end of the meal, Jan had memorized the designs on the china, the silverware, and Rob's new Christmas sweater. She even counted the drips of wax down the side of the red candle in front of her. Since she could feel Terry's gaze on her, she refused to look beyond that candle.

Jan had never heard a sweeter sound than Emily asking for volunteers to clear the table so she could bring out coffee and dessert. She leaped to her feet and began gathering dishes to take to the kitchen. She was starting back for her second load before Emily entered the kitchen with her first.

Emily laid a hand on her arm. "Is everything all right, Jan? You were awfully quiet tonight."

"Actually, Em, I have a killer headache. Would you mind very much if Rob and I passed on dessert?"

"Of course not, dear. How about I wrap some up for you to take home, and you can enjoy it later when you're feeling better. Can I get you Tylenol or something?"

"No, that's all right. I think I'll just borrow your washroom, and we'll head out."

Jordy and Terry entered with more dishes.

"Diane's changing the twins, so you'd better go downstairs," Jordy said.

"Thanks." Jan avoided eye contact with Terry, who was stacking dishes on the counter. Once safely in the refuge of the basement washroom, her rigid self-control slipped. She clenched the sink with both hands and closed her eyes.

What did you think was going to happen, you idiot? You're the one acting like an ass. You have no claim on her.

She tormented herself imagining Terry and Marika in a

heated embrace until her eyes flew open and she stared at her reflection. "Get a grip. You're going to make a complete fool of yourself if you don't pull it together."

Jan took several long, deep breaths, turned on the cold water, and splashed some over her face. She spent a few more minutes trying to find an elusive calm, then left the room.

Terry leaned against the wall, waiting.

Jan began to walk by.

Terry stepped in front and took her arm.

Jan stared at the floor and refused to look up.

"Jan?"

The sadness in Terry's voice was unmistakable, but a surge of anger rose within. Her head snapped up. "So what happened to Jesse? I thought she was supposed to be the new love of your life. Did you ditch her to sleep with Marika? That must have impressed the hell out of Jesse."

Terry blanched and dropped her hand from Jan's arm.

My God, what did I say? Jan reached for her.

Terry stepped back. "Yeah, well you know me. Why have just one woman in my bed when I can have a dozen. After all, I've got a reputation to uphold, and everyone knows I'll sleep with anything in skirts."

Before Jan could apologize, Terry stepped around her, entered the washroom, and slammed the door shut.

Bile rose in Jan's throat, and acid tears flooded her eyes. Stumbling back, she leaned against the wall. She struggled to bring herself under control, cruelly pinching her forearm in the hopes that the physical pain would alleviate her mental torment. She stood for long moments in the silent hall, fighting to regain enough equilibrium to go upstairs, retrieve Rob, and escape from this house.

When she finally went upstairs, Emily had already gotten

Rob ready to go. He had his long winter cape wrapped around him and a woollen toque pulled over his ears. He was talking with Emily in the hall by the door as they waited. Neither of them commented when Jan reached them. She hoped that the dim hallway lighting prevented them from seeing the ravages tears had wrought on her face.

Jan put on her coat and boots and embraced Emily. "Thanks again for having us over. It was wonderful as always."

Emily hugged her back. "Our pleasure. Gord, Alex, Jordy... Rob needs a hand."

The men clattered out to the hall and began their well-established routine. Jordy and Alex each took a wheel, and Gord steadied the handles as they took Rob out into the cold, down the steps, and to the van.

Emily picked a foil-wrapped parcel off the side table and pressed it into Jan's hands. "Here, I wrapped up some dessert for you. You take care of yourself, you hear? And if you need us for anything at all, just call. One of us can be there within ten minutes."

Jan's eyes filled with tears again. She choked out her thanks and fled down the stairs.

The ride home was quiet. Jan expected Rob to bring up the subject of her time off, but mercifully he held off.

It was only once they were home and she knelt at his feet to replace his shoes with slippers that he broached the subject.

"You know I'm fine now, love. I don't want you giving up your afternoons off."

Jan didn't look up at him. "I've already decided. I'll contact the agency next week."

"Stop that. You know you need that time." Rob's voice was weak but insistent. "I'm not going to let you give it up."

The unfamiliar anger swept over Jan again, and she stood, one of his shoes still in her hand. "You're not going to let me?"

"Aw, you know what I mean, Jannie. I just don't want—"

"I don't give a damn what you want. It's my afternoon, and if I say I'm not taking it, then I'm not taking it."

"For crying out loud! What the hell has gotten into you?"

The exasperation on Rob's face heightened Jan's anger. She threw the shoe at the couch and stalked out of the room.

"Jan...Jan, please. I'm sorry. Come back."

For the first time in her life, Jan ignored him. She slammed the bedroom door and threw herself down on the bed. *God, what's wrong with me?* After a few minutes, the anger subsided, though it didn't vanish. It tickled at the edge of her mind and tightened her chest.

Finally, she pushed herself off the bed and returned to Rob. Without a word, she finished putting his slippers on, emptied his catheter bag, and transferred him to his easy chair.

Rob was equally quiet until he was settled in his chair. "I really like seeing Donny, you know? I'll miss him if you give up your afternoons."

Jan was seized with guilt. *I didn't think of that.* She picked up Rob's shoe from the couch and stared at it. Finally, she turned to Rob. He was watching her with wary and worried eyes. "It's hard to have much of a fight when I can't even stomp out of the house and leave you to stew."

Rob gave her a tentative smile. "Yeah, it's not like you can even kick me out of bed to sleep on the couch."

"Don't tempt me." They smiled at each other. They rarely argued, and when they did, the disputes never lasted long.

Jan crossed to kneel at his side. "What if I just change Donny back to Thursday afternoons again?"

Rob's brow furrowed.

Jan laid her fingers over his mouth. "It's not negotiable."

He sighed and nodded.

"How about coffee and Emily's dessert? Think you have any room after all that turkey?"

"I guess."

Terry stared out the window at the dark alley.

Marika started her car and let it idle, warming up the engine. "So that was Jan."

Terry swivelled her head. "How did—?"

"Between puking on my cat and passing out, all you talked about last night was Jan. She wasn't at all what I thought she'd be."

"What did you think she'd be?"

"Aside from the fact she doesn't literally walk on water, she's not exactly your usual type, is she? But maybe that's the whole point, isn't it? It is rather ironic, though. All the women that have tried to pin you down, and you've fallen head over heels with someone who's unavailable."

Terry winced and turned away.

"I'm sorry. That was uncalled for, and I apologize."

They sat quietly and listened to the engine warm up.

Terry tried to focus on something...anything, except how this evening had strained her aching heart. From the moment Jan entered the kitchen, she'd wanted to run away. Only her promise to Marika and the awareness that she would never be able to explain a retreat to her mother kept her in the house.

I hope my performance met Rob's requirements. Terry had forced herself to be openly affectionate with Marika even as she stung from Jan's refusal to look at her.

When Jan left the room, she stared at Rob, half-expecting a look of triumph. Instead his eyes held a profound sadness.

Terry hadn't planned to confront her, but when Jan indicated her intention to give up their afternoons together, Terry had to talk to her. *And a helluva lot of good that did.* She shuddered at the memory of Jan's accusatory words. "Is the car warm enough to go yet?"

Marika put the car in gear and pulled away. When they reached Terry's house, she stopped at the curb and shifted into neutral as she left the car running.

Terry undid her seat belt and glanced over. Marika stared out the front window. "Would you like to come in for a bit?"

Marika met her gaze and for a moment Terry thought she would accept the invitation.

"No, thank you. I think I'll go home. May I have a rain check?"

Terry nodded. *What exactly am I issuing a rain check for?*

"I really appreciated tonight. I enjoyed dinner with your family."

"Even if I took you into the lion's den?"

"It wasn't that bad. Your mom and Jordy aren't too impressed with me, but everyone else was very nice." Marika smiled. "The twins certainly are adorable."

"They're quite the little dynamos now." Terry reached out to caress Marika's cheek. "I'm glad you came, too." She leaned in to kiss her.

Marika met her halfway, and they lingered over a gentle kiss before pulling back to stare at each other.

Marika shook her head. "No fireworks anymore, are there?"

"I'm sorry."

"It's all right. Your mind…and heart are elsewhere. I can accept that." Marika shifted into gear. "This bus is leaving the station. You'd better hop out."

Terry opened the door. "May I give you a call sometime?"

"If you'd like to. Maybe we can grab a coffee together."

"That would be great." Terry swung her legs out of the car and stood up. She watched Marika's car disappear down the street before turning and going up her walkway.

CHAPTER 23

S NOW FELL STEADILY FROM LEADEN skies. Rob gazed at them and longed for spring. Years ago, he enjoyed the long northern winters, but that was when he'd been able to participate in his beloved sports. *At least the opening of spring training is only weeks away.*

Familiar theme music sounded, and he glanced back to the television. The fashion news had started. He was about to call Jan to change the channel when Terry turned into their walkway.

Jan refused to come out to the living room when Terry delivered the mail. It had taken Rob a couple of weeks into the new year before he noticed that she absented herself every morning around the same time. Exasperated, he had tried calling her for assistance as soon as he saw Terry coming to their door, but Jan put him off until Terry moved on to the next house. Finally, when Jan snapped at him and demanded to know if she was allowed any time at all for herself, he'd given up.

Why does she even bother hiding? It's not like Terry ever looks up from her mail. Rob missed the way Terry used to glance in their window and give the grin and wave that had once been a daily occurrence.

He leaned his head back and sighed. *How did it go so wrong, so fast?* Sure he had won…Jan was at his side and Terry was no longer a threat to his security, but it was a pyrrhic victory. His affectionate, amiable wife had been replaced by a tense, unhappy woman who rarely smiled. In the long weeks since Christmas, he couldn't remember one time she'd laughed, and he missed their easy banter.

His gaze drifted over to the laptop sitting on the footstool in front of Jan's rocking chair, and he scowled. It had been a much appreciated gift, but he had come to hate the thing. Jan had taken to it like a duck to water and spent hours online, reading. Even as she sat only a few feet away from him, she was miles away. Hardly chatty at the best of times, she had become monosyllabic. She never neglected him, but even when she tended to his needs, her mind was elsewhere. The worst of it was, he couldn't bring himself to protest since it seemed to be the only thing that brought her any kind of peace these days.

Frustrated, Rob banged his head against his chair. He wanted to talk to Terry, but there had been no opportunity since Christmas dinner. She never came to the house anymore, nor did she call. Emily's repeated invitations to dinner had been politely declined by Jan without any consultation with him. When he finally had enough and called her on shutting out their friends, she fixed him with cool eyes and said that she didn't feel like going out. When he tried to discuss it further, she left the room without another word.

Rob growled softly, agitated that she could so easily walk away from a confrontation. He glared down at the useless body that imprisoned him, aware of the irony of his situation. His helplessness ensured Jan's continued presence in his life, even as it rendered him impotent to take any measures to ease their current unhappy stasis. He couldn't even pick up a phone and order flowers to lift her mood.

He also couldn't broach the underlying cause of her misery. She didn't know that he was aware of her feelings for Terry. Rob was afraid to acknowledge those feelings out loud for fear it would force his wife to do something he would regret.

At least Jordy still dropped by Thursdays after school when Donny was there. Donny had served in the British Army before immigrating to Canada, and Jordy sat spellbound while they regaled him with war stories.

Rob had diplomatically questioned him about Terry's absence, but Jordy was puzzled and embarrassed by his sister's behaviour. He had gotten so upset about it that Rob refrained from further inquiries.

He watched Terry make her way down their sidewalk and up the street. His gaze drifted upwards to the sullen grey sky, and he longed again for an end to this interminable winter.

In the master bedroom, a solitary figure pushed away from the corner that afforded her a view through snow-laden branches of a winter-bare tree to the walkway leading to their front door.

Terry stepped into the welcome warmth of the old house and shrugged out of her heavy parka. *Some hot chocolate, I think. It was a damned cold wind today.* In the kitchen she filled the kettle and set it on the stove to boil.

Michael's Pathfinder pulled into the alley, and Terry took down a second mug. He trudged through the new snow in the backyard as she mixed the chocolate powder with cream. She opened the cupboard and pulled out a depleted bag of mini-marshmallows just as Michael clattered into the house.

"Hi, Michael."

"Hey, Ter. I see the snow did not stay you from the swift completion of your appointed rounds."

"Of course not. Now are you going to stand there dripping, or are you going to come share some hot chocolate with me?"

"Yum, hot chocolate. With marshmallows?"

"Is there any other way?"

"No." Michael beamed as he watched Terry's preparations. "Guess what."

Terry glanced at him. "Well, judging by that expression, I'd guess that you heard from a certain oil rigger."

Michael did a couple of shuffle steps and wrapped his arms around Terry. "He called this morning. Some very important whatzit on the rig broke down, and they've had to shut down operations for a week. He'll be here tomorrow."

"That's great. It's been quite a while since you last saw him."

"Thirty-seven days, six hours, and —" Michael glanced at his watch. "Nine minutes...but who's counting? Oh yeah, don't come knockin' when the basement's rockin'!" He began to dance around the kitchen, singing. "Gimme, gimme good lovin'." Then he stopped short and stared at Terry.

Terry looked away, her eyes moist.

Michael's exuberance vanished. "Oh shit, I'm sorry. I'm such an idiot. I just didn't think." He wrapped his arms around her waist and hugged her.

Terry patted his arms with one hand and wiped at her eyes with the other. "It's all right. I'm happy for you, really. Randy is a terrific guy, and you two deserve each other."

Michael took her hand and led her to the table. He retrieved the mugs and joined her. "I need you to listen to me now. I'm worried about you. We're all worried about you. You cannot go on like this much longer. You're barely eating enough to keep a bird alive. I hear you up at all hours of the night, and I can't remember the last time you voluntarily left the house to come out with us."

"I went to Oly's with you guys just last week."

Michael cupped her hands in his. "I practically had to use a cattle prod to get you there, and then you had one drink with Lisa and Robyn and left. I wish I'd been here for you at Christmas—"

"Nothing you could've done anyways."

"Maybe not, but I still wish I'd been here. I know how hard it was for you and what an impossible situation you've ended up in. Look, I know better than to expect you'll fall out of love with Jan just because you haven't seen her in over a month, but I think you need a distraction. Rather than moping around here, why don't you use your ticket and take a holiday for a couple of weeks? Go somewhere the sun is hot, the margaritas are cold, and the beaches are full of beautiful women."

Terry considered his suggestion. Michael's Christmas present to his roommates had been an open airline return ticket to anywhere in North America. Claire had used hers to go home to Quebec for Christmas, but Terry had been undecided. Right now, a Mexican beach sounded very appealing. She managed a half-smile. "You just want to get rid of me so you can get down with Randy."

Michael smiled. "Well, there is that, too. Really, though, I think it would do you a world of good, and maybe you'd come back with some perspective on the whole mess."

"Maybe. Let me think about it for a bit."

Michael squeezed her hands, picked up his mug, and drained half of it in one swallow.

Terry poked at the melting marshmallows bobbing at the top of the mug and then followed Michael's lead. The hot, sweet liquid warmed her belly, and she closed her eyes. She had been cold for too long.

Half an hour later, Terry lay on her bed while she contemplated white sand and crystal blue waters.

The front doorbell rang, but she ignored it. Michael would take care of it.

Maybe I should go. She desperately wanted to be distracted from the constant ache of Jan's absence from her life. *Michael's right. I've pretty much gone into hibernation since Christmas.* She had even stopped going to her parents' house for Sunday dinner, ducking her mother's phone calls and putting off Jordy when he dropped by the house.

Perpetually restless these days, Terry was unable to focus on anything. Her novel sat, unedited and untouched since before Christmas. Many nights found her wandering aimlessly around the house from the basement to the kitchen to the garret.

The only solace she found was in Marika's company. Her roommates and old friends were concerned about her, and because she saw no possible resolution to her dilemma, she was uneasy in their presence. But Marika made no demands. She never questioned Terry's unannounced appearances at her door and was uncritical of the way she drifted through the days.

Marika never brought up Jan and never asked Terry for more than she was willing to give. She was open to resuming their sexual relationship, but Terry was content with their routine of occasional movies, dinners, or quiet evenings at her condo. *I wonder if Marika would be interested in heading south with me for a holiday.*

The bedroom door flew open, and Matt stood there, glaring.

He'd never come to her house before. Terry gaped at him. "What the hell?"

"You are such a jerk!" Matt stalked over to her bed.

"Why? What did I do?" Terry sat up.

"You are the most selfish, thoughtless, inconsiderate excuse for a daughter I've ever had the misfortune to meet." Matt paused for a breath.

Terry scowled. "What the fuck are you talking about? What exactly do you think I've done?"

Matt was flushed with fury, and he bristled as he poked Terry's shoulder with his finger. "I just dropped by home, and Mom's eyes were all red. She wouldn't admit it, but I know she'd been crying."

Terry batted his hand away. "Mom was crying? Why? What's wrong?"

"You're what's wrong."

"Me? I didn't do anything."

"That's right. You didn't do anything. You didn't come over. You didn't call. Mom hasn't heard from you since New Year's, and she's frantic with worry, but do you care? You don't even have enough consideration to pick up the phone once in a while."

Terry's shoulders slumped. "Well, it's not like she doesn't know where I live."

Matt gave no quarter. "You're such an idiot. Mom's doing what she's always done, giving us our space to work things out. You know you have a standing invitation to dinner. She's left messages for you to remind you of that. She won't intrude where she doesn't feel welcome, and you've made damned sure she feels unwelcome in your life."

Terry squirmed, unable to counter Matt's accusations.

"You know, the first couple of weeks you didn't come for Sunday dinner, she made excuses for you. The last few weeks, she hasn't even tried, but I've seen her watching out the kitchen window, looking up every time a car drives down the alley. Every week, she sets a place for you, and every week, she clears it away unused."

Terry had never felt as ashamed as she did at that moment. "I'm sorry."

"Don't tell me, tell Mom." Matt sank down in the chair beside the bed, stretched out one long leg, and kicked Terry's ankle. "Why'd you do it, anyways?"

"Because I'm an inconsiderate jerk."

Matt snorted. "Yeah, well that's a given." He no longer looked as if he was considering sisterly evisceration as an option.

They sat in silence for a long moment.

"Did Mom ever say why she was worried?"

"No, but it doesn't take an Einstein to figure things out."

Terry glanced at him and looked away.

"We were all at the wedding. We're not blind. Well, except maybe for Jordy, but that boy can't get past the foolish notion that you can do no wrong, though I gotta tell you, even he's more than a little pissed at you right now."

Terry winced. She'd brushed Jordy off several times in the last month. Given how he idolized Rob, she hadn't wanted any of this to touch him. *God, I've handled him badly.* Her heart sank. *What haven't I handled badly?*

Matt leaned forward with his elbows on his knees. "You're in a pickle, but just because you've screwed things up don't mean you have the right to make Mom unhappy. She never told you to go and fall in love with a married woman. I dunno how you're going to work things out, and I'm the last person in the world to offer advice on your love life, but I can tell you that shutting out your family is fucking stupid. Shit, you've been on a goddamned roller coaster ever since you met her, and if you don't shape up soon, the whole family is going to disown you."

Terry's mouth fell open. She'd been ducking Emily because of her mother's perceptiveness but had no idea the rest of her family was aware of what was going on. She stared at Matt.

He leaned back in his chair and studied her in return.

As they sat in silence, Terry's mind reeled. She hated the estrangement from her family but had been afraid they would see her distress and force her to confront it before she was ready. But not only had she been completely transparent, she'd upset everyone she loved. *Damn it. I'm such a bloody idiot.* "I kind of blew it, didn't I?"

"Royally."

Terry shook her head. She had wallowed long enough. "I'll be at dinner this Sunday."

He grunted. "And you'll call Mom to tell her?"

"Yes, I'll give her a call right away."

Matt was halfway to the door before he stopped and turned to stare at her. "I don't get it, you know."

Terry cocked her head. "What? You don't get what?"

"Christmas Day. Her."

"It wasn't like that. Marika's just a friend who didn't have any place to go for Christmas dinner so I brought her home with me."

"That wasn't how you behaved. You hurt Jan, you know."

Terry's eyes widened. "I…she…we can't… Jesus, Matt, she's married." For a second, she thought she saw a flash of sympathy in Matt's eyes.

"Do you know what I'd give for one woman to look at me the way Jan looked at you the night of the wedding?"

Terry's jaw dropped again as Matt left.

Michael entered the room and glanced back at Matt. "Are you okay? I heard all the shouting and wasn't sure whether I should grab the bat and come up here or not."

"No, everything's fine."

"Good. Well, if he gives you any trouble, you just let me know."

Terry grinned. "Michael, my love, he'd take you apart limb from limb if you tried anything."

"Tried anything?" Michael brushed an imaginary piece of lint from an impeccable sleeve. "Don't be silly. I'd just tell Randy on him."

Terry burst into laughter, tugged Michael down on the bed, and hit him over the head with a pillow.

"God, it's good to hear that. Do you have any idea how long it's been since you laughed?"

Terry rolled on her back and sighed. "Too long?"

"Much, much too long."

"I'm sorry. I've been a pain in the ass to live with."

Michael sobered. "You've been hurting. I know that. I just don't want to see you hurt anymore. I really think you should go away for a while."

"I've got a better idea. What's today?"

"Thursday, why?"

Terry smiled and jumped to her feet. "Because I'm going to do something I should have done weeks ago, that's why. This has gone on long enough. One way or another, it has to end." She checked her watch. "Not much time."

Michael sat up. "Not much time for what? What's going on?"

Terry grabbed her wallet off her desk and planted a quick kiss on Michael's forehead. "I have to go. If Mom calls, tell her I'll call her back tonight. But first I have to find Jan and set things right…if I can."

She ran out of the room and took the stairs two at a time. Within moments, she was in the car, considering her options. *Where would she go? Knowing her, somewhere with books, but where?* She ran through the possibilities but discarded the small independent bookstores they had frequented downtown. Jan loved the quirky old purple house that was home to the Women's Bookstore, but given the day's bad weather, she would probably have opted to stay closer to home.

Aware that Jan's afternoon off was almost over, Terry drove as quickly as roads and traffic permitted to the Chapters where they had gone for their first outing, but the distinctive burgundy van wasn't there. *Damn!*

Wasting no time, Terry drove to the library, but there was no sign of the van there either.

She turned north and headed for her last hope. With a sigh of relief, she spotted the van outside another Chapters. She wheeled into a space and was out of her car before the engine had shuddered to a stop.

Terry was seized by fear. *What if she doesn't want to see me? What if she's still mad at me? What if she hates me? What if – ?* Her steps slowed as her mind painted all sorts of dismal scenarios, all of which involved Jan rejecting her. She shook her head. *I have to know. One way or another, I have to know.*

She pushed through the doors and began a search. Starting on one side of the large store, she methodically checked every aisle and corner. She reached the extensive shelves of computer literature when she finally saw her. Jan sat in an armchair by the mystery section.

Terry stopped, and her gaze devoured Jan. Her heart pounded, her hands shook, and her breath came in short, rapid pulses. She moved closer and tried not to attract attention. She feared Jan would hear her knees rattling together from two aisles away.

She studied Jan's face and frowned. Her features were sharper and more drawn than the last time she had seen her. Even through her reading glasses, shadows around her eyes were visible.

Jan's gaze drifted off her book and into space. Slowly, she turned her head in Terry's direction.

Terry tensed but remained still. *Crunch time.*

Jan took off her glasses and stared at her.

Terry held her breath, convinced as the seconds ticked by in an eternity that Jan would ignore her. Her heart began to fracture.

Then Jan smiled.

Terry crossed the distance between them in an instant and sank to one knee in front of her.

Jan caressed her cheek.

Terry kissed Jan's palm.

A tear ran down Jan's cheek.

With absolute tenderness, Terry wiped the wetness away.

"I've missed my best friend."

Her soft words went directly to Terry's heart. "So have I."

CHAPTER 24

TERRY ROSE ON SHAKY LEGS. "Would you like to join me for coffee?"

"Yes." Jan glanced at her watch and sighed. "But I have to be home in half an hour."

"That's all right. We'll just grab a quick cup here. It won't take long."

Jan stuffed her book and glasses into her purse and took the hand Terry extended to her, as she rose to her feet.

They stood, inches apart and gazes locked, until Terry dropped Jan's hand and stepped back. They walked over to the in-house coffee shop.

"Why don't you grab us a table, and I'll get coffee." Terry pulled her wallet out of her pocket. "Any special requests?"

"Just plain coffee, thanks." Jan took a seat while Terry placed their order.

When the barista handed over the cups, Terry turned to walk over to where Jan sat and stopped short. Jan's gaze was fixed on her and, for the first time, Terry saw the look that Matt envied. Love and longing radiated from Jan's eyes, a shy smile graced her lips, and her whole body leaned toward Terry in a non-tactile caress.

How did I ever miss that? Terry blinked and set the coffees back on the counter. She gave her hands a moment to stop shaking, then picked up the cups again and wended her way to their table. Once seated, Terry tried to formulate her words. She didn't want to waste their limited time.

Jan's hand covered hers. "I want to apologize — "

"No. I'm the one who has to apologize. I've been a total idiot."

Jan's fingers curled around hers, and a tingling sensation skittered down Terry's spine.

"Why don't we agree that we've both been idiots and move on from there?" Jan's smile faded, and she pulled her hand away. "I have to say some things, and I need you to listen to me, okay?"

Terry nodded.

Jan drew in a deep breath and tucked her hands in her lap. "I had no right to get upset with you at Christmas. Who you see is your business, not mine. I was stupid, and it almost cost me something very precious. I hope you can forgive me. I...I was thrown by what happened at the wedding. I know it didn't mean anything to you — "

"You're wrong. It meant everything to me."

Jan's head snapped up, and her gaze searched Terry's face.

Terry reached her hand across the table and opened it, palm up.

Jan swallowed and laid her hand over Terry's.

Terry closed her fingers. "It meant everything to me, and don't you ever doubt it."

Jan's hand shook. "I don't know what to do."

"You don't have to do anything, just listen. I know this complicates things incredibly, but there has to be a way to work things out. I've been absolutely miserable without you this last month. I'm not asking you for anything you can't give me. I just want my friend back."

Jan gave a strangled half-sob and closed her eyes. Then

she opened them and met Terry's gaze. "I've been miserable without you, too. I've also had a lot of time to think these last few weeks. I've never been one for self-examination, but I'm just starting to figure some things out. I know it's a bungle, but I'm not willing to live without your friendship if I can still have it. It was like all the light and fun went out of my life, and the hardest thing I had to live with was that I did it to myself. Do you think we can get back to where we were?"

Can we go back to where we were before that night? Do we even want to? Terry was determined that there would be no more games and half-truths between them. "I'm not sure that we can pretend it never happened. I know I can't deny what I feel, but I can set it aside. I'm not going to make your life more difficult if I can help it."

"We have a lot to talk about, haven't we?"

"Not really the time or place, is it?"

Jan glanced at the other patrons, none of whom appeared to be eavesdropping, and shook her head. She checked the clock on the wall and grimaced. "Darn, I'm going to have to get going in a few minutes. Do you think we could get together in the near future?"

Terry grinned. "Is tonight too soon?"

"I think that might be pushing it a little. I've got some amends to make. I've been rotten to Rob, and he doesn't deserve that."

Terry flinched. *Stop it. He's her husband, and that's not going to change, so deal with it.* "I know what you mean. I've got to swing by the house and see if Mom's disowned me yet."

"Disowned you? Emily would never do that."

"Well, she'd be more than justified if she did." Terry scrubbed her face with one hand, too embarrassed to confess her juvenile behaviour.

Jan's eyes twinkled. "What did you do?"

"Aw, I've been ducking out of dinner and everything. Haven't seen the family in a while."

"How long is a while?"

Terry hung her head. "Since New Year's."

Jan gasped. "You haven't seen your family in six weeks? Why? I've never seen a family closer than yours. Your poor mother must be beside herself."

Terry traced her finger through some sugar granules on the table.

"It's okay," Jan said. "Heaven knows I haven't been fit company for man nor beast. I understand."

"I hope Mom does."

Jan patted her hand. "She will. I don't think there's anything Emily couldn't forgive when it comes to her kids."

"Even us?" Terry could've kicked herself. *Jesus, my mouth needs a five-second delay button.*

Jan drew in a sharp breath, and anguish crossed her face.

"I'm sorry, Jan. I didn't mean it. I mean, what's there to know, right? We're just friends. Mom can't have a problem with that."

"Your mother is more perceptive than that, and no, I don't have an answer to your question. It would hurt more than I can tell you if I were no longer welcome in your mother's house, but there's something that would hurt more, and that's denying what's going on between us. Or am I wrong about that?"

"No, you're not wrong." Terry took a deep breath. "I have a confession. What I told you that night, about going out with Jesse... I lied. I've never gone out with her, and Marika is only a friend."

Jan frowned. "Then why—?"

Terry wasn't about to disclose Rob's intervention. "I was

thrown. I didn't know how to react, what to do, so I tried to put some distance between us the only way I could think of."

"You succeeded."

Terry's chest tightened. "I know I did. But I didn't know you were going to be at Christmas dinner. I'm so sorry I hurt you. I never wanted to do that."

Jan touched Terry's hand. "It's okay. It's not exactly like I handled things any better."

Relief was palpable between them.

With a quick glance at her watch, Jan stood. "I really have to go. Walk me to my van?"

"Definitely."

They left the store and emerged into softly falling snow. Terry stuck out her tongue and tried to catch a snowflake.

Jan bent to sweep up a handful of snow and tossed it at Terry.

Terry grabbed her own handful off a nearby car.

Jan shrieked and ran, but Terry's longer legs gave her the advantage and she caught Jan near the van's fender. She grabbed her and playfully washed her face, laughing as Jan twisted and squirmed in her arms.

Jan stuck out her tongue at Terry. With snow plastered on her face, the effect was comical.

Terry chuckled and brushed the snow off Jan's eyelashes and rosy cheeks. Her touch turned to a caress.

Jan leaned into it and closed her eyes.

We are in so deep. The thought didn't ruffle Terry's joy. *All I care about right now is you. We'll deal with everything else later.*

Neither of them moved until finally Terry dropped her hand.

Jan's eyes fluttered open. "Guess I'd better go."

"Uh-huh. Guess you should." Terry stepped back

Jan fumbled for her keys. "I'm so very glad you found me today."

"So am I. I'll call you tonight, okay?"

"I'll count on it."

Terry watched Jan drive away with a grin so big that her cheeks hurt. With a light step and an even lighter heart, she went back to her car.

Now for Mom.

Terry stepped through her parents' back door. *Ugh, it feels like I've been called to the principal's office.* After depositing her jacket in the hall closet and kicking off her boots, she listened for any sounds that would give away her mother's location. "Mom?"

There was no answer, so she went to the fridge and examined the contents. She selected a cold fried chicken leg.

"The prodigal returns, does she?"

Terry jumped and thrust the chicken leg behind her back.

Emily stood at the head of the basement stairs with a stack of clean, folded towels in her arms.

Terry brought the leg from behind her back. "Um, I was hungry?"

"First time you've been hungry in six weeks?"

Terry winced. "I deserved that. I'm really sorry. Can I talk to you for a few minutes?"

"Just let me put these away first. Why don't you put the kettle on for tea?" Emily crossed the kitchen and went down the hall with the towels.

Terry put the chicken leg back, filled the kettle, and placed it on the burner. Her mother's standard answer to family problems was tea and talk at the kitchen table. It had been that way for as long as she could remember. *Mom will probably be sitting her grandchildren down for tea and talks thirty years from now.*

Terry didn't like tea, but she wasn't about to interfere with her mother's healing ritual. She took down the cups, put tea bags into the pot, and carried the heated pot and cups over to the table.

Emily returned, and they sat across from each other.

"Matt told me this afternoon what a jerk I've been, and he was right."

Emily's eyebrows shot up. "Matt called you a jerk?"

"Among other things. He really tore a strip off me."

"And you didn't hit him?"

Terry scowled. "No, Mom, I didn't hit him." She had to concede that her mother's surprise was justified. There was a time when Matt's tirade would have ended with the two of them rolling on the floor, exchanging punches.

Emily poured tea for both of them. "Huh. Well, that's an improvement anyway."

Terry accepted her cup and took a sip. "The thing of it is, I'm glad Matt yelled at me. I have been an ass—"

Emily looked at her sharply.

"Sorry…an idiot, and I'm really very sorry. I owe you and Dad an apology."

"You owe your brothers one, too."

"I do. Where is Jordy anyway?"

"It's Thursday. He's over at Rob's of course. And Terry, I meant all your brothers."

"I know, and I'll take care of it. Anyway, I want to tell you how much I regret my behaviour since Christmas. I promise that I won't do it again. If you don't mind, I'd like to come over for dinner this Sunday."

"So Matt brought you to your senses…all by himself?"

"Well, yes, that and I also spoke to Jan today."

Emily set her cup down.

Uh-oh, here it comes.

"I didn't appreciate you bringing that woman to Christmas dinner, Teresa."

Resentment flared in Terry at the unexpected reproach. "That woman, as you call her, is a friend of mine, Mother. And since when were we forbidden to bring friends by for dinner? Duncan and Karen weren't there, so I can't see that it was such a big problem to set out an extra plate."

"That's not what I mean, and you know it. I never mind if you bring Michael or Claire or Lisa and Robyn here."

"Oh, so it's just Marika that you won't allow at your table."

"Don't take that tone with me. This is still my house. I don't like that woman, and I can't understand what you're doing with her again after all the trouble last year."

"Let me tell you something about that woman. I treated her like shit last summer, but when she saw me at the end of a two-day drunk, still pissed out of my mind, she took me into her home, cleaned up my puke, fed and bathed me, and gave me a refuge, all without asking one damned thing in return. She has no family but a dumb old cat. She was planning on having leftover spaghetti for Christmas dinner, so yes, I asked her home for a real festive meal. And you know what? I'd do it all over again."

Emily's eyes widened. "What are you talking about, a two-day drunk?"

Terry closed her eyes for a second. *She might as well know the worst of it.* "I started drinking the day before Christmas Eve and didn't stop until I was kicked out of Oly's on Christmas Eve night when Marika took me home. I was so wasted, I didn't even know what day it was. That's why I missed Christmas morning here. I was sleeping off a binge at Marika's place."

"Why, Terry? Why would you do that to yourself?"

Terry couldn't force herself to answer that. She sat silently under her mother's intense scrutiny and stared at the table.

Finally, Emily reached across the table to pat her hand. "It's Jan, isn't it?"

Terry looked up. She half-expected to see condemnation in her mother's eyes. Instead, she saw sadness and sympathy.

"Oh, my daughter, what have you done? Why her, Terry? With all the women you've dated, why her? Rob..." Emily's voice trailed off.

Terry's eyes welled up. "I didn't mean to fall in love with her. I swear it. We were just friends, and I never would've pushed anything else. Rob's my friend too. I wouldn't hurt him. I didn't want to hurt either of them, but I did. And now Jan—"

"Feels the same way about you. Yes, I'd thought as much. Oh dear, what a mess. Does Rob know?"

"Yes, we talked about it the day after the wedding."

"And? What did he say?"

"Basically that he wasn't giving her up and I had to pull back. He wanted me to make it clear to her that I was romantically unavailable, but still stay friends with her."

"Good Lord. No wonder you've been so crazy." Emily came around the table and wrapped her arms around her.

Terry leaned into the hug and squeezed her mother's waist.

Emily rocked her for a few moments and then planted a kiss on Terry's hair before she returned to her seat. "Right, so what happens now? Where do you go from here?"

Terry dabbed at her eyes with a napkin. "I'm not exactly sure. I do know it was killing me to stay away from Jan, and she was just as miserable. We had coffee together today, and we're going to try to get back our friendship. You know, go out and do things again like we did all fall."

Emily pursed her lips. "Is that going to be possible? Going back to the way things were?"

"It has to be. I can live with us only being friends — I did it for months — but I can't not see her at all."

"You did it before you knew she felt the same way about you. What about Rob? You mustn't hurt that dear man."

"I have no intention of hurting him. After all, he's the one that wanted me to stay friends with her, so he should be okay with us seeing each other again. We haven't talked it all out, but Jan and I both know we can't take this any further, no matter what we're feeling."

"Oh, dear. It really sounds like you're playing with fire. I've seen how you two look at each other, and it most definitely isn't just as friends."

"I know. I'm not saying it'll be easy, but what the heck else are we supposed to do?"

Emily shook her head.

As wise and experienced as her mother was, Terry wasn't surprised that she had no answer. She hadn't really expected one. "Are Jan and Rob welcome here for dinner?"

"Of course they are, dear. They're our friends, too, and I've missed seeing them."

"Good. Can they come over on — ?"

Jordy walked in and stiffened when he saw Terry.

Uh-oh. I definitely have more fences to mend here.

"What're you doing here?"

"Apologizing for being an inconsiderate idiot." Terry refused to take offence at his truculence.

Jordy studied her. "You are, huh? Been here a long time, then?"

Terry laughed. "Are you saying that I should have allotted a few hours for apologies?"

He snorted and hung up his coat. "I'm saying you should allot the next week."

Jordy bent over to unlace his boots while Terry and Emily exchanged amused glances. Emily nodded her head at Jordy and stared at Terry.

Terry took the hint and crossed to Jordy. "I'm very sorry, little brother. Will you forgive me?"

Jordy straightened. "Dunno. Don't think I should let you off the hook that easily."

"I'll let you use my car over spring break."

"All of spring break?"

"Yes, all of spring break."

He grinned. "All right! Me and Gary can go skiing at Sunshine. Okay, you're forgiven this time—but don't do it again."

Terry grabbed him in a headlock. She knuckled his head until he squawked but hastily let go when he started tickling her ribs.

Emily rolled her eyes and took the cups to the sink to rinse out. "Will you be joining us for dinner tonight, Terry?"

Terry stopped roughhousing with Jordy. "Sounds great."

"Good, that'll give you a chance to apologize to your father, too."

Terry groaned. "I should just fill out apology forms in triplicate and hand them around."

"Yup." Jordy wrestled her into a pile of mittens, scarves, and boots.

Terry flipped him on his back and tried to pin him.

"Do try not to break anything, children of mine. That includes bones and drywall."

Terry grinned. *I'm back.*

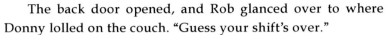

The back door opened, and Rob glanced over to where Donny lolled on the couch. "Guess your shift's over."

"Guess so, boss man." Donny rose to his feet and stretched.

"Hi, guys." Jan beamed as she came around the corner.

Rob's eyes widened.

"Hey, love. I saw Jordy driving away." Jan leaned down to kiss him. "Did you three have a good time this afternoon?"

Rob stared at her.

Jan turned to Donny. "Would you mind if we switched back to Saturdays again, starting next week if possible?"

Rob's heart plummeted.

Donny nodded. "Sure, I don't mind that at all. Fact is, I'd prefer it that way. If I'm not there, my wife can't stick me with weekend chores. Last Saturday, of all the dang-fool ideas she decided the attic needed to be cleaned out—"

As Donny rambled on about the insanity of cleaning out a space they barely used, Rob focused on Jan. Even without her request to change days off, he'd have known something happened this afternoon. In dramatic contrast to the sullen woman who had departed the house, Jan smiled easily, her eyes sparkled, and she almost bounced as she walked.

After Donny left, Rob asked, "So what did you do with yourself today?"

Jan glanced up from arranging the pillows under his feet. "I met Kate for lunch, did a few errands, and then went to Chapters for the rest of the day. Oh, and I saw Terry at Chapters, too. We had coffee together and talked about maybe doing something next weekend."

Fear closed like a vise around Rob's heart.

CHAPTER 25

MILY WATCHED HER ANTSY DAUGHTER.
Terry paced the living room, glancing constantly out the window as she waited for Jan and Rob's arrival. When the van pulled up in front of the house, she froze.

Emily wasn't sure if she was going to bolt or throw open the front door. *This is going to be so hard for her. I wish I could snap my fingers and return us all to four months ago.* Her daughter and Jan had reconciled, but Terry hadn't seen or spoken to Rob since Christmas. Despite Terry's optimistic prognostications that Rob would be pleased with the resumption of her friendship with Jan, Emily had serious doubts.

Terry snagged Jordy, who'd been bouncing around like Tigger on caffeine at the prospect of having his idol back in the house again, and the two of them ran out to help.

Emily wrapped her cardigan around herself against the cold air and stood in the open doorway while they maneuvered the wheelchair down the walk and up the stairs.

"Jan, Rob, it's so good to see you again." Emily waited until they shed their heavy winter outer clothes. She hugged Jan and bent to wrap Rob's frail body in a gentle embrace. She held him a breath longer than usual and felt him shudder. "I'm so happy to see you again. I've missed you." She drew back and studied him. *There's such sadness in his eyes. It breaks my heart.*

Emily stepped out of the way to allow Jan room to push his chair into the living room.

As the chair started to roll, Rob's foot fell off the stirrup. Terry stepped in front to halt the chair's progress and knelt down. She carefully bent Rob's leg back but didn't look at him until she rose from her task.

"Thank you," Rob said.

Terry nodded. "No problem."

The stiffness between the two was tangible. *I know she misses him – misses his friendship, but how can he help but see her as competition?* Emily sighed as she trailed after the group. *Thank heavens it's going to be a good crowd tonight. Maybe it will lighten the tension between them.* She shook her head. *Not that I'd lay odds on it.*

———◆———

With deep satisfaction, Emily surveyed the long tables extending through the dining room and well into the living room. So many people had joined them for Sunday dinner that she'd had to send Gord and Jordy to bring up an extra table from the basement.

All of her children were present for the first time this year, and Emily enjoyed the sight of her noisy brood along with their friends. She grinned as Michael stole something from Randy's plate and stifled a smile at how attentively Matt listened to Claire. *Hmm, I wonder... She's not Matty's usual type – thank heavens – but she might be just what he needs. I must remember to have Terry invite Claire over more often.*

Emily turned her attention to the trio at the far end of the table, and her smile vanished. Terry and Jan were laughing about something as Rob watched them soberly. To anyone unaware of the underlying currents, all would appear normal, but it wasn't difficult to detect the latent tensions.

Terry and Jan were trying to maintain a correct distance and demeanour, but the subliminal tug between them was clear. Quick glances, involuntary smiles, and "accidental" touches hadn't escaped Emily's attention. Worse, they hadn't escaped Rob's keen eyes either.

Emily's delight in the gathering dimmed. For a brief moment, anger surged at Jan for allowing the situation to get out of hand. She shook her head. *It's not fair to put all the blame on her. It's no one person's fault, but what a bloody mess.* Emily had wracked her brains, trying to come up with a solution that would leave all three intact but hadn't been able to find one. She knew that Terry and Jan weren't about to run away together and abandon Rob. *But how long can they keep a lid on what's growing between them? Before long, a blind man will be able to see it.*

A tiny hand tugged on her left arm. She picked up Kelly's sipping cup and tucked it into food-covered fingers.

"Hey, Jordy." Terry's voice rose above the noise. "What size are your ski boots?"

"Eight and a half, why?"

"Darn, too big. I was hoping your boots might fit Jan so she wouldn't have to rent some."

Emily's attention was instantly riveted on the far end of the table.

"When are you guys going, and what hill are you heading for?" Jordy asked.

"I thought we'd try Lake Louise next Saturday. I was listening to the ski report this morning, and they've had forty centimetres of fresh powder in the last week, so conditions should be great."

Jordy's face fell. "Aw, I have to work all day Saturday."

"You're going to get in tons of skiing on spring break since you've got my car all week."

"Mine are a seven," Karen said. "Maybe they'd fit. You're welcome to borrow my gear for the day if you'd like."

"That would be great, thank you. I really appreciate that," Jan said. "And I promise to replace anything I break. It's been quite a while since I last hit the slopes."

Terry chuckled and leaned into her. "Yeah, and I'm sure you'll be 'hitting' the slopes more than once."

Jan nudged her back. "Just don't take me down any black diamond runs. I promised Rob I'd come back with all limbs intact."

"Aw, would I do that?"

A chorus of hoots exploded from Terry's brothers. Emily chuckled as her sons retold the story of one memorable day on the ski hill when a ten-year-old Terry had led her three older brothers out of bounds and into deeply forested ravines, where they'd gotten bogged down and had to spend the rest of the day hiking out in waist-deep snow.

Under the cover of raspberries, catcalls, and laughter, Emily studied Rob's reaction to Jan's plans for the following weekend. He met her gaze for a moment, then shifted his attention to Gord at the head of the table.

I wish I knew what he was thinking. Outwardly, the affectionate interaction between husband and wife hadn't changed, but Rob was too alert not to notice the byplay between Jan and Terry. *It has to worry him.*

Painfully aware there was nothing else she could do, Emily sent a quick prayer heavenward for the troubled trio and turned her attention to Kerry on her right.

"Michael, I almost forgot," Claire said. "Lisa called earlier this afternoon and asked if she and Robyn could come over later tonight to talk to you."

"To me?" Michael canted his head. "Are you sure she meant me?"

Claire nodded. "That's what she said. I told her we were coming here for dinner, and she said she would call before they came to make sure you were home."

"Okay." Turning to Randy, Michael asked, "We weren't going out anywhere later, were we?"

Randy patted his belly. "Not likely, Mikey. I don't think I'll be able to move after this meal."

Emily suppressed a snicker. *Michael must really be in love to allow that nickname.*

The foursome clattered into the house, jockeying for space in the narrow hallway as coats and boots were tossed aside. Randy headed for the door to the basement, and Michael trailed after him.

"Don't you two start anything," Terry said. "Remember, Lisa and Robyn will be over soon."

"Aw." Michael winked at her. "Do we really have to behave?"

"Geez, it's not like I'm asking you to pledge lifetime celibacy here. Just put a knot in it for an hour or so."

Randy smiled. "Don't worry, I'll make him behave."

"Good luck. Hey, try tying him up if he can't keep his hands off you."

"Ooooh, kinky. Does that mean we can borrow your cuffs?" Michael asked.

Randy punched his shoulder and began to lead him down the stairs.

"What? It's not like I asked to borrow her nipple clamps."

They vanished down the stairwell as Terry blushed.

"Oh, that is so much more than I needed to know." Claire slipped by her with a grin.

Terry leaned her head against the wall, thumping lightly. *What did I ever do to deserve Michael?* Finally, she poked her head around the entrance to see what Claire was doing in the kitchen.

Claire was making a pot of coffee. "Want some?"

"Sure," Terry said. "You know he was just kidding, right?"

"Oui, of course. Why don't you find some clean cups?"

The phone rang, and Terry grabbed it, grateful for the diversion. By the time she had chatted with Lisa and confirmed that Michael would be home, the coffee was ready.

They took seats at the table.

"You're doing better now?" Claire asked.

Terry nodded, unsure of how much Claire knew. Claire tended to keep her own counsel but rarely missed much of what was happening around her. "I am. I'm really sorry for being such a rotten roommate for the last few weeks. I know I wasn't very easy to live with."

Claire surveyed her calmly as she drank her coffee. "What's done is done, but it is nice to be able to talk to you again."

Terry grimaced. She had been short to the point of rudeness to both her roommates since the New Year, and by the third week of her self-imposed exile, Claire had ceased even trying to draw her into a conversation. She rubbed her neck and eyed Claire. "Um, do you know — ?"

"What's been going on? Oui, Michael and I spoke about it."

When she didn't say anything more, Terry squirmed. "And?"

Claire set down her cup and leaned back in her chair. "What exactly are you asking? Whether I know about you and Jan, or what my opinion on the matter is?"

"Both?" Terry had a hunch she wasn't going to like Claire's answer.

"I didn't know that you were anything more than friends until Michael told me. I won't deny I was surprised. You may have been...active since I've known you, but I've never known you to be unethical."

Terry flinched. "We haven't done anything, you know."

"You fell in love with a married woman." Claire shook her head. "Worse, from what I understand, she fell in love with you, too. She is not free to love you, and you should not be having those feelings for her. I thought Rob was your friend, too. How can this possibly come to a good end, whether you've gone any further or not?"

"We didn't plan it." Terry stared at the table. "It just happened."

Claire's stern expression softened, and she patted Terry's arm. "Oui, je sais. Le cœur n'est pas logique. I'm sorry, my friend. I know you didn't set out to hurt anybody, but the fact is people *are* being hurt, yourself included. The bottom line is that you are contemplating adultery."

Her expressive eyes left no doubt in Terry's mind what Claire thought about that particular sin. She was tempted to defend herself with what Jan had told her about the physical aspects of their marriage, but she didn't want to break a confidence. Nor did she think that would carry any weight anyway. She was pretty sure that Claire took "till death do us part" and "for better or for worse" very seriously.

Claire picked up her coffee again. "It is not my place to tell you how to live your life, however, you asked and I'm not going to lie to you. I think you know that this is not right, or you wouldn't have been so miserable."

True, but I tried to do the right thing, and it didn't work, for any of us. As much as Terry valued Claire's opinion, she wasn't going to deny her love for Jan anymore. "Guess maybe you should light a candle for me, eh?"

Claire gave a noncommittal murmur.

Time to change the subject. "So did I see my brother chatting you up tonight?"

It was Claire's turn to drop her gaze, but a tiny smile flickered across her lips.

Terry grinned and leaned forward. "C'mon, 'fess up. Is something going on between you and Matt?"

Claire shrugged. "He talked to me. I talked back. What's to know?"

"I've known my brother my entire life. I know when he's flirting, Mademoiselle, and he was flirting with you. The real question is whether you were flirting back."

Claire took a long, deliberate sip of her coffee. "I enjoyed talking to him. I've never really spoken to him at length before, and he was quite different from what I'd imagined."

"How?"

"He wasn't really flirting in the traditional sense. He actually seemed interested in the things we discussed, and he had some unusual insights that I would not have expected."

Matt? Insightful? Huh.

Claire chuckled. "I think perhaps you do not give your brother much credit."

Terry bit her tongue. "Maybe you're right. So, are you two going out or what?"

The front doorbell rang. As Terry rose to go answer it, she winked. "I just need to know if your intentions are honourable. I wouldn't want you sullying my brother's reputation."

The sounds of Claire's laughter followed her down the hall, and she opened the door with a big smile on her face.

"Well, that's a definite improvement," Lisa said. "I was beginning to think you'd forgotten how to do that."

Terry rolled her eyes and stepped aside to let them in.

Robyn took Lisa's coat and hung it up before doing the same for her own. Her hands shook, but Lisa radiated confidence.

Terry directed them into the living room, then went to the basement door and hollered down the stairs. "Michael! Lisa and Robyn are here. Drop whatever you're doing and come upstairs." She returned to the living room. "Do you guys want any coffee before I leave you alone?"

Robyn sat bolt upright on the couch. "No, no. You have to stay." Her voice was edged with panic.

Terry blinked. "Are you sure? This is pretty personal, after all."

Robyn nodded.

"If you don't mind," Lisa said. "We both thought it might go smoother if you're here, too."

"Sure. If that's what you want, I don't mind. I'll just sit quietly over here for moral support." Terry walked over to the far easy chair and took her seat.

Michael sauntered into the room. "Ah, such a bevy of lovely ladies. To what do I owe the pleasure of your company?"

Lisa and Robyn looked at each other. "Lisa and I had something we wanted to talk to you about." Robyn gestured at an empty armchair.

Michael raised an eyebrow but sat and focused his attention on Robyn.

Before Robyn could launch into her spiel, which Terry was willing to bet was carefully rehearsed, Lisa leaned forward. "Look, we don't want you to feel pressured or anything, and we're not going to be angry if you can't agree. Hell, we know we're not exactly your kind of people."

Robyn frowned. "We agreed that I'd handle this, now shush."

When Lisa opened her mouth to protest, Robyn squeezed her arm. Much to Terry's amazement, Lisa subsided and allowed her partner the floor.

"As Lisa said, we have something to ask, but we will understand if it's not something you can do. I don't know if Terry's mentioned it or not, but Lisa and I want to start a family. We've considered all our options and would really like to have a donor who we know and respect. We both think you're a terrific man. You're smart and funny and kind, and we were wondering if you would consider being the donor for our baby."

Michael turned progressively paler as Robyn spoke. He attempted to speak, but his voice came out in a squeak. After clearing his throat, he tried again. "Uh, so what you're saying is that you want me to father a child with one of you...or did you mean both of you?"

Robyn shook her head. "Just Lisa. It would be too hard for me to keep slinging luggage if I was nine months pregnant, but Lisa can keep her office job right up until delivery." She glanced at her partner. "Besides, I don't want to stick our child with my genes."

Lisa frowned. "Any child would be damned lucky to get your genes, sweetie."

"Um, exactly how...? I mean what do you...?" Michael swallowed hard.

Terry caught the mischief in Lisa's eyes before she even opened her mouth. *Uh-oh. Michael's in for it now.*

"Well, it's like this. You know we just bought our home last year, and we're a little short on available funds, so we thought if it was okay, we'd just do it the old-fashioned way to save money."

"Turkey-baster?" Michael tugged on his shirt collar.

Lisa shook her head. "We did a lot of research into this, and the odds of successful fertilization are much higher if we go with the original method of delivery, if you know what I mean. After all, we don't want to have to impose on you too much. I figure you and me, a little candlelight and wine, and voila…the deed is done."

Terry had never seen a healthy man look so sickly.

Robyn grimaced and elbowed Lisa. "She's pulling your leg. We've already contacted a clinic and made preliminary arrangements. Your only part would be showing up at an appointed time and, um, well, you know, in a cup and all." Robyn blushed as Lisa chuckled.

Michael jumped to his feet. "I think we should have some tea." He swayed. "Or rye. Rye is good." His eyes widened. "Oh! I'm so sorry. You can't have rye when you're pregnant. Tea it is."

Lisa and Robyn gaped at him.

Terry fought to control her laughter. She hadn't seen Michael this flustered since his parents' unexpected visit.

He sat down heavily but bounced up again. "But you're not pregnant yet. Right, that's my part. Okay, tea and rye it is." Spinning to march out of the room, he promptly tripped over his feet and fell face-first at Terry's feet.

They stared at him.

Terry poked his shoulder. "Michael…Michael? Hey buddy, are you okay?"

"Just fine, thank you." He didn't move. "Would it be all right if I took some time to consider their request?"

"I'm sure that Lisa and Robyn didn't expect an answer

right away. You just take all the time you need." Terry stood and stepped over his inert body, gesturing her stunned friends to follow.

Lisa and Robyn cast worried glances at Michael and trailed her out to the hall. By the time Terry opened the front door for them, she was losing her battle to suppress her mirth and little giggles kept slipping out. She followed her friends outside and exploded into laughter. "Are you two sure you want that boy to father your child?"

They looked vaguely insulted, but gradually, a smile crept over Robyn's face and she began to chuckle. Lisa soon joined in, and, within moments, they were united in hilarity at Michael's expense.

Robyn subsided first. "Do you think we maybe should have softened him up more first?"

Terry wiped the tears from her eyes and shook her head. "Robbie, I don't think anything could have prepared him for this." Sobering, she said, "Let him think things over, guys. He just needs a little time, okay?"

Lisa nodded and slipped her arm through Robyn's. "Don't worry. We won't bug him about it. We'll just wait until he makes a decision."

Terry watched them leave and smiled at how carefully Robyn shepherded Lisa over the icy walk. *God, if Lisa does get pregnant, Robyn's going to be worse than five nannies and seven St. Bernards put together.*

She returned to the living room. Michael hadn't moved an inch. Smothering a grin, she sat down on the vacated couch.

Michael lifted his head and glared. "You were laughing at me."

Oops, guess he heard us. "Aw, I'm sorry, buddy. But you have to admit, it was pretty funny."

Michael rolled over and folded his arms under his head. "Funny? I've just been asked to father a new generation, and you think it's funny?"

Terry rolled her eyes. "For crying out loud, they aren't asking you to found a dynasty. Just contribute a few of your swimmers so they can have a baby."

Michael pulled himself up off the floor and sat beside Terry. "But that is it, don't you see?" He regarded her soberly. "God, this is going to sound so snobbish, but I don't know how else to explain it. I like Lisa and Robyn. I really do, and I think they'll make terrific parents, but — "

"But?" Terry had no idea where this was going.

"But my parents have always had certain expectations of me, in a dynastic sense I mean, and I don't think this is exactly what they had in mind."

Terry frowned. "So basically, you're saying your genes are too good for Lisa and Robyn?"

"God, no! Not at all." Michael shook his head. "You know me better than that."

Terry breathed a sigh of relief. Michael had never exhibited any illusions of superiority based on class, breeding, or wealth. He did constantly emphasize his superior fashion sense, but she had to admit that was warranted. "Okay, so what exactly do you mean?"

"I'd like to help them. I kind of like the idea of helping to bring a child into the world, you know? My concern is what happens if the parental units ever find out. I don't think Mom would take kindly to being shut out of her grandchild's life, and Dad would have a heart attack at the concept of me having children with a lesbian couple."

Terry considered his logic. "So basically, if it was just up to you, you'd say fine, but you figure if your folks find out they'll what…disinherit you?"

Michael's brow creased. "I don't know what they'd do, but I do know it has the potential to become really unpleasant. What if they sued for some sort of rights in the baby's life? It's been known to happen, and God knows they have the money to hire the best lawyers. What if they find out I'm gay and decide this is their only chance for a grandchild? Lisa and Robyn could end up cursing the day they ever asked me for help."

"I've met your parents. They're good people, especially your mother. There's no way they'd go all psycho and try to take control of Lisa and Robyn's child. Hell, the law wouldn't let them anyway. Not to mention that I can't see how they'd ever find out in the first place if you don't tell them. I'm sure, if you're worried about it, Lisa and Robyn will sign any legal documents you want giving up any rights to support for the child. That's not what they care about. They just want a terrific guy for the father, and they don't come much better than you."

"I know that's not what they want, and of course I'd help support my child so that's not even a question." Michael sighed. "I just think if my parents ever find out I'm gay, that the shock of it might cause them to do dumb things, and I know if they wanted to, they have the power to cause a lot of problems if they find out I've got a kid."

Terry scratched her jaw. *Should I tell him his mother already knows? No, I promised I wouldn't, though I may have to someday.* "I think it boils down to what you want to do, irrespective of your parents. Are you going to live in fear of something that probably would never occur in a million years, or are you going to help out some friends and do what you'd really like to anyway? It's entirely your decision. I just think you should take some time before you make it."

They sat in silence then.

Finally, Michael took her hand. "You know, if it were you asking me, I probably wouldn't have to think twice about it."

Terry grinned. "Hold that thought, buddy, I may be by to see you in a few years."

Michael squeezed her hand and stood up. "I think I'll go talk to Randy about this."

"Great idea. He's got a good head on his shoulders. You should listen to him."

Michael stopped at the doorway and glanced back over his shoulder "Do you think you can have deliveries catered?"

"Depends, do you mean the baby's delivery or your contribution?"

Michael winked. "Maybe both."

Terry threw a pillow at him.

CHAPTER 26

ROB FACED AWAY FROM THE bedside clock. Unable to roll over, he tried to guess the hour by the shadows in their bedroom, but the late winter dawn made that difficult. He had been awake most of the night and was feeling the strain of limbs left in one position too long. He'd been reluctant to wake Jan too often since she was going skiing.

He studied Jan's slumbering form. As usual, she'd shed half the covers. It didn't matter how cold the night was, Jan couldn't stand bedding up around her neck and inevitably pushed it down during the night. It made for interesting logistics because Rob preferred being tucked in. Over the years, they had negotiated a truce that usually saw their bedding angled from corner to corner by the morning.

Not that I'm complaining. Rob took a moment to appreciate Jan's smooth back, pale in the room's shadows. Then his smile slipped. He listened to Jan's deep, even breathing and grieved for what might have been and what was lost. Most of all, he grieved his inability to reach across the narrow space and touch the woman he loved.

Companion to his sorrow was a profound worry about the future. Even as his head assured him of Jan's loyalty, his heart recognized the renewed and growing connection between Jan and Terry. For the moment, he was certain that they hadn't become lovers, but always in the back of his mind was the terrible inevitability of his disease.

Rob's eyes closed, and his memory drifted back to another man with MS. Rob had befriended Harry when they were both in the hospital during a relapse. At the time, Harry was in better physical shape than Rob, but then Harry's wife left him and he plunged into a mental and physical decline. Rob tried to get him interested in the outside world by inviting him to their home for dinners and outings to the movies or theatre.

Harry refused most of Rob's invitations. He retreated into himself and hid within the safety of the hospital's walls. Within nine months, his cognitive deterioration had accelerated to the point where the once sparkling conversationalist could barely hold up his end of a simple chat. Long before his body gave out, his mind shut down. He died within two years of his wife's departure. Rob was convinced that Harry wished himself to death out of despair and loneliness.

Jan won't physically leave, but what if I become mentally disabled? MS, to the degree he had it, was usually accompanied by some degree of cognitive impairment. If his intelligence, wit, and memory were lost, would Jan turn to Terry for companionship and stimulation? *If I become Harry, could I even blame her if she did?*

Rob fretted with every minor slip of memory. He tested himself constantly, doggedly recalling bits of songs learned decades before and the smallest details of current news stories. In his darkest moments, he prayed to lose his life before he lost his mind.

He was jolted out of his melancholy thoughts when the radio alarm went off and Wynonna's powerful voice filled the room.

Jan yawned and stretched before turning to begin the ritual they'd shared a thousand times. Her eyes still half-lidded, she eased him onto his back, straightened his legs, and moved the catheter bag to the far edge of the bed.

Rob sighed with relief as cramped muscles flexed.

Jan slid in next to him, lifted his arm, and settled it around her shoulders as she snuggled into him. She snaked an arm over his sunken chest and hugged him. "Morning, angel." Her sleep-husky voice never failed to warm his soul.

"Morning, love. Did you sleep well?"

She kissed his shoulder. "Mmm-hmm. You?"

Rob didn't answer.

Jan rolled her head back to look up. "Did you not sleep again?"

He shook his head. "I seem to have forgotten that particular skill."

She frowned. "This can't go on. You have to sleep. I think we should talk to the doctor about it. Maybe she can prescribe something to help."

"Maybe. Don't worry about it, though. I'll just nap during the day when I need to."

With a muffled grunt, Jan settled back and pulled his arm back into place around her. "We will talk about this later." She cuddled back into him and closed her eyes.

Betcha she has me in to see the doctor by the end of the week. He closed his eyes and enjoyed the sensation of Jan nestled against his body as he listened to soft sounds of country music filling the air.

Reluctant to disturb their cozy nest, Rob allowed them ten minutes by the now visible clock. "Hey, love. I think we should get up now." Jan liked to ease into the day. A soft moan of protest vibrated against his chest, and he smiled. "Come on, now. Donny is supposed to be here by eight."

"Yeah, yeah, I'm up."

"You don't look like you're up." When Jan still didn't stir, Rob pulled out the heavy artillery. "I'd really like to get through my bathroom routine before people arrive."

"Okay." Jan wriggled out from under his arm and sat up. She yawned as she stretched her arms over her head.

Rob gave a wolf whistle.

Jan laughed. "Letch." She scrambled out of bed and grabbed her robe.

"Yes, but I'm your letch." Her laughter floated back to him as she vanished into the washroom. He stared at the ceiling. *How long will I be able to say that?*

<hr>

Ninety minutes later, Rob sat in his easy chair as Jan gave Donny the day's instructions in the kitchen.

A car pulled up in front, and Terry emerged. She double-checked the skis strapped to the roof carrier before she started up the walk. "Terry's here, Jan."

"Remember to make sure he lies down for a nap this afternoon." Jan rounded the corner with Donny. She walked over to Rob and tapped his nose. "And no giving Donny a hard time about it either, Major Spencer. When he says it's naptime, it's naptime. I left money on the table so you two can order in chicken for supper, okay?"

"That sounds suspiciously like a bribe to me, Mrs. Spencer." Rob's smile vanished when Jan opened the door and let Terry in.

Terry nodded at him and Donny, then stood there, shoulders stiff.

Rob said nothing.

"Did Karen drop off all her stuff okay?" Terry asked.

Jan nodded. "Everything's in the back room, ready to go."

"Why don't you give me the skis and poles, and I'll get them loaded up."

Jan retrieved the gear.

"I'll wait for you out in the car." Terry hoisted the skis over her shoulder.

"Make sure you bring my wife back in one piece," Rob said.

Terry stopped and faced him. "I'll bring Jan back intact, I promise."

They studied each other for a long moment before Terry left.

Jan gathered up the rest of her equipment. "Okay, I think I have everything." She set the boot bag down and pulled on her ski jacket, then crossed to Rob to kiss him goodbye.

"Be careful."

"I will. Don't worry; I'm not going to do anything stupid. You two have fun today. We should be back by nine or ten tonight." Jan picked up her boot bag and waved as she left the house.

Terry hurried back up the walk to take the bag from her.

"Can I get you a coffee, boss man?" Donny asked.

Rob didn't look at him. "Sure."

Terry held the door open for Jan, who smiled up at her as she slid into the passenger seat.

Long after the car had pulled away, Rob ignored the cooling coffee cup and stared out the window.

———◆———

Jan's gaze followed Terry as she walked to the doors of the Tim Horton's. She chuckled when a teenager tripped over his own feet as he twisted to ogle Terry. She couldn't blame the boy. She was doing some ogling of her own.

Terry wore a white turtleneck under a form-fitting black

one-piece ski suit with scarlet slashes on her thighs, shoulders, and sides. The suit left little to the imagination.

Jan glanced down at her outfit and sighed. Her old down ski jacket and pants would keep her warm, but they would never make a boy stumble in adolescent lust. *Not that I'd want them to.*

She settled deeper in the car's seat and watched the stream of people enter and leave the doughnut shop while she waited. When Terry exited the shop, Jan's eyes widened at the size of the cup she carried. She leaned across the car and opened the door for her.

Terry handed her a small brown bag and climbed in behind the wheel.

Jan peeked into the bag. "For me?"

"Know anyone else in this car who's crazy about blueberry muffins?" Terry took a deep swallow of her coffee.

Jan removed the muffin and tore off the top. "Do you think you have enough coffee to last you the whole way there?"

"Doubtful, but I can always stop for refills. Are you sure you don't want one?"

Jan shook her head. "No, thanks. I've had enough coffee already this morning."

"No such thing as enough."

In ten minutes, they were on the highway headed west for the mountains. Jan loved the drive through winter-browned prairie and rolling foothills toward snow-covered peaks looming on the horizon. It was a near-perfect day for their trip. A minus-twelve-degree temperature would make the skiing comfortable, and a skiff of new snow overnight would give them fresh powder to play in. The sun broke in and out of clouds and revealed patches of azure that gave her hope for clear skies later in the day.

They passed the miles in lively conversation, teasing and joking until Jan's sides ached from laughter. Terry seemed quiet when she had picked her up, but her mood had improved dramatically. *She probably just needed some caffeine as a pick-me-up.*

They had passed Canmore, a beautiful little town overshadowed by the towering mountains surrounding it, when Terry started squirming.

Jan glanced at her. "Do you want to pull into a service station?"

Terry shook her head. "No need, thanks."

Jan smiled but kept her counsel.

By the time they passed through the gates to the national park and paid their daily entrance fee, Terry was in obvious discomfort.

By the time they turned off at Lake Louise almost an hour later, Terry was practically driving with her legs crossed. "Ugh, why did you let me drink so much coffee?"

Jan raised an eyebrow. "Let you? You're a grown-up. I didn't 'let' you do anything."

They slowed as they approached the parking lots, and Terry groaned as the traffic controller motioned them down the road to the farthest lot. "Damn. I knew we'd have to park out in the back forty on a Saturday. I'm never going to make it in time."

Jan diplomatically kept her mouth shut but gathered her gear to make a rapid exit once they stopped.

Terry found a spot on the far end of the plowed lot, scrambled out of the car, unsnapped the skis, and retrieved their poles from the trunk. Jan looped her poles over her ski tips, balanced them on her shoulder, picked up her boot bag, and waited. Terry grabbed a small backpack out of the trunk and picked up her equipment.

They set off at a rapid trot across the huge parking lot, but Terry stopped before they reached the far side. With a look of panic on her face, she thrust her gear at Jan. "Gotta go — *now*." She scaled the ten-foot wall of snow that had been plowed up at the edge of the parking lot and vanished into the thick forest.

Jan balanced both pairs of skis and ignored the curious looks of other skiers walking past. When Terry reappeared at the top of the snow wall and slid back down to the ground, she burst out laughing. "Feel better now?"

Terry grinned sheepishly as she shouldered her gear. "Never, ever let me drink that much coffee again when we're going somewhere."

"Okay, but you remember you said that. I don't want any whining that I'm depriving or abusing you."

"Ooooh, you can abuse me all you want."

Jan rolled her eyes. "You are incorrigible."

"You have no idea."

Terry's low drawl sent a tremor through Jan's body.

They reached the large log structure, which bustled with skiers. They leaned their skis and poles against the stands and went inside the lodge to change their footwear and secure their street boots.

After stuffing boots and Terry's backpack into a locker, Jan pressed fifty dollars into Terry's hand. "Can you pick up the passes while I find the ladies' room?"

"Sure. But you could have had the tree beside mine. There was no waiting line."

They met up a few minutes later, and Terry handed over a bright pink day pass.

Jan affixed the pass to her jacket zipper and glanced at Terry. "Where'd you put yours?"

Terry was bent over her skis but stood and held out her

glove, which had a pink triangle dangling off it. "Rather appropriate, don't you think?"

Jan smiled and pulled her skis off the rack. They tugged their toques around their ears and adjusted sunglasses, then skied to the multiple line-ups waiting for the high-speed quad lift. Despite the long queues, loading went quickly and they were soon seated with another couple.

As the chair rose into the air, Jan peered at the skiers down below.

Terry glanced at her. "Nervous?"

"A little. I skied all the time as a kid, but it's been a lot of years since then."

"Do you trust me?"

"Absolutely."

Terry smiled and gave her hand a quick squeeze. "I'm not going to take you anywhere you can't handle. We'll start with slow, easy runs, and if you feel more confident later in the afternoon, we'll find something a bit more challenging."

Jan relaxed against the back of the chair. "Thanks. I appreciate that." She surveyed the wide, moderately inclined slope beneath them. "I don't think I'll have any problems handling something like that."

"Then that's the one we'll start with. I'll bet you find it all comes back to you by the time we finish our first run."

The trip to the top went quickly. They slid off the chair, skied out of the way, and stopped to adjust their poles.

Terry stooped to tighten a buckle.

Jan wrenched her gaze off Terry's butt and took in the other view. "My God, it's amazing." From where they stood, the panorama of mountains and valleys spread below them as far as the eye could see.

Terry pointed to a solid white area down the valley to

the west. "That's Lake Louise over there. We're on Whitehorn right now, and you can see about a dozen peaks from here that top ten thousand feet. It is pretty awesome, isn't it?"

Jan nodded, overwhelmed with the sheer majesty of it. Despite the multitude of skiers that passed them, there was no sensation of crowding, only of all the space you could ask for.

"Let's get moving before we freeze. Follow me, but stop as many times as you want while your legs get used to this." Terry pushed off and began a controlled descent down the slope.

Jan followed and was delighted when muscle memory kicked in. Her technique was a bit rusty, but she easily kept up with Terry.

When Terry slid to a stop on the far edge of a cluster of moguls, Jan swooshed to a halt and sprayed her with snow.

Terry grinned and brushed snow off her ski suit. "Hey. You're getting pretty cocky there."

Jan laughed. She'd forgotten how much she loved this sport. Impulsively taking the lead, she heard Terry's squawk behind her as she started down the run. Within moments, a black streak flashed by her, and Terry whooped at regaining the lead.

The next few hours flew by. Terry increased the difficulty of the runs she chose, and Jan adapted as her skills returned.

They paused midway through one run and stood together on the edge of the trees. Terry pulled back her glove and checked her watch. "It's past one. Do you want lunch soon?"

Jan had been having so much fun that she'd forgotten about eating, but now she was hungry. "Sounds good. Did you want to stop at the base lodge or the one halfway up?"

"Well, actually I had something else in mind, but we do have to make a pit stop at the base lodge."

Jan was willing to go where Terry led. "All right, o mystery woman. Why don't you pull out the stops for this run, and I'll meet you at the bottom."

"Are you sure? I don't mind sticking with you. I'm having a great time."

"You know you're dying to cut loose. Go ahead, I'll be fine. We've done this run three times now. I can find my way."

Terry wavered.

"Go." Jan pushed her shoulder.

"Bossy woman. Okay, I'll meet you at the lockers."

"Right behind you. Better watch your six, because I'll be on it."

"Ooooh, promises, promises." Terry pushed off into a semi-tuck and gathered speed.

Terry had been holding back for her sake. An expert skier, she flashed over the snow, barely seeming to touch the ground and never missing a beat as she soared over a jump.

When Terry disappeared around a bend, Jan pushed off and took the same route at a more sedate pace. By the time she reached the bottom and skied over to the equipment racks, Terry was nowhere in sight. She found her waiting by the lockers, backpack in hand.

"Be with you in a moment." Jan went to the ladies' room. When she returned, she grinned at Terry. "Are you going to be looking for trees again this afternoon?"

"No, ma'am. I just had so much time to kill waiting for you that I've already been." Terry snickered as Jan hip-checked her. "Hey, careful. I'm carrying lunch here."

"You made lunch?"

"Geez, even I can handle sandwiches."

"Okay. Right now I'm so hungry that just about anything would taste good. Are we going to eat on the deck?"

"Actually, I want to take you somewhere special."

"A surprise? Great." Jan followed her to the ski rack to retrieve her skis and poles.

Back at the summit, Terry led off on a run they hadn't tried previously. It was more difficult, but Jan handled it competently, up until Terry stopped and pointed off into the trees. "We're going to go cross-country for a little bit. Follow me and go exactly where I go, okay? We'll take it slow."

Jan blew out a breath. "I will." She trailed Terry into the forest, and within a few minutes, they were side-slipping their way down a steep hill and between trees. She was about to call a brief halt, as her legs ached from the strain of maintaining rigid control, when they broke out into a clearing.

Jan slid to a stop, and her eyes widened. They stood atop a large granite outcropping with a panoramic view of the valley below them and the mountains rising on the opposite side. Thick forest surrounded them and deadened the sounds of other skiers, giving the impression that they alone inhabited the mountain.

Terry knelt and snapped out of her bindings. She sank into the snow but waded forward to the back edge of the outcropping and drove her skis in deep and vertical. "Here, give me your skis."

Jan shook off her amazement and handed over her skis.

Terry slammed them into the snow beside hers and rested her back against the skis with her legs propped on the snow-covered granite.

Jan settled beside her. "Wow, this is incredible."

"Worth putting up with my sandwiches for?" Terry opened up the backpack.

"I'd eat cat food for this view."

"Sorry, no cat food. I must've left that on the kitchen table."

Terry handed over a thick sandwich and a napkin and took one for herself.

Jan unwrapped her lunch and bit into it. "Hey, these are great." She savoured the nutty bread laden with roast beef, turkey, cheese, lettuce, tomato, and pickles.

"Wait 'til you see what I brought for dessert."

They ate in contented silence.

Jan couldn't take her eyes off the view. The sun broke through scattered clouds, and the rays descending to the valley floor were reminiscent of Renaissance paintings. As they ate, the clouds cleared, and they were bathed in sunlight.

Terry took a bottle of sunscreen from the backpack and handed it to Jan. "Better put some of this on, paleface."

"Thanks. I can already feel it." Jan applied the lotion and handed it back.

"Want another sandwich?"

"This one should hold me." *What else does she have in that magic bag?*

Terry pulled out a bag of huge cookies and a silver thermos. "Triple chocolate chip." She took one, handed over the bag, and twisted off the top of the thermos. After filling the cap, she handed that over, too.

Jan inhaled the intoxicating aroma of rich, hot chocolate and took a sip. "Aren't you having any?"

"There's only one cup. I'll have some when you're done."

Jan held out the cup. "I don't think it'll kill us to share."

Terry accepted, and they passed the cup between them and munched on cookies. After lunch, they gathered up their debris, replaced it in the backpack, and leaned back on their skis.

Jan soaked in the sun like a contented cat. "This is wonderful. How'd you find this place?"

"I discovered it when I was a kid. I had a thing about going off runs to explore, and I was by myself one day when I found it. I never told anyone. I used to come here when I needed to think." Terry gazed out over the valley. "In fact, I was sitting in this exact spot when I finally figured out why I hated my best friend's boyfriend so much."

"And you hated him because...?"

"Because I loved her. I couldn't have her, but he could, and I hated him for that." Terry's rueful chuckle still echoed with a long-ago pain.

Jan reached for her hand. "That's when you knew?"

"Yes and no. I was starting to put together the equation that falling in love with my best friend wasn't the norm for most girls, but the pieces fell into place for good a few months later."

Fascinated by this glimpse of Terry's youth, Jan forgot about the scenery. "What happened?"

"Sure you want to hear this?" Terry asked with a sideways glance.

Jan nodded.

"I was fifteen, but athletic and tall for my age. The senior girls' coach recruited me for the basketball rep team, and I ended up travelling to tournaments with them. This one time we were going to a season-ending tournament in Vancouver. There were a bunch of teams from all over the West, and they had us booked into dorm rooms for the week. Normally, you bunked with a teammate, but flu swept through the dorms, and they ended up sorting out the sickies from the non-sickies. Luck of the draw, I ended up in with an older girl from Regina."

Terry stretched out her legs and waggled her boots. "Jodie was a free spirit, and she sort of took me under her wing. My teammates always treated me like the kid because I was a couple of years younger, but Jodie treated me differently. Within a couple of days, whenever our teams weren't playing, we'd hang out together. Half the coaches were down with flu, too, so nobody paid much attention to what we were doing."

Jan squeezed her hand. "You don't have to tell me if you'd rather not."

Terry lifted Jan's gloved hand to her mouth for a kiss. "No, that's okay. I'm sure you know where this is going. The tournament was due to end on Sunday, and by Friday we were inseparable. We snuck out of the dorms that night. We counted on no one being around to check on curfews. We just went to a coffee house, but we spent about four hours there. We made wildly unrealistic plans to stay in touch and get together once we were home again. We couldn't stop touching each other, you know?"

Jan glanced at their interlocked hands.

Terry smiled. "Anyway, by the time we got back to our room, we were all over each other. I had no idea what I was doing, but Jodie did. Let's just say she spent the rest of the night teaching me. My coach was so pissed off at me the next afternoon. I could barely move, I was so sore and exhausted to boot. I've never played so poorly or cared less that I did. Jodie was waiting for me when I left the locker room, and we picked up where we left off. By the time we had to say goodbye on Sunday, I was crystal clear on my orientation."

"Did you ever see Jodie again?"

"No, we kept in touch for a while, but by the end of that summer, we'd drifted apart. All in all, not a bad way to lose your virginity, though."

"Mmm-hmm."

"Your turn. Was Rob your first?"

"No."

Terry's eyes widened.

Jan held up a hand. "We need to talk, my darling girl."

Terry sighed and looked down at her boots. "I know."

Gently, Jan cupped Terry's face and turned it to her. "You know how much I…care for you, right?"

Terry nodded. There was resignation in her eyes.

"No, don't look like that. I need you in my life. You're my best friend, but you're so much more than that. God, Terry… I've never felt like this, and I'm not sure how to handle it." Jan got on her knees and took both of Terry's hands in hers. "I love Rob. You know that I do, but you're in my head all the time. I can't stop thinking about you, wanting to be with you. I mean it's you I see when I — "

Terry chuckled. "Do the laundry?"

Jan blushed. "Yes."

Terry's eyes brimmed with such love and passion that it took her breath away.

"Oh, woman, you have no idea how you haunt my midnight hours, too," Terry whispered.

Jan's heart pounded furiously.

Terry leaned toward Jan, who met her halfway. Their lips merged, and they wrapped their arms around each other.

Lost in Terry's embrace, Jan barely noticed when the skis fell over and they sank back in the snow. She was overwhelmed with the delicious pressure of Terry's body moving against hers, Terry's lips possessing her mouth, and the gasps and pleas emanating from her own throat.

When Terry finally pulled back, Jan's whole body was on fire.

Terry sat upright, wrapped her arms around her knees, and rocked back and forth. "I'm sorry. I'm so sorry." She rested her head on her crossed arms. "I didn't mean to — "

Jan sat up and grabbed Terry's arm. "No, stop right there. It's just as much my fault. I wanted that as much as you did."

"I doubt it."

Jan scrambled to wrap her arms around Terry. "You listen to me. I love you. I want you like I've never wanted anyone before. I'm not playing with you. You're not an experiment. You are a part of my heart. If I were free, I'd be in your bed before you could blink an eye, but, my darling girl, I'm not free."

Terry hung on her every word, and Jan gentled the intensity of her tone as she voiced what needed to be said. "I also love Rob. I can't hurt him. I won't leave him. I honestly think he would die without me, and I'll never abandon him."

"I know."

Terry's soft words both reassured and saddened Jan. "He can't know about this, love. It would devastate him." Terry stiffened in her arms. *Surely she knows we can't tell him what we're feeling?*

She shuffled around until she was facing Terry, who refused to meet her eyes. "You do realize that, don't you? He would be terribly hurt if he knew I loved you. As far as he's concerned, we're just friends." She studied Terry's downcast face. *What is she thinking?*

Finally, Terry met her gaze. "You're right. He can't know."

Jan exhaled and sank back down beside Terry. "You know I don't expect you to be... well, you know... celibate or anything." She winced, the thought of Terry in another woman's arms too painful to contemplate. "Just don't tell me, okay?"

Terry stared at her before a rueful smile spread over her face. "I hate to tell you this, Jan, but you've put a rather sizable crimp in my love life. God, I haven't been with anyone since... since last September, I think."

Relief swept over Jan. "Aren't we too bloody noble."

"It's got nothing to do with nobility. It just so happens that I love you, too. In fact, I'm crazy about you, and being with someone else doesn't hold any appeal. If we can't be together, I'm not looking for a cheap substitute."

Jan's eyes welled up, and she stroked Terry's leg. "Oh, my darling girl, aren't we a pair?"

"Guess we're both going to be doing laundry overtime, eh?"

"I think I'd better buy a super-sized detergent." Jan glanced up. The winter sun was getting lower in the sky. "If we're going to get a few more runs in, we should probably get going."

Terry checked her watch and whistled. "Wow, it's almost three. Where did the time go?"

Jan raised an eyebrow and looked at the snow, which still held the impression of their bodies.

Terry flushed. "Oh, yeah." She stood up and recovered their skis. She handed Jan hers and snapped boots into the bindings.

"Since you provided such a wonderful lunch, dinner's on me," Jan said.

"Sure. I know a terrific steak house in Banff we can go to."

"Sounds great." Jan surveyed the terrain doubtfully. "All we have to do is get out of here in one piece."

"Would I lead you astray?"

"No, you wouldn't." *And I don't know whether I wish you would.*

Terry's eyes sparkled, and she began a slow descent through the trees, angling back to the nearest run.

Jan cast one wistful glance over this little piece of paradise and turned to follow.

CHAPTER 27

TERRY SPIED A PARKING SPOT near the steak house and pulled in. *Lady luck is with me today.*

They exited the car, and Jan stopped in mid-step as she looked down the street.

Terry checked over her shoulder. Three winter-shaggy elk ambled down the road, ignoring a car that tried to edge past them. Locals walking by on the sidewalk barely glanced at the large animals; they took their customary presence in stride.

"Um, Terry, are those — ?"

"Elk? Yeah, they wander all over the town. They're not a big problem at this time of year, though you don't want to mess with them when they're rutting. It's just part of living inside a national park. They know they have nothing to fear from us."

The elk were now within five metres, and Jan backed away.

Terry walked around the car, put herself between Jan and the animals, and steered her toward the restaurant.

Thick, rare steaks and dark microbrews proved the perfect après-ski. The next couple of hours flew by until they reluctantly agreed it was time to return to Calgary.

When they arrived home, Jan asked, "Do you want to come in for a bit?"

As loath as she was to end the day, Terry shook her head. "Thanks, but I'm pretty tired. I think I'll go home and soak in a hot bath."

"I know what you mean. I had a fabulous time, but my muscles are talking back to me right now. They're not exactly used to this."

"Then we'll have to do this again…just so they can adapt, of course."

"That's so kind of you to be concerned for my muscles. I don't suppose you could recommend a good masseuse."

God, could I ever. Terry took a deep breath and looked away.

Jan touched her arm. "I'm sorry. I shouldn't tease. I'd better get going."

"Are you coming over for Sunday dinner tomorrow?"

"No, we can't. It's John's birthday, so we're going to Kate's for dinner. Why don't you give me a call in the afternoon — or e-mail me."

"How about I call and e-mail you?"

Jan brushed her lips across Terry's cheek. "You do that." She pushed open the door. "Thank you for an incredible day. I can't remember the last time I had so much fun." She closed the door and started up the walk to her house.

Terry stared after her, touching her cheek.

Terry entered her bedroom and tossed keys and wallet on top of the desk. When she stretched, her muscles served notice of how hard she'd pushed them that day. She sat on the bed to peel off her thick socks. *I haven't had that much fun in ages. I wonder if she'll be able to get away for another ski day before the end of the season.*

Terry tossed her socks toward the brimming laundry basket, then stood and unzipped her ski suit. She was down to her thermal long johns when a knock sounded at her door.

"Yes?"

"It's Randy. I just wanted to say goodbye."

"Come on in."

He opened the door and poked his head around.

Terry waved him in. "Are you heading out now?"

Randy sat down beside her. "Yeah, we're going to the airport in about ten minutes. I'm catching the last flight out tonight. Gotta be at work tomorrow morning."

Terry squeezed his knee. "I'm really glad you made it down for the week. It was great seeing you, and I know Michael was thrilled to have you back."

His face fell.

"Randy? Everything all right?"

He stared at the floor. "Sure. I'm glad I could make it, too. It's gonna be a while before I make it back, though. You keep an eye on that boy of mine now, okay? Try and keep him out of trouble."

She studied Randy. "Okay, what's going on? Don't tell me there's trouble in paradise."

"No, no, nothing like that. It's just hard having to go away all the time, you know? Mikey's not very happy about it. Sometimes I worry he'll just give up on us and find someone more reliable."

Terry snorted. "They don't come more reliable than you. But look, if being away in the oil patch is causing a problem, why don't you consider something here in the city?"

Randy scrubbed a massive hand over his face. "All I know is being a rigger. I don't have any other skills to offer an employer."

"You know if you were serious about staying here, I'll bet my dad and brothers would take you on in a flash." She held up a hand. "I know you don't have any experience in construction, but that doesn't mean you don't have anything to offer. You're strong and reliable. You work harder than any three men put together. My brothers witnessed that when we moved Lisa and Robyn into their house. You could learn the skills you need on the job. I'll bet Dad would jump at having an employee like you. You say the word, and I'll talk to him. They always need more men come summertime. You'd have to start at the bottom, but it wouldn't take you long to work your way up. You could even go after your journeyman papers eventually if you want."

Randy's brow furrowed.

He's not saying no. "Just think about it, okay? I know it's a big decision and you'd be leaving a lot of money for a smaller paycheque, but this way you and Michael could have a future."

Stark misery flashed in Randy's eyes. "We don't have a future. Look at me. I'm a rigger with a grade-ten education. Michael comes from the finest schools in the country. He's old money, and his dad already has a seat lined up for him on Bay Street once he has his MBA. The only reason he's out here at all and not in Queen's is because he somehow convinced his parents he needed space before he settled down. His family has plans for him, and there's no way in hell they could ever include me. Best I can hope for is that Mikey will stick with me until he's done with university, and even that's a pretty far-fetched hope."

Terry had never heard the placid giant so pessimistic. "Jesus, Randy, Michael loves you —"

"No, I love him. I even told him so this week, but he couldn't say it back. He got all flustered and red, so I laughed it off. Told him I musta had too many beers."

"No, now come on. I saw how he acted when you were coming back. Michael does love you."

Randy got to his feet and patted her on the shoulder. "I know he cares, but he's more of a realist than you are. You don't harness a thoroughbred to a draft horse and think it'll last forever. But hey, I didn't mean to lay this on you. I just wanted to say goodbye and thank you for the hospitality. I'll see you next time around, okay?"

Terry stood and hugged him.

Randy returned the embrace. "I'll give serious thought to your proposal, all right? It might not be a bad idea to find a new career in town. I would've had to one day anyway, so this could be a good opportunity." He closed the door behind him.

Terry's earlier euphoria ebbed away. *Michael, Michael, Michael…are you screwing up the best thing to happen to you?* She stripped off the last of her clothes and grabbed a robe and a book before going downstairs for a bath.

An hour later, her mood much improved by bubbles and a good mystery, she returned to her room and flopped on the bed with her book.

Ten minutes later, she realized she'd been rereading the same paragraph and set the book aside. Her thoughts turned to their day and tryst on the side of the mountain, the sweet pressure of Jan's lips, the taste of her mouth, and the way Jan writhed beneath her. Terry's nostrils flared, and she opened her robe. One hand trailed across her belly and down her thigh. Her legs parted as arousal began to coil within.

She summoned the image of Jan, auburn hair spilled over the snow, ardent green eyes reflecting her own passion, wet lips parted and inviting. In her mind, Terry slowly lowered the zipper of Jan's ski jacket, inching it down to expose…multiple layers of thick sweaters and cold weather wear.

Terry's eyes snapped open, and her wandering fingers stilled. *Shit! Okay, let's try this again.* She took a deep breath, closed her eyes, and reset her fantasy. Now Jan reclined on the bed, arms outstretched to welcome her.

Breath quickening, Terry traced a line up the centre of Jan's body and around the lower curve of one breast. Jan slowly followed instructions and unbuttoned her blouse, exposing a black satin teddy —

Jan looked down and then back up at Terry, raising one eyebrow. "A teddy? Really? I've never even owned a teddy."

Terry groaned, her fingers stilling again, just as they had reached an eager nipple. *All right, no teddy...but you're wearing a black lace bra.* Instantly, her fantasy lover was clad in a black lace bra, and Terry sighed happily. Her hand slid deep between her legs just as Jan lowered her pants over a black thong that barely covered a nest of dark red curls —

A knock sounded at the door.

Terry hissed. She hastily pulled her robe together and re-tied the sash.

Michael pushed open the door. "Hey, Ter. I saw your light on. Hope you weren't asleep or anything." He ambled over to sit beside her on the bed.

"Nope, not sleeping." Terry dried her hand discreetly on her robe and grabbed her novel. "Just doing a little reading before I turned out the lights." *Please don't be let it be a long heart-to-heart tonight.*

Michael kicked off his shoes, grabbed one of her pillows to tuck under his head, and made himself comfortable across the foot of the bed.

So much for that. Terry sighed. *C'est la vie.* "Randy's off then, is he?"

"Yes." Michael picked idly at her duvet.

She nudged him with her foot. "Hey, gloomy Gus, he'll be back soon. In fact, he may be back sooner than you think."

"He told me about your proposition. It was really sweet of you to offer."

"Then why so glum? If this works out, he could be back in town for good before summer. Isn't that what you want? To have Randy around all the time?"

Michael rolled on his back and stared at the ceiling. "Of course it is. It'd be great to have him working in town."

"Uh-huh. So why do you look like Cindy Lou Who just discovering that the Grinch stole Christmas?"

He didn't say anything.

Terry gave him time, watching his face.

Finally, he rolled back toward her. "Randy told me that he loved me a couple of days ago."

"And? Isn't that a good thing?"

Michael covered his face with his hands. "You'd think so, wouldn't you? I couldn't even say it back. I'm such an asshole."

"No, you're not. If you don't love him—"

Michael sat upright. "But that's the thing, Ter. I do love him. I've never met a guy like him before. He doesn't play games, you know? He's the most honest, strong, straightforward man around. With Randy, what you see is what you get. He makes me feel safe and so loved…"

Terry's brow furrowed. "So if you do love him, and he obviously loves you, what's the problem?"

"It should be so easy, but I froze. As soon as he said that he loved me, I froze. Couldn't say a damned thing. And the worst part was, I could see the hurt in his eyes, but he still tried to make things easy for me by laughing it off. God, I don't deserve him."

Terry ran a hand through her hair. "I'm sure Randy's okay. I mean he's seriously thinking of moving into town, so he must want to be with you. I'll bet that he knows you just need time, and you'll say it back to him when you're ready."

Michael hung his head. "I'll never be able to say it to him."

Terry blinked, and a growing indignation rose within. "Why?"

"It's the same thing as with Lisa and Robyn's request. I have to think of my family. You know that."

"You do, do you? So because you're one of the Toronto Seatons, you can't tell a decent, honourable man who thinks you bloody well walk on water that you love him…when you do?"

Michael scowled. "It's not like that—"

Terry glared at him. "The hell it's not. You're not even living your own life. You're taking an MBA when you have zero interest in business because Daddy has a partnership waiting for you. You've balked at fathering a child for two wonderful people when it may be the only chance you ever have, because your parents might find out about it. You were even thinking of marrying a woman you don't love to meet your social obligations, being totally unfair to both of you. And now, when you admit you're in love, you're rejecting a wonderful man because he doesn't fit into your father's plans? Jesus, Michael! You're completely fucked up."

"I'm fucked up? Christ, you're in love with a married woman who loves you too but will never leave her husband, and you have the nerve to say I'm fucked up? You won't even have a discreet affair with her. What the hell are *you* going to do? Spend the rest of your life playing with yourself while she heads home to her husband every day?"

His furious words shocked both of them, and they stared at each other.

Michael blinked first and patted Terry's ankle. "Aw shit, I'm so sorry. I didn't mean anything by it."

"No, you did, but it's okay. You're right. We're both messed up." *Jesus, now* I'm *depressed.* "To answer your question, rhetorical or not, I don't have the vaguest idea what I'm going to do. All I know is that I love her, and I'm going to take it day by day."

Michael hopped off the end of bed and came around to hug her.

Terry returned the embrace.

"Here, shove over and make some room, you bed hog." He wiggled onto the bed beside her.

Peace restored, they reclined against the pillows, shoulders braced against each other.

"So what do I do?"

His plaintive question tugged at Terry's heart. "I don't have the answer for you, sweetie. Hell, I don't even have any answers for my own life. No way am I going to take on the Seaton dynasty."

Michael's head dropped to her shoulder. "I don't want to take them on either."

"What do you want? I mean if you didn't have to worry about your family and nothing else was a factor, what would you do about Randy and Lisa and Robyn?"

Michael looked at her wistfully. "I'd get Randy a ranch in the foothills where he could run the horses he loves. I'd father as many children as Lisa and Robyn wanted to have and be the best uncle to them that I possibly could. It sounds so simple, doesn't it?"

"Maybe it is that simple. Maybe you need to figure out exactly what will make you happy and forget about everything else. I know your family has had expectations of you from the moment you were born, but it's your life. You only get one. Do you really want to waste it doing what everyone else expects of you rather than what you truly want?"

Michael shook his head.

"Is it the money? Are you afraid of being cut off from the family fortune if you don't toe the line?"

"No. I mean I like the money. I've always had it, so it'd be weird to be disinherited, but to tell you the truth I'd still have my grandfather's trust fund, so I wouldn't be broke."

Terry sat up straighter and jostled him. "Then what's stopping you? Why don't you do exactly what you want to do, regardless of your parents?"

"I guess... I don't know, Terry. I...I suppose...I could, couldn't I? It's all possible if I really want it to be. I can make my life out here. I don't have to go back to Toronto, do I?"

"Not if you don't want to. Last I looked you were a grown man with the freedom to choose."

Michael's expression dimmed. "But I might lose Mom and Dad. I do love them, Ter. They're my family. It's always been the three of us, you know?"

God, I wish I'd never made that promise to his mom. "I can't claim to know your parents well, but I swear to you, if you decide to be honest with them, I have no doubt that at least your mother will understand, and I'll bet you anything that she would help your father eventually accept it, though it might take a while." She stared at him intently. *C'mon, man, read between the lines.*

Cautious hope dawned in his eyes.

Maybe I got through to him.

"Do you really think so?" Michael asked.

"Yes. I really think so, with all my heart."

He searched her face, then gave a noncommittal grunt.

Terry didn't press him further. *The seed is planted. We'll just have to wait and see if it blooms. I did my best, Randy.*

Michael settled back beside her. "Now that we've solved my life, what are we going to do about yours?"

"Not much we can do, is there?" He frowned, and she shook her head. "No, it's okay. I'm really happy just to be friends with her again. I had a fabulous time skiing with her, and I'm looking forward to our next day together."

"Is it enough?"

"Has to be, doesn't it?"

"Mmm-hmm. I've got a hypothetical question for you. If she wanted to make love with you, would you say yes?"

"She does want to make love with me. But she's too loyal to Rob and too honourable to do that to him. I don't blame her. Hell, I even admire it…not that it makes it any easier."

"No, that's not what I mean. If someday she does decide that you and she can have a quiet affair without anyone finding out, what are you going to say?"

"Well, not that I think that'll ever happen, but if she ever said yes, I don't think I'd be strong enough to say no."

There was no trace of judgment in Michael's eyes. He nodded, then a big yawn overtook him.

"Haven't been getting much sleep lately, Mikey?"

He smacked her shoulder "Hey! Only Randy gets to call me that."

Terry punched him back. "And doesn't that tell you everything you need to know?"

"Maybe. Thanks, Ter. I feel a lot better. I'll let you get back to your book now. See you in the morning."

After he left, Terry set the abandoned novel aside, took off her robe, and slid under the covers. She turned the lamp off and stared into the dark.

If someday she does decide that you and she can have a quiet affair without anyone finding out, what are you going to say?

CHAPTER 28

TERRY ROUNDED THE CORNER WHILE she sorted the bundle of mail in her hand. She glanced up the block at the Spencer bungalow and froze.

An ambulance was parked in front, and two men in dark blue uniforms extracted a gurney from the rear.

She bolted up the street, heavy mailbags thumping against her sides. Her adrenaline-fuelled sprint ended when she burst through Jan and Rob's front door and slammed to a stop.

Four surprised faces looked at her. One of the attendants stood beside Jan, his pen poised over his clipboard. The other attendant squatted by Rob's recliner.

Jan shook off the surprise first. She crossed to Terry's side and placed a hand on her shoulder. "Hey, are you okay?"

Terry sucked in deep gulps of air. She glanced from Jan to Rob. Both looked fine. "I saw…the ambulance."

"And you thought something was wrong. No, nothing's wrong. It's actually a private ambulance that does patient transfers. We saw Rob's doctor yesterday, and she arranged for him to have a sleep study at Foothills. She also detected a few minor crackles in his lungs, so he's going to have a course of IV antibiotics for two days to head off trouble before it starts."

"How come you're not taking him to the hospital in the van?"

Jan rolled her eyes. "Because the van died on me. It's been

giving me some trouble lately, but I've been putting off getting it into the garage. My own stupid fault, but naturally, when I needed it most, it wouldn't start."

Terry shrugged off her bags. "I'm glad it's nothing serious."

Jan turned back to the attendant who was tapping his pen on his clipboard.

Terry walked over to Rob's chair. "Man, don't scare me like that." She impulsively leaned over and hugged him.

Rob's eyes widened. "Well, geez, that's what you get for jumping to conclusions. But thanks for caring."

Terry knelt as the other attendant left to retrieve the gurney. She laid one hand on Rob's arm and looked at him steadily. "I've always cared, Rob. I never stopped." Her words were quiet, meant only for his ears.

"Thank you." Rob's eyes glistened.

She patted his arm and stood.

"Terry?"

She looked down at him.

"Neither did I."

They looked at each other for a long moment, then she smiled. "I'd better get back to work." She shouldered her bags and glanced at Jan. "Anything I can do to help? Will you need a ride home from the hospital?"

"Thanks, but I don't know how long I'll be. I want to make sure he's settled and that the sleep clinic is all teed up for tonight, so I'll just take a cab when I'm ready. I'll give you a call later, okay?"

Terry nodded and looked at Rob. "Take care of yourself, okay? Jordy and I'll pop by for a visit tomorrow night."

"Bring me a chocolate milkshake?"

"One chocolate milkshake as ordered, and if you're really good, I may even coax Mom into making you cookies."

Rob winked. "I'm so good I can get affidavits to prove it."

Terry laughed and left the house. *Note to self, ask Mom to make Rob his favourite cookies.*

She was drained by the ebbing adrenaline but relieved that her fears had been misplaced. She picked up her route where she had left off. A short while later, the ambulance pulled away.

For the first time in months, Terry felt a ray of optimism that the tension between her and Rob might ease. They had both been on their best behaviour around Jan, but she missed the easygoing camaraderie that marked the early months of their friendship.

Neither could overlook the adversarial subtext between them, but since they were inextricably bound by their love for Jan, they couldn't avoid each other.

Even a détente would be better than the way it's been. Here's hoping...

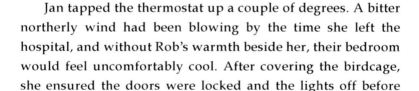

Jan tapped the thermostat up a couple of degrees. A bitter northerly wind had been blowing by the time she left the hospital, and without Rob's warmth beside her, their bedroom would feel uncomfortably cool. After covering the birdcage, she ensured the doors were locked and the lights off before going to bed.

She shivered as she slid between cold sheets. Jan was hopeful that the sleep study would pinpoint why Rob's slumber was so erratic, but she missed him. *At least he won't be in the hospital too long this time.*

Jan didn't know what woke her hours later, whether it was a sound, a light, or the simple sense of another's presence pervading the room. But without conscious decision, she sat upright, arms locked around her knees, and looked at Rob standing at the foot of their bed.

How did he get up without waking me? Wait a minute... Rob could not be standing there or anywhere.

She stared at the robust figure rocking back on his heels. His hands were tucked in the pockets of a dark blue flight jacket that fit snugly over broad shoulders and a forage cap was pushed back on thick brown hair. Blue eyes shone at her, filled with love. *He's so tall.* The inanity rattled in her mind as she strove to make sense of it.

Instinctively, she reached out to him, but he shook his head and she let her arm fall. He ran his hand through his hair and adjusted his cap. His hand entranced her, its sturdy muscularity so different from the frailty she was used to. A light gleamed dully off the gold band she had placed on his finger so many years ago.

Rob beamed at her, and she was struck by his cheerful vitality. Then his smile faded, and he regarded her urgently.

"What is it?"

"I love you, Jan."

The words he had spoken thousands of times sounded strange to Jan. The voice was his, but as she had never heard him — deep, husky, resonant.

Rob smiled. "I know you know that, my love, but I couldn't leave without telling you one more time."

"Leave?" Sadness sliced through her and was echoed in his face.

He nodded, and they gazed at each other for long moments, words superfluous as they reaffirmed the love they shared.

Tears filled Jan's eyes and obscured Rob's image. "I'll miss you, angel."

"As I will you, Jannie, but you'll be okay. My love...thank you." His words were softer now.

"No." Jan dashed away the tears, but it didn't stop his image from fading. "Please don't go."

His gaze caressed her as his form lost substance.

Then he was gone, and she clung to the afterimage burned into her memory. "Save me a dance, angel." In the dark and silent room, Jan buried her head in her arms.

When the phone began to ring on the bedside table, she didn't start. She made no move to pick it up. She didn't need to. She knew who it was and what they had to tell her.

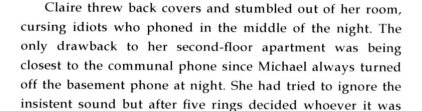

Claire threw back covers and stumbled out of her room, cursing idiots who phoned in the middle of the night. The only drawback to her second-floor apartment was being closest to the communal phone since Michael always turned off the basement phone at night. She had tried to ignore the insistent sound but after five rings decided whoever it was wasn't giving up. She went down the stairs and grabbed the hall receiver. "Allo?"

"Claire? I'm so sorry to wake you, but I need to speak to Terry, please."

Claire almost didn't recognize the anguished voice, but alertness set in as she identified the caller. "Jan? Are you all right?"

A muffled sob met her inquiry.

"Just a minute. I'll go get her."

She set the phone down and dashed up the stairs. When she reached Terry's room, she flung open the door and flipped on the light.

"What the hell?" Terry sat upright and looked blearily at the clock. "For crying out loud, it's only four thirty."

"You have to come right away. Something's wrong."

Terry swung her feet out of the bed. "What are you talking about? What's wrong?"

Claire grabbed her arm and hustled her out of the room. "Jan's on the phone, and there's something very wrong."

"Jan?"

"Oui, Jan. Hurry."

Terry took the stairs in giant leaps and thundered down to the main floor.

Claire followed close behind at a safer pace. By the time she reached the main floor, Terry was on the phone.

"Oh, God," Terry said. "I'm on my way, sweetheart. Just hang on."

Michael popped his head out of the basement door, sleepy eyes taking in the scene. "What's going on? Sounds like a damned herd of elephants up here."

Terry dropped the receiver in the cradle. "Rob died tonight. I've got to get over there."

Claire and Michael gasped as Terry ran back up the stairs. Claire sat down heavily in the hall chair, and Michael crouched beside her. She reached for his hand. They stayed there until Terry dashed back down the stairs moments later. She was still wearing her sleep shirt atop her jeans. She jerked her jacket out of the closet and fumbled with her boots.

Michael asked, "Do you want me to drive you over?"

Terry shook her head; tears ran down her cheeks. "No, thanks. I have to get going. I have to get to her." She was up and running down the hall to the back door before they could utter another word.

Claire sighed. "This is so terribly sad. There is no way I'm going back to sleep."

"Me neither. Do you think we should call Terry's family?"

"Oui. Emily would want to know, and Terry may not have

the chance to phone her. Why don't you make the call, and I'll make the coffee."

Terry barrelled around the corner, grateful that nearly empty roads facilitated her race through city streets. She swerved into the curb, ripped the keys out of the ignition, and ran up the path before the car stopped rumbling. Flashes of her last frantic sprint less than twenty-four hours ago streaked through her mind, but with the inescapable knowledge that there was no happy ending this time.

She fumbled to fit her key in the lock and pushed open the door. Suddenly apprehensive, she took a deep breath and stepped inside.

Jan was curled up in Rob's chair, clutching his favourite plaid blanket. Her eyes were red, and tears rolled down her face.

Terry crossed to her, knelt, and took her in an embrace. "I'm here."

Jan's body shook, and Terry's tears soaked Jan's shoulder.

They stayed like that for a long time until Jan calmed.

"Tell me."

"He was finished at the sleep clinic, and they transferred him back up to his room. He was settled in by two a.m., and the nurse said he was fine. Somehow, he slipped away between then and when she next checked." Jan's eyes filled again. "They didn't try to revive him because of the DNR on his records from the last time. God, Terry, what if they could've brought him back if I hadn't let them put that on?"

Terry shook her head. "No, sweetheart. There's no way you should feel guilty about this. Remember what Rob's wishes were, and remember what they told you would probably happen if he did have a stroke or heart attack? You know damned well that he didn't want to hang on hooked up to machines. That wasn't Rob."

"I know. It's just…how could this happen? He was just in for a sleep study."

Terry stroked Jan's back. "Do you remember telling me that you always hoped he'd slip away easily in his sleep rather than lingering in some hospital hooked up to tubes and machines? Well, that's what happened. He went to sleep and didn't wake up."

Jan ran a hand over her eyes. "But I'd always hoped I'd be there for him, you know? I wanted to hold him, send him from this world to the next knowing how much I loved him, how lucky I was to have met him and to have shared my life with him."

"He knew that. How could he not? You lived your love for him every day."

Jan looked up at her pleadingly. "I want to see him."

Terry stood and offered Jan her hand. "Then let's go see him and say goodbye."

"He already said goodbye." Jan's words were so soft that Terry almost missed them.

The drive to the hospital was quiet, both lost in their thoughts. When they arrived, a sympathetic nurse escorted them to Rob's room.

"We'll be moving him soon, dear. But since he didn't have a roommate, we thought we'd leave him until you arrived." The nurse, accustomed to the rhythms of life and death, patted Jan on the arm and left them alone.

Jan stared at the quiet form covered by a white sheet.

Terry struggled to push her own grief aside, determined to be strong for Jan. But when Jan peeled back the cover, Terry lost her battle. The tears flowed unchecked, her sorrow compounded by a growing sense of guilt.

Jan caressed Rob's face, pushing back his stubborn forelock and rubbing at a bit of leftover gel on his temple.

Terry had never seen a dead body before and was struck by the absolute stillness, the absence of…everything.

Jan whispered, "Thank you, too, angel."

Terry was about to retreat to allow Jan space when she turned and took her hand.

"He's not there, Terry. That's not him."

Startled, Terry glanced at the bed.

"No, I mean that's only a shell that he left behind." She pulled the sheet up, rested her hand on Rob's chest for a minute, and led Terry out of the room.

Terry grinned and dabbed at her wet eyes. *God, he's got a million of them!*

Eric stood at the front of the funeral chapel as waves of laughter rolled through the crowd over another of his Rob-stories.

Terry had been surprised to learn that the irreverent jet jockey was a lay minister in his church, but Eric had not only arrived with an impressive collection of Rob's brother pilots, he was conducting Rob's service with equal parts laughter and tears.

Eric reached inside his suit jacket and extracted a sheet of paper. "I want to wrap this up today by reading a letter, one that Jan wrote Rob the day he died." He fumbled with his reading glasses.

"My dearest Rob. It's only been a few hours since you said goodbye, and I still can't believe you're gone. A huge hole has opened in my heart. I hope you can hear me because I need to tell you this. I was a thousand times blessed to have you in my life. Countless times through the years I was awestruck at your courage as you handled every obstacle thrown your way with incredible grace. Beloved, you made us laugh when any other would have sobbed at what your own body inflicted on you. You had no time for self-pity, and no one else thought to pity you, for your very nature demanded so much more: respect, admiration, love. For the rest of my days, your life will be my shining example of how to live to the fullest the human spirit is capable of. Beautiful man, I love you... I miss you."

Terry's tears flowed anew, and Jan shuddered next to her. She took her hand and squeezed it gently. On the other side, Kate patted Jan's leg.

"That wraps up this part of the service. We're going to move to Springfield airport now for those who wish to join us, and then we'll gather at four thirty at Jan and Rob's home to toast his memory and tell more stories." Eric took off his glasses and wiped his eyes. "Heaven knows we've got an endless supply of them." He stepped down from the podium and led the way out of the chapel.

Terry stood and kept a supportive hand on Jan's back as she followed Kate, John, and Kevin out of the pew. Emily waited to exit the next pew with the rest of the Sanderson family. "I'll see you out there, Mom. I'm going to drive Jan."

Emily nodded. "We'll meet you there."

"Jordy —" Terry couldn't say it, but he nodded.

"I've got it. Don't worry."

When they arrived at the airfield, Terry couldn't help flashing back on the last time she'd been there for the air show. Her throat tightened, and for the hundredth time she forced back her grief and guilt. *No. This is not the time to wallow.* It didn't stop the tears, though, and Jan handed her another tissue, sympathy in her eyes. *Jesus, and I'm supposed to be strong for her. Doing great there, Sanderson.*

They walked to the tarmac where a funeral wreath stood, enclosing Rob's photo. Eric stood next to it, flanked by Tom and two of Rob's former wingmen.

Terry glanced over, pleased to see Michael and Claire standing with the entire Sanderson clan, along with Lisa and Robyn. Donny and his wife were there, as was Rob's family, who had come from the East for the funeral.

Jordy stepped out from where he stood beside his parents and walked to Jan, carrying a bronze urn. He stopped in front of her and extended the urn.

Jan laid her hands on it and bowed her head for a long moment, then nodded.

Jordy joined the group of pilots and climbed into the small plane with Eric.

Terry was struck by how he had grown these past few days. Despite his grief, Jordy was steadfast in standing by Jan and helping her in every way he could. It was his way to honour Rob's trust in him. In turn, Jan asked him to take charge of Rob's ashes, and he accepted the responsibility with grace and dignity.

The four small aircraft taxied to the runway, led by Eric's and Tom's red and black bi-wings. Jan edged closer as the formation began to roll and lifted off. Terry wrapped an arm around her shoulders as the flight banked and turned west. Once over the mountains, Jordy would open the urn and let the wind pull Rob's earthly remains to their final rest.

The small crowd waited and conversed quietly until Donny spotted the formation returning.

Jan straightened under Terry's arm.

As the flight approached the airfield, a lone aircraft broke away, soaring heavenwards as Rob was honoured with the missing man formation.

Everyone was silent when the planes roared overhead. Then the crowd began to drift apart as people made plans to regroup at Jan's home for the reception.

Emily walked over to them. "I'm going to head over to the house. Kate, did you want to join me and we'll get everything set out before people arrive?"

Kate gave Jan a quick hug and walked off with Emily.

Terry turned and took Jan's hand. "How are you doing?"

Jan's eyes were peaceful. "I'm okay. It really was a beautiful send-off, don't you think? He'd have loved his friends' tribute."

"It was perfect."

Jan slipped an arm around Terry's waist. "Thank you for being here for me. I don't know how I'd have gotten through these last few days without you and your family."

"Always."

CHAPTER 29

TERRY STROKED SPOOKY'S FUR. IT had been months since the Christmas insult to the cat's dignity, and he appeared to have fully forgiven her. "Good thing you don't hold a grudge, buddy." She glanced up as Marika returned from the kitchen with a refill for her coffee. "Thanks."

"You're welcome." Marika resumed her seat across from Terry and curled her legs beneath her. "So, do you think it's serious with Matt and Claire?"

"I think it's serious for Matt, but, honestly, Claire is not making it easy on him. She has no intention of becoming one more notch on his bedpost."

Marika smiled. "I take it that she's looking for a relationship with a little more depth than he's used to?"

"I think he's going to have to go to Quebec to pass her family's inspection before he sets one foot beyond her bedroom door. You know what the best part is, though? He's so crazy about her that he'll jump through any hoop she sets. I caught him reading *What Women Want* last week. He was so embarrassed, but when I didn't tease him, he actually asked some questions. I never thought I'd see the day when Matt would choose chivalry and cold showers over an easy conquest."

"Yes, it's amazing what love will do." Marika met her gaze steadily. "So, did you hear back from the publisher?"

"I did. Unfortunately, it was another rejection slip." Terry shrugged. "If it's meant to happen, it will. I'm not going to lose sleep over it."

"That's a very pragmatic view given how hard you've worked to get the manuscript ready."

"Everything else in my life is going so well that it's hard to get upset about something I have no control over. Speaking of which, did you ever find a replacement for your assistant?"

Marika groaned.

"I'll take it that's a no?"

"Not only is it a no, but I only have a few weeks until Marion starts her maternity leave. I have to find someone fast so they can be briefed before Marion leaves. I'm so swamped with cases I haven't had time to do more than glance at resumes."

"Don't you have a pool of assistants at the firm?"

"No, every lawyer has their own assistant, though we do share floaters, depending on the workload. I'm going to end up hiring the first person who shows up for an interview, just to get it over with. Anyway, let's not talk about it. It'll just ruin my weekend. On a much brighter topic, did you say that Randy is due back in town soon?"

"He starts working for my dad at the beginning of the month."

"I imagine Michael is pleased?"

"You could say that. He hasn't been this excited since Lisa and Robyn broke the news that his swimmers had done their job. God, I thought he was going to have a coronary that day. You should have seen Sunday dinner that week. I don't know who was the prouder papa-to-be, Michael or Duncan. You'd have thought both of them did it all by themselves. But the best part was when Lisa and Karen looked at each other, rolled their eyes, and started telling the guys exactly what was going to happen in about seven months time. By the time they were done, Michael and Duncan were as green as the broccoli. Sure shut 'em up, though."

They laughed, and Terry cocked her head. "Did you ever think of having kids?"

Marika coughed as her coffee went down the wrong way. "I'm not exactly the maternal sort, in case you hadn't noticed. Spooky's just lucky that he's reasonably self-sufficient. No, I don't think motherhood is in the cards for me. Why, are you thinking about it?"

"Maybe someday. I'm not in any hurry."

"Well, you're not exactly ancient, so you have lots of time. How's Lisa doing anyway?"

"Pretty well, actually. Not a lot of morning sickness, so she got off lucky, unlike Karen. Robyn is driving her crazy, though. She won't even let Lisa carry groceries from the car. Lisa wanted to play ball as long as she could, but Robyn put her foot down. First time I've seen that happen, and darned if Lisa didn't back down. We sure miss her at shortstop. Our record's only two and two without her."

"Does Jan play?"

"No, but we put her to work as the equipment manager."

"So things are going well with you two?"

Terry flinched. "Mmm-hmm."

Marika sighed. "You know, you can't avoid this forever."

"I'm not avoiding anything."

"Sure you're not. It's been three months now since he died. I know you love Jan, and from what you've told me, she loves you, too. So when are you going to do something about it?"

"Like what?" Terry refused to meet Marika's gaze.

"Oh, for heaven's sake." Marika shook her head. "Do I really have to paint you a picture?"

"Well, it's not like we're not together all the time. We go

out and do things, and we spend hours on the phone when we're apart."

"Yet here you are on a Friday night, keeping me and Spooky company when you should be making love to the woman you adore."

"She had a meeting tonight. Besides, maybe I like hanging out with you and Spooky."

"And maybe you're just scared spitless. Have you even gone any further than kissing her?"

Terry flushed and shook her head.

"I'm pretty sure you know what comes next. So what exactly is holding you up?"

"Geez, she just lost her husband. I don't want to rush her before she's ready." Terry's reason sounded feeble even to herself.

Jan mourned Rob's loss deeply but hadn't let it prevent her from going on with life. With no pressing financial need to work, she filled her days volunteering with the MS Society, the food bank, and a hospice. Terry often caught Jan's curious looks when they parted after an evening out and knew Jan was waiting for her to make the first move.

Marika levelled a stern gaze at her. "All right, enough bullshit. Exactly what is going on? This isn't like you at all."

Terry hung her head. "I feel guilty."

"Excuse me? Guilty about what? You didn't cause Rob's death."

"What if I did?" The thought had haunted Terry ever since she'd seen Rob's body under white sheets in his hospital room. "What if the stress of knowing what was going on between Jan and me ended up killing him?"

"Good lord, Terry. Surely you don't really think that?

From what you've told me, Rob lived on borrowed time for years. This is in no way your fault."

Terry leaned forward, and Spooky jumped to the floor. "Even if I didn't directly cause his death, what about how unhappy I made him the last couple of months of his life? I interfered with the only thing that mattered to him. He gave my family and me nothing but kindness, and how did I repay him? I got involved romantically with his wife. For God's sake, Marika, he was a helpless invalid, and I stabbed him right in the heart."

"But you two didn't do anything. You didn't have an affair."

"Not physical, but definitely emotional. It was agony for him knowing that we were in love."

Marika arched an eyebrow. "And that's why you won't have sex with Jan? Because you feel guilty for falling in love with her?"

Terry nodded, her throat thick with emotion.

"That's just about the dumbest reason I've ever heard."

Terry scowled. "Hey — "

Marika stood up. "Out."

"You're kicking me out?"

"Yes. It's for your own good. I'm not letting you hide here anymore." She took Terry's arm.

"But, but — "

Marika pressed Terry's jacket into her hands and opened the door. "I love you dearly, but you're driving me crazy with all the moping around. Go see your lady and straighten this out. I don't want to see you darken my door again until you do." She kissed Terry's cheek. "Besides, some of us do have a life. I have a date tonight, and you're not invited."

"You have a date?"

Marika rolled her eyes. "It does happen from time to time. Now go. You have business to attend to." She shut the door in Terry's face.

Terry stared at the closed door for a few moments, then turned and walked down the hall to the elevator. "A date. She has a date."

When the elevator arrived, Terry shot a forlorn glance back down the hall and stepped inside.

————◆————

Still moping over Marika's bluntness, Terry ignored Michael's laughter and the soft hum of voices in the living room and headed up the stairs. *Guess he's entertaining tonight. Well, I'm not in the mood to see anyone, including him.*

When she walked into her room, she stopped short. "What the hell?" The usual heaps of clothes and damp towels had been collected and removed. Her bed was neatly made, and even her carpet appeared to have been vacuumed. "Guess Michael couldn't stand it anymore." He'd been vociferous about her lack of housekeeping when he'd dropped into the garret the night before. "I owe you one, buddy."

Terry crossed the room and opened the window, which let in the fragrant spring air. She slouched on the window seat, legs folded under her, and looked out over the backyard. As she gazed at the old crabapple tree covered in brilliant pink blossoms, her thoughts drifted.

Her current romantic stasis couldn't go on forever, but she didn't know how to break out of it. Every time she contemplated making love to Jan, an image of Rob as she had last seen him came into mind. She hated that guilt was crippling her. *God, how long is Jan's patience going to last?*

"You look like you're a million miles away, love."

"Aack!" Terry teetered toward the open window.

Jan grabbed her arm and pulled her around until her feet were safely planted on the floor.

"Damn, you scared the life out of me. The screen wouldn't have stopped me. I'd have gone right out the window."

"I'm sorry." There was an unrepentant twinkle in Jan's eyes. "I wouldn't let you fall."

Terry sat down and tugged at the neck of her shirt. "I thought you had a meeting tonight."

"I did, and somehow your mom and I were maneuvered into being on the organizing committee for the summer food drive." Jan smiled. "Tonight Emily asked me to sit with the family for Jordy's grad next month."

Terry kept a nervous eye on her. "That's good. I'm glad you two get on so well."

Jan drew one finger down the middle of Terry's shirt. "Emily's a terrific person. A lot like her daughter, actually. Anyway, the meeting was over a couple of hours ago, and I decided to drop by and see my favourite girl."

"Good. I'm glad you did." Terry wiped her palms on her jeans. Something was different about Jan tonight. The charged atmosphere excited and unnerved Terry in equal measure. When Jan met her gaze, she forgot to breathe. Tingles ran through her body and settled between her legs. *Uh-oh.* "Room."

Jan blinked.

"Don't you think my room looks great? Michael cleaned it up for me."

Amusement rippled over Jan's face. "Michael cleaned it up for you, did he? That was awfully nice of him."

"Well, yeah. At least I think it was him. I mean, who else would clean it?"

"Maybe somebody who thought a tidy room and clean sheets would be conducive to…a good night's sleep."

"Oh. Ohhh!" The full import of what Jan said sank in, and Terry's mouth dropped open.

Jan reached out and gently closed it. "You'll catch flies, darling."

Terry gulped, and her heart raced.

Jan traced a path across Terry's hairline, along the side of her face, and down her throat. "So soft." She glanced up and hesitated, studying Terry's expression. Her hand fell away, and she took a step back. "What's wrong? Don't you want this anymore? Have...have your feelings changed?"

The pain in Jan's voice galvanized Terry. She jumped to her feet and pulled Jan into her arms. "No! Oh God, no, Jan. I love you. With all my heart, I love you. Please believe that." She clung to Jan and ached for the hurt she'd caused.

"Then why? I don't understand."

Terry eased her back so she could look into uncertain eyes. "I love you. I want nothing more than to lead you over to that bed and spend the rest of this night making love to you. And then I want to do it all over again the next night and the next and the next, until I've spent a lifetime loving the woman I adore."

"Then why...?"

Terry released her, turned to stare out into the gathering dusk, and tried to collect her thoughts.

Jan laid a hand on her back. "We have to talk, my darling girl."

Terry lowered her head and rocked forward on her toes. "The last time you said that we were on the edge of a mountain."

"Yes, we were, and a lot has changed since then. But one thing hasn't. I love you, and I long for your touch as much now as when we melted the snow that day."

"One big change — Rob's gone."

"Yes, he is." Jan was silent for a long moment. "That's what this is all about, isn't it?"

Terry nodded and stood motionless, afraid to move...afraid to say anything. *Please don't let me screw this up beyond repair.*

"Terry, you listen to me. Our love does not dishonour Rob. It doesn't diminish the love he and I shared. Even knowing what I do about myself now, I wouldn't change my choice to marry and care for him. I'll always cherish what we had between us, even if it wasn't a conventional marriage."

Terry shivered.

Jan took a step closer. "But as you said, Rob's gone now. I'll miss that dear man for the rest of my life, but I will not deny what I feel for you. I love you more than I've ever loved anyone...anyone, Terry. I want to be with you, tonight and every night. Tell me, how long would you have me wear widow's weeds? Three months? Six months? A year? Do you really think Rob would deny me a chance at happiness? Do you think he would take pleasure in me sitting by myself at home, weeping for him? Or would he delight in knowing that someone loved me...and that I didn't have to be alone?"

The truth of Jan's words was suddenly clear to Terry. The one thing never in doubt had been Rob's love for his wife. The love that he had fought for so fiercely in life wouldn't condemn Jan to loneliness after his death. *Jan loves me.* Terry knew that with every fibre of her being. She wasn't helping Rob by denying them the expression of that love now. She was hurting the woman she loved. *That's unacceptable.* Terry's shoulders straightened, and her head came up.

Jan pressed against her back and slipped her arms around her waist.

Terry froze as Jan undid the top button of her shirt.

Hypnotized, she stared as each button was unfastened and her shirt tugged out of the front of her jeans.

Warm hands ran over her belly, and Terry's chest heaved. Jan cupped and caressed her breasts and teased her nipples through the fabric of her bra.

Terry's knees weakened and her mouth dried as Jan drew her shirt back over her shoulders and down to her elbows. Her eyes closed when Jan unclasped her bra and slid that, too, down her arms. The evening air flowed over her naked torso, but before she could protest her exposure, Jan's hands covered her breasts.

She tried to speak, but all that came out was a whisper as soft lips grazed the nape of her neck and a trail of kisses seared across her shoulders. When Jan slipped a hand down her belly and under the waistband of her jeans, Terry's knees gave out.

With a delighted laugh, Jan caught her and pulled her back against her body.

Panting, Terry clung to Jan's hips. "I think we'd better lay down before I fall down."

Jan turned her and kissed her before she ripped off Terry's shirt and bra. Then she took her hand and led her to the bed. She fumbled with the buttons of Terry's jeans, her mouth devouring Terry's.

Terry's head spun as her clothes were stripped away and she landed on her back with Jan astride her hips. "Hey, one of us is way overdressed here." She ran her hands over Jan's thighs and unbuttoned her pants.

With excruciating slowness, Jan crossed her arms and pulled her sweater up over her head before tossing it to the floor.

Terry sucked in her breath and stared at the ivory satin bra cupping generous breasts. She was a fifteen-year-old again, awed with desire and ready to burst at a single touch. She raised her gaze to find ardent eyes locked on hers. Terry struggled not to cry as the full impact of Jan's love sank into her heart. She stretched out a trembling hand and touched Jan's face.

Jan closed her eyes and leaned into the caress with a tiny sigh.

That sound steadied Terry. She unfastened the bra and tugged it away, unzipped Jan's pants, and pulled her forward.

Jan gasped as their bodies came together.

Terry ran her hands down Jan's back and under her pants. Cupping Jan's buttocks, she slowly rocked against her.

Jan whimpered. "Please—"

"Let's get these off." Terry pushed Jan's pants down as far as she could, then rolled her to the side and divested her lover of the rest of her clothes. "God, you're beautiful." She traced her fingers down the centre of Jan's body.

Jan blushed and turned her head.

Terry cupped her face and gently turned her back. "You are, my love. Never doubt it."

"I'm not eighteen anymore." Jan glanced down to the soft curve of her belly.

"I'm glad." Terry took possession of Jan's lips. Her earlier urgency ripened into a need to love Jan without reservation, to fully convey all the pleasure she took in this act of consummation. By the time they slept, Jan would have no doubt how glorious she was in Terry's eyes.

Terry eased on top of Jan. She began to explore her lover and delighted in Jan's quiet exhalations of pleasure. She lingered over soft curves and hardened nipples and drifted down until she rested between Jan's legs. Then she slipped her tongue into the wet heat.

"Yes, Terry… God, yes—"

Terry slid a finger inside and coaxed Jan higher, her own excitement mounting as Jan panted and writhed under her touch. She increased her pace until Jan stiffened and called out her name.

Extracting herself, Terry crawled back up the bed and took Jan in her arms. She rolled onto her back and held Jan, stroking her back.

"You sure made me wait, but, sweet Jesus, it was worth it." Jan's throaty tones vibrated against Terry's neck. "I've never… It was never like this."

Terry smiled at Jan's uncharacteristic incoherence. *I wonder how long before we can do that again.*

A few minutes later, Jan raised her head and flashed her a grin. She slid down Terry's side, into the space between her legs, and then up Terry's length, dragging against her sensitized flesh. She stopped to lavish attention on her nipples, and Terry arched her back.

Jan's laughter rippled against Terry's breasts. "Eager, are we? That's the problem with you youngsters. No patience." She wriggled higher and nibbled on Terry's neck.

Terry was already on overload, but when Jan glided a hand down and began to stroke her clit, she gasped. Writhing, she pleaded for more, but Jan kept her rhythm and pressure light. Every nerve in Terry's body vibrated with arousal.

Suddenly, Jan came to rest between her legs.

Terry almost wept with relief at the caress of Jan's tongue. Long, rapturous moments later, Jan sent her over the edge, and the sounds of her pleasure filled the room.

The exquisite thrumming still wracked her body when Terry opened her eyes. Jan hovered over her, a look of such love on her face that Terry was filled with devotion. "God, how did I get so lucky?"

Jan kissed her and sank into Terry's arms.

Long moments went by before Terry asked, "Are you all right, sweetheart?"

"Very, very all right, my darling girl."

"I thought you were new at this. Some beginner. I may have to nominate you for rookie of the year."

Jan's laughter shook their conjoined bodies. "I read a lot, especially over these last few months. You'd be amazed what you can learn from books and online."

"So what you're saying is that you had the theory down cold, and you just needed the practical experience?" Terry delighted in their banter, relieved that becoming lovers hadn't altered the bedrock of their friendship.

Jan tickled Terry's ribs "Uh-huh. Did I mention that you were the perfect guinea pig?"

"Well, anytime you want to put in more lab time, just let me know."

There was silence again as they basked in each other's arms, until Jan rolled her head back against Terry's shoulder. "I feel like I've finally come home."

Terry smiled. "I know exactly what you mean."

####

ABOUT LOIS CLOAREC HART

Born and raised in British Columbia, Canada, Lois Cloarec Hart grew up as an avid reader but didn't begin writing until much later in life. Several years after joining the Canadian Armed Forces, she received a degree in Honours History from Royal Military College and on graduation switched occupations from air traffic control to military intelligence. Having married a CAF fighter pilot while in college, Lois went on to spend another five years as an Intelligence Officer before leaving the military to care for her husband, who was ill with chronic progressive Multiple Sclerosis and passed away in 2001. She began writing while caring for her husband in his final years and had her first book, *Coming Home*, published in 2001. It was through that initial publishing process that Lois met the woman she would marry in April 2007. She now commutes annually between her northern home in Calgary and her wife's southern home in Atlanta.

Lois is the author of four novels, *Coming Home*, *Broken Faith*, *Kicker's Journey*, *Walking the Labyrinth*, and a collection of short stories, *Assorted Flavours*. Her novel *Kicker's Journey* won the 2010 Independent Publisher Book Award bronze medal, 2010 Golden Crown Literary Awards, 2010 Rainbow Romance Writer's Award for Excellence, and 2009 Lesbian Fiction Readers Choice Award for historical fiction. *Broken Faith* (revised second edition) was published in winter 2013. *Coming Home* (revised third edition) was published in spring 2014.

Visit her website: www.loiscloarechart.com
E-mail her at eljae1@shaw.ca

OTHER BOOKS FROM YLVA PUBLISHING

http://www.ylva-publishing.com

BROKEN FAITH
(revised edition)

Lois Cloarec Hart

ISBN: 978-3-95533-056-9
Length: 415 pages

Emotional wounds aren't always apparent, and those that haunt Marika and Rhiannon are deep and lasting.

On the surface, Marika appears to be a wealthy, successful lawyer, while Rhiannon is a reclusive, maladjusted loner. But Marika, in her own way, is as damaged as the younger Rhiannon. When circumstances throw them together one summer, they begin to reach out, each finding unexpected strengths in the other.

However, even as inner demons are gradually vanquished and old hurts begin to heal, evil in human form reappears. The cruelly enigmatic Cass has used and controlled Marika in the past, and she aims to do so again.

Can Marika find it within herself to break free? Can she save her young friend from Cass' malevolent web? With the support of remarkable friends, the pair fights to break free — of their crippling pasts and the woman who will own them or kill them.

WALKING THE LABYRINTH

Lois Cloarec Hart

ISBN: 978-3-95533-052-1
Length: 267 pages

Is there life after loss? Lee Glenn, co-owner of a private security company, didn't think so. Crushed by grief after the death of her wife, she uncharacteristically retreats from life.

But love doesn't give up easily. After her friends and family stage a dramatic intervention, Lee rejoins the world of the living, resolved to regain some sense of normalcy but only half-believing that it's possible. Her old friend and business partner convinces her to take on what appears on the surface to be a minor personal protection detail.

The assignment takes her far from home, from the darkness of her loss to the dawning of a life reborn. Along the way, Lee encounters people unlike any she's ever met before: Wrong-Way Wally, a small-town oracle shunned by the locals for his off-putting speech and mannerisms; and Wally's best friend, Gaëlle, a woman who not only translates the oracle's uncanny predictions, but who also appears to have a deep personal connection to life beyond life. Lee is shocked to find herself fascinated by Gaëlle, despite dismissing the woman's exotic beliefs as "hooey."

But opening yourself to love also means opening yourself to the possibility of pain. Will Lee have the courage to follow that path, a path that once led to the greatest agony she'd ever experienced? Or will she run back to the cold comfort of a safer solitary life?

KICKER'S JOURNEY
(revised edition)

Lois Cloarec Hart

ISBN: 978-3-95533-060-6
Length: 472 pages

In 1899, two women from very different backgrounds are about to embark on a journey together—one that will take them from the Old World to the New, from the 19th century into the 20th, and from the comfort and familiarity of England to the rigours of Western Canada, where challenges await at every turn.

The journey begins simply for Kicker Stuart when she leaves her home village to take employment as hostler and farrier at Grindleshire Academy for Young Ladies. But when Kicker falls in love with a teacher, Madelyn Bristow, it radically alters the course of her tranquil life.

Together, the lovers flee the brutality of Madelyn's father and the prejudices of upper crust England in search of freedom to live, and love, as they choose. A journey as much of the heart and soul as of the body, it will find the lovers struggling against the expectations of gender, the oppression of class, and even, at times, each other.

What they find at the end of their journey is not a new Eden, but a land of hope and opportunity that offers them the chance to live out their most cherished dream—a life together.

HEARTS AND FLOWERS BORDER
(revised edition)

L.T. Smith

ISBN: 978-3-95533-179-5
Length: 250 pages

A visitor from her past jolts Laura Stewart into memories — some funny, some heart-wrenching. Thirteen years ago, Laura buried those memories so deeply she never believed they would resurface. Still, the pain of first love mars Laura's present life and might even destroy her chance of happiness with the beautiful, yet seemingly unobtainable Emma Jenkins.

Can Laura let go of the past, or will she make the same mistakes all over again?

Hearts and Flowers Border is a simple tale of the uncertainty of youth and the first flush of love — love that may have a chance after all.

COMING FROM YLVA PUBLISHING

http://www.ylva-publishing.com

CONFLICT OF INTEREST

Jae

Workaholic Detective Aiden Carlisle isn't looking for love—and certainly not at the law enforcement seminar she reluctantly agreed to attend. But the first lecturer is not at all what she expected.

Psychologist Dawn Kinsley has just found her place in life. After a failed relationship with a police officer, she has sworn never to get involved with another cop again, but she feels a connection to Aiden from the very first moment.

Can Aiden keep from crossing the line when a brutal crime threatens to keep them apart before they've even gotten together?

MAC VS. PC

Fletcher DeLancey

As a computer technician at the university, Anna Petrowski knows she has one thing in common with doctors and lawyers, and it's not the salary. It's that everyone thinks her advice comes free, even on weekends. That's why she keeps a strict observance of her Saturday routine: a scone, a caramel mocha, and nobody bothering her. So when she meets a new campus hire at the Bean Grinder who needs computer help yet doesn't ask for it, she's intrigued enough to offer. It's the beginning of a beautiful friendship and possibly something more.

But Elizabeth Markel is a little higher up the university food chain than she's let on, and the truth brings out buried prejudices that Anna didn't know she had.

People and computers have one thing in common: they're both capable of self-sabotage. The difference is that computers are easier to fix.

IN A HEARTBEAT

RJ Nolan

Veteran police officer Sam McKenna has no trouble facing down criminals on a daily basis but breaks out in a sweat at the mere mention of commitment. A recent failed relationship strengthens her resolve to stick with her trademark no-strings-attached affairs.

Dr. Riley Connolly, a successful trauma surgeon, has spent her whole life trying to measure up to her family's expectations. And that includes hiding her sexuality from them.

When a routine call sends Sam to the hospital where Riley works, the two women are hurtled into a life-and-death situation. The incident binds them together. But can there be any future for a commitment-phobic cop and a closeted, workaholic doctor?

Coming Home
© by Lois Cloarec Hart

ISBN: 978-3-95533-064-4

Also available as e-book.

Published by Ylva Publishing, legal entity of Ylva Verlag, e.Kfr.

Ylva Verlag, e.Kfr.
Owner: Astrid Ohletz
Am Kirschgarten 2
65830 Kriftel
Germany

http://www.ylva-publishing.com

Second edition: 2005 PD Publishing
Revised third edition: March 2014 Ylva Publishing

Credits:
Edited by Sandra Gerth
Cover Design by Streetlight Graphics

Lightning Source UK Ltd.
Milton Keynes UK
UKOW04f1345020215

245509UK00001B/92/P